Selected praise for
Sleepwalking in Daylight

"Flock draws astute parallels between the alienated Cammy and Sam—living in a sexless marriage, bored with driving to endless soccer practices and sick of being the devoted mom... Filled with perceptive, dead-on insights into both teenage angst and the common pitfalls of marriage in the middle years."
—*Booklist*

"Elizabeth Flock offers us a haunting look at the challenges and responsibilities of raising a small family in suburban America. This is a cautionary tale about the perils of narcissism and living in denial. Once you pick it up, you can't *not* read it to the very last page. *Sleepwalking in Daylight* will be remembered for a very long time."
—*New York Times* bestselling author Dorothea Benton Frank

"Elizabeth Flock's *Sleepwalking in Daylight* is a painfully emotional mother-daughter story told in the voices of Samantha and Cammy, in alternating chapters. Samantha is so wrapped up in herself that she can't fathom Cammy's unhappiness. Cammy secretly tries to find her birth mother, certain that her 'real' mother will understand her as Samantha does not.... Flock tells a disturbing family story in two authentic voices."
—*Boston Globe*

"[A] terrific novel...[Samantha] is still married but she's fallen in love with someone else—and is desperately trying to reconnect with her goth-obsessed teenage daughter."
—*Parenting* magazine, "Recommended Read"

"Elizabeth Flock is a skillful storyteller, and the suspense is genuine as we watch Cammy sink deeper and deeper into her pain. Samantha is indeed 'sleepwalking in daylight' and the reader wants to scream at her to wake up."
—*AuthorMagazine*

"Have you ever opened your eyes and realized that you've been sleepwalking through your life? If so, this is the novel for you. *Sleepwalking in Daylight* is heartfelt and poignant, unique and memorable. Elizabeth Flock's characters feel real, her dialogue is first-rate. The story is rich and resonates long after the last page has been turned. This novel isn't about the perfection of life, but rather, how life's imperfections make it all the more precious."
—John Shors, bestselling author of *Beneath a Marble Sky*

Sleepwalking in Daylight

elizabeth flock

MIRA®

MIRA

Recycling programs
for this product may
not exist in your area.

ISBN-13: 978-0-7783-2734-9

SLEEPWALKING IN DAYLIGHT

www.MIRABooks.com

Printed in U.S.A.

For Jill Brack

Samantha

We haven't had sex in eleven months. Just shy of a year. More time than it takes to grow a human being. I know it was eleven months ago for two reasons: one, it was on our wedding anniversary and on wedding anniversaries sex is a given and two, the next night was the incident with the family room light. I was reading a book about a missionary family in Africa I ordered after Oprah plugged it. I keep track of what I read on my calendar and plus I remember wishing it weren't our wedding anniversary because I was at the good part but instead I had to pretend I didn't know Bob was simply going through the motions required of husbands celebrating their wedding anniversaries.

So there we were the following night, in the second floor room that is, after the kitchen, the nerve center of our house. Bob was at the computer in the corner searching eBay for tennis rackets even though it'd end up costing more for one on eBay when you factor in the shipping and handling.

"Why don't you just go to Sportmart?" I'd asked earlier in the evening.

"I'm looking for the old wooden ones," he said without looking up. "The old Wilsons."

I shrugged and went back to my book. I became so engrossed I remember looking up and feeling shock that no, I wasn't in a civil war in the Congo, I was actually in my tidy three-story house on Chicago's North Side. I remember smiling and thinking I love it when that happens. When a book's so good you forget who and where you are.

I'd heard Bob sighing and pushing back from the family desk littered with half-finished homework, field-trip permission slips and school reminders on brightly colored paper. He crossed the room and flicked off the light as he left and it took me calling "hey" for him to come back, switch it back on with an "oh, sorry, I forgot you were there." The worst part was he wasn't doing it to prove some point. He truly forgot I was in the room with him. Which is exactly the point. We haven't had sex since.

I know it seems like a silly thing, the light incident. But everyone has that final straw, that moment of clarity when you can't put your finger on it, you just know there's been a shift, a ripple in the atmosphere. The little things have added up and finally you can't take it anymore. We've been quietly drifting into our own worlds for a while, Bob and I. I've just been ignoring it. Up until now. And I can't take it anymore.

Just last week I got buttermilk for the pancakes I decided to make for no real reason. A special treat. I felt like making an effort for once. I got the buttermilk because I know Bob likes it when the pancakes are richer. *Swanky pancakes* he used to say in a tone that thanked me for going the extra mile back when something like buttermilk was considered going the extra mile. Last week not only did he *not* notice we were having something other than cold cereal, but when I carefully slid a stack from the spatula onto a plate waved me off and he said, "None for me. There's that construction on Irving Park so we've gotta get going. C'mon, guys."

Sleepwalking in Daylight

Our eight-year-old sons, Jamie and Andrew, were still chewing when they grabbed their shin guards and soccer cleats. Sometimes I wonder if they really are twins, they're so different in looks and personality. Jamie moves slowly and deliberately like he's thought out every step he takes. Before breakfast he lined up his guards and shoes neatly by the backdoor. He put out two bottles of water, just to the side. He remembers the second one because Andrew never does. Jamie has freckles across his nose. His skin is so milky white   you can see blue veins through it. His delicate features I think will translate into a refined face later on. He is small for eight and many people assume he is younger than his brother. Andrew is solid and stocky with thick brownish-red hair and a *Dennis the Menace* cowlick. He is exactly what you think of when you think of an eight-year-old boy: messy, unkempt, fearless. If he falls down and cuts his lip he spits the blood out and keeps going. He's got a short attention span but he was tested for ADHD and came up clean. I've had to tell Jamie not to pick up after his brother, which he does on the sly because he can't bear to see his twin in trouble. In trouble Jamie looks wounded. Andrew just tips his head back to roll his eyes at the ceiling and sighs at the futility of parental warnings. Nothing gets through to Andrew; everything gets through to Jamie.

"You know which field it is, right?" I ask Bob.

"I know which field," he says, annoyed but pausing for a sneeze of a second while he considers double checking.

"I'm just saying. It's changed this season and you haven't been yet. Boys, you know which way to go, right? Take a right from the parking lot and go over the hill, remember? Show Dad the way, will you?"

"Bye, Mom!" Andrew calls out.

"Tie your shoes, Andrew. Bob, get him to tie them up before he gets out of the car. He'll trip."

"Yeah yeah yeah, tie your shoes," Bob says. "Let's go guys."

The soccer ball is wedged between his arm and ribs. He drops the keys and bends like a pregnant woman to pick them up, careful not to tip the plastic grocery-store platter of doughnuts I got for halftime.

"Don't forget the dry cleaning on the way back," I tell him. "Hey—you want steak for dinner? I'm going to the market."

"Yeah, fine, whatever. Jamie, get a move on, kiddo," he says from the door to the garage.

Our backdoor opens to a stone path Bob and I laid when we first moved in almost twenty years ago. We were house poor but thrilled to own in what was then an up-and-coming neighborhood. We'd brought a boom box out back and played the only radio station that came in. Jazz music. I lost steam halfway through the job that was supposed to take only a day but stretched out over two whole weekends because the pavers we'd chosen were mismatched. There were countless trips to and from the outdoor landscaping center. The second Saturday I lay back on the grass in the sun listening to Miles Davis and Bob whistling then cursing. I remember staring up at the clouds like a kid, smiling at life. We had a great house, there was a light breeze and I was lying on land we owned, my bare feet on *our* grass. I remember shading my eyes to watch Bob with a mathematician's concentration size up stone after stone over the shallow hole he had dug. His college T-shirt was new then. It was a Squeeze concert tee from when they played on campus. Our second or third date. Sophomore year. Boston College. 1981. After the concert we got drunk at a keg party at his friends' off-campus house.

I was all over him back then. I thought it was sweet that he wanted to take it slow. He said I was different. He said he didn't just want sex, he wanted to "go the distance." He said he didn't want to do anything to "mess us up." So we took it slow. We fooled around but nothing major. We slept squeezed into my single bed under my Marimekko comforter to the smell of ramen noodles and beer. I remember wishing he weren't so sloppy a kisser, but I figured it'd get better over time. It never did get better, but I figured there were more important things in life than having to wipe my mouth with the back of my hand after kissing him.

Our friends loved being with us because we weren't the kind to couple off and make the single ones feel worse for being single. We were the fun ones. We went to parties and split up to talk with this friend and that—we didn't need to be together every second. In fact, it was not uncommon for us to go a few days without seeing one another. Like during midterms. Still, we'd always know where the other one was. We had our schedules memorized. Sometimes I'd wait for him after his sports-medicine class and get coffee at the student center cafeteria filled with flyers with roommates, band members, used books, tutoring. We had so much in common there was very little learning curve. We were both from Chicago, we'd both gone to parochial high schools, we were both only children. My best friend—my freshman roommate, Lynn—became his best friend. We double-dated with Lynn and her various boyfriends. When she found herself in between boys Bob fixed her up with his friend Patel from Delhi, India, but she can be embarrassingly difficult if she doesn't like someone and she didn't like Patel and Bob swore he'd never fix her up again but he did because I begged him to and finally she clicked with Michael who she ended up marrying and Bob was best man and I was maid-of-honor and it was all perfect. Storybook. We got married when Lynn and Mike got back from their honeymoon. We laughed and said we were like Fred and Ethel and Lucy and Ricky. Then we'd argue about who got to be Lucy and Ricky and who had to be Fred and Ethel. I'd imagined we'd live in houses next door to one another. Lynn and I would quit our jobs to raise our kids together. We'd have coffee after carpooling. Bob would play weekly pickup games with Mike and they'd talk about how cool their wives were. I imagined Bob and me spooning every night like we'd done in my dorm room. I wanted the white-picket fence. I was sure we'd have children, but at the time, being so young, I felt indifferent about it.

But somewhere in there I had doubts. I began to worry on the honeymoon actually. We were happy in the Caribbean, Jet Skiing, parasailing, snorkeling, sunset booze cruises with other honeymooners, but I started to notice we were running out of things to talk about. Like we'd had a set amount of sentences in the bank and by the time the honeymoon rolled around that savings account was empty.

On the beach one afternoon, gloomy clouds turned day into night and dumped rain like they were punishing us. It happened so quickly we didn't have time to rush to the car, so we waited it out under our rented Heineken umbrella that was as useless at shielding us from the tropical shower as it was from the brutal white sun.

"Are you upset about something?" I asked him. "You've been so quiet."

He shrugged and stared out at the kidney clouds.

"What is it?" I asked him. "I'm freezing—will you pass me the extra towel in the bag?"

He was mechanical. His arm bent at the elbow, dipping into the bag on his right, clutching the towel, passing it across to me on his left like claw-a-stuffed-animal machines at supermarket entrances.

"It's just…" he said, fixing his eyes at the clouds rolling away to refill themselves. "This is it."

"Wait, what? What're you talking about? Are you freaking out? Do you wish we hadn't gotten married or something? Here, get under the towel." I pressed closer into him. "Aren't you cold?"

"I'm fine. Forget it. It's stopping. Want to go back to the hotel?"

"What does 'this is it' mean?"

He said, "Just forget it, okay? Forget it," with a rattlesnake's venom, so I backed off. I was young and figured it'd all work itself out. I thought it was a gloomy rainy day kind of mood.

I did wonder why we weren't in the bedroom more. Our room had a king-size bed with big fluffy pillows and equally soft robes in the closet. Turn-down service included rose petals sprinkled on the bed. The hotel catered to honeymooners. Lots of finger foods. Chocolate-covered strawberries. I chalked his mood up to being exhausted from the swirl of wedding planning. Bob's always been an active guy so I knew going in it wouldn't be a languid lie-on-the-hammock kind of trip. On the last night of the trip we went to a tiki-hut bar on the beach. We got a bucket of beer and listened to the steel-drum band, nodding to the beat, looking out at the ocean. Bob moved from beer to scotch. I'd only seen him drink scotch once when he was with his fraternity brothers at a homecoming party senior year. We watched the sunset. He jingled the ice cubes and drained the rest of his drink, holding up the glass to signal the waiter for another. I went to the bathroom, washed my hands, looked into the mirror and thought, *I think I just made a huge mistake.* There was no one to talk to about this but I worried. I worried and worried and worried myself into a thick inertia that kept me canceling plans with Lynn and Mike for nearly two weeks after we'd gotten home. I hadn't wanted Lynn reading my mind.

elizabeth flock

The stone path isn't a straight line. We thought it would be prettier winding to the garage like a miniature Yellow Brick Road. Now we all use the direct route across the grass. Lynn and Mike bought a house two streets over in our tree-lined neighborhood that feels like the suburbs but is just a few minutes from downtown Chicago. The two- and three-story houses on our street are similarly designed with small squares of grass, front porches, patios, decks and grass out back. Two-car garages that open to a long narrow alley that requires a tap on the horn and a wave to someone waiting politely to back out. Barbecues with large spatulas and tongs. Brick chimneys. Wreaths and roping in winter. American flags in summer. Indian corn in the fall. On any given week there can be three, four visits from Boy Scouts selling wrapping paper or magazine subscriptions, clipboards held by crunchy-granola college kids wanting to save the planet, a local guy down on his luck offering to clean up leaves with a flimsy rake he carries with him from house to house. In the winter he comes to shovel snow off our short walkways up from the sidewalk. He says we can pay him whatever we think it's worth.

By the late 1980s Mike and Bob started losing their hair and watched their midsections thicken. Bob got glasses, Mike got contacts. One day I looked at my husband and realized he looked old. Not old old but...*old*. Like a grown-up. It was hard to see the college kid I'd married. Lynn and I stayed in shape together, enrolling in the same health club up the street, the one with aerobics classes that were only just catching on around the country. We got the Jennifer Aniston haircut just like everyone else. Then we grew it long and straightened it. Just like everyone else.

"Bye, Mom." Jamie turns to give me a hug before trailing off after Andrew and Bob to soccer. "Thanks for the pancakes."

When the door slams shut I pour the buttermilk batter down the sink and run cold water to dilute it. Cammy shuffles in rubbing her eyes, smudging the leftover makeup she never takes off before bed. The cabinets bang open and closed. The jars and bottles on the door of the fridge clatter when she pushes it shut with her foot, balancing milk in one hand, a bowl of cereal in the other.

"It smells like pancakes in here," she says. She shimmies onto a high counter stool and hunches over the bowl, shoveling food into her mouth while she stares at the cartoon riddles on the back of the box, tipping it back to read the upside-down answers at the bottom.

Cammy's most beautiful in the morning, still soft from sleep. Her skin is olive-colored and gets deeper, more Mediterranean looking, in summer. It's flawless. She is petite with bird wrists and a graceful neck. Bee-stung lips. Large brown eyes. Her natural hair color was a deep rich brown before she dyed it. It looked like a caramel apple. Wavy and thick with bangs she used to trim so they didn't catch on her eyelashes like they do now. She looks younger than sixteen. Until she layers on makeup that's more like face paint. Hard teenage edges build up when she gets dressed. Her black clothes look like Halloween costumes.

She finishes her cereal and, climbing down from her stool, she almost trips, milk almost spills. She is all limbs, lanky, knobby knees, flat chest, unsure of where her arms and hands should go when she's standing. Her lashes curl and her teeth are straight without having had braces. Now in the grip of the rebellious stage, she is fighting anything attractive about herself. She shrinks if she thinks someone's staring at her and is horrified when someone says, "Wow, Cammy Friedman? I can't believe it. I haven't seen you since you were this big. Look at you."

When Cammy was young she had a natural impulse to hug. Like Jamie now does. When she was a little girl I was still in the habit of crying on Mother's Day. One year—I can't remember how old she was—I'd thought Cammy and Bob were down making me breakfast in bed but then I felt a hand on my shoulder. I sniffed back my tears and turned to her, she put her arms around me and patted me on the back saying, *It's okay, Mommy.* Then she quietly left me to blow my nose and screw a smile onto my face in preparation for the lumpy pancakes coming up the stairs on a rickety wicker breakfast tray with a handful of wilting dandelions bobbing in a jelly jar.

About a decade later and she flinches at any human contact. When forced into a hug she bends forward so her shoulders and arms are the only things touching, keeping the rest of her body as far away as possible. It annoys Bob but then everything seems to annoy Bob these days.

We see things differently, Bob and I. I look at people's eyes. Sometimes, not often but sometimes, I'll catch the eye of a stranger by accident and there's a feeling of depth or recognition, a strange familiarity like we're the same breed of dog. Usually it's people who have the same eyes I do: wide set and round and a shade of dark brown that deepens to match my pupils when I get upset.

But Bob sees everyone as feet. As in, "You mean Eddie with the Hush Puppies?" And I'll say, "No, Eddie with the penny loafers you think have holes in the soles," because I speak shoe now too.

To Bob, crowds are simply approaching feet. When he walks down the street he looks down. Nikes. Flip-flops. Manolos. Payless knockoffs. In winter, Uggs and L.L.Bean. When it's someone in sneakers his eyes follow each step like it's a beautiful woman he's checking out but really he's always watching heel impact. He majored in sports medicine. We had dinner with Mike and Lynn and toasted his new job at Nike and for a while he was bubbling over at the end of every day, telling me about how he was working on things that would make a tremendous difference for the next generation of runners. Somewhere in that first year he stopped bubbling and started drinking. Not too much but just enough to amplify his growing cynicism. Lynn said once that it was weird to see someone in their twenties so jaded, but I got all defensive and she dropped it. She and I both knew she was right, though.

Bob's business is sport shoes, as they're called in the industry, but mostly I tell people he designs sneakers. Before he started working at the top sport-shoe company in the world I never knew "shoe architecture" existed. Of course I'd read somewhere about how Nike started with a running coach and a waffle iron, but beyond that I was ignorant of all that went in to building a cross trainer.

The feet in Bob's world can be divided into two categories: healthy and unhealthy. Healthy means equal wear and tear through from the ball to the heel. Unhealthy is everything else and to Bob most feet are unhealthy. So he speaks in declarations that sound like fortune cookies at a foot-fetish restaurant.

"Whoever thought of taking flip-flops mainstream?" he asked his bewildered dinner partner at a school fund-raiser.

And:

"That guy has no idea that in ten years he'll be seeing a podiatrist for collapsed arches," he said to me while we were Christmas shopping at Old Orchard Mall.

And:

"In a perfect world, we'd outlaw high heels and everyone would wear orthotics."

He said that to the principal at Cammy's school after a tense meeting in which the headmaster told us she was on probation again. The principal, Mr. Black, looks like the doctors used forceps when he was born. His pinched face matches his prim boarding-school Oliver Twist personality. I can't stand him mainly because he seems not to be able to stand me. Or my family. Even before Cammy was in trouble, Mr. Black acted like we were a *problem*. Like we were *high maintenance*. When Cammy was in first grade we'd gone in to talk to him about moving her to another class with a more patient teacher and he started shaking his head halfway through our request and held up his hand. He said, "It's a poor sportsman who blames the equipment." I wanted to wring his neck. We tried talking to him about Cammy's special needs and he waved us off like it was all bullshit. Bob said, "The kid's in first grade…what could it matter?" And Mr. Black leaned across his desk and hissed, "Exactly." Bob said, "No, I mean, what's the big deal about her going into Miss Landis's class. We hear she's great with—" But before Bob could finish, Mr. Black stood and said, "We'll see what we can do." We were dismissed. Being new parents we actually thought he'd come through, but now that I know him I know he didn't give us a second thought. Son of a bitch.

So, years later, Mr. Black was walking us to the front door on his way up to a class he needed to audit and I knew he was trying to mask the click of my shoes in the empty hallway when he halfheartedly asked Bob how work was going. He made me feel embarrassed to have such loud footsteps when they're just footsteps, for Christ's sake. Bob had us standing inside the front door for nearly five minutes talking about the latest in heel air cushioning until I saved the impatient principal by taking Bob's arm and saying, "Honey, we've got to get going." I purposely avoided what I knew would be grateful headmaster eyes because after all he'd just slammed my daughter and anyway he'd always been a son of a bitch. I guess, then, I was saving myself from having to hear Bob's foot philosophy. Again.

"Jesus Christ, what're we going to do?" I say on the way to the car. "I swear to God I honestly don't know what else we can do. We've grounded her a million times. I've tried to get her to open up to me…she's just always so angry. Why the hell is she so angry all the time?"

"Allen Edmonds shoes," Bob says, reaching for the keys he'd given me to hold because he insists they make his gait uneven. Four keys. Like he's running a marathon at the Olympics.

"The guy's got good taste in footwear, I'll give him that," he says.

"Bob. Focus. What're we going to do about Cammy?"

"He's being way too harsh," he says, starting the car and adjusting the rearview mirror even though he was the one who drove us there. "Probation? For ignoring a teacher?"

"I swear to God I can't believe it. How'd we get to this? And Bob, she didn't just *ignore* Mrs. Cummings. *You* know that death stare she gives. That Goth stare is crazy scary. I guarantee you she was clamping her jaw shut and doing that stare. I'd send her to the headmaster, too, if I were her teacher. When that look comes over her it's like a cloud or something. And that's not even the issue. She's been cutting class. She's smoking on school property. What the hell? I've never smelled smoke on her, have you?"

"I think it's a little much to suspend someone for a death stare," he says, looking to the right then the left before inching out of the school parking lot. "And kids cut class from time to time. Give her detention, for God's sake, but suspension?"

Right and left again a second time. You'd think he was

pulling onto the Daytona Speedway the way he looks for cars before moving. Like they're going to whiz at him at triple-digit speeds and send him spinning into the boards.

"He's not suspending her," I say. "He's putting her on probation. You're fine on this side, by the way."

"Suspension, probation, same thing. They both look bad on her school file."

"Exactly my point," I say. "It's green, that's why everyone's honking."

"Will you just let me drive?"

"All I'm saying is we've got to be a united front when we get home." I turn in my seat to face him because I can't bear to watch him drive. He's terrible behind the wheel and the worst part is he has no idea. Completely clueless. Cars will slow down alongside him, the drivers' faces gnarled in anger, mouthing swears, but he doesn't see them.

"What's the party line?" he asks.

"She's grounded, for starters. No computer. No cell."

"How's she going to call if something gets canceled or she needs to be picked up from somewhere?" he asks.

"What good is taking away the computer if she still has her cell? All she does is text. We've got to take it if the grounding's going to have any impact. Besides, what's so wrong with her finding a pay phone if there's an emergency or she needs a ride? I don't know why you're worried about that part of it anyway since I'm the one who does all the picking up."

"What the?"

"When was the last time you picked up Cammy or the boys from anything other than a random weekend soccer game? They're your kids, too, Bob."

He looks ahead and I find myself wondering how upset I'd

be if he died. I'd be worried about the kids growing up without a father, but me? I don't know that I'd feel much.

"I think it's about the adoption," I say. My stomach twisting up tells me this is not a good time to bring it up, but there's never a good time to bring it up.

"Oh, my God, so we're blaming everything that goes wrong on the adoption? Are we going to dredge this up for the rest of our lives? Jesus, let it go."

"You want to know what I think? I think most of everything that's gone wrong with her is because of how she found out about the adoption."

"Oh, please…"

"You know exactly what I'm talking about. To tell a little girl the reason why she feels like she looks different from her brothers is because she's not our 'real' child? Honestly? What the hell, Bob. How many years ago was that—ten years? No, eleven. For the last *eleven* years she's been feeling like an outcast in her own family."

"Stop. It's not like that and you know it," he says. I feel our speed increasing and we are uncharacteristically in sync with the other cars along Lake Shore Drive.

"Oh, yeah? What's it like then? Huh? You're saying you didn't blurt it out? You're forgetting that we had a plan…that we were going to talk to her together at an age-appropriate time like the books say? You just plunge in *without me* and say something *without thinking it through* and then you scratch your head in amazement like you're surprised she remembers it word for word after all these years and then you sit here all smug and tell me *it wasn't like that?* It was *exactly* like that, Bob. Exactly."

Bob slows down and once again cars are swerving around us. A guy in a Prius gives Bob the bird and I wonder whether it's because we're the enemy now in our hateful gas-guzzling SUV or that Bob is driving under the speed limit or maybe just maybe he sees me spitting angry words at this man in my car, this man I no longer recognize, and he flips him off for me.

"Things have gotten so out of hand with her," I say, backing off the adoption subject like I always do. "I don't even know where to start. I put my finger on one leak and another one spouts."

"I know," he says. He's lying. He doesn't know. At least not when it comes to the kids, and frankly I'm sick of hearing how awful work is every single day. The boys crave time with him. Lately it's taken me nagging him to get him to spend any kind of time with them. We ride the rest of the way in silence, which is fine by me.

I look at him and honestly? Honestly I am not in the least bit attracted to him. So that brings me back to my point:

Not one of my friends wants sex. Seriously. Not one. Well, not any of the ones with kids. I look around at other forty-something moms and they fall into two categories. One group has surrendered to the uniform of motherhood: sensible shoes, mom-jeans, sweatshirts, bulky full-length gray Michelin Man parkas in winter, shapeless old T-shirts in summer.

The second group is the pilates group. They're *hot*. They wear jeans their daughters covet. They have defined biceps and flat tummys. Oh. And abs. Six-pack abs. Working out is a full-time job for them. It's like there was a secret memo to do yoga, be in the best shape of their lives and shop in stores that carry tight T-shirts with plunging necklines, but the irony is there's nowhere to go with it since *no one's having sex*. I love a good crisply laundered white shirt, button-down like a man's but formfitting. My jeans aren't too tight but they aren't baggy. My favorite shoes are a pair of old Gucci loafers I splurged on years ago when Bob got a great Christmas bonus. The best buy I've ever made: they're well made so I've never had to have them resoled. The leather's buttery and camel colored. They go with every pair of pants I own. Mostly though I wear skirts. I've never understood why more women don't wear skirts. At school pickup not so long ago, Ann Slevick looked me up and down and said, "You're always so *put together*," and I thanked her but she didn't smile. So the next day I made a point of wearing my jeans with the holes in them.

Sometimes at night when I'm changing into Gap boxers and an old Mount Rushmore T-shirt with holes and yellowed armpits, I inspect myself in our full-length mirror. I've got a decent hairstyle: that shoulder-length layered cut everyone seems to have. I haven't overcolored it, so the brown looks natural, which is lucky. My ass isn't so bad. Not for a forty-five-year-old. I've seen worse. It's the front that bugs me. I hate my stomach. Lying down it feels flat if I don't run my hands along my hips. It actually feels like it used to be before the boys. So all in all I suppose my body hasn't started the middle-age decline *yet,* but it's only because I'm tall and my limbs are long and there's something deceiving in that. In old class pictures I would be the one standing on the side of the bleachers where all the kids were neatly sitting in rows. Our teacher stood on the other side. I cursed my height and wished I could stop shooting up like the Jolly Green Giant. It felt like a creepy magic trick, the way I grew taller and taller. It felt like *Guinness World Records* tall. My classmates looked like Lilliputians to me and I hunched over, folding into my chest to try to compensate. Like Cammy, I had knobby knees and clumsy bruises. With no spatial reasoning I found myself cutting the corner into another room, my whole right side hitting the door frame on the way in. I finally stopped growing at five feet nine inches

elizabeth flock

and boys started reaching and then passing me and all was forgiven, but I still have to remind myself to sit up straight.

"Have you guys heard about all these sexless marriages?" I ask my book club. We've been together for about five years now. It started with me and Lynn and Ginny from down the street. Ginny's sweet. Maybe too sweet, but still. She's thirty, fifteen years younger than me. She and her husband, Don, live in a bright green house everyone calls the Traffic Light. She's the one I call when I need another set of hands for something around the house. Like hanging the drapes I sewed. She's always home. While I never set out to, every once in a while I end up talking to her about life and I'm reminded why I like her so much. I think we bonded when she left her job as an investment consultant at a downtown banking firm about four, five years ago. Around that time on a summer night in white wicker chairs on my front porch we talked about what we really wanted out of life. I said I wasn't sure but I knew it hadn't happened yet. I remember this: she seemed startled. When she said, "But you have children," I realized why. I used to think the same way. That life would make sense once we had children. Ginny mentioned she and Don had been trying to have a baby. She talked about finding something else in her life. Something with purpose. Something she could feel proud of. I told her what I wish someone had told me. I told her not to be in such a hurry to have children. I told her sometimes it's not all it's cracked up to be. She nodded and sipped her wine. There wasn't a hint, even a twinge of judgment from her. I knew this was something she'd share with Don in bed that night. "She doesn't really love her children," she'd marvel. "I never would've guessed it."

Most people I know think the sun rises and sets on their

children. They orbit around them like planets. So it was a big deal to feel open enough with someone other than Lynn about something so personal. I told Lynn we needed to let her into our friendship. She balked at first but after a little while, months maybe, she admitted Ginny's pretty great.

So book club started with the three of us. Then Ginny asked if she could bring a friend she works out with, Leanne, who is kind of a pain in the ass but I don't mind her. She's funny but she doesn't seem like she has a whole lot of depth. Or intelligence. I've always suspected Leanne cracks the bindings on her books to make it look like she's not only read them, she's *studied* them. She might even dog-ear them then flatten out the folded triangles on random pages. Teresa Wdowiak came in along the way—I can't remember who brought her. Then Sally Flanders cornered Lynn when Lynn was weeding some years ago and asked if our book club was accepting new members and if so could she be one of them. What choice did we have? There's no stopping Sally Flanders.

There are eight of us here tonight, which is uncommon. Typically it's four or five but we're reading *The Kite Runner* this month and everyone wants to weigh in. Last month someone recommended *A Hundred Years of Solitude,* but no one got past the first fifty pages so we canceled. Actually that's not true. Kerry Kendricks read it and fought the cancellation, but she's a show-off and no one wanted to sit there and listen to her lecturing us about South American literature.

We're in Sally Flanders's living room. I hate being in Sally Flanders's living room. It's like walking into Pier One through a curtain of the smell of potpourri and scented candles. I'm pretty sure I see a Glade plug-in across Sally's living room, next to a grandfather clock that's got an irregular tick. Sally favors floral design and needlepoint animal pillows. She tells us where to sit—that's weird enough as it is—based on what pillows are there. She calls them her "cute critters." Tonight I've got "Lucky Lassie" wedged between my lower back and the spires on the back of this, the most uncomfortable chair in the world. Lynn is rolling her eyes at something Leanne's saying about the snickerdoodles she brought—she always wants a medal for her cooking, saying stuff like, *Oh, it's so easy,* and then rattles on about how much trouble she went to for all of us. Special in-gredients blah blah blah. Her cooking's not even very good and Lynn usually finds a way to point that out. Tonight she eats one tiny bite of the cookie and leaves the rest on her empty plate, which she puts on the coffee table where Leanne's sure to see it. I don't know why Lynn lets Leanne get to her.

"I just read this article in *MORE* magazine or something—maybe it was *O*—that said forty-year-old women are just getting started," I say. "It said something like we're secure with our bodies and vocal about our needs. I can't remember the exact wording but that was the gist."

The laughter interrupts me.

"What?" I look around at them. "I'm being totally serious. Don't you worry about this?"

"No, she's right," Lynn says. "There was something on the *Today* show about it yesterday. They showed one couple who had sex on their honeymoon and that was it. Guess how long they've been married? Just guess. You won't, so I'll tell you. Twelve years. Twelve years and no sex. I don't know how she pulled it off, but I'll have what she's having."

More laughs.

"What's all the fuss about anyway?" asks Ginny. "We still have sex."

"You're in your thirties!" Lynn says. "Of course you're still having sex. Wait'll you turn forty."

Paula, who complains anytime the conversation becomes social, mutters "off topic" in a tsking tone, hoping it will steer us back to book talk, but it rarely does. She usually sits there with her arms crossed and her lips tight. Tonight, though, she weighs in: "I'm so tired all the time."

Everyone stops and looks at her. It's an unspoken assumption that Paula's asexual. She's got a Dorothy Hamill haircut and what a doctor would definitely term morbid obesity. I've never seen her with anyone but her three-legged English bulldog, Freddy. I think Paula is about fifty pounds away from being housebound. She's all business but I kind of like her for that. In the blackout a few summers ago she organized a candle drive so the elderly neighbors would be okay. She puts together a neighborhood newsletter on her computer. Birth announcements, who's moving in or out. Want ads you can e-mail to her. A ten-speed for sale. Babysitters needed. Does anyone know a good plumber? That sort of thing. She's the kind of person neighborhoods don't realize they need. She's the one who goes to the monthly Neighborhood Watch meetings and writes up safety information we already have. Lock your doors. Keep your front light on all night to discourage burglars. I respect Paula. In an emergency I like knowing she's at arm's length in her house with gray vinyl siding she hoses off every spring.

"I don't know what *you're* worried about." Ginny looks at me and rolls her eyes. "You're always so *together,* you know? Like you've got it all figured out. Plus, you and Bob are like the golden couple. I bet you have sex, like, every other day."

I open my mouth to say, "Are you *crazy?* You can't be serious!" but Lynn interrupts.

"As far as Michael knows, I have my period every day of the month," she says. The laughter bounces off the cuddly critters or whatever they are, mixing with advice for what to say to get off the sex hook and then a juicy story about a sex-addict husband of *someone we all know very well,* according to Kerry Kendricks, who, when Lynn asked her if *she* still has sex, says:

"Who has the time?" Kerry Kendricks is on every committee at school and not once have I heard her called by just her first name.

Ginny: "Let me ask you something." She looks at me. "Do you all think it's the women or the men? Do women want sex and the men don't or is it the other way around?"

Everyone's talking at once so it doesn't matter that I don't answer. I don't tell them that neither of us wants sex. Only Lynn knows I haven't stopped trying with Bob because I think it could still save us from being total strangers to one another. I haven't stopped trying for sex even though I don't want it any more than Bob does.

The next morning after the kids are off to school Lynn pulls up a kitchen chair and shakes a packet of Sweet'n Low into the tea I put in front of her.

"Before I forget, will you sponsor me for the breast cancer run?" I slide the form to her. "I know, I know. I swear this is the last time I'll hit you up this year."

"Breast cancer, Go Green, Save the Whales…" She sighs, fitting her name into the allotted space. "Sheesh, is there anything you *don't* raise money for? Here you go."

"Thanks, and for the record it was a Greenpeace fund-raiser not Save the Whales and it was about ten years ago." I laugh. "Thanks for this. I really do appreciate it."

"You should've taken it to book club last night," she says. "I would've loved to have seen how much Paula gave, since she loves breasts more than anyone, I bet."

"I don't think she's a lesbian," I say. "You heard her."

"Don't be so sure," Lynn says.

"So how about what Ginny said?" I settle across the table from her and just to make it seem like I'm bringing it up casually, I brush nonexistent crumbs off the table.

"What, you mean how they still have tons of sex?"

"Yeah, that," then I pretend to remember something else Ginny said, "Oh, and then there was that comment about me...what was it?"

Lynn narrows her eyes at me. "You actually think I'm buying your little show? You really want to talk about Ginny's sex life?"

"I don't know what you're talking about." I barely finish the sentence without laughing. "Okay, okay. You're right, you're right."

This is the best part about Lynn. She's pretty much always right. The worst part about Lynn is that she knows it.

"You know why everyone thinks you're so together? Because you *act* like you're so together," Lynn says. She's blowing on her tea, waiting for it to cool.

"Everyone really thinks I'm so together?"

"Yup."

"I'm not so together."

"*I* know that and *you* know that but I'm telling you, people think you're so together."

"Wow."

"Yup—" she takes a sip "—little do they know. Shoot! There's the recycling truck and I forgot to put the bins out. Got to go."

"Don't forget dinner tomorrow!" I call out to her. At a school fund-raiser/silent auction last spring, I bid on dinner for two at a new sushi place downtown thinking it'd be a good date-night thing to do with Bob. SushiMax is the hardest reservation to get according to *Chicago Magazine*. I forgot all about it until they called to reconfirm, and of course Bob found some excuse to get out of it until I came out and asked if it was just that he didn't want to go and he shrugged and said, *"You know how I feel about sushi,"* so I asked Lynn and told Bob he had kid duty.

I *have* been acting. Of course. I haven't thought of it as acting but that's exactly what I've been doing. But doesn't everyone put on a good face? Is anybody my age really happy? I've stretched my mouth into a smile for so long it's become natural. And sometimes it *is* natural…with the kids, especially when they were smaller. With Lynn. I know there are other times, too, I just can't think of them off the top of my head. Oh. After yoga, when I make it to Imogen's class. That's another genuine smile. On the rare nights just Bob and I have dinner, it's so silent I restrain myself from upending the kitchen table just to jolt us out of this stupor.

Bob once said, "The only constant in our marriage is the edge of the cliff we're hanging on to, killing time until we tire ourselves out and give in to our inevitable collapse."

It was fairly early in our marriage. We were reading in bed. We'd been married probably three years by then. I think it was during the fertility nightmare, but that's a whole other story. I remember it was summer and all the windows were open because the air conditioner didn't work. When we'd moved in, Bob had said, priority number one was central air, but the months ticked by and two, three years later there we were with a broken window unit and air so humid I was sweating just lying there.

"Listen to this," he said. I put my book down to wipe my palms on the white sheet while he read a sentence aloud.

"'The only constant in our marriage…'" He recited more while I was staring up at the ceiling thinking a ceiling fan might not be such a bad idea after all.

"Are you listening?" he asked. Then he read it again and that time I heard it.

I turned on to my side and flattened the pillow so I could see him, his expression. I remember wondering if he was simply impressed with the writing—sometimes he read passages aloud to anyone within earshot just to marvel at the sentence structure. Or was it something else? He'd put the book down and was staring into the room so I only had his profile. Then, almost to himself, he said:

"So I guess things could be worse."

I waited for a laugh but there had been no sarcasm in his tone. It was as if he was comforted knowing at least we were doing better than the couple hanging on to the cliff, if only a little bit better. That's the way he said it. Like he hadn't realized anything could be worse than what we were living through.

I couldn't think of what to say. I remember struggling to find words but none came. After a few minutes of dead silence, both of us lying there, our books splayed facedown across our chests, he said, "We should get a ceiling fan." He paused to consider the idea. "I don't think they're that expensive. It wouldn't be so hard to install. Probably only take me a day. Victor could come over and help me with the electric. What do you think?"

I'd shut my eyes and when he glanced over for my opinion I pretended I'd fallen asleep. I faked a few random muscle twitches. I heard him sigh then felt him shift to reach the lamp. His book fell on the floor, more shifting, and I thought maybe he'd gently lift my book off my chest, but soon there was snoring. I realized I'd been tensing every muscle to stay still until I had the night to myself to think about what Bob had just said. It was a bombshell, no doubt about it.

Around the time my eyes adjusted to the dark—I remember

this part because I was staring at the ticky-tacky drapes I'd never gotten around to replacing, when it hit me. It wasn't a bombshell. Things could be worse but not by much. I just hadn't wanted to see it.

But here's the rub: once he said it out loud, after that night, I couldn't get it out of my mind. I still can't.

Cammy

This is so stupid. I'll read this back later and it'll be totally gay and I'll just end up throwing it out but whatever. I'm supposed to be writing an essay on who I think is the most helpful to the environment in today's world but fuck that. I have no idea who's good for the environment and I don't care anyway. Nothing's ever going to stop the planet from going to shit so what's a stupid essay supposed to do but show the waste of time put into writing it. Oh, and by the way, it wastes paper on top of it so isn't that just perfect. Write about the environment and kill a tree in the process.

Will came by the other night at like two in the morning. He climbed up the tree that's right up along the house—the tree Dad says is wrecking the foundation. I told him my mom would shit bricks if she caught him in my room but he said "she should just chillax. It's not like we're doing anything." I wanted to say "oh, so putting your dick in my mouth isn't doing anything? Then get the hell out." But I didn't say it and he left as soon as I finished.

This whole thing with Will makes me feel small like I want to crawl into a cave. Or onto my mom's lap. Like I want to be a little kid again and this time do it right. I look at faces in every crowd like I'm gonna see myself staring back at me but that's so ridiculous. Like I'm really going to see a mirror image of myself. This whole thing is ridiculous but I can't stop looking at faces in crowds. At the mall. In line for a movie. It's just weird knowing my real mother is out there somewhere, maybe looking for me too. I bet she's beautiful. Graceful. Elegant. I wonder if she regrets having me. I wonder if she regrets giving me up. I picture her out there searching for me, trying to find me. Like she knows she made a terrible mistake. Pinning up Have You Seen This Girl posters on telephone poles. It was probably an impulse. Maybe it was me crying too hard. She couldn't handle the pressure. She had postpartum depression I bet and she didn't know where to turn so she gave me up to have some peace and quiet. I bet she changed her mind the next day but it was too late. Samantha and Bob Friedman took me away and didn't tell her where. And she's lived with a hole in her heart ever since. In my mind I find her and she pats her lap and even though I'm much too big for it, I crawl onto her. I want to start over with her. From the very beginning.

My parents are freaking out about me. They think I can't hear them through the walls but in this house you can hear everything from everywhere so it's like they think I'm deaf or something. Maybe that's part of it like maybe they know my birth mom was hard of hearing and so I probably am too but they don't want to tell me. Who cares. Last night I heard them through my iPod. They're all Cammy this and Cammy that like they aren't screwed up enough they've got to use me to keep from going insane in their boring lives.

I'm never getting married. Maybe I'll be gay. In front of his friends Will calls me a dyke and I know it's because I don't have boobs yet, not like the sparkly cheerleader types that suck off the football players but I wouldn't want boobs if that put me in their category. Sometimes I wonder what it must be like to be that pretty. Those girls can pick and choose and not have to worry about grades or being ignored. They're never ignored. The guys all treat them like they're made of glass, they're all gentle and nice to them like they're Princess Diana. Or no, idiot, she's dead. So not Princess Diana but someone alive who's like that, looked up to. Like Missy Delaney.

Missy Delaney's the first one who said I don't match my family. That's what she said in her squeaky ferret voice: *you don't match your family.* Like I'm a purse and they're the shoes. It was like eight years ago I think and because she was around other people she made it sound like it was a compliment like I'm prettier than my family or something but she and I both knew it wasn't meant to be nice. I think she was the first person who didn't like me. And I really don't know why she picked me not to like.

Now I get it. I mean, if we met today I wouldn't blame her. It's like we're from different planets. Different galaxies. When I dyed my hair black she told everyone I was a dyke in training and then when I got my nose pierced she said I passed my graduation and was now a card-carrying lesbian. Not the lipstick kind, either, she squeaked to all her little worshippers. I can't wait to forget her after graduation.

I'm totally used to the fake cough–blow job–fake cough thing they all do when I walk into a classroom. I'm used to everyone laughing. I'm even used to the knob of tongue pushing back and forth from the inside of Max's cheek every time I walk by him to my desk. I mean, it used to bug me but whatever. They used to call me Marilyn Manson but then Monica said *at least Marilyn Manson gets laid* and they shut up after that. I hate my life.

Monica's the only one who gets it. She moved here in time for the start of freshman year but since no one knew her from elementary school she had like zero friends. The thing about Monica is she doesn't care if anyone likes her. If she does she hides it pretty well. Even then, two years ago when we were fourteen, she was talking about stuff like *self-expression* and artistic integrity. She'd sleep over and we'd stay up late talking about the stuff I think about all the time. Like how what we look like on the outside never matches what's inside. She goes *well, at least I'm not a hypocrite. I wear all black because that's who I am inside: dark. I don't buy into all this shiny happy shit.* We went shopping one weekend back then and I spent all my allowance on new clothes kind of like hers even though I wasn't copying her. I was just ready for a change. She still thinks I copy her but I so don't. Her parents aren't around much…I've never seen them…so I think she likes having someone to talk to about everything. Like at school and stuff.

It's like my parents don't care what I think. It's more like they care who I come from, which figures since that's kind of what I care about, too. I know I don't belong to Samantha and Bob anymore. It's so hilarious how me calling them by their first names makes them all mad. Like "oooh, Cammy's acting up again" when it's just their own first names. Everybody else not related to them calls them by their first names so why not me. I didn't mean for the boys to start doing it so I can't really do it to their faces anymore. It's not the boys' fault I don't belong. They don't care what color my hair is or what's pierced or how much makeup I wear, they treat me normal. Like I'm their sister. I don't want them to find out about me for a while. They're too young for it now and whatever, like they'd really care anyway? The only people who notice the difference are Robert—Bob. Dad. Whatever.—And me. Oh, and Missy Delaney.

Here's a poem I wrote today in class and I think it sucks but whatever. I'll put it here for posterity, in case I blow my brains out or something. In case I go all Columbine on everyone.

Different

He looked at me with eyes that said "wow I thought you figured it all out by now"
Like I'm so dumb it never occurred to me.
Puzzle pieces fitting together at last.
Mystery solved only not that day.
That day felt small and dark like a cave I couldn't climb out of.
The solving of the mystery only recognized after emerging from the cave of childhood that ended there in the car on the way to soccer on a day that started like every other one before it.
The answers lying in front of me there, in the middle of growing up.
I take this with me like a rock I picked up on the beach and put in my pocket so I can remember the sand even when I'm home from the vacation.
Even when I'm under snow.
Even when I'm in a dark cave.

That's my stupid-ass poem.

Samantha

We're on our way home from a new couple's house. We met them at an open house at the boys' school. It was set up so the parents attended mini versions of the classes their kids take and this was lunch hour so we were in the cafeteria standing over a plastic tray of grocery-store crudités with wilting lettuce garnish, dried-out baby carrots and blue-cheese dip that had a film over the top of it. That night Dave and Susan Strong seemed terrific. He looked about as happy to be there as Bob was, but she was upbeat, and because they are new parents she peppered me with questions about school. When the bell rang we shook hands and I said we should get together sometime. The next day I got an e-mail from her with a list of dates they were available and I thought it was wonderful…. I'd been planning on following up, too, because I hate those empty offers. Finally we nailed down a night. I was happy to be able to bring someone new into the mix. I've been trying to shake things up and what's pathetic is that I thought something like having dinner with new people would shake things up. It took an act of Congress to get Bob to go. He never wants to go out, period.

In the car on the way home from dinner Bob turns to me at a red light and says, "Please tell me we don't have to get together with them again. He wears man-clogs, for God's sake. Even male nurses don't wear those anymore. They're the most dysfunctional couple I've ever seen in my life. Did you hear what he said to her about the chicken?"

"I couldn't believe it. In front of everyone. Did you see her face when he got to the part about how she always screws up dinner?"

"They must've been in a fight," Bob says. In the glow of the brake lights ahead of us, I can see Bob's tongue sucking food particles out of his teeth. I look away when he nibbles at something he worked loose.

"Yeah, but to have it in front of people they barely know? I wanted to die. So did everyone else. You know that was a red light, right," I say.

"It was yellow when I went through it. You want to drive?"

"I'm just saying."

"Did you hear him when he said, 'Oh God, not this again,' with that sneer when she said she had a great story about the principal at their last school?" Bob says.

"He's a jerk," I say. "I can't stand either one of them. She's racist, by the way. I don't know if you caught that, but she might as well've had a white sheet over her head."

"We're done with them, right?" Bob asks. He's at a green light but he's sitting there as if it's red.

"You can go, it's green. Yeah, we're done with them. Boy oh boy, they bicker bicker bicker. Let's call them the Bickersons."

We both laugh and maybe it's because we both realize it's been a long time since we laughed together that Bob reaches across for my hand and gives it a squeeze before placing it back at the two-o'clock position on the wheel. Ten and two…he rarely drives with one hand.

I'd thought Dave and Susan Strong would be different.

Secretly I'm kind of sick of our group of couple-friends. Except for Lynn and Mike, of course. I feel bad saying this especially because I used to be just like this, but to most, if not all, of the people I know, raising children is the greatest gift in the whole wide world. Leanne. Kerry Kendricks. Sally. If you ask how someone's doing they'll answer with something their kid's just said or done. Nothing about themselves. Sometimes I catch a glimpse of myself and realize I'm just like them. I hate that. *Hate.* I'm sick of my brain going to mush, of lying in bed wondering what I'll make for their school lunches the next day. Or whether I need to pick up another case of juice boxes at Costco. I'm sick of car pool. I'm sick of being the devoted mom. I'm tired of shuffling the kids to piano, guitar (Andrew just started weekly lessons), soccer, tutoring. The homework they bring home takes an ungodly amount of time and effort. Now that the time has changed we leave in the dark and we get home in the dark. I've tried making good square homemade meals but lately I've been throwing in frozen chicken nuggets and heating up canned peas. The kids seem fine with it (*Chicken nuggets! Wow! Thanks!* only makes me feel guilty for feeding them crap). But there's not enough time. This is what we all talk about. Everyone I know. This is it. This is what our lives are.

We talk about those women who leave their kids in day care or with nannies while they work full-time. Why have kids? someone will say. And we all nod like it's so true, *it's so selfish of them.*

They'll regret going back to work when their kids grow up to be delinquents.

Having coffee and pie at a tacky café with sticky plastic tablecloths, someone will mention Dale Harmon who was left alone a lot and ended up accidentally shooting himself with his father's gun. Someone *always* mentions Dale Harmon. No one ever let their kids play over at the Harmons' house because everyone knew Evers, Dale's father, had guns. So there you go: if his parents hadn't been working all the time Dale would still be alive. That was the prevailing thought. But I'm not quite sure Dale's mother, Tally Harmon, was working at the time. I think she might have gone back to work *after* Dale died. To get out of the house. The Harmons' house stayed on the market for ten months before they had a buyer from out of town who wasn't familiar with the family. No one in town wanted to move into a house a child died in. But the thinking was, *If Tally had been a good mother she would've been there.* Once she went back to work no one really saw her anymore. I was convinced that secretly she was relieved to have an excuse to go back to work.

I used to be a pharmaceutical rep. Right out of college I got a job with a company that'd just introduced an antidepressant *TIME Magazine* called "The Pill That Changed Our Minds." I was part of a massive hiring and nearly every one of my clients placed huge orders. I was voted sales rep of the month for a straight six months. I didn't particularly like my job but I loved the money, and my dad would exaggerate to all his friends that I was in line to take over the company. I remember limping home in high heels to Bob and our shitty three-room apartment uptown, off Wilson. I'd soak my feet in Epsom salts at night, talking to Bob from the edge of the tub about how the paycheck was worth it. I ended up hating all the walking and talking and schmoozing and handing out samples or free ballpoint pens with drug names on them. Most of the doctors hit on me and it grossed me out but I couldn't do anything about it. They were good clients. I ended up quitting just after Bob and I got engaged. It was a pain-in-the-ass kind of job, I thought. Until about a year later, I really didn't miss it at all.

It was the late '80s and every place we went it felt like I was looked down on because I didn't work and didn't have kids. We'd go out for beer with Bob's friends from work and they'd all ask what I did for a living. I'd say something stupid like, "oh, volunteer work and stuff," but it was a lie. I didn't volunteer. I sat around our suffocating apartment doing nothing in particular, wondering why I quit selling antidepressants. Wondering if I *needed* antidepressants. I was relieved to start house hunting. It gave us spark. Purpose. It was fun imagining what our lives would be in this or that house. Then we moved and I threw myself into unpacking. Feathering the nest. I felt—we both felt—grown-up. We'd lie in bed with our new roof over our heads, listening to the unfamiliar sounds of an unfamiliar house. We had so much to talk about back then. We chattered on and on about light fixtures and hardware-store runs and door handles and leaky faucets and catch basins and finished basements and crown molding. I knew where to find the nails at Home Depot (aisle five) and Manuel in the paint department (halfway down aisle seven, to the right) asked how the green was working out in the bedroom. Bob and I came to know which steps were the squeaky ones and we'd politely avoid them if one of us was sleeping.

I started wanting kids because I was bored. I was twenty-eight when we went to our first fertility clinic. The doctor sent us away with a laugh, saying we were young and still had plenty of time to try the natural way.

"You look like it's a death sentence, Pam," he said. "You're newlyweds, for goodness' sake! That's all you're doing anyway, right?"

He took a sip of his coffee and got up to show us the door. I never corrected him on my name.

Then it was 1991. Month after month I held my breath as

my period approached. If I missed a day I'd pull another stick out of my economy pack of pregnancy tests. I'd gone through over a dozen by the time we were in front of another doctor asking about shots to stimulate egg follicles. In early 1992, we were talking in vitro. By then it had become a full-time job. Bob was exhausted from the emotional and physical roller coaster but I was focused and determined and a little crazed. Bottoming out every time I saw those telltale stains on my panties. Bob called this time "the door in the floor." It got worse when people asked when we were going to start a family. No one knows the pain of that question when you've just had the ultrasound that shows your third in vitro has failed. By then Bob had checked out. Our fights got louder and meaner and always ended with him storming out and me crying like we were in a country-music video. He started staying away longer and longer and when he rolled back in he'd reek of cigarettes and beer. A double whammy since the doctors all said smoking and drinking decreases sperm count and motility. I've always suspected he was trying to sabotage the whole thing even though in the beginning he seemed happy about the idea of us being parents. Back when he'd whisper, *I'm gonna make you pregnant right now,* in the middle of sex and it would turn us both on. That lasted about two months.

In mid-1992 I gripped the arms on the chair next to Bob's across from our third fertility doctor who cleared his throat, looked up from my chart and said, "You might want to start considering adoption."

Cammy

Every once in a while Q-101 has commercial-free weekends and this was one of them and every single song was good. Not just a few—every single one. Ricky and I looked at each other by the time the Plastic Rabbits came on and it was like we were both thinking the same thing at the same time...like, why isn't there TiVo for radio stations? If there was, we would've maxed it out today.

Someone should invent that, he said. Ricky was lying with his head in my lap and it felt all coupley at first but it's not like he thinks of me that way so it's totally fine. I used to have a crush on him but whatever, it went away in like five minutes so it's all good. It's not weird or anything. I almost never think anything about it. Anyway, the only bad thing about his head in my lap is whichever leg it's on ends up falling asleep. We watched this group of old couples doing tai chi in the park and Ricky kept calling it *ching dong* and I laughed so hard Diet Coke came out my nose. And right then is when Missy Delaney walked by. Fucking Missy Delaney. She's such a bitch and the worst part is no one knows it yet. I feel like I have X-ray glasses on, like night goggles or something. Like I'm the only one who sees her face when their backs turn and her smile goes right into a frown. Not a fade-out but straight to black, like a scary movie and she's the killer. She has big boobs so all the guys like her of course. Even Ricky. Normally we agree on everything but when it comes to Missy it's don't ask don't tell.

I'm wiping the Diet Coke off my nose on the shoulder of my shirt, so I don't see the look he always gets when she walks by. He's all cool and shit and there she is Miss Priss only she's a total slut. Thank God I didn't see his face get all red and blotchy like he's been slimed at Nickelodeon. I can't take it anymore.

"I heard she got with some Lane Tech guy on Saturday night," I said.

I kinda feel bad about saying that because even though I did hear it I know it's probably not true because we saw her with her family when we went for family dinner at Giordano's. My mom stopped by their table and tried to get me to stop there too but no way. I just went to the table and waited for her to do her little social-butterfly thing.

"Bullshit, she did not," Ricky said.

Here's the thing—if it'd been someone he didn't have a crush on he'd have laughed and agreed with me or he would've blown it off or something but he got all pissy so that's how I know he's crushing on her. Big-time. Plus, the minute he saw her he sat bolt upright out of my lap like we'd been caught having sex. Whatever. Of course he sticks up for her.

"Why do you even like her? I mean, seriously?" I asked him.

"I don't *like* her like her," he said.

"Yeah, right."

"I don't," he said. "But I don't hate her like you do so sorry."

I wonder if he dreams of her sucking him like I do to Will. I wonder if he'd still be friends with me if I told him how last night Will said "go faster" and pushed himself so far into my mouth I gagged. I wonder if Ricky'd call me a bitch like Will did. I wonder if Ricky even knows about me and Will.

So I said, "I just can't believe you buy into all her shit. Little Miss My Father's Been on the Cover of *Fortune Magazine* and Yours Hasn't. Jesus, like that's something to be proud of. He's like Mr. I Own the Universe and I'm Going to Save the Environment."

"He knows Bono and shit," Ricky says.

"Everyone knows Bono."

"I mean he *knows* him. Like, personally. They're friends."

"Yeah, well, big fucking deal."

"Goddamn you're a bitch these days," he says.

"What're you *talking* about? I'm exactly the same as I've always been."

"It's like you're in this cult with Monica or something. You, like, *copy* her."

"Fuck you, I do not!"

"Yeah? Well, you always swore you wouldn't pierce your nose."

"That was when we were in, like, *fourth grade,*" I say. "Besides, you're the one who's all hot for Monica."

"Whatever."

"You know what I did last night?" I changed the subject. "I took two Benadryls. It was *awesome.* Seriously. Get the Severe Cough and Flu ones. It says to take one but whatever. Take two."

"You're a freak," he said.

Then he tried to dummy-wrestle with me 'cause that's his way of saying sorry and I knew it was only because Missy was way out of sight so there was no danger of her seeing him being all over me. Then it hits me—I've got to go to the friggin' movies with my mom…the last thing I want to do.

About a month ago my mom and I were in the car trapped like rats in a line at the place where they test how much exhaust your car puts out and the line was like a million cars long so there was pretty much nothing to do. Nothing good on the radio and my iPod was out of juice. I had finished my homework in study hall last period because Ricky was out sick 'cause his parents wanted him to have a day with his grandfather visiting from Phoenix so there was no one to pass notes to and I pretty much had to do my homework because Mrs. Cummings was staring holes into my head. It was the longest day of my life, swear to God.

Anyway, there's Mom babbling about how when she was young she and her mother would go to the drive-in movies on Sunday nights, just the two of them. I said that was what they did in like the fifties—like all *Grease* the movie and she said they still had drive-ins in the seventies. Whatever. She's all *we should have a mother-daughter tradition, too* and *I used to love Sunday nights with my mom.* Then she got all quiet like she was going to lose it and I don't know how it happened but next thing I knew I was saying yeah, sure, and she was off and running like she won the lottery. I feel bad I'm such a bitch and so hard on her—it doesn't take that much to make her happy if she's all freaked up about a Sunday-afternoon movie matinee. She looked at me like it was the best idea anyone had ever come up with since the dawn of friggin' time. She's all *it means so much to me that you're suggesting it.* I didn't suggest it but she wanted me to think it was my idea so I couldn't take it back. Whether she knows it or not, she's always made a show of overloving me, like she's keeping me from noticing how her love came so naturally with the boys. She's not so polite with them. She's careful with me. I've always felt this way. It's like she thinks I'm temporary. The boys can't up and leave but I can. I'm not her blood. I don't remember a time when I didn't feel this way.

All my life I've felt them watching me. Like a rat in a lab experiment. They threw me into their mix of DNA and they're curious about nature and nurture. We're talking about that in school now. Nature versus nurture. They'd never in a million years admit it but they treat me differently. I've always felt no matter how hard they hug me, when the boys came along they hugged them closer. Their hugs lasted longer with the boys. Like they were relieved. Like they were thinking: *phew—for a second there it looked like Cammy was the best we could do.*

Out of nowhere, this morning I wanted to tell my mom how pretty she is. She's so pretty it almost hurts to look at her. She never really wears makeup. She doesn't need it. She's naturally pretty. I really wish I looked like her. She must look at me and wonder what she would've gotten if she'd had her own daughter.

Samantha

The first time we heard Cammy's voice she was screaming *mo peas* over and over, crying so hard she was practically choking. The social worker told us it meant "more please" and wasn't it great, she yelled over Cammy's two-year-old voice, wasn't it terrific she already had manners. *She says thank-you, too,* the lady told us.

Cammy's foster mother was bobbing her up and down, wrenching her bottle away so we could get a better look at her face. The more she pulled at the bottle, the harder Cammy cried. *Isn't she beautiful,* she yelled over her. *Here, now come on, Cammy, let them see those beautiful eyes of yours,* she said. She was being patient because we were in the room. No telling what she'd be like alone with Cammy. It was all I could do to keep from grabbing the toddler, but I didn't want to look crazed. Like a baby-stealer. On our way out of that third fertility clinic I was so hysterical Bob said I was one step away from walking into a hospital and stealing a baby.

"What's in that bottle?" Bob asked.

I hadn't noticed it was brown but the crying was so loud I couldn't think of anything other than *please just hand her over to me. For the love of God let me hold her.* I'd read all the *What to Expect in the Toddler Years* books, but somehow it didn't register that Cammy was still on a bottle. She was already underweight for her age so it was easy to forget this was a two-year-old who should probably be on solid food.

"It's Coke," the foster mother said. "Don't give her the diet kind. She only takes the regular Coke."

I felt a flush of excitement that she told us this like Cammy was already ours. Like the adoption agency had already approved us.

"You're giving her *Coke?*" Bob said. I worried his tone would piss her off but then I remembered the foster parents have nothing to do with the adoption. She couldn't stand in the way just because she was insulted. And she was insulted.

"Yeah, well, *you* try feeding a crack baby, how about that? If you can find something better—go for it. Be my guest if you think you know it all. It's Coke or go deaf from the constant screaming. It's around the clock. Say goodbye to a good night's sleep."

The social worker cleared her throat and said, "Yes, well, the Friedmans have been brought up to speed," and then she leaned over to me and whispered, *"As you can see, this particular foster family is a tad bit overwhelmed. They have a houseful of children. It's really not so bad."* I can't remember the social worker's name, which is so weird because I had her phone number memorized back then we spoke so often. She spent every parenting class passing notes to us like *this is important* and *that will come in handy* when the group leader talked about how to raise a crack baby.

I've always hated that label. There must be something better. *Child born addicted* is what was first offered to us. The wait for healthy infants was so long. Crazy long. So we went to a private lawyer Mike found for us. Mike called him a fixer. Someone who *got the job done. Greased the machine.* He worked *within the system.* He *expedited things.* Bob and Mike whispered about it and I knew it meant money was changing hands under the table but I didn't care. I just wanted a child.

We knew we'd be looking at pictures on our second appointment at the adoption agency. I was wearing my gray slacks because they were the only ones that still fit. I'd lost a lot of weight from all the stress. It was six-thirty in the morning when Bob turned to face me in bed. We blinked at each other and he touched my cheek and said *let's go get her* like our little girl was waiting to be picked up from school. Which was exactly what I was thinking when he said the words. The way he said it, the smile he smiled, the feel of his hand on my face, pushing my hair out of my eyes, all of it made me cry and laugh at the same time. He was really trying to be a good sport and I knew it even then. Deep down I knew it was hard for him to muster up excitement that day. He sure did try though and I felt grateful for it. We scooted closer to each other. He rearranged the comforter over us. I ran my hand down his chest. He stopped me when I got to the waistband of his boxers. He kissed my forehead and said, "You want the first shower?"

It didn't hurt my feelings as much as it made me sad. Looking back, I think I sensed that we'd turned a corner and we'd never find our way back to where we started. I couldn't put my finger on it at the time. All I knew was that once we decided on adoption, sex felt redundant. Irrelevant. We'd come to hate sex by that time. Because of all the fertility visits. Bob disappearing into a stuffy room to "make a deposit," they called it. Into a plastic cup. He said they had old *Playboy* magazines he wouldn't touch because he said they looked sticky. They had lotion from a pump dispenser on the wall and a box of tissues and a Magic Marker to write your name on a sticker on the cup. There were the bruises on my belly from all the shots I had to give myself to boost my egg count. The ovulation kits.

Having sex during surges like it was all one big science experiment, which of course it was.

We were half an hour early for the appointment at the adoption agency. The receptionist smiled and said a lot of people do that on picture day and then she said *that's a good sign it's the right decision for you.* Bob squeezed my hand.

When our adoption counselor told us there were "alternatives" to waiting on the list, however short it was thanks to our shady lawyer, Bob mumbled "alternatives are never good," and I guess I should've paid more attention to that but I was single-minded. I elbowed him and he smiled across the desk like he knew I wanted him to. They look at everything, those agencies. Any hesitation could set you back. I don't know why I was in such a hurry, but I remember it felt like time was flying by and we'd be passed over and never have children and a childless couple was something I didn't want us to be. Sometimes I wonder what would've happened if I hadn't pushed and pushed us to have a family. Actually I wonder that all the time.

I was convinced we'd find her that day. Picture day. I'd gotten Bob a key chain engraved with the date so I could give it to him over dinner. The date we had our first child. I remember happily paying double for the engraver to rush the job. We'd only just gotten the call to come into the agency. Two weeks after submitting our application.

I stopped turning the pages in the photo album when I saw her. She was scowling at the camera and the downturn of her mouth looked like my mother concentrating on something. My mother made this same Charlie Brown face when she was cooking and checking a recipe or when I stayed out past curfew or if my father was late and missed dinner without calling from work.

There she was. This beautiful head of wavy light brown hair on the verge of being blond.

"That's her," I said. I thought when the time came I'd feel a rush of…something. I don't know. Some kind of lightning bolt. Instead, it was as natural as looking at the sky. It was as if I'd known her all my life. Like I'd willed her to us.

Bob put his hand on my shoulder and leaned in closer to see. I slid the album over so he could get a better look. I traced the line of her face and looked at him and caught a flicker of something I'd rarely seen in him. He hid it when he felt me turn to him, but there was no mistaking it. He looked defeated. Resigned. I opened my mouth to say something but closed it because I couldn't think of what to say. He'd folded into himself like a bat. His hands tucked into his armpits. Feeling the heaviness of the silence the adoption counselor said:

"I'll give you two some privacy."

She closed the door quietly behind her.

"What?" I asked him.

"Nothing," he said. He didn't look at me. He pulled the book over and smiled at her picture and then turned his face up like he was trying to make up for the grimace.

"You made a face," I said.

"No, I didn't."

"You made a face. If you've got something to say just say it," I said.

"No. Yeah. I mean, she's beautiful. Clearly. But—"

Maybe I was too quick with the defensive/offensive *"but what?"* but I was upset. How could he be backing off? We'd come this far. We'd talked about adopting a child with special needs. He seemed to think it was a good idea before picture day. He told me that if it would make me happy then fine. Okay, so he was doing it for me, but is there anything wrong with that?

I think it was because he saw that I wanted it. He knew I

wanted to be extraordinary. Not ordinary...*extra*ordinary. Making a difference in a child's life is one thing...making a difference to a child with special needs—that felt *right* to me. Lynn kept asking me if there was any rhyme or reason to it. Had my mom worked with retarded kids? she asked. What the hell did I think was going to happen? she'd asked. Did I think I'd win some award or have a street named after me? she'd asked. I couldn't explain it. Not to her and I suppose not to Bob. Not well enough anyway.

So there we were staring at Cammy in a three-ring binder.

"But what? Finish your sentence," I said.

"Nothing."

Then he cleared his throat the way he does when he has something to say.

"It's just—" more throat clearing "—I mean, are we sure we can take on a crack baby?"

"I hate that term."

"You know what I mean. A child born addicted. Whatever. It's a huge thing."

"We talked about this," I said. "We've been over this. I thought you were good with it. We were on the same page. I can't believe you're changing your mind."

"Sam, we only started talking about it when we heard there was a long wait."

"Yeah, so?"

"So...it's only been a few weeks, four, tops. It's a big thing. Maybe we should take a little more time..."

"But here she is! She's the one. She's our girl. I don't care what she's got in her system. And up until now you didn't care either. At least that's what you said. Were you lying?"

"Jesus no. It's just that it's...real."

"Yeah, well, having children is real, Bob. We've spent how

many thousands of dollars trying to make one of our own. That was real, right?"

"You know what I mean. This is a child with addictions…"

"…and they said it wouldn't be long until it's out of her system altogether. They said the lasting effects are minimal. So she'll have trouble concentrating in school. We'll hire tutors."

"You really want this," he said. Like it was a Christmas present that cost a little too much but that he'd be willing to buy to make me happy.

"I really want this."

He looked at her picture, smiled up at me and touched her photo like I had.

"Welcome home, Cameron Friedman," he said.

I threw myself into hugging him. I hadn't asked him if *he* really wanted this. I figured me wanting it was enough for the both of us.

My mother used to say there's no such thing as too much love. But what happens when there's not enough love? What if, when you look at your husband you feel blank like a piece of notebook paper?

I remember my mother leaning over the bathroom sink applying coral lipstick, checking her teased hair to make sure the bouffant was not too big because big is tacky. I would sit on the edge of the bathtub, watching her wave wet with nail polish fingertips, getting ready to go out with my dad. Even when she wasn't in it, the bathroom smelled like nail polish, Joy perfume and White Rain hair spray. Her closet had sachets so her clothes all smelled like roses, so that's what she was: petals and softness and color.

Mom'd say things like, "Rule Number One, never ever leave the house without lipstick." She put it on right after brushing her teeth and as soon as I was allowed to wear it, I did the same thing. She told me Dad never ever saw her without it. She said in a fire there are two things you need to do before you run out, lipstick and mascara. I started having all kinds of nightmares involving fire and she told me that Dad always kept fresh batteries in the smoke detectors, *he's that kind of father,* she said. For a long time if someone mentioned their father I'd ask if he changed the batteries in the smoke detectors.

I remember she'd tell me I was meant for greatness and boy oh boy just wait something special was surely in store and boy oh boy would I look back and laugh at how I never believed her. I didn't believe her when she said I would meet someone who I would love more than chocolate. I didn't believe her when she said I would love being married just like she did or when she said *just you wait, Samantha. You'll see. The love you'll have for your children will be beyond your imagination.*

It was definitely beyond my imagination the work it took to live day to day with Cammy. Lynn's son, Tommy, was only a few months old at the time, so we hadn't been able to spend time together, with or without the kids. Forget babysitters. No one had the patience for Cammy. Our social worker said the more exposure Cammy had to other kids her age, the better off she'd be. I thought I'd try the Mommy & Me class at our health club.

When you have a child born addicted to drugs you notice things you never before gave a second thought to, like taking Cam to the club. I'd never heard the loud music pumping bass like a punch, coming in through the revolving doors, which alone were confusing to her, I could see. I hadn't thought of lights being particularly bright, but they were suddenly blinding. The line of people checking in felt interminable— had it always taken so long?

All this made Cammy hysterical. Hysterical. People turned around. They stared. Some shook their heads like I was a criminal for bringing her here. I found myself embarrassed. Looking back, I wish I'd said, "Really? Really. You're upset about the noise my daughter's making and you don't mind Wang Chung blaring overhead?" Deep down, though, I couldn't blame them. I was one of them not so long ago.

By the time I signed us in, my arm was breaking under the constant squirm of frantic Cammy. My other shoulder was pinched in the straps of the baby bag I hadn't been able to readjust. I was sweating, passing the spin studio. The pilates room. The office for personal trainers. I was walking past my former life. By the time we made it to class I was exhausted. I looked in through the window in the door and all the moms were talking with each other. So pleasant. Then I looked at their kids. The class was for mothers and their two-year-olds. They were strict about the age apparently. So when I looked in at them I was shocked to see they were nearly twice Cammy's size. I looked from her to them and back at her. They were healthy of course. They'd been breast-fed healthy milk. They'd had carefully scrutinized pregnancies. The babies were all bobbing up and down happily on their mothers' laps, waiting for class to start. I turned and whisked us both out of there and never again went to the health club.

Bob and I went days without talking. It was a dance. Bob somehow sleeping through the cries in the night. Sometimes I knew he was faking sleep. He was teaching me a lesson. I was the one who wanted this baby. This child born addicted. If I wanted her so badly, he snored to me, I should be the one taking care of her. I felt in over my head but I wouldn't admit it. I couldn't bear to hear Bob say I told you so. I also wondered if he'd suggest returning her. Picking out another. Like a too-tight pair of shoes you need a half size bigger.

We passed each other silently. He'd dress for work while I stroked Cammy's belly, trying to calm her. The house was in a constant state of Cammy's moods. When we did speak it was never above a whisper. And our conversations weren't conversations but directives. Bullet points.

"How's she doing today?" he'd whisper on his way through the kitchen to the front hall to hang up his coat and change to house shoes. He never waited for an answer. Or, "We need diapers," I'd whisper. He'd act like this was quite the imposition. Like it was the final straw when really he did the bare minimum. Or, "Can you pop this in the mail when you go out?" He'd tap the bills into a pile.

I was too exhausted to ask him for help. I was too tired to fight with him about it. I should have said something. Maybe I did. But nothing changed.

Sometimes I'd make more of an effort.

"How was work today?" I'd whisper.

All of this while Cammy either slept or squirmed in my arms. I held her constantly. I developed biceps. Bob would try to hold her, but if she cried too hard he'd hurry her back to me and stalk out of the room.

It takes years to realize the impact an event has on your life. You don't see it at the time. Then much later you have perspective.

Not in this case. I knew, as it was unfolding, that it was tragic. The whole thing. I'd bitten off more than I could chew with Cammy. Maybe I could've done better if Bob had helped, but that wasn't in the cards. I didn't know the man moving in and out of our house. He wasn't even a roommate. He was a stranger. With Cammy asleep in my arms I'd look across the room at him and cock my head in wonder at his coldness. I knew he was hurt that our life had become all about Cammy, but I couldn't have imagined he'd take it out on her. I never thought he'd withdraw completely. Many times I'd cry right along with Cammy. I remember the ache of it. I remember feeling lonelier than I ever had in my life. Lynn made efforts to relieve me, give me a break, but I shooed her off. She had Tommy to worry about. Besides, no one could handle Cammy as well as I could, I told myself. It was true. Other friends stopped by with baby gifts, but they'd back out the door within minutes, Cammy's cries were that primal and unstoppable. Never-ending. So when the door closed behind my well-meaning neighbors and friends, I'd cry right along with my daughter.

Fast-forward in time and here I am, living a life I never imagined. I lie here in bed and I feel the sheets move to the rise and fall of my husband's breathing. I listen to the clicking his mouth makes when his tongue gets stuck to the roof of his mouth and I wonder how long it will take him to come to the surface of sleep just shallow enough for his brain to remind itself to create more saliva. Click. Click. Click. That is the sound of our marriage. Like the ticking of a clock. His mouth makes the noise of our marriage.

Sometimes I wish my mother was dead. I wouldn't want her to die painfully or anything. Just, like, in her sleep. Only because…it's just that…I mean, if she was dead no one would blame me for wanting to find my real mother. If Samantha was dead I wouldn't hurt anyone's feelings. My real mom would say things like *I knew they'd be good parents* and *I know I can't replace her but I'd like to be whatever kind of mother you'll let me be.* Bob would be fine with just the boys, and with Samantha gone I wouldn't feel like I'm betraying them, like I sometimes do now. Bob and the boys would come over to my real mom's house and we'd make them dinner and fill her in on all our stories.

Monica's brother has ADD and she stole his Ritalin. The whole freaking bottle. She gave me half the pills. This stuff is amazing. I'm trying to pace myself. I'm trying not to take it too many times a day because I don't want to run out. Anyway, this stuff helps me focus on *not* thinking about her. My birth mother, I mean. Also all the school shit. This tiny pill makes me concentrate on other shit. I even get my homework done, miracle of all miracles. I'll do anything to keep from going insane wondering where that goddamn letter from the adoption place is.

My biggest fear is them calling the house. I'm pretty sure I didn't write our home number on the form but I'm not positive. I get so focused on the Ritalin and then at night I zone out with Benadryl and it's all good. Three Benadryl knock me senseless.

I just think if Samantha left us, like divorced Bob and left us and started her own life, I could relax a little. I know I'm going to hell for saying this but whatever. I'm a bastard child so I'd be going to hell anyway. Plus, this is my diary and no one's ever gonna read it but me. I'll end up burning it when I move into my own place. I do wish she was dead sometimes.

Samantha

My mother died when I was in high school. Sixteen years old. She never saw me graduate. She never knew I was an honor student in college. She never met or knew Bob. She never met my children. I wish I could turn back the clock. I wish my mother had paid attention to her cholesterol and stayed away from all that fried food. I wish she'd listened when the doctor told her she had high blood pressure and should cut back on all the smoking. I got hold of her medical records from her last couple of doctor visits and there it was in writing, *Patient has been informed of the risks involved with her smoking and her high cholesterol. Patient urged to begin an exercise regimen and urged to have regular physicals.*

Nowhere in the file is a record of her following up with any of the doctor's suggestions. The same recommendations were made on subsequent visits.

If I could wind the clock back, I would pick the day I first noticed her holding on to the banister. That day I could hear her raspy breathing. I could hear her sigh.

"I must've stood too quickly," she said when she caught me staring.

I wish I could go back in time to explain to her that she was killing herself. I was too young to know all that at the time. It was unimaginable to me that she would disappear from my life.

"Mom, we're going to the doctor," I would say. "Get in the car."

And then I would get her a health-club membership and we'd work out together.

"You're so young," I would say. "You shouldn't be having so much trouble going up and down stairs. I've made an appointment, so there's no getting out of it. The car's out front. The air conditioning's on. Let's go."

I don't know if my father ever did this. He withdrew so quickly when she died and then years later I didn't want him to feel bad about it so I never asked. I'm sure the thought, the regret, occurred to him. I wonder if it haunted him. As for me, I think about her every day. It's a skipped heartbeat when I get to the family-history section on medical forms. To have to say *yes, heart attacks do run in my family—my mother had one.*

Then to have to answer the inevitable *how's she doing* with *oh, she's passed.*

It killed Dad when Mom died. I wonder if it would kill me in the same way if Bob died. I would feel sad, certainly, but would I *die* without him? Absolutely not.

Cammy was six and a half when I sat Bob down and asked him about trying for more. I'd been thinking about it for a while but we were never in one place together for long enough to have that talk.

"Oh, Jesus, not again," he said when I asked if he ever thought about having more kids. Cammy was asleep, the dishes were done and Bob was still awake. The trifecta.

"This time it'll be different," I said. "We've got Cammy. If nothing happens it won't be the end of the world or anything."

I truly believed that. More kids would be better for us. Bring us closer together. Yes, I truly thought that.

It only took one round of in vitro and voilà we were shopping for a double stroller for the two boys. Jamie and Andrew. I got blankets and towels monogrammed and Bob hunkered down at work and I hardly ever thought about the distance between us.

I rubbed anti-stretch mark cream on my huge belly. I bought maternity blouses with busy patterns that would help camouflage my monstrous popped-out belly button. I waddled to the baby stores, buying the tiny clothes, the bassinets, the cribs. In the sixth month I started to have the sick feeling it was all a big mistake. I wanted my mother to tell me everyone felt that way and it was only natural to be scared. I wanted her to warn me to keep track of the space between Bob and me, to make sure it didn't widen too far.

He started going gray in my eighth month. We were young but suddenly Bob seemed weary and creaky in his movements. And he started hating work. One night I made macaroni and cheese and Cammy was uncharacteristically quiet, so as I was pouring the unnaturally orange cheese powder onto the slimy pasta, I asked him how his day was. Usually he'd say "fine" and that would be it, like a television series in the fifties.

"Yeah, how was your day, Daddy?" Cammy asked.

I smiled at her and looked at Bob, but he didn't seem to think it was that cute. Lately she'd been echoing everything I said, so I'd started watching my swearing.

"It stunk," he said.

"It stunk," Cammy said.

"Don't say that," Bob said. He was on his first scotch, but if I didn't know better I'd say it was number two.

"So it wasn't a good day workwise?"

"That's why they call it work. If it was fun it'd be called something else."

"Remember when you used to love it?" I said.

"Yeah. So?"

"What changed?" I asked.

"The industry changed, that's what," he said, loosening his tie. "Shoes used to be designed. Now it's all about athlete endorsements. If some high-school draft pick likes black stripes on his basketball shoes, that's what we spend weeks drawing up. Straight stripes or are they angled up from the heel to the laces? Then we've got to send the PDF to the kid's agent to see if he likes what a whole team of us has been agonizing over. That's where the money is. Endorsements. Never mind that we had to switch to foam and felt inserts because the kid wants the stripes in leather not nylon. Eighteen years old."

"I'm hungry," Cammy said. "Is it ready yet?"

I turned the burner off and spooned the mac and cheese onto two plates for us, a little plastic plate for Cam.

"Ten years ago the kid would've been laughed out of the conference room and now we're bowing and scraping like he's the I.M. Pei of the shoe world."

"Why don't you quit?" I asked him.

"To do what?" he snorted. "What else am I qualified to do? And what about this *little family* of ours?"

"Jeez, Bob. Nice talk," I said.

"Nice talk, Daddy."

"Never mind," he said. "Sorry. I just had a shitty day."

"Swearword!" Cammy shot out.

I tried to rally back. To ignore what he'd implied.

"What would you do if you could do anything in the world, if money wasn't an issue?" I asked.

"I'd invent a time machine so I could go back and actually *design* shoes instead of decorate them."

I called Bob when my water broke but his secretary told me he was on his way to a meeting. It was 1999 and not many people had cell phones. The people walking and talking on them were considered pretentious show-offs. I called Sally, who was wearing a sweater with baby ducks and Easter eggs on it. I vividly remember that sweater. Sally has a theme sweater for every occasion. For Halloween. And Christmas. The Fourth of July one has a hidden battery to light up the flag across her chest so she has to keep it buttoned up and I've always wondered if she regrets the purchase on those sweltering sunny summer days. The minute the first leaf falls in September or October, Sally changes a seasonal flag that hangs over their front porch. The summer one featuring two beach chairs at the edge of the sea is switched to the fall one with pinecones the day after Labor Day.

We took Sally's station wagon with labeled bins in the back (Soccer, Volleyball, Frisbees/Misc.) and I felt bad the whole way to the hospital because I was sure I was getting her seat wet. I didn't know if it was bloody water or not (I couldn't remember what the books had to say about this), but either way her car had upholstery instead of leather and I kept envisioning unspeakable stains, so as we turned into the parking lot for the emergency room, I offered to have it cleaned.

"Don't be silly, of course not," she said.

But I saw her glance at the seat when I hauled myself out of the car and even during a contraction it occurred to me that she would drive directly to the car wash that minute.

Bob came running in through the automatic double hospital doors that make everyone look like they're making a grand entrance. He hurried alongside my wheelchair on the way to our assigned labor room. I ignored the fact that he smelled like perfume. It wasn't the first time I wondered about him cheating, but I wasn't about to bring it up on a gurney giving birth to my twins. Our twins.

A nurse named Doris was just wonderful during labor. I remember she was wearing scrubs with little teddy bears holding bunches of balloons and was the kind of person who strokes your head like she would a Labrador puppy. Doris repeatedly told me that an epidural was just moments away and she and I both knew she was lying because I hadn't dilated enough but I appreciated her efforts to keep my mind off the pain, which was excruciating. There is nothing I can add to all the stories about labor pain. It's terrible and mine was no different than anyone else's. I stupidly wanted to experience natural childbirth.

"You're doing great, just great," Bob said, and I remember him grimacing from my squeezing his hand so hard.

"How could you have thought this was a good idea?" I screamed at Bob. "This is a nightmare I'll never wake up from!"

The linoleum floor bounced the words up and back into the air of the hospital room and for a second it seemed as if everyone had stopped moving. It was like that game I used to play with Cammy—Red light, Green light.

"Honey, you're in pain—she's in pain," he said to me and Doris the nurse. "It'll all be okay in a little while. Just get through this and it'll be fine."

I think about that day in the delivery room and how I felt like the air had been pulled out of the room by a giant vacuum. Now, years later, I'm driving my regular route home from the kids' school that insists on frequent fund-raisers and pep rallies. I steer the minivan past a long boarded-up carpet shop promising same-day service. A garage on the other end of the block advertising fast oil changes sits empty. They are two ghosts bookending a sprawling Barnes & Noble towering over the middle of the block like it's flexing its muscles. Like it's challenging someone to a fight. It swallows up everything nearby and for good reason: why go anywhere else when you can eat your lunch, take advantage of free Wi-Fi and play with your kids in the children's book section that's become an amusement park with puzzles and blocks and stuffed animals all for sale. I inch left, onto Lincoln Avenue, pausing for a man in a suit talking on his cell phone, unaware the light has changed and I have the right-of-way. He doesn't break his stride, as if he is alone on the sidewalk and road. Waiting for him to reach the other side of the street, I glance into my rearview mirror at the boys, quietly watching a DVD. Their heads cocked at identical angles, their smooth little legs splayed open, each holding a corner of the DVD player because by now they know I mean it when I say if they can't share it I'm taking it away. I love them. Those hours in that suffocating delivery room are long past and I cannot imagine life without these children of mine. But that space, that distance between Bob and me? It's so wide right now it's like a river where you can't see the person on the opposite shore. We're dots to one another.

I accelerate to make up time but it's futile: I hit every red light. The radio traffic reporter is saying Lake Shore Drive is *free and clear in both directions* but the on-ramp from Belmont is jammed and, inching up to get onto the Drive, I can see all three lanes are jam-packed. No one's moving.

"Shit," I say, catching myself, looking into the mirror to see if my swearing registered with the boys. I've got to work on my swearing.

There's nothing I can do about the traffic so I switch from news radio to NPR. *All Things Considered*. A gentle voice is quietly reading a story about carrier pigeons. It's a miracle, really, how these birds fly distances specifically calculated by their owners. There are long pauses between sentences to better hear the coos of the pigeons and I start to feel sleepy, like I always do when I listen to NPR. I switch to the classic-rock station programmed into the number-two button on my radio. The guitar part of "Whole Lotta Love" wakes me right up. On cue the cars around me start moving like all they needed was some Led Zeppelin to hurry things along.

Saturday is nonstop. Bob takes the boys to soccer. I throw in a couple of loads of laundry and make it to Whole Foods before the crush of confused-looking stroller-dads who've promised wives they'll take the kids to do chores on the weekend. Their wives aren't sleeping in, though. They're doing all the stuff they've been meaning to get to all week but haven't been able to because of the kids. I remember to send flowers to Ginny, whose mother died of pancreatic cancer a few days ago. I call the florist as I pull in to a parking space at the Jewel for a paper towels/toilet paper run. All the non-food things that're prohibitively expensive at Whole Foods. Do we really need ten-dollar geranium-scented organic counter cleaner? I mean, come on. I pick up dry cleaning and stop by Alamo Shoes to return Jamie's Crocs because I accidentally bought him the wrong size. I check off all these things at a stoplight. The pen pokes through to the steering wheel, so I don't bear down too hard crossing off.

At three, Bob breezes in with the birthday present we need to bring to Kelly Voegele's party at Waveland Bowl at three-thirty. The one errand I've asked him to do and he's acting as if he should have a laurel wreath placed on his head. The boys want to go to Kelly Voegele's party only because it's bowling not because it's Kelly who they call a dork. I wrap the gift in sixty seconds and gather the boys up and we're out the door piling back into the car. Charlie Spencer's parents are picking them up at the end of the party, so we've got a break.

"Want to rent a movie or something?" I ask Bob when we get home. "It's Saturday night, Cammy's in her room and we both know she's not going anywhere and the boys are eating dinner over at the Spencers' and I give it an hour until they call asking to spend the night there. So for all intents and purposes we've got the house to ourselves."

"I'm not really in the mood, sorry," he says. "I've got to hop online for a while and motor through some stuff I didn't get to this week so…"

"Aw, come on…we have the house to ourselves. It's like all the planets have aligned and for a split second the earth is standing still."

"Honey, I've got so much to do it's crazy," Bob says.

"I could help get rid of some of that stress for you." I do a slinky belly-dancey kind of move toward him.

"Seriously…" he says. "I'm not in the mood."

"But you haven't been in the mood for months." Bad move. Bad move, Sam.

"Months?"

"I don't know. Yeah, I guess it's been a while. Maybe eight or nine months?" These words are a cartoon balloon over my head and I know we won't be having sex tonight. Good job, Sam.

"I didn't realize you had a calendar out. I didn't know you were keeping score."

"I'm not," I say. "Forget it. I was just thinking maybe something's wrong." The question mark of another woman, another bedroom, threatens to clip the thread that's holding us together.

"You know what? You saying that puts me in even less of a mood."

"Bob, come on…"

"Come on, what? I'm going upstairs."

I wait a few minutes and go up after him.

"Honey, please," I say.

He spins his desk chair around. "What do you want?"

"I don't know why you're so mad at me, first of all. What did I do?"

"Nothing, just forget it," he says.

"I just feel so disconnected from you," I say. "I'm not *keeping score,* I swear. I just feel…okay, wait. Let me rephrase it. Sometimes do you feel lonely? Like even when you're here at home? Like this isn't really your life, you're just going through the motions?"

"Nope," he says.

"Really? Even a quick flash of a thought that maybe this isn't what you pictured your life would be?"

"Can you get to the point?" he asks.

"It's just," I say. "Every once in a blue moon you don't get the teensiest panicked when you look around at your life?"

"Panic? Jesus, Sam, where are you going with this? Our life *panics* you? Are you *serious?*"

"Okay, okay, maybe *panic* is the wrong word—"

"Sam…"

"Surprised! Maybe you look around and you're *surprised* you have this life. Don't you ever feel that way?"

"Not really, no," he says. "I don't feel that way. Obviously you do but I don't. What's so surprising? This is what we always wanted, right? A family, healthy kids, friends, a nice house…"

"I know, I know," I say. "Maybe I'm just— You're turning back to the computer now?"

"What else is there to say? You feel panicked and I feel fine. People can disagree, you know. It's not the end of the world."

He turns back to the screen again.

"It's because…can't we talk about this?"

"We just did," he says. He shrugs and starts tapping on the keyboard again.

"What're you looking at that's more important than talking to your wife about your marriage?"

I look over his shoulder. "Real estate? You're looking at houses?"

"I'm looking at comps," he says. "I want to see what the Silvermans' house is listed for. Is that okay with you?"

"Bob, seriously. I only want you to let me in. It's like pulling teeth to get you to open up and I'm so tired of it."

"Jesus, Sam," he says. "Every other goddamn day you talk about how you feel about this or that. You're asking me how I feel about this or that—"

"Because you don't talk to me! And it's not every other day." I want to say, *I bet you talk to* her. That's if there even is a her. Maybe there isn't, I don't know. I don't want to know.

"Let me finish. I'm just…" He trails off, trying to form the words. "I'm sick of it. And now you're telling me you're panicked? I've told you how I feel. I feel nothing. You happy now? *I feel nothing.*"

That last statement throws us both into silence. He looks startled and sorry the words have come out of his mouth. WHOA! bubbles into the space between us, freakishly huge like the POW! and ZOWEE! from the old Batman and Robin fights.

"Thank you," I say. "*Thank you* for finally saying that out loud."

"Sam, wait—"

"I'm being totally serious," I say. "I'm not picking a fight.

I'm relieved, actually. It's a relief to hear you admit it. You feel nothing. No—don't get huffy—you said it. I wanted you to tell me how you feel and you just said it all."

"I don't feel *nothing* like the way you're thinking," he says. "I don't mean I feel nothing toward the kids. Or you."

"No, no, no—I totally get it. I think I've known it all along. But I want to ask you something. Don't shut down again, okay? Just hear me out. Do you think it's possible…wait, just listen! We haven't talked about it in months, so don't roll your eyes like that. Do you think maybe you're depressed? You don't sleep well at night. You don't have a sex drive—don't get mad, I'm just saying it's a sign of depression. Nothing makes you happy anymore. This is sheer inertia."

"Here we go…"

"Couldn't you just entertain the thought? Why do you have that look on your face? What're you thinking?"

"I'm thinking I'd like to know what the Silvermans' house is listed for."

I walk away and replay the sting of his words, letting them sink in and it is too big to cry about. That's all I can think: that it's too big to wrap my head around. This is where we are. I want so badly to know how we ended up like this. Yes, okay, sure, we never really had that spark, that chemistry, but we were best friends. Pals. Now we sit here in silence. It may be chaotic with the kids, but with us? Silence. That, or fighting. I wonder how he describes me to her. If there even is a her. Maybe there isn't, I don't know. Everybody argues and says things they maybe wish they hadn't, but this isn't that. He's wrong—this isn't all I think about every single day. I stay busy. Busy busy busy. I'm so busy I can barely think about what to make for dinner. Busy. I go to my school meetings and I pick up the dry cleaning and I cook and clean and do a million other things I can't remember I've done at the end of each day. I am the queen of multitasking. I organize my errands efficiently. I buy flats of impatiens to plant only after May fifteenth when the frosts are guaranteed to be over. I help out with school fund-raisers. I run Race for the Cure every year. I plant mums in the front on October first. I pick out the freshest roping to swag on the front of the house for wintertime. In between I do just about everything you need to do to keep a house humming along. That's who I am. I'm busy. I am every other mom in America.

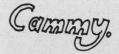

They always fight. They don't think I hear it but I do. I've always felt like my parents adopted me thinking it might stop them from fighting.

For a long time I'd say "don't fight" and that would be enough. They'd look at me and they'd remember the original purpose of me: to make them better. A little girl to bridge the gap between them. A trial child. Like when couples get a dog before they have a baby...to see if they can handle the responsibility. I'm their experiment. The thing is I don't know how they could've thought they did a good enough job with me to move on to the real thing. They had Andrew and Jamie on purpose so obviously they figured they did something right with me. But really all they do is fight. I don't know what that *something right* was.

I'd say "don't fight." I remember seeing my mom's eyes fill with tears and I'd hug her to make it better. Then I started getting sent to my room or outside to play even though there weren't that many kids my age on our block at the time. I was eight or nine maybe. They'd raise their voices, remember I was there and one or both of them would send me out of sight so I wouldn't remind them their mission failed. Adopting me only made things worse between them. I was a walking reminder of the fact that they once had hope for something better. I was supposed to be that *something better.* I'd send me outside or up to my room, too, if I were them. I'm definitely not something better. I'm something worse.

Samantha

A day after the nothingness of our marriage is finally acknowledged, on Sunday night, I find myself in a bathroom stall at the deep-dish pizza place with my head against the cold metal stall, crying. Back outside, across from our table, there is a young couple trying bites of each other's pizza and laughing at each other's jokes and listening intently to the other's stories. Did we used to be them? Now we are nothing, Bob and I. We are *nothing.* And here I am sobbing, pulling out squares of toilet paper piece by piece because the roll is locked in place. Someone in the next stall sniffs a signal that I'm not alone.

When I get back to the table Cammy of all people sizes me up and leans over and asks me if everything's okay. It's the first time in weeks she's looked out from the curtain of her oily hair. I tell her I'm fine, just blew my nose. I think I'm coming down with a cold I say.

"We ordered a large cheese and a small veggie," Bob says, folding his menu. "If you want a salad the guy's right over there putting in our order, just go tell him."

The next day I'm at the sink wiping the counter clean of cereal dust from the Cheerios box Jamie shook clean. I put the milk back in the fridge and slide the English-muffin crumbs from under the toaster into the palm of my hand. The air in the house is pressurized like when only one car window is cracked open. The vacuum of nothingness. Shit! Nothing? Shit. Do I feel nothing? I feel nothing. I can't really remember what it was I thought was so great about him. Why did I marry him? I was in such a rush. Why the hell was I in such a rush? No. Stop it. Stop thinking, Sam. Just stop.

I should take the toaster apart to empty it clean, it's been ages since the last time, that'll keep me from nothing. The metal tray on the bottom pops off easily. I'd thought I'd have to pry it off so I used too much force and the seeds and burnt edges and shriveled-up raisins from toasted bagels scatter on the floor.

We were in such a hurry to grow up. Maybe that was it. God, what were we *thinking*. Stop it. Stop *thinking*. I sweep the toaster debris into the dustpan and it strikes me that the floor hasn't been swept in a while. I get to the bar stools and I figure I might as well get them out of the way. Mom always used to use that cliché: anything worth doing is…wait, how does that go? Huh. Anything worth doing is worth doing well? Does that apply to marriage or chores? Maybe it was some kind of code she slipped me. Did she know she was going to die before I'd understand it? Did she hope I'd remember so it could help me at a time like this? Did she really think marriage was something worth doing? Of course she did. She of all people.

The phone rings. It's Lynn.

"What're you doing?" she asks.

"Cleaning the kitchen," I say. "Hey, how does that expression go? The 'anything worth doing' one… How does that go again?"

"Anything worth doing is worth doing well," she says. "Want to come over? I'm bored."

"I've got stuff to do. Come over here."

"Fine," she says. "I'll stop over after Whole Foods. You need anything?"

"No, thanks."

Our marriage isn't *nothing.* How could he feel *nothing?*

I've got to stop thinking about it. The couch cushions haven't been plumped in a while. I'll plump the couch cushions. On the shelf next to the TV the DVDs have gotten out of hand. None of them are in their boxes. Good project: I match all of them up but Spider-Man 2. It must be caught in a web somewhere I'd say to the twins if they were here. Jamie'd laugh and Andrew would roll his eyes, but inside he'd be smiling. I clean up the debris of a busy weekend—lacrosse sticks, dirty soccer socks, iPod headphones tangled in a hemp necklace Cammy wore in her crunchy-granola phase.

Here's Lynn cutting across the grass from her car.

"We just seeded! Get off the grass!"

"Oh, please." She waves me off. We both know my lawn's too shady for grass, but every year Bob gives it a shot. She walks past me to the fridge. "I'm starving." She smells it and twists her face up. "This is disgusting. It smells like feet in your fridge, just so you know."

She closes the door with her foot, picking olives out of a plastic container as I pour her a cup of tea.

When she looks up she says, "What's going on with you? You look terrible."

I love Lynn. I absolutely do. But every once in a while, she annoys the hell out of me. Today would be one of those days.

"Nothing's going on," I say.

"Something's going on."

There's this moment I think everyone has. A moment when you try to decide if you have the energy to wade into the muck of *what's really going on.*

"Talk," she says.

"Oh, fine. We had a fight last night. Me and Bob."

"Which one? Which fight?"

"*Which one?* We don't fight that often. Don't give me that look, we don't."

"Why can't you leave the sex thing alone?" She shakes her head. "What're you, a nympho or something? Get a vibrator and be done with it, for Christ's sake."

"It's not the sex thing. We're totally disconnected."

"What does that mean, *disconnected?* I'm serious, what do people mean when they say they're disconnected?"

"That just proves you and Mike have a good relationship," I say. "Disconnected means you don't know what the other person is thinking or feeling. Bob won't talk. We're like two ships passing. We're like roommates. Ever since…God, I don't even know…"

"When you started trying for Cammy," she says. She's heard all this before but she's a good friend so she lets me tell her all over again.

"Yeah. I could tell. Even at the time I could tell we were going our separate ways. Like a deal you make without saying the words."

"What was the deal?" she asks. "Pass the Triscuits."

They're stale. They're barely crunchy. Plus, they're Triscuits, for God's sake. Triscuits always seem like a good idea but they never are.

"Have some grapes." When I push the bowl over to the middle of us, fruit flies scatter.

I watch her lightly pinch through the bunch, looking for the firmest grapes. I'd say something about her getting her fingers all over them but I need to throw them out anyway so I don't.

"Here's the thing," I say. I burn my tongue on my tea. "Shoot!"

"What's the thing?" she asks.

"I just don't get it. I spend a fortune on organic food at Whole Foods. I've cut down on giving the kids fish that feed on the bottom because of mercury poisoning. I've had them tested for celiac disease and considered going gluten free because wheat's supposed to contribute to ADD. You know Jeremiah Pilson?"

"That smelly kid with the pug nose? Oh, my God, that kid's an asshole," Lynn says.

"Don't call a child that!"

"He is, though."

"Okay, fine. Anyway, remember how he used to be all over the place? Going a hundred miles an hour? Well, his mom— I can never remember her name—she told me he's got ADHD and they found out he's allergic to gluten so they totally cut it out and *poof!* he's a totally different kid. She said they even took him off Ritalin."

"What's the point?"

"I've done everything for this family," I say. I get up to wipe off the breakfast crumbs I missed. "I've put everyone first. I've disabled the passenger air bags. I replace the bike helmets when they outgrow them…"

"And she's off to the races…" Lynn tells me I talk too fast when I get on a tear.

"They've informed every decision I've made in my adult life."

"It's called *having kids,*" she says.

"You know what I mean. Even before we had children! We chose this neighborhood because it's in a good school district and we knew someday that'd be important, but you know what? I kind of wanted to live in one of those sleek high-rises downtown for a while. At least when we were younger."

"Have you ever noticed how everything's symmetrical in

those apartments?" Lynn settles back into her chair. "Pictures are hung two on this side of the doorway, two on that side of the doorway. Or if it's not even numbers it's three. Three candles. The pillar kind—all the same size and equally spaced out in the middle of the dining-room table. Those three balls in a bowl. You know those balls? The shell-covered ones, seed ones. They make balls with everything on them."

"You're totally missing the point."

"I'm still waiting for the point."

"I'm just saying. What about me? I've been reading the same five pages of *Eat, Pray, Love* for a month now because I fall asleep and the next night I can't remember whether she's in Italy, India or Bali."

"So you want more time to read?" Lynn is sarcastic in a sitcom way.

"You're not listening to me! I've put my whole life on hold for this family. I've made them the center of my universe and that's fine. That's what you do, right? You put the kids first. But no one's putting *me* first. No one's looking out for me. We remodeled the kitchen into this huge open space so I could watch the kids while I'm in the kitchen, but guess what? I want my sunroom back. I loved that sunroom."

"That sunroom smelled like mildew," Lynn says.

"I loved my herb garden. You know how much fresh dill is now? Almost seven dollars. For a little plastic container."

"So you're asking what's in it for you," she says.

"I'm asking what's in it for me." I can tell she's serious now. I'm not going to get some Aaron Sorkin line. "Does that make me selfish? Am I being selfish?"

Lynn sits with her left arm crossed, her right hand in a loose fist like *The Thinker*.

"Does this mean I'm crazy?" I ask.

"No," she says. "This means you're middle-aged."

I looked at the table and back up at her for confirmation I guess.

"You're halfway through your life, more or less," she continues. "It's what happens when we turn forty. We have midlife crises. Why do you think all those self-help books are multiplying like rabbits? Everyone's wondering the same thing. The whole 'is this all there is?' thing."

"*You* don't. I never hear you complaining about the deals you made when you had the kids."

"What was the deal you made?" she asks again.

"That we'd try for a baby even though Bob didn't want one. He went along with it so I'd leave him alone afterward and he could have his big career. Wait. That's not it exactly. I don't know. It's hard to describe."

"Yeah. I know."

"You do not."

"I do, too!" she says.

"Give me one example of a deal you guys have made. I'll know if you're making it up, so don't lie."

She buys time by taking a sip of her tea and holding it in her mouth before swallowing.

"Forget it," I say. "Also, Cammy's in trouble."

"What now?"

"She's on probation. We had to go in to talk to the principal on Friday."

"What'd she do?"

"She's been cutting class. She's being *disrespectful* to her teachers."

"Yeah, but in Black's opinion if they don't say *sir* or *ma'am* that's being disrespectful," she says. "He's got a stick up his ass the size of a baseball bat."

"And cutting classes?" I say. "I mean, let's just face the facts.

Look at her. *Look* at her, Lynn. It's not normal the way she dresses. The makeup. Swear to God, in a million years I never thought…"

"Did you guys know any of this was happening? The cutting-classes thing. I mean before? You never said anything about it before."

"When she started hanging out with this new girl from downstate I smelled trouble."

"Who's the kid?"

"Monica Carter. You don't know her. She's freaky looking. Pierced cheek. Pierced eyebrow. I'm pretty sure her tongue's pierced, too."

"That's so gross," Lynn says. "P.S. Doesn't it hurt when they eat—doesn't the food tug at it I mean?"

"Focus."

"Sorry, sorry," she says.

"I went to pick up Cam from school the other day and I see her slouching next to this girl who looks like Cammy times a million. She looks like she hasn't taken a shower *ever*. Cammy walks to the car like I've got all the time in the world and this girl nodded at me and gave me the peace sign when I introduced myself. That's another thing, Cammy didn't introduce me. I had to lower the passenger window and say 'You're Monica, right? Nice to meet you.' She smokes. She holds her cigarette like she's Steve McQueen."

"Okay, first of all, sixteen-year-olds don't introduce their parents to their friends," Lynn says.

"Okay, well, fine," I say. "The point is, I don't like this girl. I saw her smoking in front of the 7-Eleven. She goes to the soccer games from time to time and hangs way off behind all the parents, leaning against a tree with her arms crossed like she's *soooo* cool. She's got a brother on one of the teams I guess. Cammy thinks she's God's gift. We can't ask her any questions

about Monica without her stomping off saying we're so judgmental and we don't like her just because she looks different.
She's got that Goth eye makeup and she wears long black Grim
Reaper clothes. And right on cue, Cammy's wearing the same
makeup. I had to switch to paper napkins because black lipstick
doesn't come off in the wash."

"It's what they all want us to think. They're all antiestab-
lishment, antiparent, and Cammy's wondering why you don't
like it?" Lynn says.

Lynn's cell phone rings.

"Yeah, well," she's saying into her phone. "I'm not picking
you up early again. No. Because you're not sick! Go on back to
class."

"You don't even say goodbye?" I ask her.

She cocks her head to the side like *do you know me at all?*

"You're losing me on this story," she says. "Where's the fight
with Bob in all this? And by the way, didn't Cammy get her
nose pierced pre-Monica Carter?"

"Nope. Post-Monica. So the fight. It started after they told
us about the probation. That was Friday. Then on Saturday
Cammy starts in again with us hating Monica because she
looks different. *She looks different,* get it?"

"Am I supposed to know what that means? Hold that
thought. If this is Tommy again, I swear to God… Oh. *Unless
you're throwing up blood I'm not picking you up early.*"

She turns back to me. "He's got an algebra test last period
he didn't study for so he's pulling out all the stops. Sorry, keep
going. The fight with Bob…"

"Don't you remember years ago when I found Cammy in
the bathroom crying? Remember what she said? She said she
wanted to look like the rest of us. She was tired of looking different from us, she said."

"So you're mad because…" she says. "I mean, that happened a long time ago, that thing in the bathroom."

"I'm mad because when Cammy was three and a half Bob decided—*without talking to me about it first*—he unilaterally decided to tell Cammy she was adopted. He told her she wasn't our *real* child, his words. She wasn't even four years old! And we'd decided we would wait longer, talk to professionals beforehand to find out the best way to do it."

"Shithead."

I hate it when Lynn calls Bob that. She does it all the time now. "I hate it when you call him that."

"You're the one who fought with him!"

"I know, but he's my husband and…it just doesn't feel right."

"All right, all right, I'll stop. But why's it coming up now?"

"It's coming up now because now's the time she's acting out. He messed her up. I've been waiting for this to happen. I knew we wouldn't see it for years and here we go. Right when it matters most. Right when they're becoming who they're going to be. He messed her up and I can't do a thing about it. She won't listen to me anymore. And I don't know when *that* happened either…"

"Oh, stop," she says. "This kid, this Monica, she looks different, too, so it makes sense Cam would hang out with her. Maybe it's good they have each other. Oh, honey, don't cry."

"I sound like such an old lady saying this, but she's always been such a good girl," I say. In the bathroom off the kitchen I pull a tissue out of the Kleenex box but it's the second or third to last and they all come out at once, something that annoys me every time it happens.

"We've been so close," I say through a nose-blow. "She's never talked back to me, not once. And now…"

"Now she's a *teenager*," Lynn says. "Welcome to the teen years. It'll pass. It always does."

"I don't know," I say. "Remember when she was ten and she went and got that skin lightener from the drugstore? The kind they make for African-Americans? I found the box in the trash and luckily I stopped her before she used it, but when I asked her why, you know what she said?"

"Huh."

"She said she hated her skin color. Here she is with the most beautiful light olive skin and she says she wants to be fair-skinned like Jamie and Andrew and me and Bob. *Then I'll look like a* real *Friedman,* she said. I remember it like it was yesterday."

I fiddle at the wisps of balled-up Kleenex.

"And now she's swinging the other way," Lynn says.

"And now she's swinging the other way," I say. "Exactly."

"Is Bob worried, too?"

"No," I say.

"Shithead."

The thing is, he's not a shithead.

Cammy.

I couldn't stop coughing. It was brutal. When Monica took the joint from me I went into seizure coughs. She laughed and then asked if I wanted some water which I did but I couldn't even nod my head I was coughing so hard.

Monica doesn't have fun anymore. She says everything's boring. It is. I know it is. But every time I think of things to do other than hang out in my room she looks at me like I'm a baby. Like when I said *let's go to the mall* she says *oh, my God you're serious? I thought you were kidding. The mall's all pod people with hairbands and purses.* I'm embarrassed I asked.

When I say *let's go to the lakefront and sit on the rock wall at Montrose* she's all *and what? Skip rocks? So gay.*

Then she goes *this is a shit-ass city* which pisses me off but I don't tell her that. Who hates *Chicago?* It's like the best city in the country.

Anyway today she brought a joint over and said *okay let's go to your little lake.* I thought it was a cigarette. Just for a second, but still.

My mom was out with the boys somewhere so we had to walk, which took forever. The wind was coming at us and I looked at Monica and she looked like a Halloween witch. A cool one. With her clothes blowing after her like a black wedding dress with that long train.

We get there. It's overcast and kind of cool so not many people are out. We're near the dog beach. When I'm here with the boys we always stand and watch the dogs chasing each other, swimming, fetching. It's our thing, it's what we do, the boys and I. Now, with Monica, I pause to watch this little white dog trying to wrestle a huge stick away from a Lab. I think the little one is a Jack Russell. I said *wait, look at that. That dog's crazy. Look at that.* Monica says *whatever, let's keep going.* I wanted to see if the white dog got the stick after all but she kept going and I had to half jog to catch up. Seeing it through her eyes I realize it's stupid to stand there like idiots watching other people's pets play. They throw tennis balls way out in the water and those dogs splash in and swim hard. Some of them go pretty far out. Even when it's cold. I guess I'm too old for that now. I wonder if my real mother ever had a dog. I picture her with an Afghan with that thin body and long hair. If she'd have kept me we might have brushed the dog together. We would've named it Heather. I've never seen an Afghan in person just in pictures but they're beautiful. Owners are supposed to match their dogs and I've always imagined my mother like an Afghan. The kind of person people make way for when she walks through a crowd.

There's a long cement pier with a metal antenna at the end of it and even though it's freezing and windy we walk down to the end of it. On warmer days fishermen plant themselves up and down it. The very tip is hidden by the concrete base of the metal thing so we sit there dangling our legs like it's a hot day in August.

It takes her a lot of tries to get it lit. It's that windy. I watch the way she holds it between her thumb and first finger. Like a guy. It's not like I haven't seen people smoking pot before but she looks cooler doing it than anyone I've seen. I watch her inhale and hold it in. She hands it to me before she lets the smoke out. I hold it in a pinch like she did. For a second I think *what if I let it go in the wind*. But she'd be pissed and she's already at the end of her rope with me. I don't think I'll do it right. And what if I fall in the water because I'm so stoned.

I blow all the air out of my lungs and inhale but the smoke goes down too fast. I go into a choking cough. She grabs it out of my fingers like it's a diamond I might drop. The coughing gets worse every time I try to take in air.

"You want water or something?" she says.

But she doesn't have any with her so I don't know why she offers.

"You've never smoked pot before," she says.

I manage in between coughs "yeah, I have," but I can tell she knows I'm lying.

"With who? Your little friend Ricky?" she says. "Dubious."

She takes another drag and hands it to me. It's a test. She's looking out across the lake but I know she's sizing me up. I wish I could wait a little longer. My throat's on fire.

This time I don't suck it so deep. I hold it in.

She goes: "You barely got any that time."

I don't think that's true but I'm aware that I'm just holding it in my mouth long enough to not have to answer her so maybe it's true.

"This is good shit," she says. It's her third drag. The joint's almost gone, she's pulling it in so hard.

"Last call." She hands it to me.

This last drag I do it right. I can feel it. I have to pinch it using the very tips of my fingers because it's nearly out. Monica takes it back carefully and sucks on whatever's left then she tosses it in the water. The paper's so thin it disintegrates within seconds.

"You know who you have to meet?" she says. "You've gotta meet this guy Paul."

We're still dangling our legs. I'm kicking mine in and out like a kid.

"Who's Paul?"

"Just this guy. What're you doing later?"

It's Saturday and I know I'm grounded but I can crawl out so I tell her *nothing* and she says to meet her at the 7-Eleven at nine.

When we stand up I almost fall in and she laughs and pulls me close to her. We shimmy close to the antenna base and she goes *race you back to the beach*.

I run after her. Our clothes are whipping in the wind. She looks back to me and for a second I see what she must've been like before all this. Before all the black. Back when she was normal. When she was a kid.

By the time we reach the sand we're out of breath. I feel light and happy and I laugh and she does too.

She's not bored. I'm not either.

On the way back to my house I realize I've passed the dog beach without looking over at it.

Samantha

"Jamie, go up and get your sister. Oh, shit." I'm making lunches at the last minute as usual and as usual I make a mess that could have been avoided if I'd made lunches the night before like Kerry Kendricks does. A glop of jam splats onto the floor. "Shit."

"Double swear!" he says. He checks to see if Andrew's around so he can rub it in. "That's fifty cents!"

I'm crouching over the sticky patch of floor I made worse by using a too-wet paper towel that's only smeared it into a larger sticky patch of floor. "You have exactly two seconds to *go get your sister!* Wait, throw me the sponge, will you? Good job. Now go."

"Cammy! Mom says come down!" he hollers from the foot of the stairs.

"Go up and get her!" I holler to him. "She's going to miss car pool!"

I've run out of peanut butter. Great. I don't hear the thumping of Cammy's music anymore, but Jamie and Andrew are the only ones to appear.

"What? Where is she? Andrew, grab two juice boxes out from the pantry."

"But they won't be cold," he whines.

"Cammy wouldn't come out," Jamie says. He looks like he's tattling and to Jamie that is a horrifying offense he takes great pains to avoid.

"There's Mrs. Kempner honking." I hurry to the front door to wave that they're on their way. "*Cammy! Car pool! Now!* Okay, good, coats on, backpacks… Andrew, did you get juice for both of you? Good. *Cammy!* Boys, go go go. Have a good day at school! *Cammy?*"

I hold up a finger letting Eileen Kempner know to wait another minute and I nearly trip on my robe rushing up the stairs to bang on Cammy's door. The music is cranked high again so shouting is futile. Over some emo noise I don't even understand I can hear Eileen tapping on her horn. On my way downstairs I remind myself to Google emo music. Or I'll go to iTunes.

Back at the front door I mouth *sorry* and wave Eileen on.

Cammy's music is so loud the doorknob vibrates in my hand. Of course it's locked. No shaking or beating works and my blood is boiling so hot I'm breaking a sweat in my pajamas and robe that's too heavy and a very ugly flannel but the kids gave it to me for Mother's Day so I'm doomed to wear it for the rest of my life. I call her cell phone from the phone by my bed and I'm about to hang up because I remember we confiscated it but it's ringing. It doesn't go straight to voice mail. Aha. The music is turned down and she answers, not realizing the call's coming from a few feet away since we've blocked our number from caller ID.

"If you don't get out here right now I swear to God…"

I hear her door open. She's fixed a look of amused bewilderment on her face, like she has no earthly idea what the fuss is about.

"You realize you missed your ride to school, right?"

She brushes past me and glides down the stairs without a care in the world.

"I'm talking to you!" I'm about to storm after her but I hurry to my closet to throw on sweats and whatever shirt my hand lands on so I can drive her to school. Cammy's attitude du jour is just the kind of thing that gets under my skin and she knows it.

"Get in the car." I don't bother locking the door. I'll be back in twenty minutes. "Hurry up.

"I'm so sick and tired of your games, Cammy, I swear to God. Oh, hi, Mrs. Ainsley!" I fake a smile and wave through the window to our elderly neighbor walking her dachshund. Back to Cammy. "Give me *one good reason* I'm driving like a banshee to get you to school when it's not my day to drive. Huh? Can you speak?"

She shrugs and I fight the urge to screech the car into Park so I can wring her neck. She *shrugged*. What do I do with that? She's looking out her window.

"I wish someone would tell me what I'm supposed to do with you. What am I supposed to do with you?"

I shouldn't have beaten the steering wheel. I shouldn't have yelled. I shouldn't have yelled *that*.

"I hate you," she says.

She doesn't spit it in anger. She doesn't raise her voice even. She says it calmly, like "gee, isn't it a lovely day out." Like it explains everything, which, I guess, it does. I'd been waiting for this cliché moment of teenagedom—you hear about it, read about it, see it in Lifetime movies, you know it's coming, but nothing prepares you for the punch of it.

"What?" Maybe I didn't hear it correctly. "What'd you just say?"

"Nothing. Whatever." She sighs, turns on the radio and goes back to studying the apparently fascinating scenery.

At the stoplight I feel the look of the driver next to me probably wondering what kind of a mother has a freakish Goth daughter. They all judge me. *How is it okay for that daughter to be like that—where's her mother, for God's sake?* That's what they all think. So I put on my show. I tip my head back and smile as if I've just heard a wildly entertaining story. I turn my head to him. I make sure the smile slowly fades so he thinks, *Oh, I guess I didn't realize they're actually really enjoying one another's company what a lovely mother and daughter actually they look so close and happy.* Yessiree, we're having a *marvelous* time in here. We always have a marvelous time together. I smile into his eyes and nod. I know what you're thinking, buddy. I'm one lucky mom, in the company of her chatty daughter who's so sweet she just might look over at you and wave. That's the kind of girl she is. The kind that waves at total strangers just because she's naturally friendly.

"It's *green.* Jesus frigging Christ, the light's been green for, like, an *hour. God.*"

Ah, yes, she's naturally friendly.

The rest of the ride is a vacuum of oxygen and sound. The kind you notice. I exhale when her door slams shut. Back at home I clean up the rest of breakfast, start a dishwasher load and pick up random boy-debris scattered throughout the downstairs before I straggle up to shower and change for a day that already feels half over and it's not even 9:00 a.m.

A couple of hours later I'm waiting for the cable guy to come. I hate waiting. Hate it. They've given me a four-hour window and I should be going through my list of things to do, e-mails to write, calls to return, but I'm staring out the front window instead. I don't know when I've just sat here, staring out the front window like this. Probably before Cammy. Three cars have driven down our street. I recognize none of them.

We live on a street you'd have no reason to come down unless you live here or were visiting someone who lives here. It's not a cut-through. It's not really on the way to anywhere anyone wants to go. Then again, I'm rarely staring out the window for any length of time. A Roto-Rooter van pulls up in front of the Flanderses' house. Sally's showing them in. She's still in her robe even though it's eleven in the morning. Soon they're snaking a hose from the van in through the front door. I wonder if she sits here like this, looking out the window all day. Maybe that's why she drinks too much.

I jump at the sound of a knock at the front door. Thank God they're here. They'll fix the cable box upstairs and I can get going.

I open the door and instead find two serious-looking teenagers in matching white shirts, thin black ties, neat backpacks, holding bibles. They're probably Cammy's age. Normally I would have politely said *it's not a good time* or *I'm on the phone could you come back,* knowing I'd screen door knocks the rest of the day. I've signed a petition now and then but generally I close the door pretty quickly. Today I find myself inviting them inside. They look neither surprised nor pleased to have a shot at saving me. They look like this is exactly what would happen at this house in this nice neighborhood with its nice yards and nice families.

"We'd like to talk to you about our savior Jesus Christ," the thinner of the two says. They take their backpacks off at the same time. They are standing at attention in our small front hall. I hold my arm out for their jackets and drape them on the coatrack. It's hard to keep them up for all the fleeces and raincoats. I remind myself to sift through our coats later to free up some hooks.

"Come on in. Have a seat. Would you guys like something to drink? I've got Coke. And juice," I say.

I want them to stay. I don't know why but I want to talk to them. Maybe this will lead me to some awakening. Maybe this will be the change I've been waiting for.

"No, thank you, ma'am," the other one says. He is hefty. He wears Buddy Holly glasses. He has terrible acne, the kind he'll need sandblasted off later. "Can I ask you about your spirituality?"

I sit across from them on the chair by the fireplace.

"Make yourselves comfortable." I say this because they're perched on the edge of the couch. Like they're prepared to be shown out within minutes. I wonder why, then, they didn't look pleased to have made it into this living room. "Are you hungry?"

"No, thank you, ma'am," the thin one says. He has a buzz cut and between the two of them I feel like I've been transported into the fifties. Which is about right. A bored housewife waiting for a visitor. Happy and eager to entertain whoever happens to stop by.

"Are you on a pilgrimage?" I ask them. I don't know why but I find myself interested in why they're here. "Did your parents travel with you? I don't really know how it works. Like is it Buddhist monks spending a year traveling without worldly goods?"

I'm aware I seem silly. Part of me wishes Cammy were here. The old Cammy. I could make her sit down with us in the living room. She could learn something. See the bigger picture. I wouldn't feel so alone.

"It's not exactly like that, ma'am," the thin one again. They speak robotically. Like they've memorized a script.

"Do you get scared going door to door like this, without any family with you?"

"We're each other's family, ma'am. That's kind of the point," the pimply one says. "The Church of Latter-day Saints is one big family. We support each other spiritually and emotionally. And, if need be, financially."

"Mostly we stand shoulder to shoulder looking up to our savior Jesus Christ," the thin one says. I see him looking at the palm of his hand and I realize not only is he nervous but he's cribbed notes there.

"Is this a mission then?" I ask them.

"It's a calling," Hefty says. "To share knowledge we've received by revelation from the Holy Ghost regarding eternal gospel truths."

"It's an opportunity to serve," Skinny says.

I don't find their memorized speech creepy, like I might have on another not-so-lonely day. It's comforting. These two boys comfort me. They fill the silence.

The doorbell rings and I jump. They blink at me with their innocent eyes. Sheltered boys who have enough courage to go into strangers' houses. They've seen nothing of the world and here they are in Chicago going door to door. I'm assuming they're from Salt Lake City but maybe they live nearby, come to think of it.

"Just a sec," I say. "It's the cable guy. I'll be right back."

What the hell am I doing? These could be robbers casing the joint. Dressed like Mormons. Genius when you think about it. I walk to the door and think *fine. Let them take whatever they want. I don't care about any of this shit. They can have whatever they want.*

The cable guy has a huge key chain clipped to his wide belt. I wonder what a cable guy needs with all those keys.

"Hi. It's the box upstairs. In the bedroom," I say. "It just stopped working all of a sudden." I hurry him upstairs so I can get back to the Mormons.

"Sorry about that," I say. "What were you saying?"

"Can we ask you about your spirituality? Do you believe Jesus Christ is our savior?"

It's not that easy, I think. You don't know it yet, I want to say to them. Life hasn't broken your spirit yet. A savior? Please.

"I guess I do, yes." I don't know why I say this. My parents were lapsed Jews. Jesus Christ doesn't exist for Jews. But if I tell them this they'll leave and I'm desperate for them to stay. Why, I have no idea.

"Ma'am?" the cable guy calls from the top of the stairs. "Yeah, I found your problem."

"Just a second." I hold up a finger to the boys.

The cable guy starts talking while I'm hurrying up the stairs. "See, you got yer box and yer switch and you got yer restart and there's a difference no one seems to notice. And here's yer situation, someone turned the box off. Maybe they thought they were powering the TV set off, maybe not. Who's to know. Anyway, lemme show you how to boot it back up in case for next time."

He shows me the tiny restart switch. I sign his papers and he jingles his way out of the house leaving dirty footprints on the cream-carpet mistake in the upstairs hallway.

"Okay." I plop back into the living-room chair. "Sorry about that."

It appears they've been reading their bibles.

"Have you received the sacrament? The blood and body of Christ our Lord?" Skinny asks.

I don't care about the sacrament or any of that shit.

"Let me ask you something," I say. "What does your religion say about family?"

"Family?" Hefty looks defensive, as if I'm bringing up the whole polygamy thing. Or maybe he's skeptical. Like I might be a lost cause and maybe they should leave and try the next house over. I want to tell him they're all lost causes. Everyone on this block. I can't think of one person who'd invite them in like I have.

"Yeah, family. Busy families who don't have time for anything anymore. Or, um, families that aren't close. You know. Fighting. That sort of thing."

The skinny one elbows the other one and quickly leafs through his book. He's thought of the answer.

"We believe in," he says, still flipping for the right page, "ah, we believe in—here it is!"

"Oh, yeah," Hefty mumbles. He looks disappointed he wasn't the one to think of it first. "Family Home Evening."

"Here we go," Skinny looks up to make sure I'm listening. He starts reading aloud. "'Family Home Evening is an evening set aside for family activities, discussions and instruction. Church leaders do not schedule meetings or activities on Monday nights so that families can be free together.'"

He's proud he's answered my question.

"Monday nights," I say. "Huh."

I cannot imagine us doing this. I try to picture us gathered around a Scrabble board fingering the wooden squares. Rearranging them on our stands. I'd spell out N–O–T–H–I–N–G. I wonder how many points I'd get for that one.

"Do you guys do that with your families? I mean, do you actually practice that?"

They both shift in their seats. Hefty says, "Well, we try to. Yeah. I mean, yes. We do have family nights."

"What's your position on piercings?" I ask. This comes out of nowhere. I hadn't expected to ask it. Now that I have, though, I'm curious.

"Piercings?" They look at each other. I think they're glad to be tested like this. They're used to being quizzed. Looking to their book is familiar. They're in school still. This is not so different from that. This is their community-service project I bet. They can report back that they enlightened a heathen.

Hefty is the one to look it up. He wants to read aloud this time.

"'Church members are encouraged not to disfigure their bodies with tattoos or piercings.'" He looks up at me, making sure this is what I was asking about then he continues. "'If girls or women desire to have their ears pierced, they're encouraged to wear only one pair of modest earrings.'"

He closes the book. They look at me expectantly. Like they're at a batting cage, waiting for the next ball to shoot out of the machine.

The phone rings.

"Maybe we should come back?" Skinny says.

"One sec. Just one second. Let me see who it is, in case it's one of the kids."

It's Cammy's school.

"Hello?" I'm watching the Mormons whisper to one another.

"Mom? Can you come get me?"

Her voice sounds funny.

"Cam? What's wrong?"

"Just…can you just come get me?"

"It's not even lunch period yet. Are you sick?"

I can hear her sniffing. She's crying. She's not calling from her cell. She's in the main office. If she were in trouble, though, someone else would've called me.

"Mom?"

"I'll be right there. Watch for my car. Or…do you need me to come in?"

"I'll be out front."

"Stay inside. It's chilly out."

"Just...come, okay?"

"I'm leaving right now."

A knot cinches in my stomach. I grab my purse and keys from the kitchen counter.

"Ma'am?" one of the Mormons calls out.

"Oh God, I forgot! I mean, gosh." I'm already halfway out the backdoor. I hurry back inside. "Sorry. I'm sorry."

I rush back through the living room to the front door to let them out. "This is so rude of me. Sorry."

Hefty is struggling to get his arm through the second backpack strap. Out of habit I reach out to guide his arm. I'm a pro at untangling children's limbs from all sorts of objects. The Mormon flinches, mutters "I *got* it" and whips around to face me like I was going to stick a Kick Me sign to him. Oooooh. He was the kid everyone picked on in school.

Skinny's halfway down the front steps when he turns and gives it one last shot.

"Mrs.—um—Ma'am?"

"Yes?" My fingers are already gripping the car key with the serrated edge facing up so I don't have to waste time fumbling in the dark garage.

He waits for me to give him my full attention, which is kind of ballsy for a timid clip-on-tied Mormon. It occurs to me that he probably feels more confident talking God outside, where he can beat a fast retreat if he's shooed away or challenged, which I'm sure he probably is. Somewhere along the timeline God became controversial.

"Can I ask you one last question?" Skinny squeaks when he talks and I'm guessing that given his age the puberty ship's already sailed, so every day he wakes up knowing there's no hope for a voice change. These two are quite a pair.

"What?" I ask. *Hurry up hurry up I've got to go I've got to go I've got to go.*

"Do you believe in God?" His head's tilted up like he's daring me to answer.

I consider how to answer and settle on short and sweet.

"Nope," I tell them. "No. I don't believe in God."

I've known this for a long time. I've ignored it because I want the kids to believe. I want them to go to church…oh, screw it. That's not it. I've ignored it because it's not what you're supposed to say. At least not in my world. You're not supposed to say you don't believe in God. It's not what you're supposed to think.

They both look like I have shot a puppy in front of them, so I'm guessing even though Skinny had looked defiant in asking, neither of them realized they were talking with a *bona fide heathen*. I bet that's what's ticker-taping through their heads right now. *She doesn't believe in God?* will ping-pong back and forth between them, their own lore from this journey or quest or whatever it is.

Cammy! Shoot, I've got to get going.

"You don't believe the Lord is our salvation?" Hefty looks as if his merely whispering this is blasphemous. Skinny looks from him to me. I remember they're just kids. Kids starting out on what will surely be a fruitless Laurel and Hardy pilgrimage.

"Actually, *that's* really what it is," I say, jingling my key chain in the universal signal that it's time to go. "I don't believe in God, but more than anything, I don't know that I believe in *salvation*."

I close the front door on the Church of the Latter-day Saints and hurry through the backdoor to about the furthest thing from a Latter-day Saint I can think of.

Turning right onto Clark I think to myself that if I'd had time I would've explained that no, that's not it either. It's that I'll believe in salvation if our marriage works. I try to make the yellow light but don't. A hunched elderly woman has to push her walker in an arc around the front of my car. The guy behind me isn't letting me back up so I'm stuck in the middle of the crosswalk. If I'd had more time I'd have told the Mormons my whole belief system has been shattered. Mothers dying, children struggling, love vanishing, a marriage so fragile it could splinter in a light wind…where's God been for all this? Huh? That's what I'd have said to the Mormons if I'd only had more time.

I don't see her at first. I slow to stopping across from the front door expecting her to come hurrying through it, but I notice something stirring by the garbage can by the hedgerow along the side of the building. It's Cammy. Her face is streaked. Her lips are blue from the cold. She's more crumpled than usual. She rushes to the car like it's a sniper zone.

She smells musky, like sweat. Close up I see it's mascara streaking her cheeks. "Oh, my God, Cam, what happened?"

Once the car door closes she's crying. "Go. Can we just go home?"

I pull away from the curb. "Okay. Okay, we're going home."

It's hard but I give her a little space before I start asking questions.

I wonder whether I should turn on the radio. Usually that calms her. Gives her the background noise she sometimes needs to get her talking, although that didn't seem to do the trick this morning so I decide against it.

"Honey? Cam?" At the stoplight I reach across to push the curtain of hair behind her ear. Instead of flinching and backing away from my touch like she does these days, she lets me stroke her head. "What is it, honey?"

She cried the whole way home. I tried everything I could to get her to tell me what was going on but she wouldn't. She kept shaking her head no.

"Did someone do something to you?" I ask as we pull in to the garage. Her cries stop at my question. I've landed on it.

"You can tell me," I say. "What did they do to you?"

She's never said so, but I'm sure she takes a lot of heat from the other kids about the Goth thing.

She's looking down at her hands. She's picking her black nail polish off. Her fingernails are chewed below the quick.

"Cam?"

She looks over at me. I can see the makeup around her mouth is gone. About the shape of where a clown would paint a huge red frown.

"What happened to your face?"

She looks back down. She wanted me to see.

"Nothing," she says.

"Something happened, Cammy. Please tell me. *Please.*"

I scramble for the right questions to ask. I'm at a loss.

"Did you get in a fight with someone?"

"No."

"Did someone hurt you?"

"I'm going inside."

"Talk to me, Cammy. Tell me what happened."

She climbs out of the car, dragging the black bag she wears crisscrossed. A messenger bag she saved up for when backpacks became "retarded" last year. It has a pin that reads I Hate Everyone on the strap.

I rest my head on the steering wheel. I need to follow her inside. I need to push gently, get her to open up. Make her forget she hates me. I need to be a good mother. I need to pull myself together.

I'm so tired of this.

CAMMY

The Vicodin's taking forever to kick in. At least I think it's Vicodin. Paul said it was but you never know with him.

I never thought we'd start doing it at school. Will waved me over to his car when I went out back to smoke during free period. I don't buy cigarettes. I bum them from this girl Waverly who looks like she watches too much Japanese anime. She wears her hair in two little-girl buns and red-and-white striped tights with oversize black romper-stomper boots. I don't really know her but she doesn't care that I ask her for one, like, every day.

Anyway, there's Will leaning against the side of his car smoking, nodding for me to come over so I'm like wow finally we're going to hang out in daylight instead of like vampires. But then he's like *get in* and he's in the car and the next thing I know he's got his pants unzipped. Right there at school. I told him I had to go and he's all *yeah, right*. Then he's got his hand on the back of my head and he's strong. Plus, he's got a fistful of my hair so I couldn't get away anyway. It kind of hurt the way he was pushing and pulling my head but I couldn't say anything obviously. I choked at one point because I couldn't breathe all that easily he was going too fast and pushing me too hard and he's like *do it right, bitch*. After, when I sit up straight,

I see Missy Delaney walking back across the parking lot from cheerleading practice or something and right when I'm wiping my mouth we lock eyes. She knows. She looks at Will then back at me. She looks over her shoulder at me again before she goes through the backdoor.

Will goes *get the fuck out* and I ran in to the office even though free period is over and I have to go to calculus. I'll get a demerit for cutting out but I don't give a shit. Missy Delaney's already told half the school by now. At least my mom didn't give me too much shit about leaving school. She's all *what happened? Did someone hurt you? Let's talk* blah blah blah. No way am I going to talk to her. She'd totally freak out and I'd get a life sentence and besides nothing would change. Will would still be Will and Paul would be Paul and I owe him so much money there's no way he'd let me out of it. There's no way out. That's why sometimes I wish I were dead. That would solve everything. Last night, though, God, it was so weird. I had this dream that I finally got up the courage to tell Mom everything. Like everything. She hugged me like I was a little girl and then she said *everything will be okay, I'll take care of it from here, we'll move away and you can start over* something something something. Oh! I remember! She goes *stay here I'll be right back*. I was all like yes! with my fist in the air like a cheerleader. And I'm waiting and waiting for her to come home and tell me what happened. I'm thinking oh, she probably went and got the police—in my dream I'm thinking this. Like she got Will and Paul and all them arrested and they didn't know who she was so they couldn't figure out it was me who told on them so it was perfect. But she takes forever to come home—this is in the dream—and when she did I'm still sitting cross-legged on her and Dad's bed and I'm like well? And she says…I remember this part perfectly… she says *was I supposed to do something?*

When I woke up this morning I really thought it'd happened. I lay there thinking about it and even when it hit me that it was just a dream I still thought—I still think—that's exactly what would happen if I told her for real. She's on another planet. She doesn't care. I mean, she asks questions but then she says I'm like this problem or whatever so what I'm going to make things worse for myself? They're already in their own worst-case scenario the way they fight all the time even when they aren't saying anything out loud they're totally toxic. That's what Monica would say. *Toxic.* And anyway, what happened in the dream is exactly what would happen—she'd totally forget about me and it'd be *oh, was I supposed to do something?*

So last week they sent letters from school saying now there's a *suggested dress code* and it basically means I have nothing to wear. Everything they put in the *inappropriate* column is hanging in my closet. From now on, no T-shirts with any words on them, nothing ripped or torn, no black, blah blah blah. It's like they singled me out and you know what fuck them. It's not like they can make me. I don't give a shit what they want me to wear. It's so retarded: like what we wear is going to change what we are inside or what we think. Like if we wear these perfect cookie-cutter clothes we'll lead perfect cookie-cutter lives and think perfect cookie-cutter thoughts. What a freaking joke. Mrs. Flanders from down the street is off her ass drunk every day. Mr. Murphy is an online-porn addict—Billy told us he went to use his dad's computer because he was too lazy to go upstairs to use his own and he finds all these sites and does some digging and it turns out his father has subscriptions to like fifty porno sites. Billy says it explains why his father's such a jerk-off. Everyone laughed but me. That's what they want us to be, little suburban cookie cutters with pretty lawns and perfect little houses and smiles and tea parties. But everyone has freak-ass problems.

Samantha and Bob sat me down for a family forum only the boys weren't there so they might as well have stamped THIS IS ABOUT YOU AGAIN, CAMERON on their foreheads. On the mantel is an old picture of us at Disneyland with the boys in matching Mickey Mouse-ears hats. You'd think this was the best family trip *ever*. Every time I look at that picture I think it's so weird you can't tell I just barfed after riding Space Mountain and the boys were crying they were so scared in Pirates of the Caribbean and Mom and Dad—Samantha and Bob—had just gotten into a fight about funnel cake or something. But there's the picture in a pretty silver frame with the word *family* engraved on the bottom, front and center above the fireplace that only looks like a fireplace. Well, it is one but you just turn a switch to get it going, you don't have to do any Girl Scout work with the sticks and the paper and the dry wood. It's all fake.

Mom and Dad sat down across from me and talked about how this is actually a good thing, how this means we'll get to go shopping for new clothes, Samantha said. She smiles so brightly at me sometimes I want to punch myself, I feel like such a jerk. I really try not to be a fuckup. At least I used to try. But I end up screwing everything up anyway. All I want is to wake up out of this stupor of a life.

I feel like I'm waiting for something to happen. Something that'll get me away from these wide mouths opening to show teeth, twisting up like oooooh aren't we lucky we're alive? Mom Samantha whatever said *we'll make this a mother-daughter outing we could have lunch and go to the mall* and then she's talking about the Cheesecake Factory like I'm five and I still like that place. *You used to love the beeper they give you when you're waiting,* remember? *Remember how the hostess would have to trick you into giving it back to her…honey, what'd they give her? Oh, yeah, it was just a mint but you thought it was so cool to have candy before dinner. Remember?* Bob goes *I don't remember that* and Samantha says *you were never there* and Bob blew air out of his mouth and rolled his eyes like he'd heard that a million times. That's like all he does now. He looks like he's condemned like how the warden yells *dead man walking* when the guy's going to the electric chair. We watched that movie in civics class last spring. *Dead Man Walking.* After that's when they started saying "dead girl walking" whenever I walk down the hall in between classes. So retarded. Like *oh, yeah I get it I have a pale face like a dead person ha ha ha you're so original.*

My punishment for not conforming to what they think I should wear is I've got to go to the mall with my mother. Fine but I'm not going into the fucking Gap. And you can kiss that Abercrombie shit goodbye, too.

So that's number one. Number two is bigger and worse. I got nailed for cutting class. I can't believe it. Mr. Keesler is practically in a coma he's so sleepy during class. He never glances around the room so how he knows I've been missing is beyond me. I've been getting a good grade in trig anyway so what's his friggin' problem. I've got to come up with a plan, though, because I can't let things fall apart now… I'm so close. Any day now the letter will come. I'll find her. Zoey Nickerson from down the street is home from college because she got mono and gained like twenty pounds so she's around during the day and I'm going over there in a little while to ask her if she can pinch-hit for me. The trouble is she tells on people. She used to babysit us when she was in high school and she was the worst of all of our babysitters. She made us go to bed exactly when our parents said to. Marly from two blocks over always let us stay up late and watch TV on school nights as long as we didn't tell that her boyfriend came over. They made out right in front of us all the time. Anyway, if I got in a fight with the boys Zoey'd say things like "I'm going to have to separate you three" and even the boys were disgusted I think. They were pretty young but still. Then she'd tell on us when my parents got home, like that was going to get her more money or something. Once I heard them laughing at her after she left and I thought it was cool I had parents who thought the same way about the babysitter I did. That was back when I was eight or something. Maybe ten or eleven.

So now I've got to think of something legit that will get Zoey to stop by every day because I can't cut out to do it anymore. Come to think of it, the mailman goes to the Nickersons' house before ours so maybe I could work it so she wouldn't have to come over. But the mail is a federal thing and I don't know if they'd let her take someone else's mail. Shit. I've got to think this through. I don't understand why it's taking them this long anyway…the letter should've been here by now. I could put a three-day hold on the mail and that'd buy me three days before having to go to Zoey. She's just the kind of girl who'd blackmail me over it so I really don't want to have to ask her.

Ricky can't do it, which pisses me off because it was his idea to contact the adoption agency in the first place. He's the private investigator one. I'm better at following his orders but now he's in his own private hell because his mom made him take out his nose ring and the hole got infected and she bought him all these preppy Easter egg-colored shirts and he *has* to wear them because she's best friends with one of our teachers and they'd tell on him for sure. So I guess I can't blame him for being upset. But where does that leave me? If the letter comes and Samantha gets it I'm up the creek. It could go two ways: one, she keeps it and never says a word about it so I'm screwed and I'll never know. Two, she and Bob get all freaked out and sad and they'll be all don't you love us enough and she'll be all *you're lucky you* have *a mother…you can't even imagine what it's like to grow up without a mother.* She'll cry and talk about her mom and I'll be the shitty daughter who makes her mother miserable. What else is new.

Samantha

At least the kids don't know how bad things have gotten between Bob and me. You can say a lot about our marriage but we're both good parents. I've always thought it's better to keep the fights away from where the kids can pick up on them— what good does it do to have it out in front of them? So at least we've got that going for us.

There was this horse I rode on a family trip we took last year. The Grand Canyon. What a bust that trip was. The boys fought over Game Boy the whole time (Jamie forgot to bring his and Andrew refused to let him take turns). Cammy complained nonstop: why wasn't there any cell service in the area (in the Grand Canyon? I asked. You've got to be kidding me) and why couldn't we have gone to the Bahamas where all her other friends were going. Of course these are the friends she dropped when Monica Carter came to town, but I didn't point that out. Bob complained about how it cost two hundred dollars for two hours on horseback along the outer ridge even though we're a family of five and no family activity's ever cheap. I argued it was a bargain but he moped anyway, just like the kids. My horse's name was Lightning and I took him because if he lived up to his name I wanted to be the one with the broken back instead of one of the kids.

Turns out Lightning was anything but. He trudged along the beaten-down trail, following inches behind Flossie, Andrew's horse, without once looking up. His air of resignation was so complete that I hated every minute of the ride and gave him extra sugar cubes the guide handed out at the end of the ride. The tickle of the weary velvet nose nibbling on the palm of my hand broke my heart. Call me crazy but I remember looking into Lightning's eye and feeling that click, that flicker of recognition, pass between us and I looked away and said "let's go" to everyone. Andrew beat a path to the rental car, shouting it was Jamie's turn to sit in the middle, and Cammy sighed a disgusted sigh and not one of us thanked Bob for forking over the two hundred dollars.

I think of Lightning from time to time, when I'm standing in line at the grocery store stepping in front of the cashier where the person before had just stood. Pushing the loaded cart to my car. I think of Lightning as I inch my car forward in the line to pick up the kids from school. I imagine the car in front of me is Flossie. We're all on this trail we've walked so many times there are grooves in the ground. We could do it in our sleep.

Tuesday is soccer practice and I have just enough time to get the car washed after dropping Andrew off at the lakefront. The car-wash guy motions me forward to tighten up the gap between me and the dirty Mercedes in front of me. He's too quick with the snake-cord vacuum and I know I'll find crunched-up leaves or crumbs on the mats. I turn off the radio. In the rearview mirror I watch the antenna fold into itself. Then I inspect my face. I've got to remember to pick up that cream Lynn says works on dark circles. I'm reapplying lipstick in the rearview window when the guy knocks on my window.

"Tires done this time?"

"Yes, please."

"Wax?"

"Yes."

The guy passes my receipt through my window like he does every Tuesday. I line my tires up to the rails and shift into Neutral. The car knows what to do from here. Like Lightning did. The plastic strips slap suds on the hood. The buffers move out along the sides of the car. The whole operation feels like one of the boys' Transformers, the way everything moves out, does the job and tucks back into place as if nothing happened in this tunnel. The air blower pushes drops of water off. I pay at the end and drive away with the windows up so they won't streak. I am behind two other gleaming cars at the exit. We are all moving along slowly, as if the air alone will dirty us up. One by one we follow the trail of the driveway to the road.

"Honey, kick the mud off your cleats before you get in, I just got the car washed."

Jamie does but Andrew is incapable of getting mud off of anything and anyway it takes two seconds for the inside of the car to smell like hormonal, sweaty, preteen boy.

"Hey, Mom? Can Ryan come over for dinner?"

"It's a school night," I say.

"I know I know I know but we'll do homework and his mom says she can pick him up whenever we want."

Kerry Kendricks knocks on the window and I have to lower it after all. "They just sprung this on me, too," she says. "We can do it another night if you'd like."

"Oh no no, it's okay," I say as the boys *yessss* and bump fists in the backseat. "We're getting pizza so it's no big deal."

At home I make Jamie sit and finish his homework which is like trying to put Scotch tape on a dam leak, he's so fidgety, barely able to stay in his seat at the kitchen table, turning to watch Ryan toss an imaginary baseball to Andrew who swings an imaginary bat while they whine for him to *just get it over with come on let's go come on hurry up.* When he erases the seven he put in the blank after "4+2+2=" and scribbles a sloppy figure eight, he leaps up and the three of them tear out of the house so fast I practically see cartoon speed lines. I hunt for the cordless phone that's never in its charger so I can make the phone calls I've put off all week. I'm always relieved to get answering machines for calls like these: a reminder to Adrina Ibrahim to bring Gatorade and pop for the class picnic; a call to Max, the stay-at-home dad, to ask where the next away game is; I'm three for three with answering machines with a message to Sally Flanders to find out the name of the gluten-free cookie company she'd raved about recently. This way I can throw out the *TIME Magazine* story about how too much gluten affects kids' learning and concentration, even if they're not allergic to it. Let's see…what else can I get rid of? A discount flyer for a now not-so-new yoga studio I swore I'd try out—gone. Adrina's recipe for butternut squash—let's face it, I'll never get around to it—gone. I'm skimming something I cut out of *O Magazine* when I hear Bob coming in. He closes the door hard. A slam. Like an announcement. Like I should line the kids up tallest to smallest.

"What's for dinner?" he asks, looking in the fridge, still holding his battered multi-pocket soft leather briefcase.

"Pizza. And I'm making a salad." I'm still sifting through my pile. "Did you ever call John back? He left a message about golf a while ago."

"Oh, yeah, pizza Tuesday," he says. "I'm going up to change."

"Can I throw this note out to call John?"

"I don't care," he says. He scans the Sports section before tucking it under his arm.

"Well, did you call him or not?"

"I called him, I called him."

"Cammy's going to hit you up to be able to go over to Zoey's house, of all places," I tell him.

"What's wrong with that?"

"She's *grounded,* remember? Jesus. And when was the last time she went over to *Zoey's?*"

"Good to see you, too," he says.

"Nice tone."

"Nice way to greet your husband," he says.

"Your first words were *what's for dinner* so I wouldn't talk. Do you want sausage on your side of the pizza?" I ask.

"I guess," he says, glancing at the stack of mail. "Holy shit, how many more catalogs can we get?"

"You said a swear, Dad." Andrew appears behind both of us. "Twenty-five cents. Mom, can we play Nintendo?"

Bob's standing at the fridge, I can feel the cold air at my back.

"Twelve ninety-nine for a pint of chicken salad?"

"It's organic," I say. I make a note to follow up with Sally on those cookies before I stop at Whole Foods again tomorrow. It takes two or three calls to hear back from her.

"It's bullshit."

"Swearword! Twenty-five cents!" Jamie calls out.

"No way," Andrew turns on him, "I hit you to show you he swore. It's my twenty-five cents. I heard it first."

"Yeah, but you didn't call it."

"Boys, cool it," I say. Oh, I have to pick up the cleaning. Another note to self.

"He didn't call it," Jamie pleads his case to me.

Bob's picking up containers looking at bar codes and prices.

"Five ninety-nine for strawberries? Jesus, Sam."

"Swearword!" they call out at the same time. Now they're listening to every word, waiting for the next quarter.

Ryan twists his arm around so he can pick a scab on his elbow while he asks the boys, "Why do you call it when you hear swears?"

"You want pesticides on your children's food? Pass me the cucumber, will you? Bottom right."

Jamie answers Ryan, "We make money every time our parents swear."

Ryan wipes the blood from his re-opened wound onto his shorts and studies his elbow again.

"Slice thinly," Bob says. "Make it last because that's the last million-dollar cucumber we're eating."

"It's awesome," Andrew is saying to Ryan, "they swear a lot. I bought a transformer with the money I made last year."

"I wish my parents swore," Ryan says. Now he's licking his bloody finger. "I want that new iPod nano."

"Boys! We do not swear a lot," I say. Great. Just great. Kerry Kendricks'll find a way to make it seem like we're horrible parents. "Stop picking at that, Ryan. You need a Band-Aid. Let's wash it off first, sweetie."

"Ryan just drank his own blood," Andrew says to the room. "Dad. Did you see that? Dad. Ryan's like a vampire. He just licked his own blood."

"I'm serious, Sam," Bob says. "No kidding."

"Boys, go on upstairs, I'll call you when the pizza gets here. Jamie, get Ryan a Band-Aid when you go up will you?"

"Can you get out the tomato?"

He leans in and lowers his voice. "We're hemorrhaging money."

"The other tomato. I think that one's not ripe yet."

"Seriously, Sam. We've got to cut out the spending."

"You still want me to buy the scotch? Now, *that* would save some money. Cutting out the liquor."

"Fuck you," he mumbles, twisting the cap off.

The boys race in from the living room.

"Swear!" "F word!" "That's fifty cents!" "I said it first it's mine." "No way!"

I look up from the chopping board to see Bob plink the quarters down in front of the boys and stalk out of the kitchen.

"Can we play Nintendo?" Andrew yells from halfway up the stairs.

I stare out after Bob.

"Did you straighten your room like I told you to do yesterday?" I ask.

"Yeah. Can we?"

"Yes. You can play until dinner. Don't run too hard up the stairs."

Soon, Ryan gets picked up and the night fills with busy emptiness punctuated by parental barking. "Brush your teeth." "Pick out a book we can read before bed." "Go tell your sister to come down here." "Well, bang on the door until she hears you. Tell her I said to turn the music down." "Clothes go in the hamper guys, not on the floor."

The other side of the bed is empty; Bob's at the computer. The sheets are cool. We don't say good night to one another anymore. Fine with me.

Shoot, did I set my alarm?

For the first few minutes of going to sleep it's that airplane kind of sleep where you're aware that you're drifting but you're not quite in deep sleep yet. But then a random muscle twitches and your head jerks and you realize maybe you were sleeping after all. It's during that, before the jolt, that my mind circles around whatever's been bugging me during the day. I want to call out to Bob to come, to turn off the computer and come to bed. I want to tell him I'm sinking. *We're* sinking. We've become that couple I always felt sorry for, the couple with nothing to talk about. It's too hard worrying about *us* all the time. Worrying *alone.* I want to tell him I need help, I didn't think this would be so hard. I want him to hold me and tell me everything's going to be all right. I want him to tell me he'll take care of everything for a while.

I'm pretty sure I set the alarm. I better check. I have a parent meeting before school starts tomorrow and Kerry Kendricks is a bitch if you're late. Then lunch at Spiaggia. I can use the parking lot in the Bloomingdale's building. Or wait, I should take the train down.

It's Wednesday and I have to meet three gossipy women I'm on a school fund-raising committee with and frankly I'd rather jam a chopstick in my eye than go but I've canceled twice so this time I have to go. For about twenty minutes we'll talk about the event—a 5K walk/run that's meant to raise money for new auditorium seating. The rest of the time will be spent picking apart this parent or that. This kid or that one. I mostly listen and try to fly under the radar so I'm not a target when I'm not with them, even though no one's safe. Bob calls them the harpies. Sandy Kweller will end up drinking three glasses of wine and Marty Kozlowski will end up pretending she has to drive Sandy home because she wants to see the new curtains in the living room even though we all know it's because Sandy's too drunk to drive. No one talks about Sandy's drinking.

I'm glad I decided to take the el because parking's a nightmare downtown so this is easier. The train pulls up and I take a seat while a recording announces, "This is the red line. Bryn

elizabeth flock

Mawr is next. This is the red line." The recorded voice is calm and nonethnic. Not robotic, just nondescript. I wonder what he looks like and how long it took him to record all these street names. I wonder what kind of feat in engineering it must have been to create the system that trips off the announcements. "We are approaching Bryn Mawr. The doors will open on the right at Bryn Mawr." Across the aisle from me is a well-dressed woman about sixty-five with her look-alike daughter who is probably about my age. The mother is listening intently to her daughter who is explaining how difficult it is to get home from work at a decent hour so she can spend at least a few minutes with the kids before they go to bed. This younger mother is impeccable. She is wearing low heels with a toe that curves just right. Her Godiva-chocolate brown bag is far too large for her frame, which means it too is perfectly current. She has a severe haircut, but it suits her. Her mother is murmuring something to her about day care or nannies and whatever she's saying is agreeing with her daughter, who is nodding her head.

I wish I could ask my mom to save me from the mess I've made of my life. She'd know exactly what to do to make it right. I'd tell her this isn't exactly how I pictured my life. She'd have seen the warning signs years ago and she'd have sat me down and told me how to keep from capsizing. I close my eyes and picture her under soil and silt and grass and dandelion roots, random foot-steps thumping overhead every once in a while. I picture her casket lowered into the ground in Graceland cemetery at the corner of Clark and Montrose where buses idle, so it feels more like a construction site than a final resting place. I hate visiting her grave so I never really do. Before Cammy came along I would go on Mother's Day, but that was too depressing so I tapered off and as Cammy got older the day was taken over with hearts and cards with backward letters and uneven pottery made in art class.

At the next stop a man in a suit takes the seat next to me. He comments he's running late for work. He slides his leather briefcase into the space between his feet and I look at it and think it's pretty gross to do that. The floor is filthy. In front of us a sleeping janitor still in his uniform from a night shift wakes suddenly to check the stop. When I pull my purse off the seat to make room for my seatmate I notice he's handsome. Very handsome. I push a loose strand of hair back behind my ear and then I remember reading somewhere that when men and women are checking each other out they touch their hair. Oh, Jesus, now he thinks I'm checking him out. I go back to reading—I have to finish this book before book club next week and I don't particularly like it so it's taking me forever to slog through. *A Ghost From Afghanistan.* Homework reading. All the names are similar and I have to keep backing up to see who's who. Two stops later he shakes the front section of the *Wall Street Journal* closed and takes a sip from his commuter cup of coffee.

"Man, that's good," he says to himself mostly, but I can tell from the way he's shifted in his seat it's meant for me, too. He's the chatty type. I hate that. I try to keep reading but I can't concentrate. What the hell.

By the time we pass Addison we've half swiveled in our seats in friendly conversation. Turns out he and his wife had looked at a house two doors down from us but didn't buy because it had mold in the basement. I tell him about the Silvermans' house for sale up the block from us but he says they already bought a house nearby. The train stops midway between Addison and Belmont and the conductor comes on to say that the train in front of us has some mechanical difficulties so it would be a few minutes before we start up again. Could we please be patient? he says. My seatmate introduces himself.

Craig. Craig Riggs. He looks like he stepped off the cover of *Men's Health* or *Runner's World*. He looks like he'd be more comfortable on a mountain bike or rappeling off a cliff than in a suit on the way downtown. He's charismatic. Good posture. He talks about his work at a foundation he started a decade ago, and what strikes me is how passionate he is about it. Some kind of environmental mission. Cleaner water, more efficient fuel sources. I haven't met that many people happy with their jobs at this stage. Our friends all say they wish they'd done anything but what they ended up doing. Just last week Lynn's husband, Mike, said he dreams about killing his boss. I can't remember the last time Bob said anything positive about his job.

I ask Craig about his children and he tells me his only child, a daughter named Lexi, has just had her fifth birthday.

"A princess tea party," he says.

"That's the best age," I say and he nods.

He asks random questions about me. Have I always lived in Chicago (pretty much), how long have we been married (nearly twenty years), where did I go to school (Boston College), do I ever go to Cubs games (yes, but not that often). There's my hand darting up to check my hair again. Damn—it's like I have no control over it. Thank God I'm not in sweats. I have a blemish on my left cheek and I don't want him to see it. I knew I should've put something on it last night. My mom used to say toothpaste was good for clearing up skin but I flip over in my sleep and the toothpaste would be all over the sheets and the bed would smell minty fresh. When I saw it in the mirror last night I figured who cares, I'm not the vain type. Slowly I sneak more glances at him. He has a wonderful smile that changes the whole shape of his face.

We have the same sense of humor and soon we're laughing about everyone on the train.

"Oh, my God, it's Donald Rumsfeld," he says quietly. "What's he doing getting on the train at Lawrence?"

"There's J-Lo," I say. "Actually if J-Lo and George Stephanopoulos had a love child that would be her."

Why did I have to reference J-Lo? It sounds like I'm trying to be younger than I am. All his references are political. When he brought up Paul Wolfowitz I nodded and laughed and said, "That looks exactly like him!" even though I'm not sure who Paul Wolfowitz is. World Bank? And what *is* the World Bank anyway? I've always wondered. I hope it wasn't a test. Naw—he doesn't look like the type to try to catch someone in a lie.

By the time we get to the heart of downtown I have laughed harder than I have in I don't know how long. Something about the whole thing makes me feel like a kid in high school. I feel light. The taped voice calls out, "We are approaching Lake Street," and I feel heaviness, all the things I've forgotten about in this half-hour ride start seeping back into my brain.

A few seconds before we get to our stop he turns to me and says:

"Can I ask you something?"

I laugh in anticipation of another joke. "Sure."

"No, seriously," he says. The train is inching to a stop.

"Okay," I say. "Shoot."

His eyes are wide-set and deep brown and lock onto mine but not in that uncomfortable way so I don't look away. He's searching my face. His eyebrows furrow then lift in a question.

"Do you ever want to walk away from your life?" he asks.

"Doors open on the left at Lake Street," the recorded man says.

The train is a sneeze away from stopping and he is searching my face for a reaction.

"Do you? Do you ever think this life is not exactly what you had planned?" he asks with urgency. "Do you ever crave something, *anything,* that could wake you up?"

I clear my throat and stand up, pushing my purse straps onto my shoulder. I'm caught between wanting to burst into tears and wanting to break into a run.

He says, "Sorry. I thought maybe…"

"No, no, it's fine," I say, fiddling with my purse, looking at the seat to make sure I haven't left anything behind. I brush a make-believe hair off my shoulder.

"I just got the sense…" He trails off.

I clear my throat and wait for the doors to open. I don't know why this has thrown me. We're standing in awkward silence, facing out.

For lack of anything else to do and because it seems like a polite thing to do, on the platform we exchange e-mail addresses. He stands aside so I can walk down the steps first. We wave at each other at the corner of Lake and Michigan. But then I stop before I cross the street.

"Craig!" I call to him. He turns around from halfway across the street. "Yes," I yell over the people still crossing. "I feel the exact same way."

It's a relief to say it out loud. Now the tears come. Why the hell am I crying?

He walks back to me fast, with purpose, with intent, and it makes my breath stop. I don't know what he'll say.

And right there, on Michigan Avenue with lunchtime crowds pouring out of buildings lighting cigarettes, he envelops me, this stranger from the train. We say nothing. He squeezes me before letting me go. We nod at each other. He's gone before I can figure out what to say.

I can't get his question out of my mind. I'm preoccupied during lunch with this strange question that does not strike me as strange at all. Sandy semi-slurs the words *pledge sheet* and *Kinkos at cost* and I'm wondering how can this man ask me something like that, something so personal? Marty clicks her pen shut indicating "business" is over, time for fun, and I panic that I seem so obviously unhappy. I must if a complete stranger is asking me if I want out of my life. And that hug. Oh, my God, that hug. On the way back home on the train I look for him but I know he won't be there. I finger the paper with his e-mail address on it, looking at his name, constructing an e-mail in my mind.

It's wonderful to have a few hours with a crush. What's wrong with that? Here is another soul walking around the world feeling the same way I do and he's not afraid to talk about it with a complete stranger. I can honestly say he was hot. Thick hair that makes him look younger but salt and pepper to add character and sexiness. Great hands. I watched his hands when he was talking about when he and his wife first moved to Chicago from Seattle and I don't remember what he said, I just remember wondering why he doesn't wear a wedding ring. That's kind of tacky, men not wearing wedding rings. It's sort of playerish. Like he's trolling. Maybe he's that guy. The guy that says he doesn't wear a wedding ring because he doesn't like wearing jewelry but then wears a watch. Or maybe he uses the "we don't need a material symbol to prove we're married," but I'll bet his wife wears something material. Something big and shiny and bright. He doesn't need a symbol of his love but she does? Um, no. Married men should wear wedding rings, period.

But he thinks about the mess of his life, too. That look, those eyes of his, the completeness of that hug…that's not something a player does. It was more friendly than steamy. I wish I hadn't worn these pants. I always forget how they make me look like I have a huge stomach because they pucker out when I sit down. I was so preoccupied I didn't think to smooth it out. Great. Now he thinks I'm fat.

I walk in the door and listen to messages. The school called, Cammy is in the nurse's office feeling nauseous. She's been sick a lot lately and I make a mental note to get her to the doctor. Bob called and said he can't pick up Jamie from piano because he has a conference call with some famous basketball player. So it's a scramble to race down Broadway to Cammy's school. Then to pick up the boys, drop Jamie off at piano, run Cammy and Andrew home, throw dinner together for later, pick up Jamie, stop at Staples for poster board, then home and and and.

I've set a new record with the smoke alarm tonight. It's gone off three times and I know I'll forget to put the nine-volt battery back in and we'll all end up charred in a burn unit somewhere because I'm too scatterbrained to reload it.

Bob's behind me at the sink drying the roasting pan. We'd had pot roast for dinner and I always regret having pot roast for dinner when I'm scrubbing the pan. I fight the urge to throw the damn thing out.

"Oh, I forgot to tell you," I say, "I've gotten fifteen hundred dollars in pledges for Race for the Cure. And I still haven't asked anyone in book club yet!"

I turn to look at him. He's propped himself up against the counter, lost in a smiling thought.

"What're you thinking about?" I smile and turn off the water.

When he focuses back to our standing there his smile shadow fades, his eyes harden. I fight the impulse to ask if he is daydreaming about another woman. I won't ask him that. There might not even be another woman, I don't know.

"Huh?"

I take his arm. "Come with me."

"Where?"

"Just leave that and come with me." I take his hand and lead him into the garage—the only place that's quiet and somewhat private.

"What?" he asks once we close the door behind us. "Is that goddamn ceiling panel peeling back again? Are we getting water in here?"

I pull my sweater over my head. I'm wearing my good bra—the push-up one that cuts into my shoulders.

"What the hell're you doing? Jesus, Sam…"

"Come here," I say.

"You're going to scratch the hood of the car. I'm going back inside, it's freezing in here. Sam, seriously."

"Come here…just for a second."

"I'm beat," he says.

The door closes behind him and I pick my sweater up off the concrete garage floor. I shake off the sawdust we sprinkled to soak up a leak. From the small window facing the house I can see him trudging back in and I want to run after him and shake him out of his stupor and say *what're we doing?* I want to yell *where did we go?* I want to ask him why we ended up like this. I consider throwing the sweater away—it's never really been flattering. I take a deep breath and open the door to the golden warmth of the kitchen. I step back into my nice little life.

Back inside I find him sorting through mail. He looks up and says, "Sorry, it's just I'm tired."

"I'm tired, too," I say. "I had back-to-back committee meetings at school this morning. By the way, Bill Wendel's going to be calling you to see if you'll join the audit committee. I had to get downtown for lunch." *Do you ever want to walk away from your life?* "I had to pick Cammy up early. She was sick again. Then I had to drive Jamie to piano. I went on a Staples run, oh, yeah, I put those file folders upstairs on your desk. Then I drove the kids home and scrambled to make pot roast for dinner. I'm tired, too. But…"

"Another night, then," he says. "We're both tired. It'd be nice to have an early night."

"Wait. I'm not saying I'm *too* tired. I'm just saying I've been going full guns all day and I still make an effort—"

"And what do you think I do all day, huh?" His mouth distorts and spits the words at me. "You think I'm standing around telling jokes at the watercooler all day, shooting the breeze? Sorry if I don't feel sorry for you listening to the radio and bopping around town all day."

"Okay, first of all, I never said you don't work as hard as I do," I say. "And for the record I don't *bop around* all day. I ferry *our children* to and from about a million different things every day. Your clothes don't exactly dry-clean themselves. And how do you think that food ends up in the fridge?"

"Forget it," he calls over his shoulder on his way upstairs to help the kids with whatever the kids need help with. I know he wants to get away from this because he rarely helps the kids with homework.

"Hang on," I call to him. "Come back for a second."

"What?" He sticks his head back into the kitchen to keep from committing to a long conversation.

"It's just…"

"Yeah, I know."

"Do you? I mean, do you really, because…wait, can't you just come into the room all the way so I don't have to talk to a disembodied head?"

"What?" he says.

I almost ask him Craig's question. Almost.

"Never mind," I say. "Forget it."

I feel a mix of relief and triumph, as if an invisible abacus has slid another point in my favor because I pursued sex but was turned down yet again. It makes me wonder if I keep asking Bob for intimacy knowing I'll be turned away so I can keep racking up the points that will, in future arguments, be used as evidence of our decline. It's entrapment and I'm seeing a meanness I never thought I was capable of. I don't even want sex with him, now that I think about it. It's not normal to go this long without it, but I don't want him.

After dinner I'm officially off the clock, but all that really means is that I "get" to open mail, pay bills and balance my checkbook before I drag my body upstairs where there's laundry on the bed that needs to be folded before I can crawl into it, which is maybe my favorite part of the day. Then I wake up and do it all over again the next day. By nighttime yeah, sex is the last thing I want to do. I know how he feels. But at least I'm trying to make an effort. Or if I'm going to be honest, I'm trying to look as though I'm making an effort.

The school-benefit committee has been eating up a lot of my time so I sit at my desk and clear papers off my keyboard to return e-mails. My desk is in a kitchen nook crammed with junk and piles of paper and Cammy's old retainer. I've been meaning to organize the cookbooks on the shelf above the computer but there's never enough time. I put the mouse on a stack of library books I need to return. Sliding it across Harry Potter's face, I boot up.

I dig up the list of people I have to e-mail and when I log on *there it is.* Craig! My heart stops beating. My palms get tingly with sweat. This is silly. Ridiculous. I'm a grown married woman. But when I click on it and read his words I nearly faint. Six words:

I cannot stop thinking about you.

Cammy.

I think Samantha is bipolar or something. I don't know, maybe just depressed. Either way it's weird how she's so different now. Not that I care but whatever.

One day she's all over me to get new clothes and have a mall day with me and once I agree to it she's totally forgotten. I mean, I guess I wouldn't have minded going shopping with her. We haven't done that in like forever. Just so long as it was Old Orchard and not Water Tower where everyone I know goes to hang out on the benches near Hollister and Abercrombie. I don't go there, it's not my crowd. So Old Orchard would've been fine but whatever. She forgot.

I wrote this poem today in history, which is my least favorite class, and Ricky says that's ironic since all I care about is my own history. Anyway, here's the poem:

YOU

You think
You own me.
You think
You know me.

You think
You care about me.
You think
It's all about YOU.

I think Ricky and I are stopping being friends. We're so different now it's scary and I'm sick of trying to act like I'm someone I'm not. Yesterday I was across from school in the park where everyone goes to smoke during free periods and he comes up to me and like freaks out because I'm on the swings at the playground part. He says *ooooh, you're such a rebel smoking your joints and fucking clove cigarettes and swinging like you're dying to get kicked out by some mom. Maybe you'll get arrested and then you'll be like the queen of your new loser friends.* He doesn't like it when I smoke reefer but I don't give a shit. I don't like it when he drools all over Missy, so we're even.

Ricky's panties are in a wad over Paul and his group. Paul got kicked out of Lane Tech for setting off the fire alarm one too many times—at least that's what he says. Everyone else knows it was pot. Which is so hypocritical because all our parents spend a shitload at Whole Foods where they buy hemp stuff and organic food and *natural supplements* and here's pot which is the most natural thing in the world. It's actually good for you—doctors give it to patients. Paul says doctor shit is the strongest you can find and there they are prescribing it.

Anyway, Ricky hates Paul but he won't admit it. All he keeps saying is that I become like this weird person when I'm around Paul's group. He wants us to stay like we were in fourth grade...best friends who wanted to get married (we never told our parents that part and Ricky denies he ever said it in the first place). I can't believe I used to rehearse what we'd tell our kids: *we sat next to each other in fourth grade and your father laughed at everything I said and I knew we'd get married.* I used to think about how many kids we'd have and whether they'd look like me or him. I knew we'd never adopt.

Now it's like we're going in opposite directions, like the new preppy clothes he's wearing have leaked dye into his bloodstream and gotten all the way to his brain and changed him into a pod person. He keeps asking me when I'm going to get my new clothes with my mom and yesterday in the park he said *man your feet are so dirty. Why don't you wear shoes? It's disgusting.* He's such a priss now. Like a little girl.

He didn't seem to mind it when I got the tattoo. He didn't mind me squeezing his hand blue when the fat guy with a Mike Tyson claw tattoo on the side of his face started in with the needle. We'd hung out at his house and his parents were away in Cabo and they trusted him to be alone with his older brother Adam because they didn't know Adam's the biggest partyer on the planet. Anyway, Adam gave me two shots of Jim Beam before we left for the tattoo parlor. Liquid courage. Ricky said it was funny to see me drunk. A few minutes later I was leaning forward with the back of my shirt up feeling the cold wipe of an alcohol cotton ball just above my butt and I wasn't sure if it was me being drunk or me being scared that made me throw up. The guy acted bored, like everyone does it. He tossed Ricky an almost finished roll of paper towels and said to call him when we were serious about *pinning some skin.* That's what he called it. I was fine since I'd barfed up the Jim Beam so he came back and had to sit with his legs wide apart because he was so fat his stomach had to hang between them. The bandage was thick. I couldn't take a shower for two days and I had to sleep on my stomach for a week. My parents never suspected anything since it was on the small of my back right above my butt.

This was before Ricky the prep, when he was Ricky the

normal. He kept saying I can't believe you went through with it and the way he looked at me it was like I'd invented the iPod. Then one day he leaned in and I thought he was finally going to kiss me so I closed my eyes and tilted my head up because he's like a foot taller than me but he was only bending down to get a closer view of it from over my shoulder because I'd been obsessing that summer was coming and if my mom or dad hugged me they could look down and see it. So he's coming close and there I am about to reach up and put my arms around his neck. My eyes were even starting to close automatically. I'll never forget it. He laughed and went, "What a dork! I'm not kissing you, you freak."

I shook my head to get my face back to normal but I knew it was too late, I'd already fucked it up. We didn't talk for like a week after that and we talk like fifteen million times a day so a week is like dog years. Then he came up to me in the hall and said, "I've been thinking about it and I've got an idea. Meet me after sixth period at the back stairs."

Here's the worst part of the whole thing. I thought he was thinking about how I wanted to kiss him and he'd changed his mind. Will never kissed me. We skipped that step. So I bummed a piece of mint gum off of Natalie from the south side because I remember I had something gnarly for lunch and my breath stunk. At the end of sixth period I crunched a zillion Tic Tacs I got from Sara with the backpack she wears all day until she's hunched over like a *National Geographic* village woman. Sara never goes to her locker in between classes like everyone else because someone always sticks signs on it like Bloody Sara and To do: buy tampons! Sara got her period on a day she was wearing tight white pants and she didn't know she had a bloody crotch until third period but the damage was done. Sara left at the end of the year. I heard she went to Payton but I'm not sure. Anyway, she had Tic Tacs in her backpack so I downed a fistful on my way to meet Ricky. I was all freaked because my hands were sweaty like a Judy Blume book.

"You want to find your birth mother, right?" Ricky said the second I pushed through to the outside landing.

I remember trying to act normal like that was exactly what I thought he'd say but I think he looked at me weird.

"I could help you find her if you want," he said. "In science we were talking about DNA and medical history and *bam* I think we could fake a doctor letter like it's from your parents and they'd have to give you the info on her. We could totally find her if you want. I mean, only if you want."

I said I wanted to mainly because I wanted to leave and go back inside away from him. And it's true I've always talked about finding her. I just never really thought about following through. That night Ricky Googled adoption agencies and then it was too late to turn back. Not that I want to or anything.

Samantha

"I've got a couple of names of people downtown," Lynn says, "and one who's kind of near us. I don't know much about that one though."

"Did you tell Sally who you were asking for?" I ask. The thought of Sally Flanders knowing I'm looking for a couple's counselor mortifies me. "I swear to God if you told her it was us…"

"For Christ's sake, of course I didn't tell her," Lynn says. "Listen, she doesn't want anyone knowing about her drinking any more than you want her knowing about you and Bob. Do you have a pencil? Let me give you these names."

I scribble down area codes 312 for the downtown ones, 773 for the one by us. I shove the paper into the front pocket on my too-tight jeans I can't wait to change out of. I think this every time I squeeze into them. I need to put them in the Goodwill pile, but they're finally soft and worn in and I'm terrible about throwing things out. I have a pile of old T-shirts dating back to grade school and I'd love the shelf space in my closet, but I'll never get rid of them. They're like a scrapbook of my life: Bee Gees concert T-shirts, Santana, the Dead. The half marathons, the charity runs, See Rock City, Niagara Falls, they're a photo album I'll never get rid of.

"Everyone goes through this, you know," Lynn is saying into the phone. I readjust it on my shoulder while I snapshake a sheet still warm from the dryer. I halve it then quarter it and say,

"It's the loneliness that kills me," I tell her again. "If he'd just talk to me about anything…"

"Be careful what you wish for," she snorts. "I'd kill for Mike to shut his mouth every once in a while. The guy never stops talking. Ever. He wakes up talking and doesn't quit until lights out."

"What do you guys talk about?"

"I don't know. The kids. People at work. He's got the memory of an elephant so he's always talking about something or other we did years ago."

"I feel like we're in this vacuum. It's so quiet between us. You know how if you only open one window in the car there's that pressure on your ears until you crack open another one? That's what it feels like when we're alone."

I've put all the socks into one big pile and am holding the dark ones up to the light because the navy ones look black. Recently I've started folding them in half instead of balling them up, because I was watching a Bravo show on reorganizing your home and it turns out sock balls take up twice as much space.

"Then it's good you're seeing someone," she says. "Hell, everyone should go."

"You guys haven't."

"Yeah, well…" She trails off and I can hear her mind clicking for something helpful to say.

It makes me feel better having taken the first step but

honestly I don't know if I'm making too much of this. Maybe Lynn's right: it can't hurt to go to someone impartial.

The fact that I'm obsessing over an e-mail from a stranger I met on the train means we've got a problem. And boy oh boy am I obsessing. Those six words: *I cannot stop thinking about you*...six words and I'm literally floating. No. We've got to see someone, Bob and I.

In the meantime, it's rude not to reply to Craig's e-mail. Just something polite to show I'm not blowing him off. What if we ran into each other at a social thing—how awkward would *that* be if I had left him dangling out there having sent such a bold e-mail. What to write, what to write. *It was great meeting you on the train today.* No. Too sophomoric. *I so enjoyed our talk on the train today. Our chat on the train? Our conversation...* No. This is ridiculous. Maybe I shouldn't write him. But then his question lingers in my brain. That question...I cannot stop thinking about that. He is walking around thinking the same thing I am.

I go to the bedroom to change out of my jeans and the second I lower the zipper and see the imprint of the button and the waistline on my skin convinces me I've got to get rid of them. It'll be good for me. Cleansing. A new leaf. My sweatpants feel like a cloud. I fold the jeans and place them neatly on the floor of my closet so I won't forget to add them to the Goodwill pile Bob's started out in the garage. At the last minute I remember the slip of paper in the pocket and put it in my underwear drawer so I can remember to call in the morning. I could call today but...

When you think about it, I've already made a move toward marital counseling, what harm would it do to push the envelope now, since Bob and I are going to get fixed soon anyway? This guy doesn't seem dangerous or like a stalker who won't back off. *I cannot stop thinking about you,* he wrote. *Do you ever want to walk away from your life? I cannot stop thinking about you.* Here I go:

Nor I, you.

My finger slides the mouse over to the send button. What the heck. I double click and zip, it's gone. It's done. Nothing I can do about it now. Why not have a little harmless flirting? That's all it is.

A day has passed and it's taken all the willpower I can muster to stay away from the computer. I'm married to Bob. My husband, my family, comes first. When Bob gets home we'll talk, really talk.

Beef stroganoff is the kind of meal that leaves a certain kind of mess. Rings from the bottom of the sour-cream container need to be scrubbed off the table. Dirty pots and pans tumble together in the sink like a dish-cleaner commercial. I survey the damage. Bob is late. My wine is still cold so I sit and sip and think about Craig.

I wonder what brought him to this same point. Is this a midlife crisis? I wonder if everyone feels this way. Lynn still sits on Mike's lap from time to time. I've brought it up with her but she's always pithy about it. Quick with the sarcasm. She says she feels the same way I do, but there's no way. She claims she's not but she's happy. Happy people don't feel like walking away from their lives.

The backdoor opens and Bob comes in. He smells like the outside air but somehow the sheen of work lighting is still there. Bob hasn't gotten a raise in two years. He won't talk about it but I know it stings and yes, it worries me. We've tightened our belts as far as they go (except for eating organic, but just the other day I bought a regular cantaloupe so there's that). He had his performance review a couple of days ago but that night he'd been running late so we met at the Y rec center for the boys' basketball game. With the ref whistles and clapping we couldn't manage a sentence between us. George and Stacy Wilmot were sitting on the bleachers next to me. When Bob hurried in, stepping one, two, three over the benches to us, the Wilmots were talking about their recent trip to Napa. I keep meaning to make friends with them. They're sweet and always have something going on. Easy to talk to. At the end of all the games, we do the dance "let's get something on the books," "we really *should*," "call me and we'll schedule something" and they shuttle their son, Jordan, out and we pile the boys and their backpacks into the car and I forget all about the Wilmots. Until the next game.

So I haven't had time to hear about the review. I fix him a plate and say, "So? How'd it go with the review?"

"Don't ask," he says. He holds up his hand to stop further questions. I feel a pit in my stomach. He's loosened his tie and rolled up his sleeves. An upper-middle-class version of *A Coal Miner's Daughter.* Grim. Beleaguered. Trapped. I feel sick with it.

"It didn't go well, I'm guessing," I say. I wince knowing he'll bite my head off. I'm his wife, though. Aren't we supposed to be talking about this stuff?

"What did I just say?" he says. "I don't know what else I can do. They want the impossible. *Everybody* wants the impossible. Why are you staring at me like that?"

"I'm not staring," I say. I'm careful now. "I'm listening."

He forks a chunk of beef. He's eating because it's in front of him, not because he has an appetite. His elbows on the table.

His head hanging not far from the plate. His mouth opening to take in the heaps of food.

"Fuck it," he says under his breath. Looking at his plate. "Fuck the whole thing."

"What'd they say?" I ask him, trying not to wince at the bite of his words.

"Sam, I told you I don't want to talk about it. Drop it."

I sip my wine. I don't know why I hadn't noticed before that it was too bitter.

"Pass the salt, will you?"

The subject is closed. No raise again this year.

I hand the salt down to him over crumpled napkins and half-finished glasses of milk. He shakes it across the plate and shovels in another bite. He's staring at a spot on the wall.

"Is there any rice left?"

I get up and pour the rest of the wine down the sink. The rice that's left is gunky. Stuck to the bottom of the pot. He doesn't care, pausing midbite for me to spoon it onto his plate.

I keep thinking I'll stop getting my feelings hurt. I keep telling myself it's not personal. But my feelings do get hurt. And it is personal. And this will keep on and keep on until I'm crying again. I'm so tired of crying. I'm exhausted by this.

I walk out of the room. I listen to him scrape the chair away from the table a few minutes later. The refrigerator door opens, closes, a bottle cap pings onto the counter.

"Has Cammy's report card come yet?" Bob comes in holding a fresh beer. "Oh, I looked into her volunteering at A Foot in the Door, that place that gets old shoes to homeless people trying to find jobs. It'll look really good on her transcript."

"I can't wait to hear you pitch *that* to her," I say.

"Listen, we've got to round her out," he says, "colleges want the whole package and so far she's got nothing on her record but probation and semigood grades. At this rate she'll be lucky to get into a junior college."

"Put that on the list of things to talk to her about," I say.

"Have you talked to her teacher about backing off of the whole thing so we could get it off her record?"

"What's she going to say?" I ask him. "'*Oh sure, no problem. Your daughter can treat me like shit but I won't ever do anything about it.*'"

"Can't hurt to try," he says.

"Why don't *you* try talking to Cammy," I say. "I hate always being the bad cop."

"She's a teenager. No teenager likes to talk to her parents. Oh, by the way, can you take my car in for servicing?"

"Sit down," I say. "Let's curl up on the couch."

"Don't forget to remind them to change the oil this time," he says, tapping the mail into a neat pile in the palm of his hand. "I don't know how they managed to forget that the last time."

"We could put on some Coltrane," I say.

"I forgot to tell you, Sonny's going to pitch my high-top design to the guys in from Tokyo."

"That's great," I say. "Couch. Coltrane."

"Dad! Where's the plunger?"

"Oh, Jesus. I'll be back," he says. He sighs and yawns as he crosses the living room to the stairs. His feet clomp up to the second floor, slow deliberate trudging.

I squish one of the end pillows under my head and stretch out my legs, careful to keep the soles of my shoes off the seat cushions. I'd take them off, but they're new, and Bob will notice the high heel, but before he starts on his lecture I'll tell him they're Aerosoles. We go back and forth on Aerosoles—he says they're a crock but when he feels the inside of them like he did with my loafers he cocks his head to the side as if he's impressed and when he doesn't say anything I feel victorious. I arrange myself so my skirt doesn't get wrinkled and I wait. Staring up at the ceiling I remind myself to call the painters to take care of that cracked and peeling corner where we had water damage last spring; I wait some more. While I'm thinking about it, I should make a list: I need to take the portrait of my mom to get reframed, I need to get my highlights retouched and I keep forgetting to get the plumber over here for the catch basin—I'm pretty sure it's time for him to clean it out. Now my waiting is a test: how long will it take Bob to remember we were in the middle of something? Now the test has become an indictment—I will not leave the couch until he happens by and realizes his mistake. I know I'll forget all the things I need to get done if I don't write them down now but I don't want all this waiting to go to waste now after so much time. I can't risk getting up to get something to read because knowing my luck that will be the precise moment Bob will come back down through the living room and I want him to see me waiting. I'm not going to let him skate by that easily. Not after putting in half an hour. It seems like an hour has passed but it's probably half that. Certainly the toilet has been taken care of in this amount of time. So I sit here and find myself daydreaming about Craig. I wonder what he's doing. I wonder what his marriage is like. I wonder if he is thinking of me right now. Here comes Bob coming down the stairs. At the last minute I decide to sit up straight so I'll look uncomfortable and he'll feel worse.

"Hey. What're you doing, just lounging around?" he says. He doesn't even stop on his way to the kitchen.

"Remember Coltrane?" I call out. I don't budge, hoping he'll put two and two together that I've been waiting for him to return. He's probably in the kitchen doing the "I coulda had a V8" hand smack to his forehead. But instead, "Hey, honey? Where's that ruler that was in the top drawer, you know, the hardware drawer? Never mind. I found it."

He passes me and heads back upstairs. I log on to the computer. Screw it.

Hey there. This is out of the blue but I'm wondering if you want to meet for coffee? I'm scoping out a nonprofit not far from you on Friday. What about Starbucks?

Sure, I write. I could do it Friday. What time are you thinking?

Friday comes and I change outfits four times. I settle on my jean skirt because it's a skirt, but the denim keeps it grounded so I don't look like I got dressed up for him. I put on my good push-up bra but then I take it off because it might make me look too busty and it feels weird wearing it during the day and also it's black and the shirt I want to wear is yellow and I'm pretty sure the black would show through the fabric. So I have to wear my tired old everyday bra that doesn't do much for me, but then I don't want to look obvious. The yellow shirt is a button-down, pinched in at the waist, with little cap sleeves that make it girlie and feminine. The shoes take the most time to pick out. Flats make me feel dumpy but heels are way too much of a statement and I don't have any that really go with my jean skirt, so that limits me considerably. It's going to have to be ballet flats. The ones with little bows on top coupled with my shirt are too Laura Ingalls Wilder. The gray plain ones aren't terribly flattering but they're the only ones that go and I remind myself I'm supposed to be fitting this coffee into my busy day and gray flats are just what I'd wear on a busy day so gray flats it is. I spray on some light perfume that wears off in twenty minutes usually but the hint of it is all I want anyway. Who puts on perfume to run errands? Me. I put it on every day. It's a little thing but it makes me feel put together and most days I'm not.

I get to Starbucks too early so I drive around the block a couple of times because I don't want to look too eager. I want to blow into the room like I'm making a grand entrance. Then again it's hard to stride in flats so maybe I should go in first after all. Also, tables get taken over by the laptop crowd, so I should definitely go in and grab one. I don't want to have to sit on those bar stools facing the street. Not that we're doing anything wrong, it's just I don't want to be nervous the whole time—it'd be just my luck to have Sally Flanders walk by and see me with this handsome man in the middle of a weekday when I'm normally rushing in and out with grocery bags and dry cleaning.

I go in and snag the last free table for two. I'll wait to order coffee until he gets here. I can't risk losing the table by going up to order. A Johnny Cash tribute CD is playing, stacks of them in a tree that also offers five or six other CDs, some indie, some jazz, some seasonal.

I forgot what he looks like. I forgot how gorgeous he is. How his thick hair makes him look masculine and virile and younger than most of the husbands in my group. And look how easily he wears his clothes. That's a strange observation but it captures him perfectly. He's comfortable in his own skin. He is so handsome I forget I haven't eaten all day. I forget I have a million things to do. And this next thought makes me embarrassed for myself: I forget there is anyone else around us in this busy Starbucks. He strides in and owns the room without realizing it. *His* is a grand entrance.

"Hey. Sorry I'm late. I always forget how bad parking is on this block."

"You better get in line now," I manage to say. "There's a group of about ten high-school kids and they're headed this way."

"What can I get you?" he says.

"Coffee. Black. Grande's good. Thanks."

I fumble in my purse for my wallet because that's just what you do, you offer to pay even when you know the other person is going to. He doesn't waste time with the formality of "put your wallet away," he's already up at the counter ordering, looking over at me and rolling his eyes at the crush of high schoolers. The baristas shout out orders like they're landing planes.

He comes back within minutes, blowing on his cup.

Now that we're sitting across from each other I have no idea what to say. It feels like a date. So I guess I do have something to say.

"Um, this is awkward to say," I tell him. He looks worried but then I don't know this guy. Maybe worried is his natural expression.

"I really liked talking with you the other day," I start, "but is this weird? I mean us meeting for coffee? I'm married. You're married."

"Married people make new friends all the time."

"True," I say. "It's just, oh, I don't know."

"Look, I know what you're saying. I do." He leans back and crosses his leg ankle to knee. "But it's just coffee, for God's sake. So I went to this nonprofit and listen to this, they've raised enough money to send a class of eleventh graders on an exchange program to South Africa. They're looking for funds to bring the kids they've been writing to—it's a pen-pal program—here. Two weeks of switching lives. Cool, huh?"

And just like that it's easy. Normal. Enjoyable. Interesting to hear about. Nothing weird about it at all. He talks about traveling down to "Jo-berg" for a site survey. And how he ended up on a trek into Zambia and happening on another school with even more severe needs.

"I feel bad," he says. "I haven't asked about you. What do you do?"

Oh, Jesus, here we go. The conversational black hole.

"Nothing," I say. "I mean, I'm a stay-at-home mom."

"That's not nothing," he says. "That's harder than what most people do."

"Yeah, yeah, yeah, everyone says that. But I'm not exactly jetting around saving the world. Educating African kids. I'm so boring it's sickening."

"You're not boring," he says.

"How do you know I'm not boring? You don't even know me."

Then it occurs to me…

"If you're so happy doing what you're doing how come you said you thought about walking away from your life?"

He uncrosses his legs and sips his coffee.

"There's always more to the story," he says with a shrug. "*You* know that."

"How are you so sure about a complete stranger? You keep acting like you know me."

He locks eyes with me. We have the same eyes. Deep, wide set. Unveiled, open.

"I don't know," he says, again shrugging. "You're right, I don't know you. It's nice talking to you, though."

I look around. At a table for two along the amber-and-purple-painted wall is a silver-haired man hunched over a laptop, a weathered leather briefcase tilted on the empty chair across from him. He must feel me looking at him because he sits up and I can see his collar and I wonder why a minister is sitting in a Starbucks pecking at a keyboard in the middle of the day. I look back at Craig and feel his glow of energy and light and happiness and in being near him, close to him, I absorb it. What's so wrong about that?

I feel at ease. My smile at him is natural. I get a prickly feeling like I did years ago when I saw the trailer for *Steel Magnolias,* knowing it was going to be my favorite movie of all time, which it was. Until I saw *When Harry Met Sally.* Then it was a tie.

He talks about how he used to be an adrenaline junkie but had to scale back once the baby was born. I take in the sound of his voice. I watch his lips as they form words that hang in the air like exhaled smoke. He talks about how he'd always wanted to go fly-fishing in Chile and I follow the line of his face with my eyes, noting his strong bone structure. Then there's shooting the rapids on the upper fork of the Salmon River, he's saying, but that went on hold when they decided to bump out the kitchen to fold the family room in so it's more of an open-floor plan. His shirt is longsleeved and casual, like a sweater but not a sweater. Oh, my God, how long has he been silent? He has caught me checking him out. I look away.

"I've been rambling. Sorry," he says.

I honestly don't know what to say. What did he leave off with? Jesus, Sam, *say* something. Anything.

"Yeah, we haven't taken a trip in a long time." That's all I can think of? *We haven't taken a trip in a long time?* Pathetic. Say something else. Throw *something* out there. "I mean, without the kids. We used to talk about going to Egypt, a boat ride on the Nile. Somewhere along the way we forgot about it and now with the kids and all..."

"I know," he says. "Funny how that happens, huh?"

We both smile.

"For me it's not so much about travel, though," I say. "It's that connection. That closeness we used to have."

"Exactly," he says. "That's *exactly* like us."

"I just—this sounds horrible and I don't mean it to be, but sometimes I look at my life and I can't believe this is all there is. I always thought something major would happen to me, you know? I know it's stupid."

"It's not stupid at all," he says.

"What did you want to happen in your life that hasn't happened?" I ask him. "From my side of things I can't pinpoint it. I just wanted something huge. I know, I know…"

"No, no, I know what you're saying," he says. "I thought maybe I'd go into politics. I truly thought I could change the world blah blah blah. Make a difference. You know the drill…"

He chatters on about some of the things he would've gotten involved in: welfare reform, education. He's big into fundraising now, for candidates who've become friends.

"Oh, jeez, look at the time," I say.

"You can't come up with a better one?" He laughs at me. "Please. I've been talking too much. Evie tells me that all the time. Sorry."

"I'm serious," I tell him. "I've got to pick up the kids. It's been great talking with you."

He stands to help me with my coat.

"I'm sorry, I, um, I forgot today's an early pick-up day. Okay, bye."

I look at him and he has that same look on his face that he did on Michigan Avenue a few days ago. Searching. Serious. And yes, a hint of sexiness he can't help.

"Um, okay, see you later," I say.

"Bye, Samantha."

A few hours later, after the kids are asleep, I decide it's time to channel that commercial where the woman's rubbing on body lotion and her husband's watching and pulls her into bed before she's even done. The takeaway: lotion is so sexy, good luck applying it in front of your man. I time it so right when he gets into bed and puts on his reading glasses, I perch, naked, on the edge of the foot of the bed, my Jergens at my side. Going to bed naked is out of the ordinary in and of itself, so I assume Bob will be turned on by that alone, but I keep my back to him so I can go on with the show. After my arms are good and moisturized he says:

"What the hell? Since when do you do that outside the bathroom?"

I half turn and make a point of pumping more lotion into my hands.

"You're going to get that all over the comforter," he says.

"Want to help?"

"You can't put lotion on yourself?"

"Maybe we could do it together," I say.

"I'll pass," he says. "You know how I hate getting lotion on my hands."

I want to scream, You know what *I* hate Bob? I hate that you make me feel like I should cover up. Like my body repulses you so much you can't even touch it with lotion. Or without, come to think of it. I want to yell, I want out! You hate getting lotion on your hands? Well, I hate how depressing my life is. How about *that* shit, *Bob?* I could throw stuff into a duffel and walk out and you'd never have to worry about fucking lotion ever again! Instead, I pull on my robe and go downstairs to the computer.

The e-mail waiting for me was sent only minutes ago.

It was great seeing you today.

This time I don't reply right away.

We're friends. Friends who meet for coffee. I probably won't get together with him again. It was kind of boring, actually. All he did was talk about himself. I still don't get what would make him want to walk away from his life. That's not something a lot of people say, period, much less to a stranger. What the hell.

Thanks for the coffee, I write back.

In two weeks we've met for coffee four times. I guess that's a lot, but it doesn't feel like it. In between we e-mail. Simple stuff. Like what's going on, what our days are filled with. He's becoming a close friend.

On our fifth meeting I switch to chai tea latte.

"Lemme ask you something. Do you tell your wife about me?" I ask him.

He hands me my drink and settles into his chair. It's the same table we always get.

"Do I tell my wife about you?"

"Yeah. Do you?"

He finger combs his hair. "It doesn't really come up. I mean, you know."

He brushes the crumbs of his coffee cake off the table.

"Why?" he asks. "Do you tell your husband?"

"It doesn't come up."

"There you go."

We're friends. Guilty friends who have nothing to feel guilty about. We meet at Starbucks. We e-mail. We talk about our kids. Books. Movies. What's so wrong about that? So why haven't we mentioned one another to our spouses?

"Hey, by the way, any chance you all would want to adopt a kitten?" I ask.

"A kitten?" He smiles. I get the feeling he's glad for the subject change.

"A cuddly, orange-and-white little ball of fur…"

He laughs. "Laying it on a bit thick, aren't you?"

"She's so cute you can't believe it. Lexi would flip over her."

I said the magic words.

"So unfair." He smiles again. "Little girls and fluffy animals. Nice touch. Why don't you guys keep it if she's so damn cute?"

"Bob's allergic. Cammy came home with her the other night. We've been feeding her with an eyedropper, she's that small. The kids are heartbroken we can't keep her, but…"

"Bob's allergic," he says.

"I've tried everyone I know."

"Maybe Bob's *conveniently* allergic," he says.

But I can tell he's seriously considering it.

"If she doesn't work out I can take her back," I tell him. "I could find her another place, I guess."

"I thought you tried everyone you knew."

"That's true," I say. "But I don't want to put you on the spot."

"You know what? It's your lucky day. I'll take her."

Bob will be relieved—he thinks I'm conspiring to keep the kitten, but I wouldn't do that to him. Not with him sneezing and tearing up all the time. He's been getting an angry rash on his arm. The kids will just have to deal with it.

I jump up to hug Craig without a thought. He seems surprised. He smiles but is definitely surprised.

"Thank you thank you thank you," I say.

He's awkward. He shifts in his chair.

"So, what else is new?" he finally asks.

I wonder what he'll tell his wife about the kitten. Where it came from. I wonder what I'll tell Bob and Cammy. Shoot. What do I tell Bob? I'll just tell him I found a family who wanted a kitten. Simple. But then he'll ask who they are and how I know them and I'm back to square one. Shoot! I should've thought this through. Why didn't I think this through? Okay, calm down. You're thinking it through now, so calm down. I'll just tell him I met someone at Starbucks—which is true, technically—and we got to talking and somehow the kitten came up and voilà I found a home. Bob won't ask what we were talking about. Home free. Done.

I used to pull the minivan into the driveway at the end of the day and the kids would pile out, usually one or two of the neighbors' kids would be in the mix, and pour in through the backdoor and they'd scatter. Some to the fridge for after-school snacks. Me unloading groceries or picking up jackets tossed in the direction of the hooks by the door, some to the downstairs computer, others to the one upstairs. This afternoon I'm like a football player—I go wide and pass them as they dump backpacks and take off boots—I race to the kitchen computer to check my in-box. It's like beat-the-clock because no sooner do I open his e-mail than I hear:

"Aw, Mo-om, I need to use the computer" and "Mo-om," (always in a drawn-out whine) "how long are you going to be on? I've got to send in my essay" and my personal favorite "Mo-om? Is dinner going to be ready soon? I'm starving." I hate that one on many different levels. One: it's passive-aggressive. If you want me off the computer just say so. Two: it reminds me of Mrs. Cleaver. Like I'm not supposed to have friends I want to be in touch with…I'm just supposed to cook and clean and see to everyone else's needs. And three: coming from three kids who can easily find a snack for themselves…well, that just gets my goat. When I was growing up my mother taught me how to make dinner and clean up and do laundry and a million other things my kids don't have a clue about. I know, I know, I'm to blame. Now I realize how smart it was for our mothers to do this, not because it's sharing the workload (many times I feel like it would take far less time if I just did it myself without having to walk someone through it), but because it creates self-sufficiency. When I tell my kids to set the table I watch while they open the wrong cabinets for dishes and glasses like they're in an unfamiliar kitchen.

"Excuse me, I will be on the computer for a few more minutes," I say. "What about Dad's computer? Go up and wait for that one and I'll let you know when I'm off. Or better yet, find some other homework you can do."

"What's for dinner?" Jamie asks.

"Oh, fine." I get up and fish past several not quite entirely sealed bags of questionably edible frozen vegetables for a box of chicken fingers.

Five minutes in the microwave and we're about to sit down.

"Andrew, call your sister."

"I'm here, I'm here," Cammy says. Cammy plops down while tightening the strings of her hoodie until she resembles a police sketch. Of course, her sweatshirt is black. Of course, her skirt, baggy to the point of almost slipping off her hips, is black and full of pockets and zippers like cargo shorts. The hem, if you could call it that, is ragged from dragging on the ground nearly every day. She wears it so often there's no turn-around time to wash it and anyway she should do her own laundry, so I figure she'll be forced to when maggots hatch from the accumulated dirt.

"What happened to the whole organic raw thing?" she asks.

I poke her back with one hand, set a plate down in front of Jamie with the other. "If you want ketchup it's on the top shelf in the fridge."

"Eat your peas," I say to Andrew. "Jamie, stop pushing them

over and under the rim of your plate. I know you're trying to hide them. I'm not blind."

"Did you know Helen Keller wasn't really blind?" Jamie says.

You've stirred me awake, Craig said.

"Mom, did you?"

"Did I what?"

"Did you know Helen Keller wasn't really blind?"

"She could read if she put the book right next to her eyes," says Jamie. "Mom, Andrew just kicked me under the table. He did it again. Andrew, *cut it out.*"

Then Andrew, "Did Dad bring home the new sneakers? The Z110s? Mom?"

"Huh? Oh, no. I don't think so. Check the front hall closet after dinner."

"Can I be excused?" Cammy asks, but clearly it's said sarcastically since she's already up and scraping her plate into the disposal side of the sink.

"You didn't eat anything," I say.

"You didn't get me any Boca Burgers," she says. "You get the boys all that free-range chicken, but you don't get me Boca Burgers. They're both in the frozen-foods section, you know. I'm outta here."

"Did you know penguins barf their food so their kids can eat it?" Jamie asks.

I watch Cammy plug up her ears with the white iPod buds on her way out of the kitchen and part of me wants to stop time here to keep the future from slapping us in the face. Something's in the air, like the way you can *smell* Halloween approaching.

"Mom, Andrew kicked me again."

CAMMY.

Samantha spoils the boys. It's so obvious it's sick.

Ricky came home from school with me yesterday and Samantha practically wet her pants she was so happy to see him. She thinks he's better than Monica. Then again she'd think Hitler was better than Monica. She's always liked Ricky. Even after he got a tattoo of a celtic cross he keeps calling an Ankh like that makes it cooler. She'd freak if she knew about my tattoo but it's not like I wear frigging ponytails anymore so there's no way she'll see it on the back of my neck. It's small. A nautical star. Ricky smirked and said it's what lame sailors used to get and the bald tattoo guy with an ear lobe stretcher said *yeah, genius, 'cause it means you're trying to find your way home safely from a long journey, get it?* and that shut Ricky up. I started regretting the whole thing when he wiped an alcohol pad on my neck. I sweated bullets and since the air conditioner vents were pointed right at me the sweat made my skin cold. I knew if I backed out Ricky'd never let me hear the end of it but man I wanted to. If I ever smell rubbing alcohol again I'll barf.

So yesterday. Ricky and I hung out in the living room for some reason. I can't remember why but we did. When I kicked the boys out she came in all steamed and asked to *have a word* with me. Out in the hall she's all about not wanting the boys to see *inappropriate behavior.* What a joke! If she only knew.

Before Monica, my mom'd be pissed because Ricky doesn't do the whole act like, *Hi Mrs. Friedman how are you today isn't your dress lovely my how clean the house looks.* That's why she hates Monica. Then I don't know what happened but all the sudden she's smiley and patting him on the back and all hi, sweetie. To his face she's all, *Oh, Ricky, how are you* and *Oh, Ricky, why don't you and Cammy come hang out here in the kitchen and keep me company while I make dinner.* Yeah, right. I'd rather stick my fingers into a juicer.

They think me and Ricky are like boyfriend-girlfriend. It's so fucking hilarious. Like we'd ever be boyfriend-girlfriend. Ricky looks at me like I'm his sister and plus now he's always talking about how hot Monica is and how he could get into her pants if he really wanted to. I tell him *yeah so go for it if you're so hot for her* and he makes up something stupid like *I will when the time's right.* What a joke. Anyway, they think we're hooking up because Ricky's tattoo is a star with the letter R twisted into the letter C in the middle. They think it's like a heart with initials plussed together but it's our symbol. We designed it when we were thinking of starting a group. The beauty is it's our initials but it really stands for Rage Company. Like whatever we all do in the world, we're still raging against something. Sometimes we'll see someone who looks like he'd get it and we joke around like *oh, yeah, let's recruit him into RC* but we're too lazy to do anything about it. Also I think it'd be queer to have a group. It feels too yearbooky.

I feel like—we both feel like we're in a chain gang and whenever anybody else in our family does something we're dragged along like it or not. We're locked in with no fucking choice. Except now I have a choice and fuck it I'm taking it. Who wouldn't? It's like this escape hatch I never really thought about but now it's time for me to take it. Ricky calls it a do-over. Once I talk to my birth mother I'll be able to decide who I want to live with and it'll be like so frigging easy. Finally, things will be easy. I can be whatever I want to be without thinking this little Friedman clique is looking down on me or feeling sorry for me like *oh poor Cammy she's not one of us you know so be extra nice so she doesn't notice.* Their faces stretched into smiles. Smiles or psycho frowns when I've done something wrong again. When I need to *earn their trust back.*

Ricky says Monica's RC material and we both laugh because it's so gay to have this little club, like we're in a tree house deciding whether to let the rope ladder down for someone else to climb up but that's exactly what he wants to do. It's his way of getting me to share her with him and I hate that. Plus, the minute Monica finds out about RC she'll bail. She already thinks everyone here is like five years old. Today she said, "Oh, my God I don't know how you haven't blown your brains out yet, this place is so fucking *soul crushing.*"

She says stuff like that. *Soul crushing.* And the minute she said it I felt stupid that I haven't said the same thing out loud because I've thought it a million times but once she said it all I could do is say *I know, right? Totally.* So I look like I'm trying to copy her yet again, which is exactly what Samantha thinks I'm doing. I heard her talking to Bob about it…they think Monica's *bad news* and that she's leading me down the *wrong path.* But then Samantha told him she thought I was already on that path when Monica came along and I wanted to say *hell yeah I was* because the only thing worse than Monica thinking I'm copying her is Samantha and Bob thinking I'm copying her. Then again, maybe the wrong path is the right path, didn't they ever stop to consider that? Maybe it's good to rage, to get it out and not keep it all bottled up inside so everyone thinks you're happy and shiny.

Ricky doesn't know about Will. I mean, I don't think he knows about Will. He wouldn't care anyway, since he doesn't like me like me but still, I kinda don't want him to find out. And that's fine with Will. In the beginning, when we were at the parking lot one night with a bunch of Paul's friends, Will came over and asked if I wanted to go for a walk. I get so embarrassed when I think about it now because right when he came over to ask me I felt like I was going to pass out like one of those screaming Beatle fans. Will's hot, if you don't look too hard at his skin. He has burns on sixty percent of his body and part of them come up his neck to his jaw. It looks like he was dropped into a vat of acid if you see him in the daytime but at night you can hardly see. He's never said what happened but Ricky told me his father set fire to his house with his mom and him still in it—he locked them in and took off right after he lit the match to the gasoline. Will got kicked out of school last year but he kept a lot of his friends because he's like the ringleader next to Paul.

Anyway, he came over to ask me to go for a walk and I'm such a frigging dork I thought it was going to be like a stupid Disney movie…us walking and maybe holding hands and yeah I guess making out or something. I was such a baby. We got behind the 7-Eleven and that's when he unzipped his pants. It's totally not sex or anything so I don't know why I thought it was like the biggest deal but I didn't really know what I was supposed to do so he had to tell me. He was nice about it that night—his voice was softer than it is when he's talking with Paul and the group. Plus, if you look past the burns he's hot now that he's grown out his hair. Monica's been drooling over him since she got here and I couldn't wait to tell her we hooked up so I did what he said and I guess it wasn't so bad after all. Except it was embarrassing when we were going back around the building and I barely touched his hand and he whipped it away from me and walked faster back to Paul. At the time I thought maybe it was his reaction when something surprised him because of the fire but then I realized it's because he wants to keep it quiet. He's not the type to brag. I didn't know where to stand once we got back to everyone—Ricky wasn't there that night and Monica was grounded so it was people I don't normally hang out with and I felt like a sore thumb. So I went inside the store and got a Snapple to get the taste out of my mouth and then I walked home. I think Will was surprised to see me go or he probably didn't see me because it was dark because when I said *see ya* he looked away. Whatever.

I told Monica about it but it felt weird to tell Ricky so I didn't.

My mom would freak if she knew. She thinks I'm five. She'd totally freak and then she'd find a way to talk about her mother and I'd end up feeling like a shithead again so forget that. Like I'd ever tell her anyway.

Zoey said nothing's come in the mail yet and I trust her since she knows she's getting my iPod once she hands it over when it does get here, that goddamn letter. Actually she only *thinks* she's getting my iPod. I'm giving her my Shuffle but whatever. Ricky said that if it doesn't come by the end of the week he'll call the agency and say he's my father Bob and that we were *under the gun to get to the bottom of things* because of the *medical emergency* and maybe they could just tell us over the phone. I know for a fact that we covered all our bases with the paperwork because the Web sites for this stuff had legal pdf forms that most agencies require and we filled them out perfectly, following the examples they give you.

I feel like I'm holding on until I find all this out and maybe I'm getting my hopes up like Ricky says but I can't help it. It's like it's out of my control. I can't wait until this goddamn letter comes! The only thing that worries me, other than Zoey missing the letter and Samantha and Bob finding it, is whether they've found a way to see into my documents on the family computer. My dad's computer is locked so I had no choice— I had to use the family one. It's not like my mom knows a lot about computers but still…lately she's been on it like 24/7 and I'm starting to freak out that she's tracking me. All of a sudden she's obsessed with the computer and she's a total bitch if I'm on it. There's no way she knows what I've been doing because I wipe my footprints off the hard drive and even if there's some hidden file that I don't know about I guarantee she wouldn't know how to uncover it. She's like Amish with computers. She hurries off when she sees me coming and it makes me sick to my stomach for some reason but I really don't think she even knows about Google Desktop so I think I'm okay.

It's weird what she pays attention to, like it's priority number one to get rid of my kitten. Like a tiny kitten's gonna shift the earth on its axis. She's all *I don't know why you didn't ask first…if you had I would've reminded you about your father's allergies.* I didn't mean to cry about it—who cares anyway, right?—but then she got all whiney about how she found *the perfect family.* That's what she kept saying: *they're just perfect, Cam. The perfect family.* Well, Goody-fucking-two-shoes for them. Now they've got my kitten to make them even more perfect.

Thank God she forgot about that whole "Sam and Cammy Go To The Movies On Sundays" shit she wanted us to do. I threw out the showtimes I'd Fandango'd. I didn't want to see a romantic comedy anyway.

Samantha

SYSTEM FAILURE. UNABLE TO CONNECT TO THE INTERNET. Check your local connection and contact systems administrator.

"Cammy?" I call from the bottom of the staircase. "Ca-mmy! Can you come here for a second?"

SYSTEM FAILURE. UNABLE TO CONNECT TO THE INTERNET. Check your local connection and contact systems administrator.

The upstairs is dead quiet.
"Cammy!"
"Whaaaat?" Her tone and volume matching mine.
"Can you come down here?"
I'm back, logging on after restarting again, hoping…nope. Still nothing.
"Jesus, why are you screaming at me?" she says.
"Can you fix this? I've tried three times now and I can't get online."

"Dad's computer's offline, too," she says. "Must be the cable modem."

She shrugs her way out of the kitchen.

"Wait! What do I do to fix the cable modem? Can you do it?"

"No, I can't do it," she says, as if the mere suggestion is amusing.

"Watch your tone," I say. "And take the other earphone out, it's rude to stay plugged in when someone's talking to you."

"I'm just saying. Call the cable company or something, I don't know. P.S. They're not *earphones*. That's so gay."

"Oh, excuse me, and don't call things gay. You know better than that. What're they called if they aren't earphones?"

"*Head*phones," she says. "Or earbuds. Depending. Can I go now?"

"I'd have thought you'd be freaking out about this more than anyone," I say. "How come you're so fine with the computer being down?"

"I'm texting. I don't care."

"That reminds me, we're going to have to have a little talk about your cell-phone minutes," I say.

"Okay, but can we do it later? I've got, like, a million things due tomorrow…"

"And you're texting homework back and forth, right? Uh-huh. Fine. You're excused. But just try one more time?"

I pace behind Cammy, but after another halfhearted attempt she gives up and says, "Nope. It's dead," in a snarky tone that's become a regular thing.

I have to rummage through a shoe box of paid bills to find the number for the cable company.

"Thank you for calling Horizon Cable, the world leader in phone and cable communications, my name is Princess, how can I help you?"

"Oh, yes, hi, wait, let me take you off speakerphone," I

say, running across to the kitchen phone. "Sorry, I was on hold so long."

"Can I get the last four digits of your social-security number to verify your account information."

"Oh, sure…5421. I'm calling because I can't get online and my daughter says—"

"You live at zip code 60626?"

"Yes," I say.

"Ma'am, our technicians are working to fix the problem. It should be corrected soon. There's a cable outage in your area."

"How long until it's fixed?"

"Ma'am, we don't know yet. Sorry for the inconvenience. Is there anything else I can help you with today? Can I tell you about our money-saving three-in-one package? If you act today you can receive one month of premium cable channels free."

"No, thanks."

"Have a nice day and thank you for calling Horizon Cable."

I know he's e-mailed me by now. He had to take Lexi to a birthday party and wasn't sure if parents were expected to stay or if it was the drop-off kind. By this time of day we would have traded two or three e-mails at least. We don't call each other. Technically we haven't done anything anyone could be suspicious about but it's this unspoken agreement to communicate by e-mail. I just thought maybe he'd call my cell. So now I'm facing the real possibility that I might not see him all weekend.

This of course puts me in a terrible mood, the kind of mood that sweeps across the house like a spotlight. One by one I'm ordering rooms cleaned and straightened and Bob is sent to Costco and anyone who's ever been to Costco on a Saturday knows what kind of hell that is.

I click on and off. I restart the computer. I go back and forth between Bob's computer and mine and then, in an instant—*checking password* flashes across the screen and just as Bob's car pulls in, packed with cases of bottled water and toilet paper and restaurant-size mustard, there Craig is in my in-box. Just when the house gets busy again. Bob's got to unload so I have time to check just the one.

Have you ever seen *The Usual Suspects?* Rented it last night. It's so good you can't believe it. Just thought I'd say hey.

"Mom! I'm done cleaning my room," Andrew calls down to me. "Can I go next door?"

The second e-mail…I have to read the second one. Really quickly. Bob's still unloading the car.

"Mom? Can I?"

"Huh? Oh. No! You've got a soccer game in a few minutes!"

It's taking a second for his words to unfurl.

Hey. What're you up to? Just wanted to let you know I'm thinking about you. We're off to watch the game at a friend's house. Hope you're enjoying the day.

I check over my shoulder and while I still have the kitchen to myself I click on number three. I have no willpower.

Lexi saved us from football watching. Evie thinks she's coming down with something. I think she wanted to get home to the kitten. We named her Fluffy by the way. I use the word "we" in the general sense. Do I look like the kind of guy who'd name a kitten Fluffy? This kitten could not be more loved. Thinking of you.

"What're you doing?" Bob asks.

"Oh, my God, you scared me! I didn't hear you come in," I say, trying to find the X to close out my e-mail. I can't look panicked.

"How was Costco?" I ask him, aware that I'm trying too hard to sound casual.

"You seem happy," Bob says. "What was that e-mail you didn't want me to see?"

"Huh? Oh, nothing! Just a school thing. Was it crowded?"

"Why were you so frantic to close it when I walked in if it was just a school thing?"

"Jesus, what's with the third degree?" I get up and busy myself with a pile of papers and mail next to the computer. "Oh, yeah, did you see this thank-you note we got from Margie O'Donnell? Read it so I can throw it out."

This is a turning point. We look at each other, Bob and I do, like a game of chicken where you try to last longer not blinking, as I hold out that random piece of paper that will decide whether he can let it go or whether he'll hold my feet to the fire and get me not only to confess but to surrender Craig. And you know what? I will. If Bob gives me any sign of hope whatsoever, I will chuck the whole damn thing right then and there. So here we are, allowing Margie O'Donnell to decide our fate on this day of discount warehouses and clean rooms. Her letter is suspended between us, a gesture that carries the weight of a family with it. Bob's reaching for it, accepting it, will be a tacit agreement to continue believing in our commitment, flawed though it might be. Refusing it will force us into an unknown abyss that could heal us or hurt us permanently.

Bob takes the note from me and lowers his eyes to Margie O'Donnell's neat handwriting.

"That's a nice note," he says. He hands it back and calls to the boys for them to hurry up for soccer. To prove everything's business as usual I make a show of sorting through the pile crammed between the computer screen and a stack of cookbooks. My heart's only just now returning to its normal beat after the near miss of Craig's e-mail. In case he's suspicious, I act preoccupied with my to-do list.

"They didn't hear you," I mumble like I normally would.

I look up when he turns to call up to the boys again. I touch the mouse to reactivate the screen so I can check to make sure I've logged off completely. I have. Good. Crisis averted. Then, remembering his e-mail, I imagine Craig curling up with Lexi and Fluffy.

"Jesus, where are they? Boys! Swear to God…" Bob stalks through the living room to the foot of the stairs.

"Hey, Bob?"

"Yeah? Boys! Let's go! Get your stuff!"

"You never asked where the kitten went," I call to him.

"Huh? Boys! Don't make me count to three!" He turns back toward the kitchen. "What'd you say?"

"How come you never asked where the kitten went?"

He hunts through his coat pockets then his pant pockets for the car keys.

"Where the kitten went," he echoes.

"The kitten? The kitten you were allergic to? The one we *had to get rid of?*"

He shrugs and an aha crosses his face when he spots the car keys on the counter. "Throw me those, will you? Thanks."

I toss them over.

"You found a home for it, right?" He's feeling pockets again. "Have you seen my sunglasses?"

"Over there on the table. You never asked who took her."

"Does it matter?"

The boys stampede into the kitchen, both nearly-but-not-quite dressed in uniforms.

"Finally!" Bob says. "You can finish getting ready in the car. Let's get a move on. Go, go, go, we're gonna be late!"

"No," I say. "I guess it doesn't matter who took her." But my voice is lost under the noise of *wait, I forgot!* and *that's it, I'm counting to three* and then cleats on the hardwood floor out then back again clacking over to the fridge for bottled water.

"See you later, Mom!" Jamie calls on his way out the backdoor.

I don't know if I'm relieved not to have had to lie to Bob or sad that he simply doesn't care about anything I do. That's where we are, I guess. He doesn't care about me and if I'm going to be honest with myself...I don't really care about him.

Cammy

Everyone's talking on their cell phones. Who're they *talking* to? I know for a fact I have a signal pretty much everywhere except on Lake Shore Drive around Fullerton but after North Avenue beach I get all four bars. They're talking and driving, shopping, riding their bikes. It's like a Dr. Seuss poem— They talk when they walk. They talk when they stalk. That's stupid but whatever. It's everywhere I look. Even my mom gets more calls than I do. How pathetic is that? It's ridiculous.

I gave Will my cell number but he must've lost it or something. Ricky kind of calls me but he doesn't count really. Monica might call me if we weren't in a massive fight but she lost her phone. She's lost it so many times she used up all her replacements her calling plan allows so she says she's going Amish until she earns enough money to pay for one. She doesn't have a job, though.

Monica's pissed at me for some reason but she won't tell me for sure what. After she found out about me and Will she went all ballistic because I didn't tell her even when she was talking about how hot he was. She's all "you could've said something!" It's not like we're going out or anything. I thought we were kind of but then I saw him with Paola Desti the other day. Yeah so okay she's beautiful but she's not the be-all end-all. She fake-slapped his arm after he said something I guess he thought was funny. He gave her this bear hug from behind and she rolled her eyes but still let him walk her a few steps that way. She finally wriggled free but not before he kissed her cheek still from behind. I looked him right in the eye on my way to English and he blinked at me and looked away. He's like pretending I don't exist. Invisible Cameron. So I told Monica and she said he should find someone without a dot on her forehead. That's all she said. I guess she's pissed at me *and* Paola.

Monica passed a note to David with dreads he'd have to shave if he were white but no one in this stuck-up school wants to offend a black guy so he gets away with whatever he wants. He's one of maybe twenty black kids in the entire upper school. Anyway, David got the note in trig and read it and snorted before looking back at me—so frigging obvious. Mr. Stevens took it from him and thank God he tore it up and threw it away without reading it aloud first like some asshole teachers do. Somehow I'm the one who got in trouble. He goes: "Cammy, if you slip any further down in your seat you'll be lying on the ground and this isn't nap time." Monica and David laughed at me and I know my days with her are numbered. I'm fucked since she's my only girlfriend. Whatever. There's no one I want to be friends with anyway so the joke's on you.

Lately she's been on my case about the litmag I got a poem in. She's been calling me Little Miss Sunshine. And now she makes sucking sounds whenever I come into one of the *three classes* I have with her. Here's the piece that'll be in the May issue:

WHO ARE YOU

Are you mine?
Do you call me yours?
Do you even remember my name?
Or that I exist?

I'm twirling like a girl
In a light wind of snowflakes,
My arms helicoptering out
The smell of a winter snap in the air
Even though winter's not here. Yet.

I turn and turn in the nearness of a new season.
A new beginning of something I can't name.
I need a hand to hold.
Someone all mine.

I want to have you to myself.
I want you to know I exist.
I'm not a memory
Or an idea
Or a regret.

I want you to claim me.
I want the snowflakes to dance around both of us.
They'll melt on our tongues
And on our hats and we'll laugh
And you'll turn to me and say I'm yours.

I'm waiting for you.

Samantha

I haven't slept well for at least a week now and I have a call in to my doctor to see about sleeping pills. Lynn's taking Lunesta, Sally's on Ambien and I heard Kerry Kendricks talking about Ativan. I never used to need something to help me sleep. Now every night at around three in the morning I'm wide awake, making lists of things I need to do. At least I try to make lists. Sometimes, if I try too hard to fall back asleep I find myself flipping over onto my stomach then back onto my back and I start wondering how Craig sleeps. I start willing him to wake up. I want him to be thinking of me at the precise moment I'm thinking of him. All I want is to sleep through the night. I've been yawning through the days. The other day I thought I might fall asleep driving down Ashland, so I opened the window and cranked the radio. Kelly Clarkson saved me from an accident. Lately my eyes are puffy and even Cammy's noticed.

"You pierced the top of your ear? Just great, Cam," I say.

She's rummaging through the fridge, past cold cuts and pot-roast leftovers, muttering about the horrors of living with car-nivores. She finds baby carrots and crunches loudly and I want to say *I get it, you're a rebel, you're so tough eating those carrots like such a badass,* but I let her make her point.

She looks at me and I know her mission's been accomplished. I've had the exact reaction she was hoping I'd have. Well, too goddamn bad. So I'm predictable—shoot me.

"What's next—one of those creepy tribal holes stretched into your lobes? Jesus Christ, what's gotten into you?"

"You look like hell," she says. She cocks her head to one side like she's really thought this out. "Your eyes are different."

"I didn't sleep well last night, thank you for asking. Don't change the subject."

"You're so uptight," she says. "Half the girls in my class have piercings, it's like so normal it's not even funny. Can someone please remember to get tofu."

"If it's so normal why have only half the girls in your class done it?"

"I knew you wouldn't understand," she says. Shrugs. Walks away.

"You're taking that out, you know," I call to her.

"I'm not taking it out and plus the guy at the place said you can't take it out or it'll get infected," she yells on her way up the stairs.

"The hell you're not taking it out," I'm now yelling. "And maybe that *someone* can pick up her own tofu."

She closes the door with no flourish, like she closes it every other day. A slammed door would have been an insult hurled down at me. But this is worse: it's like I'm invisible now. I don't matter enough to warrant a loud door.

I trudge up the stairs. It doesn't even occur to me to knock.

She looks up from her cell phone, her busy thumbs pausing in the middle of a text message. Before she puts on the angry-teenager-face, I see the old Cammy sitting cross-legged on her bed. The Cammy who'd smile and scoot over to make room for me and offer me an earphone to listen to a song on her iPod. The Cammy who'd laugh and roll her eyes at the way I moved my head to the sound. The Cammy who'd call me a dork.

I notice her knobby limbs are filling out and lengthening, her sharp cheekbones have gentle curves now. It's like it happened overnight. I don't remember her having breasts last week. She's in another growth spurt. It's as if she's fighting it all. Her skin is what beauty magazines would call *dewy,* but she plasters it with makeup. Her long eyelashes are bending under the weight of clumped mascara she never washes off. Her wavy curls are scorched flat so much, the ends are splitting and breaking. Mostly it's the color people notice. She used to have movie-star auburn hair that got sun-kissed in summer with lots of hours on the tennis courts, but now it's pitch-black like a Halloween-witch wig. That's the first thing everyone comments on when they see her: the tar-black hair that shadows her pale face, the long bangs that hang like an awning almost down to her nose.

I keep hoping one day we'll be poring over old family photos and laughing at the absurdity of this phase of hers. I pray it's a phase. I wonder if my mother thought the same about me. I've studied the handful of pictures of us, looking for clues in her smile.

Was she as proud of me as she looked standing next to me and Dad at junior-high graduation or was there something she was hoping would change in me?

And that picture of the two of them flanking me on one of our summers at the rented lake house on the Indiana dunes—a photo taken by a stranger who may have marveled at the perfection of the shot. It *was* perfect. The water sparkled under a sky so bright they were squint-smiling. They were tanned. Dad was in his swimming suit, offhandedly holding the bucket of water we used to pat the sand on the outer edge of the castle. Mom was looking straight into the camera, a breeze blowing some hair loose from the ponytail that made her look twenty-one instead of thirty. She was in a one-piece that had a simple, flattering band of white cutting across the navy, just under her bustline.

By far my favorite picture of all of them is the one of me and Mom on a large easy chair that used to sit by the fireplace at my old house. I'm on her lap, maybe five or six years old, and she's reading to me, we're both unaware of dad and his camera. The book is tilted up so I can see it's *James and the Giant Peach*. I'm not looking at the clever illustrations, I'm staring up at her, leaning across her chest and twisting my head to watch her ruby-red lipsticked mouth form the words. Sometimes, if I try hard enough, I can hear her voice reading to me. Not long after she died I bought the book and split it open to about where she might have been in the picture and I read silently, every other word in her voice which was still so fresh. Now it hurts to look at because I can't conjure up her tone anymore. It's been too long. I've forgotten what she sounded like.

Here is my daughter sitting cross-legged on her bed. What would she do if I died? What if I had a heart attack—would she feel guilty about our relationship?

"Take out your earphones." I flap my arms to get her attention.

"Jesus," she says. "You scared the shit outta me. Don't you know how to knock?"

"That's it," I say. "Take out both your earphones. Put your cell phone down. Don't you dare talk to me in that tone of voice. This is stopping right now."

"What're you *doing?*" She flails her arms trying to stop me from ripping the iPod out of her hands. "Stop it! Give it *back!* What the hell?"

"I'm sick of your iPod. I'm sick of your cell phone and your thumbs and the laptop you throw around like it's nothing to you, totally replaceable. I'm sick of this fucking act of yours and yes, I just said fuck so you can stop with that look like you're storing up something to throw back at me."

"What're you *doing?* You're like *possessed,*" she screams. "What're you *talking* about?"

"You know exactly what I'm talking about," I say. "This. This whole thing we're doing has got to end. You skulking around like you've got this miserable life. The locked doors. The secrets. The hair, the clothes, the makeup. I'm sick of it."

Something clicks in her and now she's staring at me with a blankness I can't read. From whipping anger to this cold stare. She's frightening.

"Can't we just stop this little game and be real?" I don't ask it, I say it.

"Be real?" she snorts, and looks away. "That's just perfect. *Be real.*"

"What's that supposed to mean—*that's just perfect?* What's your point, Cammy?"

"Just forget it."

"I'm not going to forget it. *Talk to me.*"

"Why are you screaming at me?"

"Because *I can't reach you and I don't know what else to do.*"

"Just get out! Get out of my room!"

"This is *my* room." I match her screams. "Your father and I own this house, so this is *our* room. Don't you dare talk to me this way."

She sniffs back tears and folds over herself in a groan that sounds so much like a growl I actually feel scared, expecting a Linda Blair moment. Holding her knees snug she rocks back and forth for what's probably ten seconds but it could have been ten minutes it was so awful to see. Then she snaps out of it and suddenly she's a blur of motion, standing and whipping her iPod at me and if I hadn't ducked it would've hit me in the mouth instead of shattering against the wall like it did.

"I hate you." She bends over to get some power into her lungs.

"So original," I say.

"You're so funny." She's fighting tears. "Sorry I'm not *original*."

The crying turns to hyperventilating sobs and I watch her deflate to the ground. "Just...just leave. Please. Just leave me alone."

"Cammy..."

"Seriously, just leave." She is withered, her voice nearly a whisper; she's deflated from the yelling. "You can have my cell and my computer, I don't care. Just take them and leave."

"Honey..."

"Mom, seriously—" she looks like Alice Cooper with her mascara running down those white cheeks "—I can't talk now. Please. I'll talk later, I promise. I just can't...talk...now..."

I close the door quietly, and part of me is relieved because I'm spent, too, and I don't have the energy for any more of her. Maybe I shouldn't have left her alone, but at the end it was the old Cammy looking up at me, begging me to leave her alone. So I will. She's been so tired lately, maybe it's exhaustion.

She's driving me insane, I write. My daughter is driving me completely insane. You watch: Lexi will get to be a teenager and you'll want to jump off a bridge. I thought we'd dodge this bullet since Cammy and I were so close but no go. Just had to vent. G2G. Love, Sam

* * *

We meet the following day and he listens. Craig's elbows are on the table. He cups his coffee with both hands. He doesn't say much but then I didn't really want him to. I walk out of Starbucks feeling lighter, less burdened by my daughter. He makes me feel like skipping.

I'm aware I'm editing the things I share with him. I don't tell him about the silences. About how I listen to Bob chewing over the boys' chatter and I struggle for something to say that will elicit more than yes-and-no answers. Or how I've always marveled at my parents and how they were always talking to one another, so much to say, so much to laugh about. I don't tell Craig about the politeness I used to think was us being respectful of one another. Plenty of our friends insult or nag their husbands or wives. At first it seemed as if we were simply taking the high road. I never thought it was a lack of anything of substance to say. Politeness became indifference. As in:

"What do you want to do for dinner?"

"I don't care. What do you want?"

"I don't know. No preference. Do you want to eat in or go out? Or we could order out if you want."

"I don't care."

What used to pass for manners turned into inertia. Soon it felt foreign and selfish to say, "You know what? I really want Thai tonight," because he never did say much about Thai so I'm sure he'd agree just to be nice, but it'd ruin the meal if I thought he was suffering through something he didn't want to do. I could tell he felt the same way.

I chose not to tell Craig about Bob's feeling nothing and how I lie awake feeling the suffocation of a different version of nothingness. I haven't admitted to Bob that I feel the same way. I know he feels pigeonholed by his words and how he's issued this indictment. We're not in love. We're not out of love. We don't feel anything. Maybe we feel a longing for something more from each other, but at the end of the day that's doesn't account for much. On the digital clock by my bed, the colon separating the hour from the minutes blinks an imprint into my eyes and I feel like I'm trying to keep myself afloat but I'm hanging on to sand. In these small dark hours, lying next to him wide awake I feel a guilty triumph that I haven't told Bob the same thing. He lost his footing with his words. Lately he's been solicitous of me in that way people are when to apologize out loud would be an admission of a failure. Saying that one word—*nothing*—shifted the balance of power and I feel liberated by it. There's nobility in it.

I don't tell Craig this. To tell Craig my husband feels nothing toward me will make him look differently at me. I get the feeling he's got the same crush on me I have on him. I don't want to tell him Bob reads books like it's a contest. Some weeks he reads two. Thick ones. Biographies. It only took him five days to learn everything there is to know about Aaron Burr. It took Jack Kerouac three weeks to write *On the Road*. It took Bob three hours to read it. When he finished he rubbed his neck, put it on the pile of books he's read and moved over to the rickety old bookcase to pick out his next one. No, I don't tell Craig this.

The next time we meet I venture to the place we've carefully avoided. But friends talk about their marriages, right?

"I still don't get why you want to walk away from your life," I start. "We've talked about everything under the sun but our marriages. You seem like you've got it all together. I know you miss certain things in your life, but in general, just so you know, one friend talking to another, you seem like you've got it nailed."

"That's what it looks like on the outside," he says. "On the surface. But there's no intimacy in my marriage—I don't mean physical stuff necessarily. I mean emotional intimacy. I sound like such a girl right now, Jesus. It's just…that connection, you know? That's everything. Well, Lexi's everything. Honestly, she's what keeps me going."

I'm excited he's confided in me. I hadn't imagined he'd be this candid. Somehow I love knowing he's not intimate with his wife. Which means I'm not a true friend. True friends would want the other to be happy and fulfilled. Fuck that. We both know what this is. I'm totally infatuated. I stay on course, though.

"How can you live like that?" I ask him. "I mean, the way you are… You're so…so…I don't know. You're so full of life. But that's the opposite of what you're living day to day. How is that okay? I'm truly asking because that's what I ask myself, too. Speaking for myself, it's getting harder and harder going home after talking with you. It's like reentry from outer space back to earth. Do you feel that way? Like you're two different people—one way with me and one way at home?"

"Yes. Yes."

We're both swirling the coffee in our cups. I'm struggling with what to say. I can feel him doing it, too.

I'm the one who breaks the awkward silence.

"So how's Fluffy?"

He looks up. I can see he's relieved to be on safer ground.

"Fluffy's doing fine…."

I listen to him tell me about Lexi and the kitten and all is right with the world.

Cammy.

Dear Mr. and Mrs. Friedman,

We received the requested letter from your daughter's doctor and are saddened to hear of her condition. Because all the required documentation has been provided we are hereby releasing the information we feel is medically relevant.

Cameron's birth mother did not reveal or disclose any prior illness, familial or individual. There are notes in her prenatal report that indicate she may have acquired a sexually transmitted disease but blood tests did not confirm this preliminary diagnosis, so we can only assume the notes were from anecdotal and initial examination. Blood tests taken at the time indicate the birth mother was in fact a serious drug user and traces of methamphetamines were noted. The examining physician noted that the birth mother admitted to using mushrooms and cocaine prior to finding out about her pregnancy, but further questioning revealed that use did not stop in the first trimester of her pregnancy. She was encouraged to stop drinking alcohol, but in her file it was noted that she appeared intoxicated on at least two separate occasions during her second trimester. For that reason, the pregnancy was considered high risk.

In the years since Cameron's birth and adoption, laws have

changed drastically and have eased with regard to confidentiality of both birth mothers and adoptive parents. In cases such as Cameron's, when dire medical needs require it, we are compelled to reveal the mother's identity in order to help in your search for answers. Below please find the information you requested. We sincerely wish you well and hope for the best for Cameron and your entire family. Please contact us if you have any further questions.

Biological mother: Geraldine Wilkes

Mother's DOB: March 12, 19?? (Mother did not specify. Uncooperative)

Infant place of birth: Chicago, Illinois

Adoption papers filed: May 29, 1994

Adoption consent: affirmative

Medical examination of infant: clear

Age of child at time of adoption: 2

Biological parent contact information: none provided

"Holy shit," Ricky says when I show him the letter. He's wearing this stupid-ass button-down shirt that makes him look like he's in a boy band. "Holy shit. Your mom was a fuckup."

"Fuck you, I can't believe you just said that," I say. "I can't believe you just said that."

"Sorry. Sorry, sorry. Don't cry. I didn't mean it to sound like that. It's just…oh Jesus, stop crying. I just mean—I mean, it's weird, right? Like it must be in your blood from her."

I'm trying that thing where you swallow before a sob. It's supposed to make you stop crying right then but it gives me the hiccups. I go to my bathroom to get a glass of water to drink upside down like I've always done. It's not really drinking it upside down, it's bending over and sipping it while the tip of your head is pointed toward the floor. Works every time. My bathroom's a mess; even I can see that. The hair dryer cord's tangled with the flat iron and I must've forgotten to turn it off because it's burned a V into the floor. What the hell? I thought tile didn't burn. They're already pissed because I spilled black nail polish on the counter and even nail polish remover won't get it off so they're calling in someone to get it scraped off and I'm supposed to pay for it. What a joke since I have like zero dollars and zero cents. I dropped my black eye shadow and the shadow part cracked and got all over the sink and the floor and I forgot to wipe it up so when I stepped in it I kind of tracked it back into my room, onto my carpet. I threw one of my long dark skirts over the footprints so I'm okay for now. But the thing is, I haven't washed the skirt in like forever and it's the one I was wearing when I barfed in back of the library and since it scrapes the ground I got barf on the bottom of it so it smells and now I think it's making the carpet smell, too. Good. Maybe they'll replace it like I've been begging them to do. I want to paint my room to get these baby lavender walls over with. I wanted dark red but my dad says it looks like blood so I guess it's a no-go.

"What're you doing?" Ricky's knocking on the bathroom door. "Cam? Come out. What're you doing?"

He's loud through the wood but the water in the sink drowns him out. In the cabinet underneath I reach in back of this old lunchbox-type makeup kit my best friend in fifth grade, Hannah, gave me. I keep forgetting to throw it out. In back is an old film canister I found in the living-room closet where Dad keeps all the camera equipment and some old 35mm rolls. I decide to take whatever my finger fishes out like a fortune cookie and lucky for me it's a Vicodin. I tap another one into the palm of my hand because one doesn't work well for me.

"Cam. Come out," Ricky's saying.

"Jesus Christ, what's your frigging problem?" I say on my

way back across the room to my shitty bed with the shitty dark pink/light pink comforter I picked out when I was like eight.

"I thought you were like shooting up or something."

"Nice. Thanks."

"What're you going to do?" he asks. He's lying on the floor with his head propped up on his backpack like you see tourists doing on long layovers in airports. "We could totally People-Find her now that we have all this. In, like, two seconds we could find her. You could call her."

The goddamn Vicodin hasn't kicked in and now I remember it works faster if I've eaten something. I'm so not hungry though. I've got to calm down. What's wrong with me? I should get something to eat. Maybe a banana. Maybe I should call her right now. Get it over with. First I should plan what to say. That's gay. Maybe some yogurt. Then I remember I've got a joint Paul gave to Will to give to me which he did when he drove me to behind the Dumpster in back of the Blockbuster a few blocks from school.

"You're getting stoned?" Ricky's all freaked now. "What if your parents smell it?"

"What're you, five? Anyway they're clueless. I'll just tell them it's that scented candle they gave me at Christmas. That thing smells up the whole house when I light it. Open the window, will you?"

I stuff a towel along the bottom of the door and pull the box fan in front of the windowsill but facing out so it can suck the smoke out.

"Why don't you just try it?" I'm holding in the smoke, pulling it in deeper before exhaling like Paul does. He blows it out like he's smoking a cigarette not a joint. He calls it a stick. When he passes it to whoever he's sitting next to, he says, "Want the stick?," and he hands it over like it's a peace pipe.

No one ever says no to one of Paul's sticks. You don't say no to Paul.

"Naw," Ricky says. "The fan's blowing it back into the room, you know. You should face it the other way."

"But then it would blow more in, if it's facing inside. Shit, you're right. It's going right back. What the hell?"

"Maybe it's a sign," he says.

"What's that mean?"

"Maybe it's a sign you'll turn out just like her," he says.

"Get the fuck out," I hear myself saying. I'm not sure but I think I said it out loud. Yeah, I did, because he has a weird look on his face.

"Never mind," I think I say. "You want something to eat?"

"Yeah, whatever. You look so freaking weird right now. What do you want? I'll go down and get it."

"Peanut butter," I say. "Peanut butter and a banana. Bring a knife so I can smear it."

"Won't it be weird if I go down and like raid your fridge? What if your mom asks me why you aren't getting food instead of me. She's always treating me like a Martha Stewart guest, like she's got to be all proper."

"Just go," I say. "Peanut butter and banana."

I can feel the haze of sleepiness and happiness all twisted so I think the Vicodin's starting to work. The bed feels so soft. I reach over for the switch on the lava lamp I got for my ninth birthday. God I wanted that lava lamp so badly. It's blue but it's old so inside it isn't big bubbles melting into each other, it's just a gray blob that mostly hangs at the bottom of the triangle. I still want it on. Now I'm starving. Where's Ricky? Wait, what did I tell him to bring? Popcorn? No. Not popcorn. Huh.

"Wake up, stoner," he says, standing at the edge of the bed.

"Here. Your mom was on the computer…she didn't even hear me, so it's all good."

"She's all about the computer lately," I think I say this but I'm not sure. "At least now I don't have to worry about her finding the letter in it."

"You're shitfaced already," Ricky says. "She's not going to find the letter in the computer, idiot. You have the letter in your hand, remember?"

"Oh, yeah."

He's staring at me like I'm a volcano.

"I'm gone," he says.

"Wait, we haven't figured out what to do yet. What'm I supposed to do now?"

"Why don't you ask Paul, *dude*."

"Shut up. Seriously. What'm I gonna do now?"

"I told you. You should call her."

"I don't have her phone number, freak."

"Google her, re-tard," he says. "Duh. You've got her name. The rest is all you, loser. It'll take like five minutes."

"What's your problem?"

"I'm not the one with the problem. What, you don't know how to Google someone?"

"Why're you yelling at me?"

"I'm not yelling at you," he says. He's snarling like a Doberman. "I'm sick of watching you fuck up."

"Rage Company, woo-hoo!" I yell from the bed. I'm lying on my back. When I hold up my fist in the semisalute we used to joke about, I hear him saying shit and I think it's because he tried to open the door but he forgot about the towel so it's probably jammed halfway underneath so there's not enough room to escape. Happens to me every time. "Rage Company…" I whisper. "Woo-hoo…"

Samantha

"Hey," I say, scooting over on the faux-velour purple couch I remember thinking was such a novelty when Starbucks first started appearing. Wow, I thought, how cool: a couch so you can hang out in the coffee shop just like on *Friends*. I always see coats on it, people saving seats on it while they're up in line or asking for the bathroom key chained to a block of wood so you won't steal it, like that's exactly what you'd steal from Starbucks, the key to the smelly sticky-floored unisex bathroom that always has the toilet seat up.

"Wow," Craig says, taking off his jacket, folding it in half and draping it so it won't wrinkle, "you got the couch. Our lucky day. I'll be right back."

"Thanks, I didn't want to lose our seats, so I couldn't get the coffee."

He's back in an instant and we're balancing a plate of walnut thousand-calorie coffee cake between us. I read that if you have a piece of this and a regular-size chai latte you have consumed all your calories for the day.

"So? What's new? How'd that meeting go yesterday?" I ask him in between bites.

"It went well. More of a gesture than anything else. Favor

for a friend. Not important. I'd much rather talk about you. You're my favorite topic. How's Cammy?"

"Oh, God, I don't know," I say. It's windy out and there's a phantom hair clinging to my face tickling my nose, but I can't find it and I'm pretty sure the only way to get it free will make me look like I'm picking my nose. There's a line for the bathroom and I don't want to waste time looking in the mirror, so I scrap it. But it's bothering the hell out of me.

"Here, it's right here," he says, reaching over, and with his first two fingers he picks it up and away from my face. I'm afraid I'm blushing so I look down and worry a pull in my sweater.

"Thanks," I mumble.

"So guess what?" he asks.

The barista barks out the most complicated drink order I've ever heard.

"What?"

"I just bought tickets to South Africa. A wine-tasting tour. I'm taking my dad. You know how long I've been wanting to do that? I'm so *excited*. It's true *excitement*. I'm trying to talk Evie into taking a trip with her girlfriends while I'm gone. My mother could watch Lexi…"

"That's so great. I didn't know you were thinking of doing that. That's just great."

"I didn't think we'd be able to pull it off—my father's so hard to pin down. That's why I didn't mention it."

He's saying this like he feels guilty, keeping this from me.

"Please!" I say. "You don't have to tell me everything. Jeez!" I feel shut out and it shows.

"What a great trip." I fake smile. I'm trying not to seem envious, but I am. I wish I could plan a great trip, too. I guess I could, but it'd never fly. Not with Bob.

"But I do," he says.

"You do what?" I haven't been paying attention.

"I tell you everything," he says.

I brush invisible crumbs off my lap.

"Well…"

"It's true," he says. "Think about it. I tell you everything. It's nothing bad. I mean, what's so wrong about talking?"

My heart's beating fast. But then the momentum of this trip, of the forward motion he's starting to make, takes over and he leans in and blindsides me:

"What if we kiss—not here or anything, don't worry! I have to kiss you. I *have* to kiss you," he says. He gets up and motions me to follow.

What the?

Cheating is a choice. I read that somewhere and now I understand it completely. I stand up and watch Craig pointing out to the sidewalk to let me know he'll be waiting there for me. I look around the busy room and no one seems to notice something major is about to happen. Here is where I could turn things around and do the right thing. This is the moment I'll look back on as a defining one in my life. I should feel shaky or filled with fear and doubt and guilt. I should hesitate. I should consider ducking out the alternate door. Instead, I throw out my coffee in the square cutout on the condiment island. I'm watching myself from the ceiling. This normal woman on a normal day doing a normal thing. I'm watching myself make this choice. No bolt of lightning, no last-minute divine intervention.

"You okay?" he asks.

"I have coffee breath."

I grab my purse in search of gum or a mint. I settle for a Tic Tac I have to bang out of the plastic because its so old it's stuck.

Do I have a conscience? Am I thinking about the consequences of a simple kiss? Hel-lo? Is anybody in there?

He's reaching to me. "Here, let me get the door."

I'm following him out and on my second step away from Starbucks, right in front of the frappuccino poster in the window, I step in gum. My shoe literally grips the sidewalk and I almost do that awkward buckle forward you do when you're trying not to trip.

"Wait. Hang on," I call out to him. The wad of gum is so big it's hard to believe it could have comfortably fit in someone's mouth. I scrape my shoe on the pavement but that only creates long strings of gum that then fly up and stick to the shoe itself, so now it's not just the sole that's a mess, it's my entire right shoe. A pump. One half of my favorite pair of black heels I got on sale at Saks a month ago, after I met Craig and started feeling sexy.

"I can't get it off!"

"I heard ice water helps," he says. "I'll be right back."

He goes back in to Starbucks and just as the glass door shuts behind him I look up to see Lynn walking toward me smiling and shaking her head at the spectacle of me trying to scuff the gum off my shoe back onto the sidewalk.

"Someone doesn't want you to walk the direction you're moving in," she says.

I'm frozen, searching her face—did she see me with Craig? Oh, my God, he'll be back any second, but he'll see me talking to Lynn and know to stay away. But what if he's looking down or what if he backs out the door since now he'll be juggling his coffee and the ice water. Please God, let him go out the other door.

"What the hell's wrong with you?" Lynn asks. "You look panicked."

"Panicked? I'm not panicked. I'm pissed I've got gum on my shoe, but I'm not panicked. "Jeez."

A guy selling a newspaper written by homeless people is calling out, "*Streetwise! Streetwise!* One dollar!" Lynn's saying, "What're you up to today?" and Craig's about to walk out any second—or probably he saw us and did take the side door after all, please God. And the bus is honking at a beat-up Camry parked smack in the middle of the bus stop. Cutting in front of the bus is a huge, shiny, black SUV with all the windows down, so I can feel the bass of the hip-hop song in my stomach.

"You look nice," she says. "Where're you off to?"

"I gotta go," I say to Lynn, pulling my foot free, knowing it's useless because it will stick tightly with the next step. "I've got a million things…"

"Call me later," she says, holding her thumb and pinkie up to the side of her face. "Call my cell though because Mike's got a conference call tonight."

"Talk to you later!"

I rush to my car. The gum's still not scraped off, but at this point I don't care. My cell phone rings from the bottom of my purse and I upend the whole thing so I can get it before it goes to voice mail.

"That was close," Craig says.

"Where are you?"

"I'm in my car—look across the street. You ready? Okay, follow me."

"Where? In case we get separated…"

"Montrose Harbor, where it curves off into that dead end at the tip where all the fishermen go."

"Wow. It didn't take you long to think of a place," I say.

"I know what you're thinking and for the record no, I've never done this before. Don't worry about the red light, I've

pulled over until it turns. It's just a place I go when I want to
think. I've never even taken Lexi there. It's like this little island
no one knows about."

We pass a Jewel supermarket with posters of fresh cantaloupes
in the window. Attached is a drugstore that's open twenty-four
hours a day. A block south, next to a withered playground, is
Kentucky Fried Chicken. An animal-rights group is marching
in front, holding signs calling for a boycott. Posters of tortured
chickens from poultry mills are plastered on a folding table with
leaflets on top. I saw Bianca Wells about to pull into the drive-
through there the other day and sped up to stop her, happy to
do my part in forcing the fast-food chain to start using humane
practices. At the light I stare at the beakless bird with its head
trapped between the wires of the tiny cage it "shares" with
countless other chickens, all pecking themselves to death. The
light changes but I can't pull my eyes from the mangled bird.
How can humans be so cruel? How can we treat living crea-
tures this way? Did that bird wonder how it ended up there, in
a hell only monsters could devise?

"The light's green," Craig is saying into my cell phone.
"You okay? Are you changing your mind?"

"Why? Are you?"

"No. Not even close."

The chicken fades into the back of my mind with the influx
of endorphins.

"Me neither. Should I just park next to you?"

"Yes."

He motions across, through our closed windows, for me to
join him in his car. I touch my purse on the passenger seat, my
hand fluttering over the gearshift, making sure I'm in Park.
Then the keys. I take them out, but then put them back into
the ignition in case I have to make a Bonnie and Clyde getaway.

I take a swipe at smoothing my hair. Outside the car the wind picks up and since we're at the edge of the lake I feel the spray from a wave hitting the breaker. His door opens heavily and closes the way expensive German-car doors close, sealing us in, cocooning us, the thick glass blocking the sound of the waves but not the sound of a distant car alarm.

"Come here," he says, leaning over.

I drop my keys in the dish on the front hall table and look at myself in the mirror. I tuck my hair behind my ears and smooth my blouse. My index finger touches the corners of my mouth, wiping away any lipstick outside my lip line. *Pull it together, Sam. Hold it together.*

"Mom! Cammy's throwing up!"

"I'll be right there." I look into my mirrored eyes: *You can do this.* I wipe under my eyes once more to make sure the mascara that ran is back in place and then I walk up the steps, back into my life.

"Andrew? Get me a washcloth out of the dryer, will you? While you're at it, bring it all up and you can fold it up here."

"Why do I have to fold? It's Cammy's turn…"

"Does it look like Cammy's in any condition to fold laundry?"

"Mom?" Cammy's head is in the toilet bowl, so her voice sounds hollow. And childlike. Nausea is the great equalizer, I think to myself. It's impossible to cop an attitude when you're vomiting.

"I'm right here," I tell Cammy. "Did you eat something funny? You've been sick a lot lately… I'm calling the doctor."

"No! I don't need to go to the doctor," she says. "Please don't call him."

"I don't think you're in any condition to decide that, honey.

Do you feel like you can move to the bed and maybe lie down for a little bit? It might make you feel a little better, sweetheart."

"Mom, I'm sorry," she says. Her head's still hanging into the bowl and her voice sounds far away. "My back. It's so itchy. Can you itch it? Oh, God, it won't stop itching." Her voice bounces off the porcelain.

"People get sick, honey, it's nothing to be sorry about. In the middle? Where's it itchy? Let me take a look, maybe you have a rash. Jesus! What're all these red marks? Oh, my God…"

"Uhhhhhh," she groans and heaves. Then she says, "I had to itch it. I had to keep scratching it."

"This part in the middle's bloody, Cam! What'd you use to scratch it?"

"This," Andrew says, holding up the large pasta fork.

"Oh, my God," I say. "Okay, okay, calm down. I'll rub it, how's that. When did this start?"

"What's wrong with the toilet?" she screams into the water. "There's a tornado in the water! What's wrong with the toilet? The water's talking to me!"

"Calm down! Cammy, what's going on? You're not making any sense. Nothing's wrong with the toilet. I didn't even flush it."

She doesn't wait for me to finish, instead groaning "sorry" over and over. Then, freakishly, her groaning gives way to laughter.

"What's so funny? And what're you sorry for? Jesus, what the hell's so funny? You're scaring me, Cammy."

"Oh, my God, the water just told me to tell the floor it's beautiful. And I've never noticed it before but it is! The floor's fucking awesome. Look at that."

Just as quickly she's back to muttering, "Sorry, I'm sorry."

"You're sick, honey. You don't have to be sorry for being sick."

"That's not why she's sorry," Andrew says from the doorway.

"Andrew, get outta here!" When she yells she doesn't sound sick at all. But then she starts dry-heaving.

"Andrew, go finish folding," I say. Then I turn back to her.

"What's he talking about, Cam? What are you sorry for?"

"Don't be mad, okay? You'll be mad. Don't be mad. Oh, God, it fucking itches so bad! Don't be mad."

What parent hasn't made this deal with the devil. You want to know the truth so you agree to the impossible because you know whatever they're about to tell you is as important as it is maddening. All parents fall into this trap. If I say *I can't promise that* I'll shut her down and I'll never get the truth.

"I won't be mad," I say.

"Promise?" Another dry heave rolls across her back and of course I'll promise. "If we eat broccoli we'll turn green. The water just told me that."

"Just tell me, Cam," I say. It's delirium. That's the only thing I can think of.

"I only tried them just this one time."

"What are you talking about?"

She lifts her head and says, "See? I knew you'd be mad. You promised not to be mad. This floor is hilarious. I never noticed it before. The tiles can tell time. And they're perfectly spaced. Ten little squares inside every triangle. Do they plan it that way? It's fucking beautiful."

"Jesus, Cammy, tell me what's going on. What did you only try once?"

"I finished folding," Andrew says from the door.

"Andrew, go away!" Cammy and I yell in unison.

"The water's circling again. Make it stop! Don't flush it! It'll suck my hair in."

"Cammy, you're scaring the hell out of me. I didn't flush the toilet. We're going to the emergency room. Andrew, go get your brother."

"Mushrooms!" she yells. The sound bounces up to my ears but I still can't take it in. I am silent, trying to compute what she's just told me. I understand the words but I can't say anything.

"I did mushrooms."

I let her hair go and fall back against the coolness of the tiled wall.

She looks up through her stringy hair I notice is dirty and probably hasn't been washed in days. Hair like hers has to be washed every day. Through the black dye I see the white of her skull. Looking closer, I see bald spots. Her hair is thinning out. I reach out to touch it and am surprised to find it silky still because it looks brittle.

"I'm taking you to the hospital," I say. "Andrew, call Mrs. Shapiro and tell her I need her to come over."

"Is this so she can babysit?" Andrew asks. "Can't Melissa just come back? We want Melissa. We hate Mrs. Shapiro."

The boys have recently started speaking as a unit. *We* don't like brussels sprouts. *We* want to go to see if Tommy's home.

"Do it!" I yell at him. Then I turn back to Cammy. "Okay, we're going to get you into the car. Can you move?"

"No! Don't move me! I don't want to go to the hospital. I don't need to go to the hospital, Mom. Please, just let me stay here. The water'll be lonely. It's lonely in the toilet."

"I'm making a phone call. I'll be right back."

I race down to the fridge to the list of emergency contacts pinned to the metal door by a magnet from Mount Rushmore. I trace a line down to information for Mrs. Shapiro, an elderly neighbor I only call if it's an absolute necessity. She's a sour gossip who wears L'eggs knee-highs with skirts, but she's reliable and has a pulse and right now beggars can't be choosers. Within minutes she comes in without ringing the doorbell.

"Samantha?" She limps in. "What's the matter?" I forgot about her hip surgery. I'm on hold with the emergency answering service and the Muzak version of *Sunday Bloody Sunday* comes on. I wonder if U2 minds that it's ruining their song. I feel bad about hurrying Mrs. Shapiro over here when she's clearly not in any shape to hurry.

I hold up a finger when the nurse on duty comes on. Her voice is the complete opposite of mine, as if she's teaching me a lesson for being so urgent. I'm just another impatient hypochondriac to her.

"Describe the symptoms," she says. Her voice implies she has heard one too many patients reciting WebMD self-diagnoses.

"They're not symptoms," I say, and I quickly turn to cup my hand over the mouthpiece so Mrs. Shapiro can't hear me hiss to the nurse, "My daughter's done mushrooms."

"Is she coherent?"

"Yes, she's coherent," I say. "She's talking but she's hallucinating—she goes from sounding normal to hallucinating. And she's throwing up. No, there's no blood in the vomit. Hold on—Andrew, go up and ask your sister if there was any blood in the vomit."

"Ew, that's so gross."

"Just go!" I say. "Sorry about that. Are you still there? Oh, great. Should I take her to the emergency room?"

Mrs. Shapiro is sitting at the kitchen table with her hands in her lap as if she's at a filthy diner table that hasn't been wiped clean. She's scanning the counters and tabletop for dirt and crumbs. She looks as if she doesn't like what she sees. Yeah, well, I don't either.

"Yes, I'm here," I say into the phone. "Uh-huh. Uh-huh. He's sure? Thank you so much. Okay, thanks. Bye."

"She says there was no blood in the vomit." Andrew comes back into the kitchen breathless. "But she's still puking."

Mrs. Shapiro stands and I see that she is wearing knee-high stockings with her skirt and the one on her left leg is falling down. She looks indigent.

"Did she eat something funny?" she asks.

"I'm not sure. I am so sorry to call you over here like this, Mrs. Shapiro. Thank you so much for coming, but I guess it was a false alarm. I better get back up there, actually. Do you want the boys to walk you back?"

"I'm fine," she says. "Soda water and crackers do the trick. I can stay if you like. I'm more than happy to stay."

There is nothing Mrs. Shapiro likes more than neighborhood drama. All we need is word getting around that Cammy's doing hard-core drugs.

"No, thanks," I say. I leave her for the upstairs.

"You're in luck," I say to Cammy who is crumpled on the bathroom floor, back to hugging the bowl. "You don't have to go to the hospital after all."

"There are twenty-one little squares inside every three diamonds on the floor. It doesn't add up, though. It's pretty goddamn funny when you think about it. Twenty-one. Get it?" Her voice is threadbare, she is exhausted and weak.

"No I don't get it" is all I can manage. "Tell me how, Cam?"

"How what?"

"How did it happen? When did this happen?"

"You said you wouldn't be mad. My back. Please, my back is so itchy." She's pulled herself up from the toilet long enough to crawl to the fork.

"You expect me not to be mad when my *sixteen*-year-old

girl does *mushrooms?* Jesus Christ, Cammy. Jesus Christ. Get yourself up and into bed and I'll be back. And just so you know, in a few minutes this nausea will seem like nothing compared to what's coming."

"Are you going to tell Dad?" Then she laughs hysterically. Just like that she goes from misery to ecstasy.

"Of course I'm telling Dad. Do you realize how much trouble you're in? Where'd you get the drugs? Huh? Who did this with you?"

"Mom, please, I'm so sick right now."

"I don't care if you're coughing up a lung. Tell me where you got the drugs."

"Can't we talk about this later? Please, Mom. What's your favorite song? Oh, my God, I don't know your favorite song. Lemme think for a second. James Taylor? Is it something by him? *Soo* funny." She's laughing hard again. "I wish I knew your favorite song, Mom. Samantha. Whoever you are. Let's talk later, 'kay?"

"This *is* later. This is as good as you're going to feel, so you might as well tell me now because things are about to get really ugly. Who gave you the drugs, Cameron?"

"Paul. You don't know him."

"Where does he live? Were his parents home?"

"I don't know where he lives. We only get together at the lot."

"The lot?" I ask.

"The library parking lot," she says. "Uhhhh, I'm going to throw up again. My stomach's killing me."

"So, the times you've asked to be dropped off at the library, you've been doing drugs with this *Paul?* And last week when you were throwing up…oh, my God, Cammy. How long has this been going on?"

She is resting her cheek on the toilet seat and for a millisecond I feel sorry for her, but it passes quickly.

"It wasn't mushrooms before," she says. "Oh, God, I wish I could throw up and have it be over."

"Get in bed. I don't care if you vomit all over the sheets, get in the goddamn bed and I'll be back to deal with this."

"I told you she'd be pissed," says Andrew, who has apparently been standing behind us the whole time.

"You. Get your brother and get yourselves downstairs and start thinking about what you can do to help with dinner," I tell him. "Set the table or something."

"How come we have to do it? How come *we're* getting punished for what Cammy's done. It's not fair."

"Call for pizza if you want, I don't care. The money's in my wallet. Just take care of it, Andrew. The number's on speed dial."

"Sweet," he says and in minutes I can hear him calling it in.

"Mom? What size?" he calls up.

"Medium," I answer.

"We're hungry, can we get a large?" Jamie yells.

"Just so you know, life as you knew it is over. Period," I say to Cammy. She's crawling toward the bed and is trying to pull herself up to get under the covers and I have to restrain myself from going to help her. The crying isn't helping her, it's just frustrating her.

"The guy says the medium's only eight slices," Andrew yells. "Can't we get a large? We're starving."

"Fine, get the large," I yell. "And order a side salad! Andrew? Did you hear me?"

"What?"

"Order the side salad!"

"What dressing he's asking!"

"Vinaigrette!"

"I know you hate me," Cammy says. "I'm so fucking itchy."

I look around and for an instant, the time it would take to sneeze, I see myself like a stranger would. *How the hell did I end up here?* I'm cross-legged on a bathroom floor with my strung-out Goth daughter, a clueless husband and impatient twins. Where the hell did I go wrong? What the hell happened?

"Oh my fucking God, I'm a huge tidal wave," Cammy says.

"Language, Cammy."

"I didn't say a bad word. Did I? Did I *think* fuck or did I *say* it. Oh, my God, am I awake or asleep? Are you really there or is this like some weird Matrix shit?"

"Calm down."

"Who said that? Oh, my God, that's so weird. I think my brain just said *calm down* and I thought it was you."

I know she won't take in anything I say but still. "I don't hate you. I don't even know where to start. When did this all start? When did I become the enemy?"

"You aren't the enemy. The walls are the enemy. You can't see it but they're waiting until you leave to crush me. They're winking at me right now like that's exactly what they're going to do. Oh, my God, Mom, you can't leave. You're the ally not the enemy…"

"Oh, yeah? Well, I notice the ringtone you've assigned to me is 'The Funeral Death March.' Everyone else has some kind of rap song, but *noooo,* not me. I get 'pray for the dead and the dead will pray for you.' I used to have Avril. You used to tell me everything."

It's ridiculous to try to reason with someone who's out of their mind, so what am I doing?

"I don't always have to tell you everything," she says. "I'm not a baby anymore. And…oh forget it."

"What? 'And' what?"

"And you aren't my real mother, okay?" she says. "Whatever. Not like it matters to you anyways."

She tosses this out like it's a pebble. To me it's a boulder landing on my feet. She reaches behind her head to fix the pillow just right and she keeps going: "My real mother is out there and you and Dad have never wanted me to find her."

"Is *that* what this is all about?" I ask. "You want to find your birth mother and you think your father and I won't let you?"

"I don't know. Yeah, maybe. I don't know." Then she groans. "I'm going to puke."

"I'll get the trash can. Here. Turn to the side of the bed if you're going to—there. Okay. It's okay."

She is retching bile. The nurse says that's a sign the drug is pushing its way out of her system.

"Cammy, the only time you ever brought up looking for your birth mother was when we first told you that you were adopted and you ran away to the Andersons and said you weren't coming home until we told you where she was," I tell her. "If you want to look for her we can talk about it."

"Yeah, like you'd really want me to know," she says. "What if I've already found her? What if I already know?"

I search her face. The way she says that gives me a chill and for the first time I wonder if she actually *has* found her. How could she have tracked her down? It was a closed adoption. How could she have gotten around that? It was supposed to be ironclad. There's no way she found her. She's bluffing.

"Honey, this isn't the way to go about it," I say.

"What's that supposed to mean?" Here's the old Cammy. Here's the attitude. The emphasis on "that" signaling the beginning of an argument. So it is possible to cop an attitude when you're sick after all. Who knew. I think the best way to go here is to bring it down again. Level voice. Soft tone. Let her know I'm not taking the bait.

"Let's get through this drug stuff."

"But it's like you've disappeared," she says. She's crying now, so I stroke her hair to calm her down.

"Don't put this on me, Cammy. Don't you dare put this on me. Plenty of kids feel lonely sometimes, plenty of adopted kids want to locate their birth parents, but they don't rush out and take pills and do mushrooms. I'm going downstairs, but I'll be back up."

"You're going to check your computer, aren't you?" she asks.

"Excuse me?"

"Nothing. It's nothing," she says.

"It's not nothing if you said it. Tell me what you meant by that."

"You're so glued to your fucking computer these days."

"Watch your language! I have a lot of work going on with school stuff…"

"See? You could've told me to mind my own business but instead you got all defensive about it. You don't tell me everything just like I don't tell you everything."

"I'm getting dinner ready and I'll be back, and for your information, it is none of your business how I spend my time. I'm your mother and I don't have to answer to you or to anyone else."

Downstairs I put in a call to Bob.

"I'm on my way home," he says. "You want me to pick something up on the way?"

"Maybe some ginger ale and saltines," I say.

"Uh-oh, who's sick?"

"It's a little more than that… I'll tell you when you get home. How far out are you?"

"Ten minutes."

Forty minutes later he's pulling into the driveway. I'm waiting at the door.

"The White Hen only had those wheat thins so I had to go to the Jewel." He is out of breath. "What's going on?"

"Let's talk out here, I don't want them all hearing." Part of me wants to be outside so the air will swish away the perfume he trails.

"Jesus Christ, what is it?"

"Cammy did mushrooms today," I say.

Bob sinks to the top step and I join him.

"As in *mushrooms* mushrooms? Like Woodstock mushrooms?"

"Yes, like Woodstock mushrooms. She says this was her first time but apparently before this she was taking pills."

I start crying. Just saying this out loud to Bob makes it real.

"I can't believe it," he says. "Should she get her stomach pumped or something? Shouldn't she be in the hospital?"

"I called the doctor's office and the nurse said as long as she's talking and somewhat coherent she'll be okay." I wipe my runny nose on my sleeve.

"I can't believe it," he says again. He's holding his head in his hands. "What're we going to do?"

"I don't know," I say. My head suddenly feels too heavy for my neck to hold up. "I haven't even gotten to the second part."

"There's a second part? Jesus, what? She's shooting heroin?"

"She announced she wants to find her 'real' mother. She thinks we're against it. I give up. I have no idea what to do."

"Holy shit," he says.

"Holy shit."

I turn to face him, leaning back against the bricks of the low wall lining the stairs leading from the walkway to the front door. My arm is draped across my bent knee and it occurs to me that we look like a couple enjoying a nice conversation on a nice evening in a nice neighborhood. A squirrel ventures into the yard, hesitates at finding us then inches over to dig into a seemingly random patch of grass. Pausing with every other swipe of dirt, he finally dips his head into the hole to pull out what looks like a walnut shell. Or a peach pit, I can't be sure. He scampers off. He grips the trunk of the tree, flattening out against the bark every once in a while, the pit still wedged in his mouth.

Mr. and Mrs. Rowland wave from across the street. They've been married over forty years and still walk arm in arm every night, weather permitting. I wave back and smile, thinking how bizarre it is that my daughter is falling apart upstairs, my sons are probably playing with matches or knives inside, I am in some unnameable relationship with another man, and Mr. and Mrs. Rowland are out on an evening walk, thinking we're enjoying the night too, Bob and I.

"She'll sleep it off." Bob pulls himself up to standing and sweeps dirt off the seat of his pants. His change jingles in his pocket and I think how foreign that sounds: Bob never carries change because it makes him feel like his *equilibrium is off.* Instead, he rounds up when he buys something and leaves the balance in tip jars.

"You know we've got to do something, right," I say. It's not a question.

"Yeah. I know."

"So? What're we going to do?" I ask.

"I've got so much…so much…" he says. His voice breaks and something in it shocks me to standing.

"What's the matter? Are you okay?"

"I can't…I just can't…I don't know what's wrong with me, Sam," he says. His head drops.

"What is it? Honey?" I can't remember the last time we called each other honey but it comes automatically this time. I've leaped up and, for lack of anything else to do, I rub his back.

"Something's wrong," he says.

"You're having an anxiety attack," I say, moving to the door. "Do you still have those pills?"

"I don't know what's wrong…I don't know, maybe. I can't breathe right."

"I'm running up to find them. Here, sit down. Don't move. I'll be right back."

It's been years since his last attack. It was a cluster of them. We'd just brought the boys home from the hospital. Two or three weeks later he started feeling short of breath and from the living room I saw him grab the kitchen counter after he'd written down the feeding times on the chart I put together so I could keep track of who ate when. It was complicated, granted. I remember being pissed at him for being dramatic, when I was the one who wasn't sleeping because I was a milk cow with a boy at each breast. Then when he slumped over and started almost panting I thought he was having a heart attack. I pulled myself to standing, Jamie still attached to my nipple, and got to the phone as fast as I could to dial 911. Jamie picked up on my panic and started crying. Scream-crying. Then Andrew started and it was chaos. Over the screams and my crying the operator told me to put an Aspirin under Bob's tongue, but that didn't help so they sent an ambulance and I called Lynn and Mike so they could go to the hospital since I couldn't leave the kids. Five hours later he came home. He'd suffered an anxiety attack. Too much stress. I remember thinking You *have too much stress? You? What about me?* I resented him for it. Deep down I wondered if he was faking it to get out of helping with the babies. Still, for a couple of weeks I really tried to be careful to keep them quiet and Cammy occupied, but it was hard, and one day all three kids lost it at exactly the same moment (I can't remember the cause) and I broke down and started yelling at Bob to help me. *I'm drowning here,* I called to him. Cammy started crying harder when she heard this and started screeching, *Mommy, don't drown, Daddy,*

Mommy's drowning help! Help! Help! Bob gathered her up and she calmed down, but the boys were both squalling. Just as quickly as he'd picked her up, he put her back down and practically crawled up to our bathroom for his pills. *Daddy, come back*, Cammy started yelling again. A little while later he came down and Cammy threw herself at him and clung to his leg for the rest of the night. We've had the pills ever since. Just in case his little attack comes on again. Faker.

Fast-forward and I'm rifling through the bottom drawer on his side of the bathroom sink to find the pills I've always suspected are placebos. The bottle's tucked behind Pepto-Bismol and a box of Band-Aids. I run to the kitchen for a glass of water and hurry back out to him.

"Here." I give him two and hand over the water. He's braced himself on the top step like he's afraid he'll fall off. He takes the pills while I sit down next to him.

"Is this the first one since those ones before?"

"I know what you're thinking," he says between gasps, clutching his left side.

"I'm not thinking anything," I say. "Don't talk. Just breathe."

I don't know how long we sit like this. Fifteen minutes? Half an hour? I should be stroking his back, calming him down, murmuring things like *everything's going to be okay, don't worry*, but I don't. We sit in silence.

Craig would know exactly what to do right now. Forward motion. I bet *he's* never had an anxiety attack. Which is mean of me because I guess they're real. I just wish they didn't mean I'm left doing the heavy lifting with the kids when they hit Bob. I can't stop comparing them. Craig would stay out here with me on the front porch, brainstorming how to manage an unmanageable situation instead of shuffling into the house like Bob just did. Craig would go right up to Cammy's room instead of hanging up his jacket, carefully slipping off his work shoes like Mr. Rogers, like Bob's doing right now in the front hall. Maybe Craig would call her down to the bottom of the stairs. He'd even yell and say *that's it. Game over.* He'd tell her *we're* in charge, *we're* calling the shots, instead of slipping on his ugly Birkenstocks that make him look like a German tourist, like Bob is doing.

I don't know why they're freaking out like they didn't see this coming. I was a fucking crack baby for God's sake. I was born with this shit in me. It was only a matter of time. Like mother like daughter. I don't know who wrote that on my locker but I do know I'll never trust Ricky again ever. He denies he told anyone about the letter but he's the only one who knows about her so what the fuck? Does he really think I'm that stupid? I skipped biology to wash it all off. I couldn't go to the office to get cleaner so I had to use water and paper towels from the bathroom. I don't know what the hell they used to write it with but it took like a half an hour to get my locker clean. You can still see the waxy outline of the words where they used to be—I don't think I'll ever get that out but I keep reminding myself to bring in 409 from home to try erasing the ghost of it.

I walked by Ricky after I got to my locker in the morning and he looked so guilty. He knew exactly why I didn't say anything to him. He ran alongside me like we were in *The O.C.* and he's all, "I know what you're thinking but I didn't say anything, I swear to God."

I kept walking. He's such a liar.

"You know what I think? I think it's 'cause you've got tits now and your mom's hot."

"My mom's not hot, first of all, and get the fuck away from me, second of all."

"Your mom's a total MILF and I swear to God I didn't tell anyone about anything so it's got to be that. It's the tits, I swear to God."

I didn't mean to push him that hard, but when he slammed into the lockers Mrs. Scutter rushed up and said, "You just earned yourself a detention, young lady," so I was basically screwed out of my afternoon smoke in the park. Goddamn Ricky.

My mom's—God! Samantha, I mean—she's pretty but I would never call her a MILF. Doesn't everyone see I look nothing like her? Idiots.

Detention is so *Breakfast Club*. You sit at long tables in the library and write an essay about why you did whatever you did to wind up in detention. Mrs. Richardson the librarian monitors us and at the end she gathers up the papers and we all know they go nowhere. No one checks them, they don't get graded, and whatever you write never gets commented on. Except once when this kid Bradley wrote that he wanted to blow the whole school up he was sent right to the principal and he ended up expelled. Zero tolerance. He was probably pissed his name was Bradley. I would have wanted to blow something up if my parents named me Bradley, too.

Ricky waited for me outside the library. First words out of his mouth:

"Don't go all RC on me." Like our little inside joke is supposed to make it all go away.

"Swear to God I never want to talk to you again. You're such a scumbag," I said.

He kept going like I hadn't just called him a scumbag. "I found out who did it."

"Oh, yeah, sure, and I'm supposed to believe whatever you say."

I'm trying to walk fast since I'm grounded for life and the office secretary wouldn't let me call home to tell Samantha I was going to be late so now I'm in even deeper shit. When I tell her I was late because of detention I'll be screwed anyway.

"It was Will," he says. "Missy told me he borrowed her lipstick to write it."

"Oh, so now I'm supposed to believe *Missy Delaney?* This is such a joke. Why would Will even say that? He doesn't know my mom. Such a lie. Go to hell."

I rifle through my bag and find them on the bottom. Of course. I'm on my last two Vicodin. They get chalky even if I swallow them fast, so I've started that grape-flavor vitamin-water shit. I'm buzzing by the time I get home.

So this is what she was doing when she was pregnant. She was high like a kite. She had me inside her and all she cared about was her itchy skin. Did my real father itch her back for her? I bet he wasn't around for all that. I'm sure he took off when she told him she was pregnant. She was my age I bet. She didn't want to have a baby, didn't want to think about it even, so she blew out her brains with *mushrooms* like the letter says. I wonder if she kept at it even after I was born. She probably sold me to the adoption agency to buy crack. Two years to bond with me and she gives me up to score. I can totally picture it. I can see her holding me out to some weirdo in a suit, a duffel bag full of unmarked bills on the ground next to her. She kicks it behind her in case he dives for it. I probably started to cry. Babies always know when something terrible's happening. The guy says *shut that kid up* and she shakes me a little and says *she's your problem now* and she's gone the second he takes me and hands me back to the bodyguard, holding me away from his body like I'm a piece of smelly fish. I want to ask her how the fuck could she do something like that? How could she throw out her two-year-old daughter just for a fix…it drives me insane thinking about that. I play the scene over and over again and sometimes the guy has a gun, sometimes she's crying and changing her mind but mostly it ends with me traded for drugs.

It comes back to me in fragments. Like flashbacks. I remember now that I talked to Will about her. I was totally fucked up but I think I told him. It's not like he gives a shit though, which is totally fine. I remember him going, "You were adopted? No wonder."

"What's *that* supposed to mean?" I asked him. Now it's coming back to me. It was a few days ago and he was totally stoned so it took him twenty minutes to climb up the tree to my room. I thought for sure he woke everyone up because he fell from not too high up and started laughing his ass off. When he started up again I tiptoed to the hallway to listen for sounds of awake. No sign of life.

The time to talk to Will is right before he unzips his pants. That's when he's all nice. Lately he's always in a hurry so there's been no time to finish a sentence even, but a few days ago, when I told him about the letter, since it was one in the morning and he had nowhere to be (he doesn't have a curfew), he sat down on the bed next to me. First time he's ever done that. I know he was wasted and all but it was still sweet when he rubbed my knee and told me my pajama bottoms were soft. It almost felt like we were going out.

"No wonder *what?*" I asked him.

"What?"

"You said *no wonder,* like is it so obvious I'm adopted or something?" I asked him. He pissed me off so I pulled my legs away from him into cross-legged Indian-style sitting. Oh. Native American.

"I saw your mom at the Jewel and she's hot too but different so I just figured maybe you took after your dad," he said.

I watched him lean back with his arms behind his head like he belonged on my bed. He knows who my mom is! He thought about me and who I looked like in my family! He's totally into me! I'm hot!

I really tried to act casual, like he stretches out on my bed all the time, but when I lay down alongside him he went, "Wanna get busy?" and then I felt his hand on my head. While I'm doing it he says my name a couple of times and I know I can ask him for anything I want. Right after he says, "Oh, God," I stop and look up at him and ask him for the pills Paul said he gave him the other day.

"Keep going, Jesus, keep going," he says. His hands go to both sides of my head but I know he can't jam himself into my mouth if I'm not ready so I ask him again.

"Seriously, split them with me and I'll keep going."

"Split what?" His eyes have been closed but now he's looking down his chest at me. His T-shirt is pulled up.

"The OxyContin? From Paul? Give them to me and you can have all the blow jobs you want," I say.

"You're crazy, you know that?" he says. It looks like he's going to pull away, like he's almost scared of me. "You're a crazy bitch, you know that?"

"Are you going to give them to me or what?"

"Jesus fucking Christ. Paul said you were a trip."

"O-kaay, if you don't want me to…"

"All right all right, fuck. I'll give them to you. I don't have that many but you can have half of what I have. Just keep going and I'll give them to you…"

"Now. Just give them to me now. You always take off after so…"

He reaches into his jeans pocket and even in the half dark of the half moon I can see the lump of his hand fishing around for the pills. My head's still right there, his dick is still hard, pretty much poking me in the cheek but I'm used to that. It doesn't weird me out anymore like it used to.

"Here," he says, dropping them on the floor like they're trash. "Now keep going." He's talking now like he's ordering me. I finish up, he zips up without wiping and climbs back out the window without saying anything. I wait until he leaves to feel around for the pills, rolling them into a pile into my fist. There are six and I know it's not quite half of what he has but whatever.

All I want is to be blank.

Samantha

I forgot my cell in the car when I went grocery shopping. I've missed two calls, both from Cammy. I try her back but her cell goes straight to voice mail. She never leaves messages. So frustrating. I make all the lights and pull in front of the house.

"Hi, guys, I'm home," I call up. The keys miss the bowl on the front hall table. I go through the mail on the way to the bottom of the staircase...mostly junk. Flyers.

"Hel-lo? Where is everybody?"

"Up here," Andrew says.

"Hi, Mom," Jamie calls.

"Where's your sister?"

"I don't know. Up in her room."

Since I've got the kitchen to myself I have a second to e-mail Craig.

Hi. All's quiet here. What's up with you? Just checking in to say hi. Oh, and I heard that song you were talking about...it's great. You're right. What else is new?

Bob comes in the front door. There's lots of street parking today for some reason. His keys jangle into the bowl on the front hall table. He always hits the bowl bull's-eye.

I log off quickly and pretend to be looking for a cookbook.

"Hey," he says. He's smiling and I realize it's been a while since I've seen him smile. It looks weird almost. It's been that long. "Great news about Cammy."

"What?" I ask. I push back from the desk and stand. This could be huge. "Did she talk to you about her birth mother?"

"Even better," he says.

"Oh, my God, she agreed to go to drug counseling! How'd you pull *that* off? You're a genius."

"That's not it either."

"Okay," I say it slowly, suspicious now that Bob's idea of great news is not my idea of great news. "What is it then?"

"I talked to the soccer coach and he's agreed to let her onto the team even though they're halfway through the season. Can you believe it?" He opens his arms like I'm going to rush into a hug of thanks. "She'll have to work her way off the bench but he's willing to give her a shot.

"What?" he says. "Say something."

"I honestly don't know what to say," I tell him.

"Isn't it great? When was the last time she exercised? She needs to be a part of something bigger than herself. A team is the best way to crawl out of your head. I brought her these cross trainers and cleats. She's an eight and a half, right? I took the nines in case her socks are thick. Plus, I think it'll do a lot for her self-esteem right now."

"Cammy's self-esteem isn't the problem, Bob. Cammy using drugs is the problem." I am trying to keep my cool. Bob doesn't react well to emotional outbursts. "Cammy struggling with whether or not to approach her birth mother is the problem. Cammy hanging out with delinquent losers from God knows where…that's the problem."

"She'll get so busy with practices and games she won't have time to hang out with them. That's the beauty of it."

"That's the beauty of it?"

"Why don't you just say what you're wanting to say? What're you thinking? I'm not a mind reader, Sam."

"You want to hear what I'm thinking? I'll tell you what I'm thinking." I move closer to him so I don't have to raise my voice. "I'm thinking you're *so* clueless it'd be funny if this wasn't about our daughter. *Our daughter,* Bob. Not mine—ours. You know, the one in black? The Goth girl holed up in her room right now? She's *our* daughter."

"For Christ's sake, I know she's *our* daughter," he says. "When have I ever called her anything else?"

I hold up my hand to silence him. "Let's not even get into that right now. You're more concerned with soccer than what she's going through. Do you even hear her crying in her room at night when she thinks everyone's gone to bed? Or are you oblivious to that, too?"

"What about you, Sam? You've been out to lunch for I don't know how long. I don't see *you* coming up with anything for her. Plus, you're the one that asked me to handle it!" He matches my volume. "'Can you take this one?' you asked on the front steps that first night, remember? You asked me to take it over and that's exactly what I'm doing. If you have a problem with how I'm doing it then be my guest—it's all yours. But if you want me to do it then back off and stop micromanaging everything I do. What do you want, Sam? Tell me what you want."

I don't say it loud. Of course I don't say it out loud. But I think it.

I want Craig. I wish Craig were here.

"I want to see the look on your face when the coach tells

you she hasn't come to soccer," I say. "We both know she won't go."

"Great. Just great. Now you're hoping for failure so you can say I told you so. That's really nice, Sam."

He throws up his hands.

"I give up," he says. "I'm done. Just…just do what you're going to do. I'm done."

"I noticed."

It's a staring contest. A mean one. He leans in and in a low voice he says, "Yeah, well, in case you haven't noticed, you're done, too. You just won't admit it."

Cammy

Holy shit my life sucks. It's beyond sucking. I'm completely fucked. I just came from getting frigging nylon soccer clothes at Sportmart on Clark. Samantha and Bob wanted to punish me, mission accomplished. I HAVE TO PLAY ON THE FUCKING SOCCER TEAM.

So here's what happens: I get home from school right on time because now I have to ride in the carpool home with all the babies since I'm a prisoner. Mrs. O'Donnell's minivan is totally quiet even though it's packed with kids because all the good little girls and boys are busy doing their homework so they can have time to watch TV and IM when they get home. Mrs. O'Donnell *doesn't want to disturb them* so the radio's turned so far down it's like a dog whistle. I can't even tell what song's playing and I'm in the front seat. It's that low. Why even have it on? The only thing that keeps it from being a total nightmare is Mrs. O'Donnell not being so bad. She doesn't talk down to me like I'm in preschool. She asks me if I have a boyfriend and she doesn't seem to mind that I'm looking out the window when I answer no because I can feel my cheeks getting red. She just goes on with the next question like I'm being polite back. I don't know why I do this. I really don't mean to be rude but it feels like everyone's staring at me disgusted or analyzing me. Everyone except Mrs. O'Donnell. I'm only around her on Tuesdays and Thursdays when she drives carpool. She always seems happy to see me. And today she's asking me what kind of music I like and that's always easy to talk about so I know that's why she's asking and that's pretty nice when you think about it. Safe topic. I'm talking about The All-American Rejects and the Weepies and Arcade Fire and she's laughing at the band names and we're actually having a normal conversation. My parents haven't asked me about music like *ever* and they know how much I listen. I couldn't live without music. I seriously think I'd shrivel up and die if there was no music. Then Mrs. O'Donnell's saying, "By the way I saw you at the library the other day."

Oh, shit.

"Yeah?"

I guess I'm leaning too hard on the passenger door because she glances over and then hits the power-lock button. Like I would've put a little more weight into it and the door would've flown open. I can't look over to see how fast we're going because I don't want Mrs. O'Donnell to think I think she's speeding, which she's not but still. It feels like borderline speeding. Fast enough so if the door opened I'd fall out. I'd end up in a wheel-chair peeing into one of those bags hanging on the side.

We're passing Byron's hot dogs where you pick from a million toppings and they have the world's best French fries they put in brown paper bags to soak up some of the grease. I used to have two hot dogs and a whole bag of cheese fries just for myself (the boys always split the fries) but then I went vege-tarian and now I order the garden burger, which isn't half bad considering it's a hot-dog place.

"You were in a carrel near the librarian's desk," she's saying.

"I was in a hurry so I couldn't stop to say hi and it's a library so I couldn't call out to you. Sorry."

A little faster and I bet I'd die. If the door flew open. Even with the seat belt on I'd get sucked out by the wind like a movie plane crash and my head would hit the pavement and Mrs. O'Donnell'd be so shocked she'd take a second or two to hit the brakes, which wouldn't do any good since by then my neck would've snapped back so hard my head would be hanging by a bloody thread.

"You looked lost in thought," she's saying.

"Huh?"

"At the library. Were you working on a paper or something?"

Last week before the grounding I finally got up the courage to go inside. Ricky'd been on my case to check it out when he wasn't busy trying to get into Missy's pants and lecturing me on drugs. He was right, it took about five seconds to Google her. Luckily there aren't many Geraldine Wilkes in the world. At least not in the Midwest. Anyway, Ricky's all, *we went to all that trouble to find your mother and now you're chickening out? At least see what she looks like.*

The door felt heavy when I opened it and the springs were tight so it pretty much hit me in the ass when it shut. Totally embarrassing except no one saw. Thank God because that could've been the first time she ever laid eyes on me. My hands were shaking so bad I shoved them into my pockets and since my pockets are low on my baggy pants, the ones with the peace sign stitched on the butt, it makes me look like a frigging terrorist. I should have worn something else. It's the first time I've ever thought that…and it's only because I wouldn't have wanted to scare her and make her wish she hadn't spawned a child of darkness. People call us that. That or freaks. They think it doesn't hurt feelings and maybe some people don't care but it makes me feel like shit. I see them looking at me and staring and they wonder why I hang back. I just wish I could be invisible. I try to stay in the background but I still get the looks.

I was surprised at how nice it is in the library, all high ceilings and big armchairs facing the window. Most of them taken up by old people reading newspapers that hang on bamboo poles. There's a whole section of phone books so if you want to call someone in North Dakota, no problem. A few of the long tables have people actually doing work with big textbooks, some of them writing fast like they're taking a timed test. Everyone else is at the computer section either using them or waiting to use them. People standing around looking over the shoulders of the people but they're not really in line so I wonder what happens if two people lunge when a computer gets free. The ones pacing back and forth probably fight it out. The guy in the pimped-out wheelchair'll get first crack of course. There are a couple of blue-haired ladies so old they look like they can't eat solid food anymore. I see tons of old people like them piling out of buses at the Sears Tower, with matching plastic badges hanging from their necks. I'm sure they're waiting to check e-mail to see if their grandkids have written them. My grandparents are dead but I don't think I'd e-mail them if they were alive. In pictures they don't look like the type to e-mail. Not the cruise-ship, denture type.

I've been picturing her sitting there at the front desk with glasses on a string around her neck, quietly sitting in her chair using one of those little pencils with no eraser, the kind that are impossible to sharpen. But there are like a million librarians and they're all busy like it's a yard sale. I set myself up at the end of one of the long wooden tables. I took out my biology homework like I'm really going to work on it. Yeah right. I watch for a while but not one of the women coming and going with double-decker book carts look like me. Not one. I gave up around dinnertime because it's pizza night at home and I forgot to tell Samantha to order me the deep-dish veggie one with no onions. She'll get thin-crust cheese and the boys'll wolf it down and I'll only get two pieces and I'm sick of that.

"Is it time for midterms yet?" Mrs. O'Donnell is saying. She puts her blinker on to turn left and the ticking of it seems louder than it should. Like she's timing my answer.

"Oh. Um…no. It's not midterm yet," I say.

We pull up to our house and as usual the boys have trouble with the side sliding door because Mrs. O'Donnell forgets to hit the power unlock when she parks. They're so psyched to get home it's ridiculous. Nine times out of ten they push through the front door at the same time and since they have backpacks and coats on they get stuck until I push them all the way through.

Then I walk into the hell that is my life. Bob's home early from work for some reason and he's holding out shoe boxes to me like *ooooh, you just won the lottery.* I dump my bag and start walking to the kitchen until he says:

"Don't you want to know what's in these boxes?"

"Um, *shoes?*" Duh.

He opens them up like I knew he'd do anyway he's so obsessed with shoes he can't ever wait long enough for someone else to look inside he's like a kid on Christmas. A pig in shit, Monica would say.

And then, like he's expecting the angels to sing for the un-veiling, he pulls out…a cleat.

"Those look a little big for the boys," I say. I try to move past him to the kitchen but then he smiles his dorky smile that shows his yellowing teeth. "Dad, two words. Crest. White-strips."

He's still blocking my way.

"Dad. Move. I'm starving."

"They're for you! You're on the soccer team!"

That's when the bomb drops.

"What?" I manage to push the word out of my mouth.

"I talked to the coach and he says you can start tomorrow. Practice is right after school. You meet up outside the gym and walk over to the field at the lakefront. It goes for an hour and a half."

"Yeah right. I'm not going just so you know."

"Oh, yeah, you are."

Samantha comes in from the kitchen where I know she's been huddling by the door listening.

"I don't even *play* soccer. Nice try. I'm getting something to eat now."

Samantha says, "You *are* playing soccer. Starting tomorrow. And don't get any ideas about skipping out. The coach is going to call us every day after practice to fill us in."

For some reason Bob looks at her like she's saying something he didn't expect her to say. Whatever. I've stopped trying to figure them out.

"Why don't you just put me on a chain gang on the side of the expressway picking up trash," I say.

"We considered that," Bob says. He actually thinks he's being funny but even Samantha doesn't laugh. So he goes, "Well, I'm done" like he's wiping his hands clean and when he goes up the stairs to his goddamn computer I hear him sigh like *oh woe is me my daughter's such a fuck-up.* Samantha watches him too.

"Look, I'm sorry, okay," I say. "Please don't make me play soccer, Mom. Please."

"It's a done deal."

I hate when I cry when I'm mad. I can't control it. It makes me look sad when I'm not.

"Mom, come on. They'll kill me out there. Or in the locker room. Swear to God, they're hard-core. And I'm like…"

"What? You're like what?"

"*I'm a freak!* You think I don't know that? I see the way you look at me, you think I don't but I do. Please, Mom. Please don't make me do it. I'll do anything else but sports. I'll do the dishes for a year. I'll clean the whole house every weekend, swear to God. Please."

"Nope."

"Mom. Come on. Like I'm really going to go? I'm not going."

"Yeah, Cammy. Yeah, you are."

At least she can walk upstairs away from the shit. I'm stuck in it and it just keeps getting deeper.

I hate my life.

And I'm not going to soccer. No fucking way.

Samantha

"Andrew! Come here and let me get a Band-Aid on you."

"I don't need one," he calls back as he's coming off the soccer field toward the mini bottled waters. Other parents move in and hover but I try to give him space because the parents who move in during halftime give me the creeps. Let the kids be on a team, I want to tell them. Let them bond. Let them talk about the first half. Let them do anything but be smothered by people they see every other second of their lives.

On the other hand, here I am calling my son like that old spaghetti commercial where the mother is hanging out her apartment window calling down a city block.

"Just come here for a second." I motion him over. He rolls his head back and drags himself slowly toward me like he's a fish being reeled in.

I hunt through my purse past packets of Kleenex, tampons, lipsticks, my camera, datebook, my cell and finally find a lint-covered Band-Aid.

"Give me your arm."

"I gotta go—he's about to blow the whistle."

"Two seconds. There. Go."

From the distance someone calls *sorry* and a small soccer ball rolls within inches of me.

"No problem," I say, and a gorgeous brunette is walking toward me reaching for the ball. The sun is behind her. She flicks her shiny brown hair over her shoulder. She looks like she's walked out of a shampoo commercial. Or out of the ocean in a James Bond movie. In slow motion. Her purse swings from the crook of her arm, looking expensive. Her ballet flats have miraculously avoided the patches of mud littering the sidelines.

"We haven't exactly mastered our kicking." She smiles, motioning with her head toward her daughter. "Thanks."

"Been there," I say, smiling back. I look at the beautiful girl who looks like she'll inherit her mother's classic bone structure. "Here you go. How old are you, honey?"

"Five." She eyes me suspiciously before hiding behind her mother's thin legs.

"I have sons who're just a little older than you. Are you on the 5G team? Yes? Wow. My sons, Jamie and Andrew, are on 8B."

I hold out my hand to the woman. "I'm Sam Friedman."

"Hi," she says with a firm handshake, "I'm Evie Riggs. This is Lexi. And we better get going, sweetie, I see the coach pulling everyone together, so I think the game's about to start. Anyway, nice meeting you. I'm sure I'll see you around."

Oh. My. God. Ohmygodohmygodohmygodohmygod.

I swallow back vomit. I watch her walk away. She's *happy*. She's *stunning*. She's *perfect*. I feel nothing but pure raging jealousy. I'm in a trance, moving to keep her in sight. I walk to the end of the field by the goal so I can get a better view. I watch her from a distance, her posture, her ease with the other parents, throwing her head back to laugh at something someone says to her. Terry, Sophie's mother, is talking to me but I can't hear her. Craig's not there, thank God. I don't know how I'd deal with that, Jesus Christ. Can't even imagine. Evie cheers and claps for Lexi's team. Someone moves in toward her so I walk farther from the boys' game, closer to her field. She's talking to another woman. They look like good friends, the way they're leaning in. Someone else comes up to the other side of her…she's like the Pied Piper the way everyone's drawn to her. Damn, I can't see her now. A woman is setting up her folding hammock chair right behind her. God, she's beautiful. I can't believe he didn't mention it. Then again, what would he say? *Oh, by the way, my wife's a knockout.* Of course he didn't mention it. Not to me. I bet his friends shake their heads in awe at his luck. The two of them together are probably worshipped. Like movie stars. Their friends probably hold them up as the perfect couple. *They throw the best dinner parties or did you hear what he did for her fortieth? So romantic* or *they really have it together, so in love after so much time.* How could he not be attracted to her? I guess, now that I think about it, he's never said he wasn't attracted to her, he's just talked about how they don't have sex.

I look down at my sweatpants and my muddy old running shoes. My hair's dirty, so I have it in a messy ponytail. Here's what would happen if I walked up to her and said, *I know everything about your husband. And you. I know what side of the bed you sleep on. You don't snore but you toss and turn. I know you don't like to travel much anymore. I know you don't cook. You like tea, not coffee, and you tried to get Craig to like it, too, but he hates it. Your best friend's worried about you and you don't know it but she mentioned something to your husband about you being depressed. You like reality TV. You finished* The Odyssey *in two weeks. You like classical, not Top 40 like Craig. He's my best friend. I'm his. You don't even know this part of his life. I think we're infatuated with each other.* She'd laugh. Hard.

I mean, look at me and look at her. She's perfect. Exquisite. And me, I'm…what am I? Okay, fine, I'm attractive. I can pull it together. But I'm no Evie Riggs. Not by a long shot.

I'm openly staring at her. Memorizing everything about her. She's reaching into her purse for something. What is it? I move in front of a family waiting for the next game. She's putting her hair back. Into a ponytail. Of course it's a perfect ponytail. All her hair makes it in so it looks polished, like she's stepped out of a Ralph Lauren ad. And Lexi…she's gorgeous, too. I can see she's a happy child. The kind of happy that comes from having loving, doting parents. I want to scoop her up and swing her around just to see her laugh. To see if she has his smile. I want to hug her, hold her close, inhale her. I realize I love her, too. I love her because he loves her. I love her because she is a piece of him walking around.

"Earth to Mom! The game's over, jeez." Jamie shakes my arm. "Can we go?"

"We're hungry," Andrew says.

I crane my neck to see what she's doing. Ah. Lexi's running her tiny little legs back onto the field. Evie's clapping like everyone else.

"Don't you wanna know who won?" Jamie asks.

"Oh, sorry, honey—I watched the whole thing! Of course I know who won, silly. You guys played great. Good job! So fast down the field—especially in that last quarter, Jamie. You two are so good!"

Andrew kicks the ball back and forth all the way to the car. I don't know how I manage to walk, but somehow we're standing outside the car and Jamie's pulling at the door handle.

"I didn't play the second half," Jamie mumbles.

"Mom, the door's locked," Andrew says.

"Can we go now?"

She's cupping her hands to yell to the players then smiling. I bet she says stuff like "nice try!" or "good job" or "next time, next time."

The boys have climbed into the minivan and I hit the button that slides the side door closed automatically. As it seals shut I let myself cry. A quick, gulped-back cry. I can't fall apart now. I don't have time. Do not fall apart now. Pull it together, Sam.

But I can't. I've never felt this way about another human being. Ever. But I want…I just want…

I want to be her. I want to be Evie Riggs.

I take the long way home from the lakefront, past their house. Lately I've been doing this but never with the kids in the car. Not that it really matters, though. Craig's driven by our house, too. He confessed it to me a few weeks ago.

"Can we get McDonald's?" Andrew calls from the backseat. "Jamie, *stop*. Mom make Jamie stop poking me. Jamie, *stop*. Mom!"

"Ow! Stop it." Jamie's turn now. "Mom, Andrew just punched me."

"Boys, cut it out." The words have no muscle behind them.

"Where are we?" Jamie asks. "Can we get McDonald's?"

"Yeah. In a minute," I say, slowing to about ten miles an hour. "Just a second."

"We can?" Andrew asks. "Yessss!"

"You never let us have McDonald's," Jamie says.

"Shut up," Andrew hisses at him. "She'll change her mind."

They live in a beautifully restored Victorian with a wraparound front porch and matching wicker chairs. The hedge along the house has been trimmed the way only professionals can trim. They probably have a team descend once a week to take care of the stuff we never do. Raking. Weeding. Pushing wood chips back onto the flower beds.

"Mo-om," the boys whine in unison.

"Okay okay okay." I turn my eyes back to driving.

At the drive-through they lean forward and blurt their orders out to me: "Hamburger but no pickles" "Chicken nuggets with the honey sauce" "Can we get two fries so we don't have to share?" "Yeah, I'm starving!" "Coke" "Sprite" "Wait, they're doing Transformers—can we have Happy Meals?" "They don't have hamburger Happy Meals!" "Yeah, they do—Mom, can we get Happy Meals, the ones with Transformers?" "I want mine with a hamburger."

Somehow I get the order right and they quiet down when I pass the bag back to them. I'm letting the car drive us home. Like a carriage horse, it seems to know the route by heart. I can finally think about what just happened.

Then again I don't know what to think. I feel guilty. Wait. No, I don't. Why don't I feel guilty? It's not like we've done anything earth shattering. Then again that kiss. And if we weren't doing something…secret…I would've introduced myself to her, right? Instead, I acted like I didn't know her. So we are up to something. Wait, that's ridiculous—of course we're up to something.

At the corner of Broadway and Catalpa it hits me. *I don't care about anything but Craig.* Bob. The family. Nothing. That must be why I don't feel guilty. I'd say I don't care about Evie but I *do* care about her in the sense that I wish I had her life. I've got to pull it together. I hate being jealous. I've never been jealous. Ever. And now I'm blinded by it. I wish I'd known who it was when she walked up. I could've memorized more about her. I feel like shit. Maybe I'm coming down with something. Or maybe it's just that I look like a mess and she…she…*she* is Evie Riggs. She is married to this perfect guy and she doesn't ap-preciate it.

★ ★ ★

I'm excellent at memorizing phone numbers. Bob programmed every number we could possibly ever need into the
phone (the Chinese take-out place. The dry cleaners. Even
work numbers like his Foot Locker buyer), but I don't touch
it. Especially speed-dial number one: Mom—cell. The kids use
this one so often the number one is worn off. To me, though,
it looks like a direct line to my mother. I'm looking at it now,
tracing the tiny square button, wiping the gunk off the clear
plastic display on the base unit. My head feels so heavy with
thought I can barely lift it. What will Craig say when I tell him
about today? What if it's a wake-up call to him—he'll realize
he'll lose his wife and daughter if she finds out he kissed me
and maybe he even thinks I'm a loose cannon who might tell
her in a fit of jealous passion. We won't be friends anymore.
So I won't tell him how she makes me feel vulnerable and small.
Insignificant. A phase in Craig's life.

I finger the speed-dial button with the rubbed-off 1 and I
imagine what I'd say if I hit it and heard my mother's voice.

"Hi, Mom, it's me," I'd say. "Can you come over?"

She'd know from my tone that something was wrong and
she'd say *I'll be right there.*

Or maybe I'd say this: "Hi, Mom. It's me. I'm in trouble,
Mom. Oh, God, tell me what to do. I've made a mess of my
life. What should I do? Bob and I haven't had sex in over a year.
We barely speak to each other and when we do it's to fight.
Cammy's in trouble and I don't know what to do."

She'd ask, *what does Bob think about it* and I'd tell her the truth.
I'd tell her that the other night, after I told him about Cammy
and the drugs and the birth-mother search, he went to his
computer. I'd tell her that when I finally went inside after
crying by myself on the front steps I looked over his shoulder,

assuming he was researching mushrooms or teenage drug use, I saw he was reading something about refinancing mortgages. Something died in me when I saw that, Mom. I don't know who this person is but he's not the sort of man I want to be married to. I walked out of the room and fell asleep knowing he would still be at the computer. He'd be at that computer until one or two o'clock in the morning, searching real-estate listings. When he finally does come to bed we sleep like Gumby figures, on our backs, arms bowed out at our sides just short of touching. If I were in bed with Craig we would spoon, and to a bird looking down from above us it would look like we were riding an invisible motorcycle.

It calms Bob to look at houses. Maybe it's the stillness of the pictures. Maybe it's the stats he likes: 2bdrm, 2bthm, wdfp, finished basement. He searches and searches and searches. This is all he does. Every single day he comes home from work, interacts with the kids for a little and then parks himself in front of the computer, clicks on his list of "favorites" and visits real-estate listings like some men visit porn sites. The worst part is we aren't in the market for a new house.

"Hey, Mom?" I'd ask her. "Did you love Dad? Did you wonder if you made a mistake? Did you ever want to walk away from your life? Did you ever meet your lover's wife and wish you were her?"

That's what I'd say if I hit speed-dial number one.

Instead, I exhale and call Cammy downstairs. The boys are in the family room working on homework, I think. They've probably blown it off and are playing computer games but I don't give a shit. I fall back on the couch in the living room. Other than driving, this is the first time I've sat down all day. I'm exhausted. I hope I can keep my eyes open. Maybe she didn't hear me and I could grab a catnap. Five minutes with my eyes closed would be bliss. It's too tempting to tilt over into lying on the couch, so I move to the overstuffed club chair across from it. I trace the curve of the arms. The Oriental rug on the floor is a soft amber Tibetan hand-woven number Bob's parents gave us when we bought the house. Tea-stained, they call it. It's gorgeous…very rich looking but not over the top. It blends in perfectly with the room. The colors go well with the portrait of my mother hanging over the mantel. People think I planned it that way. I walk by this picture millions of times a day to the point of not seeing it, but now, sitting here waiting to rock my daughter's world, I stare at it. The painter caught the folds of the green taffeta dress she wore to a debutante party when she herself was a teenager. She told me how restless she was sitting for this painting, how the bone stays making her bustline look Elizabethan dug into her and left marks in her stomach for hours after her sittings. You can't tell any of this by looking at it and I wonder if the painter had to make up the half smile on her face. She is serene. Her hair was swept up, but he caught the wisps that didn't make it. The background, my grandparents' old house before they moved into a nursing home, looks regal and it seemed that way to me when we visited them. Above Mom's head is the crystal chandelier that now hangs in our front hall.

Cammy comes in and makes an elaborate show of bored condescension by falling into the couch with *I'm here what do you want*. I lean forward, putting my elbows on my knees, my hands in a prayer triangle.

"First it's the black hair," I say, "which we put up with because we know it's a phase. The clothes. The face paint. Then it's the pierced nose. Then the cartilage and I know that's a phase, too…"

"It's not a phase, Jesus, I hate it when you say that," she says. "It's me. This is who I am! Cameron."

"Oh, so you're Cameron now? When did *that* start?"

"You don't get it," she says. "You just don't understand. You don't see me. It's like you think I'm this little kid or something. I'm not a *baby* anymore." She is chipping away at the black nail polish on her fingers.

"I know you're not a five-year-old, Cammy," I say. "But you're sixteen, for Christ's sake—and you're our daughter and you live under our roof and God help me if I'm not saying the exact same thing my own parents said to me, but here it is. As long as you are under eighteen you will live by our rules. You're lucky you even have a mother to say that to you. Do you know what your life would be like if I died when you were sixteen like I was when my mother died? Do you have any idea?"

"This is so fucking ridiculous," she says.

"*What* did you just say? Don't you dare speak to me like that. You have about three seconds to change your attitude or—"

"Or what? You'll put me in a time-out? Jesus. Just like a baby..." She trails off, slumping back into the downy couch pillows so she can bite her cuticles more comfortably. Really attractive.

She's always in the process of grooming herself, and the irony is she never looks groomed. She looks like she needs the kind of shower that cleans off radioactive waste. A Karen Silkwood shower. Now she's examining her hair for split ends.

"I know you haven't been going to soccer," I say.

She doesn't even bother to look up. She just shrugs and through the curtain of dirty hair she mutters, "Did you guys really think I'd go? I mean...come on." She snort-laughs just like Bob does, but God forbid I mention a similarity between them. Cammy'd chew my head off.

"The coach called this morning to say you haven't been to

practice once this week." I don't tell her, of course, that I knew this would happen and frankly I don't care if she goes to soccer or not. *United front. United front. United front.* "Your father's going to hit the ceiling when he finds out."

She looks up at me and stares so intensely I get a chill.

"He's not my father." She says this slowly as if English is my second language. I look away. Where do I go from here? What tack am I supposed to take now? She's right to go to the bigger issue. She's absolutely right, it's not about dyed black hair or piercings or soccer. But I don't know where to go from here.

Maybe she's right about a lot of things. Maybe this isn't a phase. The person cold-staring me is a complete stranger. She's not my sixteen-year-old daughter.

In an unspoken time-out of silence my eyes travel the room, settling on a tennis ball–size mark on the wall just inside the living room. Funny, I haven't noticed it in ages. The movers left a "trail of destruction"—that's what Bob called it that night. We both laughed and wandered through the stacks of boxes, looking for other nicks and scrapes, but nothing compared to that angry dent that cut right to the bone of the house. A punch to this, our first house. Chewing deep-dish pizza, Bob said it'd be a cinch to patch over but here it is, almost twenty years later, a signpost in the trail of destruction. Huh. Fitting.

"Mom." Cammy's trying to catch my attention. "Can I go now?" She sneers and stands up, but I know she's challenging me. That girl staring daggers at me a few seconds ago would've marched out. *She* wouldn't have asked permission, sarcastic though it was. No…this is Cammy again, waiting for me to make the next move. Waiting for me to be a mother. So I inhale and jump back in.

"I want to know who goes to this library parking lot. That's number one."

Teenager 101: never let them sense weakness. Ever. So I know I'm buying time with this question, but this is part of the bigger picture. I've got to break her down, break her spirit. Then I'll build her back up. Like the military.

"I don't *know* who goes to the parking lot," she says. "Just…I don't know, just *everyone*. Different people. It's not like you know all of them anyway so why do you care?"

"I care because you're my daughter and I want to know how long this has been going on. What have you been putting in your backpack to make it look like you've been studying there?"

Question number two. Again, this is to give me even more time to think of a plan of attack.

"What do I put in my backpack? Jesus, I don't know, books and stuff. Makeup. Whatever. Why does this even matter?"

She's sniffing me out, looking for cracks in the foundation. Looking to see me agree with her on the stupidity of the question, but here is another lesson I have learned—make each question seem as though it's escalating in importance, because it'll throw them off the scent. Mix the important questions in with the irrelevant ones. They'll get so used to answering what they believe are inane questions that by the time you get to the important ones they've been lulled into a hypnotic surliness and *bam* you get the answers you never even knew you were looking for.

"It matters, okay," I say. "Everything about this matters, Cammy. Oh, sorry, *Cameron*."

"See? That's what I'm talking about. You say my name like it's some joke, but you named me so why can't you respect that I want to use a different version of the name *you and Bob gave me* without you sneering at me the way you are."

Then she considers something. I watch the wheels turning.

"You guys named me, right?" she asks. "Oh, my God, you didn't *name* me? Why didn't you *tell* me that? How could you not tell me that!"

"Just slow down," I say. "We wanted you so badly. We've told you that. I knew the minute I laid eyes on you that you were my daughter. It was so natural, the connection was instant, swear to God. I honestly didn't know it would be like that. I guess I thought there'd be a breaking-in period. But it was instant. When we first saw you, your father—don't make that face, *he is your father*—your father said, 'let's bring her home.' We loved your name. It is exactly the name we would have given you. You are a Cameron, through and through. It's a beautiful name. We adopted you as our daughter and you have our last name because you are our daughter."

"I don't *care* about my last name. Fuck my last name."

"Stop it! Just stop it. Getting back to what we were talking about... So, what, you're a druggie now? A Goth druggie. With pitch-black hair. Doing drugs, that's your thing now? Do you have any idea how *dangerous* this is? Do you have any idea what you're doing?"

She gives me a disdainful stare. Yeah, well, I see her blank stare and I raise her a glare of anger so strong I can see her recoil. She's about to walk into the palm of my hand.

"Answer me," I say. "Did you think about the consequences of what you did when you decided to do *hallucinogenic drugs?"*

Another moment of silence, but this is thick with mother-and-daughter-on-the-brink-of-Armageddon.

"Answer me, goddammit."

Teenager 201: tears always diffuse the situation. Unfortunately, they have seen the playbook on this one.

"Here, here's some tissue," I say.

sob "I don't *sob* even know *sob* why I'm crying."

I soften on this one. I remember that feeling, the wave of emotion, the mood that comes out of nowhere, the embarrassment of uncontrollable tears when all you want to be is tearless and angry.

"I want to know who Paul is," I say.

Teenager 301: tears stop on a dime.

"What? No one," she says. "He's just this guy someone knows. I don't know."

"Whose friend is he?"

"I don't know! Can I go now? I have homework and like a million other things I have to do by tomorrow."

Teenager 401: know when to step back but only do it temporarily.

"This isn't over, Cammy. *Cameron.* This is far from over. Do your homework and we'll talk later."

"Can't wait, *Samantha.*"

"Watch it."

"Whatever."

Teenager 401 Advanced Credit: never let them know you're doing detective work.

I wish Craig were here to help me—I have a small window of time because I know Cammy will find a way to reach her friends and tell them to scatter from the library parking lot. Somehow she'll get word to them. We've taken away her cell phone and her computer use but somehow she'll reach them. Like that Supermax prison, the one with the highest level of security where they're holding the Unabomber—even in there the prisoners find ways to get messages to one another and to the outside world. This is the tricky part.

I wait until Bob comes home and when I see him pull in front of the house, I throw my purse on my shoulder and race out.

"Nice of you to make time for your family," I say, pushing past him on the front walk. "Thanks for showing up."

"Fuck you, Sam."

"Nice. Really nice."

"Where're you going?"

"The boys are in the family room, I think, and Cammy's doing homework, but if anyone asks I'm going out for milk."

"Oh, Jesus, what now?"

Over the roof of the car I whisper, "I'm going out for *milk*." I use the tone you use when you're telling something in code and you want to be sure the other person gets it. "If you really wanted to know you'd come home a little earlier."

His shoulders drop and in my rearview mirror I see him dragging himself up to the house. The yellow light at the corner turns red but I run through it anyway. I roll past a stop sign two blocks away and I slam the pedal up to thirty-five miles an hour up Belmont in between lights. Luckily there's no traffic this time of night.

There are a few skateboarders practicing jumps under the yellow glow of the streetlights, but otherwise the library parking lot is empty. It looks like a movie set, no trash, perfectly painted white-striped parking spaces far outnumbering what's needed for the branch. Way in the back of the employee parking area there is a pickup truck, but that is the only car in the place. These are the kind of circumstances judo instructors talk about when describing ways to beat off a would-be attacker. Keys between fisted fingers are useless, they say, because you have to wait until they're close enough to punch, but by then they will no doubt have overtaken you. No, it's better to kick and yell "fire" even though you're facing a rape or murder. People respond to fires. I remind myself these are kids. Kids Cammy's age (then again, I can't be sure of this). Kids can't intimidate me.

"Hey," I call to a boy with what appears to be a pierced lower lip, though it's hard to tell in a shadowy casting light that makes everyone look like they have a pierced lower lip. "Any of you guys know a kid named Paul?"

I try to sound tough. Like I'm in a cop show.

"Who wants to know?" the smallest of the four asks. He's wearing jeans that are too baggy, a hoodie sweatshirt with the hood up and tied so only his eyes and lips are visible. Such a joke, this white kid trying to act ghetto. His clothes are all clean, I can tell even in the streetlamp-lit darkness. I can practically smell the detergent his mother used.

"I do," I say, matching his haughtiness. "Are you Paul?"

They snort a kind of laughter that implies not only is this not Paul but he is so far removed from Paul it's comical.

"What do you want with Paul?" a beefier version of the same kid asks.

"Do I know you? Wait, aren't you Lee Wilcox?" I ask him. This throws him off. I see him deflating and backing up at the unexpected loss of power. "I know your mother," I say. "You used to come and have playdates at my house when you were little. I think we still have your sippy cup in the cabinet."

Just like that, little Lee Wilcox turns from an unrecognizable hoodlum into a child. Oh, my God, I just used the word *hoodlum*. I *am* getting old. Still, I'm happy to see this knocks him off his game. Not only that, but from the way they're looking from him to me back to him I can tell his friends will have a field day with him once I leave. Humiliated, Lee Wilcox steps back and someone else steps up in his place.

"Tell him if he ever talks to my daughter, Cameron Friedman, again I'll have him arrested so fast he won't be able to blink. I've called the police and they'll be checking this parking lot from now on and if any of you are around they'll haul you in for questioning."

They look as though I have just spoken Czech to them.

"Am I making myself clear?"

This is surreal. As I walk away, though, the fun stops.

"Fine with me." A boy steps out of the shadows of the library overhang. He is small and wearing short sleeves even though it's cold outside. In the yellow glow I see that his Albino-white hair is thinning and the wisps of what's left look fragile, like at any minute they'll blow away and this slight child will be as bald as a chemo patient. The whiteness of him is startling. He appears to glow in the dark like he's been exposed to nuclear fallout.

"Are you Paul?" I ask him even though it's unnecessary. The others have all backed away, some flipping their skateboards, others tapping cigarettes out of packs, trying to look older, reaching for cans I am sure are beer. Somewhere in the distance a motorcycle revs at a red light, reminding me I'm not far from Ashland. I could run to the street and call for help. The light must have changed, because the hum of the engine turns and wheels screech.

"Cameron's the one who dragged us here to begin with," Paul says. His voice is unexpectedly deep and it occurs to me he might make a good DJ. A good face for radio, I imagine someone saying to him.

"What do you mean she dragged you here?" I ask.

"I mean she dragged us here," he says. "We liked the 7-Eleven better anyway, but for some reason this was the place she tells us we need to be, so whatever. Fine with me, I tell her. I'll go to the fuckin' library if that's what you want. Go where the action is. And believe me, Cameron's the action."

He didn't have to add that part. I knew from his emphasis

on *for some reason* it was the drugs. He said it slowly and punched up *some.* Like I'm Forrest Gump and wouldn't have understood. He wants me to take the bait. He's looking for a reason to call in his posse or whatever rich white kids pretending to have street cred call it. He's waiting for my reaction.

"So what're you, the dealer or something?" I ask him. I jut my chin at him. I'll play the game for him.

"Someone's got to keep Cameron going." He shifts on his feet and folds his hands into the kangaroo pouch in the front of his sweatshirt. Another fishing expedition to see what it'll take to break my calm. It's like showdown at the OK Corral.

"I'm not saying it's me," he adds. Someone in the dark chuckles at this. "I'm just saying…your girl's a good customer, know what I'm saying."

Then, for dramatic effect, he steps back and disappears into the night. I call out, "You remember what I said. Don't ever come back here. And don't you dare come near my daughter ever again. You got that, *Paul?*"

I didn't expect nor do I get an answer.

The following day after the kids leave for school I start my search.

I'm used to seeing Cammy's room a mess but this time instead of seeing it as a typical teenager's room, it's a minefield. Or a crime scene that needs to be carefully picked over but left intact.

She wouldn't leave anything important on the floor. Too obvious. Under the bed, nothing but random shoes, old makeup kits she got on birthdays past. Now to the drawers. A few thongs I didn't know about, but overall, nothing surprising. In the closet I feel like I'm getting warmer. On the shelves, sweatshirts and sweaters stuffed within reach. Her clothes are all black now. At least the ones that still fit her. Oh, my God, the shopping day. The new school clothes I promised in lighter, brighter colors. I can't believe it slipped my mind. There are seven black or brown hoodies, each one different versions of the same unflattering baggy sweatshirts. I take them off in balls so I can return them unnoticed. Nothing behind them. On the top shelf there are old shoe boxes that look promising. I go through them one by one but nothing. Old diaries with entries like *today I have to clean my room* and *Brianna is my best friend EVER* in childish handwriting I miss. Camp letters she's saved. Pen pals. Nothing recent.

Where would *I* hide something? She's so hell-bent on being an adult, fine. Where would an adult put something she wants no one to see...?

I squeeze the pockets of all the hanging clothes, the jeans, the few shirts that haven't been trampled. Nothing but some loose change and ponytail holders. The last pair of pants I get to, the ones all the way at the end of the hanging rack in between old khakis she hasn't fit into in years, something crinkles. A piece of paper, it feels like. I reach in for it. It's a typed letter, folded in thirds. A business letter.

Dear Mr. and Mrs. Friedman,

    We received the requested letter from your daughter's doctor and are saddened to hear of her condition. Because all the required documentation has been provided we are hereby releasing the information we feel is medically relevant.

What the hell is this? I turn it over and look at the envelope and can't really wrap my head around what I'm reading. It's legit. I skim over most of it but sentences jump out at me. I picture Cammy reading this and it makes me sick.

Blood tests taken at the time indicate the birth mother was in fact a serious drug user and traces of methamphetamines were noted.

Oh, Jesus, she knows.

On the floor my legs have pinpricks from sitting cross-legged. I fall back and stretch them out, staring at the glow-in-the-dark star stickers Cammy put up when she turned seven. The Beanie Babies she collected are jammed into a corner of her bookshelf. Shells from a long-ago trip to Florida are still lined up on another shelf, arranged largest to smallest so that the conch shell is first, in front of a beat-up copy of *Where's Waldo?* She's blind to these things, they've sat there for so long she no longer sees them. I realize I don't know this girl now. This Cameron is a stranger to me. Sweatshirts and long black skirts and woven shoes Bob calls Jesus slippers. Black romper-stomper boots. An Evanescence poster hanging above her bed. A picture of Jimi Hendrix making a peace sign is over her desk. Marilyn Manson. On the floor not far from where I've collapsed I see a black eyeliner digging into the carpet. An empty bottle of grape vitamin water. A crinkled-up report on Kafka's *The Metamorphosis*. She apparently got an A- on it. Figures Kafka would be her best subject. There's Visine. And a cool tin cylinder of Binaca. I muster up the energy to move. Forward movement. Momentum. I get on my hands and knees and step to standing like an old lady in a stretch class. It's dark in here. I lean down to pick up her pillow—the only straightening I do because I know she won't notice. I hold it close before throwing it back to the top of the bed. One side is wet. Not soaking but a spot that is trying to dry is at the center of the white case smudged with mascara. Without thinking twice I smell it. I know this smell. I am paralyzed. My feet are rooting to the floor like the first time off the high board at the swimming pool down the street from my childhood home, only now I can't turn around and go back down the ladder.

Is it Ricky's semen? Paul's? How are they getting in here? I cross over to the window and I have my answer. Whoever it is has been climbing up the tree outside her window. Jesus Christ. I feel sick. I run to her bathroom and hunch over the toilet. Where have I been? Who am I that I don't even know my own daughter? I know one of the only Beanie Babies she couldn't find was the pink Princess Diana bear. I used to know when her periods were. I knew she hated brussels sprouts. This was the girl who needed help tying her shoes long after her friends had been doing it on their own. The nausea has passed. I straighten up and use toilet paper to wipe under my eyes.

Sex. My daughter's having sex. And I have no idea who she's doing it with and she's into serious drugs and she's freakishly Goth and where the hell have I *been?*

Whatever forged documents she supplied to the adoption agency were probably printed out right under our noses. How she faked medical records is beyond me, but this is a child who has gotten straight A's in Computer Workshop and anyway they all know computers inside and out, so I'm sure there are places she can access that would give her the information needed to copy a doctor's letter.

I call Bob at work and get his assistant.

"Hi, Grace, it's Sam. Is he around?"

"Oh, hey, Sam. Do you want me to wake him up?"

"He's sleeping?"

"I know," she says. "A little early today. He usually turns off his phone but I can tap on the door if you like."

"What time does he normally sleep?" I ask. "I forget." I lie because I have to. Because my husband has apparently slipped lower than I'd thought.

"Oh, you know, sometimes it's two. Sometimes two-thirty."

"Right. Don't wake him. I'll talk to him later. Thanks, Grace."

I put my head in my hands. It feels like I'm right on the edge of quicksand. Bob's gotten sucked in. I could reach for him but that would only pull me in too and then what would the kids do? Someone's got to save this family.

If we have to hire a private detective, fine, but first I try to do what Cammy did online. I Google her and instantly she is in front of me. Geraldine Wilkes is all over the globe. Not *our* Geraldine Wilkes, but then again who can be sure. It takes me a solid hour of clicks and nothing. I've always assumed she died of an overdose years ago. I start out West, typing in Los Angeles along with her name, and that leads me on a wild-goose chase. San Francisco. Portland. Miami. Dallas. Boston. New York— all the same. I spend an hour on the computer and stupidly don't think to plug in Chicago. I figured she'd have left the city after giving Cammy up. Too many people would have asked her where her two-year-old daughter had gone. I would have moved away for a fresh start. Or maybe she stayed behind and fell into drugged despair but then cleaned herself up. Three names jump out at me. One is a schoolteacher on the South Side. Another is a potter who has exhibited her work in several craft fairs and, clicking on the link to her Web site, I see she is far too old to be Cammy's birth mother. The final one chills me. Geraldine Wilkes, librarian, Lincoln Park branch of the Chicago Public Library. The library. *Cameron's the one who dragged us here. For some reason this was the place she tells us we need to be.*

I don't know how the rest of the day passed but it did. I threw something together for dinner. Meat loaf I think.

After three hours or so of restless sleep waiting for morning to come, daylight has arrived and I can finally begin the day. I'm up early. In front of me is a day that is already weighing heavily, like a fight you know you're going to have to get into. To keep busy and to help time pass I uncharacteristically make breakfast, stirring pancake mix and rattling pans until the boys stumble down, sleep still in their eyes, rubbing them at the sight of me, on a school day, making a weekend breakfast. Seven a.m. feels like noon, I'm so sick with exhaustion.

"Wow, mark this day on the calendar," Bob says, coming in with two dots of Kleenex on his freshly shaved face. "Pancakes on a school day." He doesn't say it in a nice way. He takes a pancake and folds it in half into his mouth.

"Why don't you sit down like a civilized human being and eat with the kids," I say.

Any second the flurry of Cammy will descend. She'll stuff a pancake into her mouth on her way out the door to Margie O'Donnell's car. She'll do this to tweak me, knowing I'll say the same thing to her I said to her father. She'll do this to try to get back on track with me. She'll do this to regain equilibrium. She'll do this because she is a teenager and it is her job to make her parents crazy. She'll rush out the door with no idea that I'm onto her. The game's over.

"Andrew, go call your sister. Tell her breakfast is ready."

"Cammy! Breakfast is ready!" he yells from his chair at the kitchen table.

"I've got to run," Bob says, already halfway out the door. "See you tonight. Hey, Sam. You need me to pick anyone up tonight? I've got a clear afternoon."

I look over at him while I'm shoving Ziplocked baby carrots into a lunch bag. He's making an effort. It doesn't make me feel warm and fuzzy. I don't appreciate it. He wants me to but

I don't. After all this time, all my begging and pleading, it's fake and temporary. Too little, too late.

"Nope." I go over to talk to him out of the boys' earshot. "I need to talk to you about Cammy."

"Can't we talk about it tonight?"

"I thought you said your afternoon's clear."

"Sam, I don't have time to get into this now," he says. "Let's just talk about it later."

"So you were offering to pick the kids up knowing I'd say you didn't have to? You fake-offered?"

"I gotta go. Bye, guys!"

"What're you guys talking about?" Andrew asks. "Are you fighting?"

"No," we both reply at once.

"Don't talk with your mouth full. Jamie, that's enough syrup," I say.

Then I tell Andrew to go call his sister down again, which buys us a few more seconds. I lean over him to whisper as he picks up his briefcase. "Bob, listen, we need to talk about the game plan here."

Cammy walks into the kitchen. "What's up with the pancakes?"

She directs this question to the boys. They shrug in between bites. *Beats me just go with it and don't ruin it for the rest of us,* their shoulders say. She's taking the temperature of the room.

"I've got to run, see you later," Bob says. And he is gone.

"Eat quickly, it's time to get going," I tell them. "I don't want you keeping Mrs. O'Donnell waiting. Shoes, backpacks. Get coats, it's supposed to get colder later."

"I don't need a coat," Andrew whines. "It's not even that cold out."

"Take one anyway. Jamie, you forgot your lunch. No, put

it in your backpack now or you'll leave it in Mrs. O'Donnell's car like last time. Andrew, coat! Yes, okay, you can wear your fleece but don't lose it."

Cammy and I avoid eye contact. She's out the door without a word and I go to the computer to check my in-box.

Please let there be an e-mail from him.

Sometimes I want to yell IS ANYBODY OUT THERE? I feel like I'm in this parallel universe and I'm invisible. Some planet I've landed on to observe the human life-form but I can't speak the language. No one hears me. Like that kind of nightmare where you open your mouth to scream for help but nothing comes out.

Like Ricky's father. Ricky's father has a hole in his throat and talks with some machine that makes him sound like a robot. It's seriously fucked up. Ricky never ever talks about him—I can tell he's embarrassed. Like one time his dad came to open house when we were in seventh grade or something. Maybe sixth. Ricky pretended he wasn't his son but then in the hall where the parents were looking at our science projects on display his dad put the thing to his neck and said "This.Is.So.Good.Richard" and everyone stared, not to be mean but just because they hadn't ever heard something like that. That was the last time his dad ever came to school. I think about what Ricky must've said to him at home to keep him from coming again and it makes me want to cry for some reason. If I ever ask about him Ricky'll look through me like he didn't hear and then he says "Anyways…" and we end up talking about something else.

The reason I haven't burned this diary yet is that it helps me remember what I do when I get fucked up. Lately I've started forgetting. Even simple things. So I've started arranging a schedule. I try not to take the blue pill before four in the afternoon—if I take it earlier my buzz peaks at six and then starts wearing off and by then everyone's home and around and that's just what I want to escape from. Plus it's harder to get stoned even now with a lock on my door. I don't have to worry about the smoke detector…I took the battery out months ago…but stuffing the towel under the door and getting the fan to blow the smoke just right out the window instead of back in—it's all a pain in the ass. Getting stoned when the pill wears off is good but not as great as it used to be. It used to only be two hits and if I timed it right I was good. Mellowing from a mellow, like Paul says. Now it takes two bowls. But it's hard to remember what I've said or what I haven't said. Or things I've done. Like a little earlier tonight I got a text from Monica saying Stp stalking me u freak and I looked at my call log and I guess I called her like nine times this afternoon but I totally don't remember it being that much.

I just don't get why she won't talk to me anymore. She gets with everyone so it's not like me getting with Will broke her heart. I mean, NOTHING breaks her heart. She was seriously the only one who got that this place sucks the lifeblood out of you. Any original thought is beaten out of you with NOTES TO PARENTS that have tons of emoticons and exclamation points.

It has come to our attention that students are gathering behind the school at the maintenance exit during free periods. ☹ This is not allowed. Please take the matter up with your child. We have a no smoking policy that is enforced. All the rules and regulations can be found in the attached booklet, if a refresher is needed. ☺

If I see one more smiley face I'll buy a frigging gun, I swear. Now our free periods aren't free periods at all. Big Brother's always watching like a fucking globe in the sky that follows you around with a spotlight and a signal beaming back to the principal's office.

Anyway, a couple of days ago I told Samantha that Mrs. Tippet told me I didn't need my math tutor anymore because I "finally grasped" calculus. Samantha shot Bob a look across the serving bowl of spaghetti and they both looked at me and she goes, "You told us that when you got home from school." I go, "Yeah, I know. I'm just saying…" but the truth is I totally forgot. She gave Bob another look that basically said "she's fucking up again." But it got better when Bob said, "We're proud of you, Cam." I mean, not better but less awkward. I was so almost busted. Then Samantha said, "Can I speak to you for a second?" to Bob, which was fine because we were all finished anyway. The boys asked to be excused like little cult members and Samantha said, "Yes, but clear your plates, put everything in the sink. Cammy, put the place mats away. And take out the trash, will you?"

I was in the kitchen stacking the stupid plastic mats Bob brought back from some trip to D.C., the ones with the faces of the presidents in little ovals. When I was little my teacher had us memorize the first ten and I was putting them away trying to do it without looking, but right when I got to Madison I heard Samantha laying into Bob so I moved to the corner of the doorway to the living room so I could hear them better.

"You're always doing that," she goes. "You're always good cop, I'm always bad cop."

"How was I good cop just now?"

"'We're proud of you, Cam,'" she says in a high mimicky voice. "I mean…Jesus. Can't you see what's going on?"

"What? What's going on? Why do I always feel like I'm

being tested on my own kids? Like I don't know them or something?"

"Because you smooth things over so no one fights. So there's no disruption in your bubble world."

"My *bubble* world? What the hell's that supposed to mean? Why don't you *say what you mean,* for God's sake!"

"Just forget it," she says. "The point is, something's wrong with Cammy…"

"Something's *always* wrong with Cammy," he says. "Think about it, when was the last time everything was fine with her?"

I heard Samantha shushing him. The floor squeaked with her coming toward the kitchen doorway to see if I was listening. Part of me wanted to stand there and let her see that I heard everything. But mostly I wanted to go up to my room and zone out. The buzz was starting to fade, so it must've been about six o'clock.

So there it is: *something's always wrong with Cammy.* Perfect.

Samantha

I couldn't sleep last night. At about three in the morning I threw in the towel and got up to e-mail Craig, asking if we could do a Starbucks meeting. Somehow I managed to drift off because when Bob's alarm clock went off it startled me fully awake. There's that moment when you wake up and you've forgotten what it is you're worried about. That happened a few seconds ago. Then I remembered. I check e-mail while Bob's in the shower and now I'm sick at my stomach knowing that in a few hours I'll be telling Craig about meeting Evie at soccer. After lunch. One o'clock. Of course I'll tell Craig I met Evie. I've got to tell him. I do have to tell him, right? Of course. What am I thinking? So the question is…how. Part of me wants to start off being indignant that he kept her beauty from me. My saying it aloud might convince him that *yes, it's true, I am married to a breathtaking woman, so what am I doing here with Samantha?*

The other part of me is afraid. Petrified. He'll be shocked at the collision of his separate lives. He'll look at me like there's a real possibility I could tell her everything. This will inevitably upset the balance in our relationship. He'll become careful with me, careful to keep me happy so I won't tell on him. On us.

I've taken four swigs of Pepto-Bismol this past hour alone. I've changed clothes twice. I'm not sure how I should look: casual, like it's just another story I'll tell him (jeans and a light sweater) or dressyish, like *hey, I'm a grown woman, there's no way I'd blow your cover and by the way I can look good, too* (pencil skirt, black boots, white shirt). I compromise on black jeans, low boots and the same white blouse but untucked. So I'm half and half. Which is how I feel.

I look in the full-length mirror. It's only ten in the morning. I have three hours to kill and a million ways to do it but I don't. I sit on the couch with my hands on my lap like I'm waiting to go into the principal's office. Enough. This is silly. I'll mow through the pile next to my computer. That'll keep my mind off of it.

There's a chain e-mail from an old college friend. Some warning about deodorant and breast cancer. Another friend forwards a joke that promises good luck if you send it to ten friends including the one who sent it to you. Another sends a long-winded story about a little girl dying of cancer whose only wish is to get letters. That girl's been dying for years now, I remember the same plea from a few years back. Maybe the letters kept her alive. Yeah, right.

An e-mail from Ginny reminding us that book club is next week and could she get a count of how many people will be there. I let her know that I'll be there, but otherwise there's nothing else I need to respond to. I return phone calls, I make orthodontist appointments for the boys, I schedule Cammy for a physical.

Somehow it's noon. I nibble on cold leftover spaghetti out of the Tupperware. That's what I'm doing when the front door opens. I jump and freeze right here at the open fridge.

"Hel-lo? Sam?"

It's Bob.

"Oh, my God, you scared the hell out of me," I say, walking to the kitchen doorway to see him jingling his keys onto the front hall table. "What's going on? What's wrong?"

"Why does something have to be wrong?" he says.

"Um, well, because you never come home in the middle of the day. Has something happened? Is everything okay at work?"

"I thought I'd come home for lunch."

"You thought you'd come home for lunch."

"Anything wrong with that?"

We both look at the container in my hand. The refrigerator door is still open. Somehow I feel guilty about eating from the Tupperware. Like he's caught me in the act.

"Want some spaghetti?" I open the cupboard for a plate. "We don't have much else."

I check my watch. It's 12:20. I've got to be out the door at ten of one. He's got to eat fast and go so I can be on time.

"Looks good," he says. He's thrown his tie over his shoulder and scrapes the bar stool back and I realize I'm supposed to be serving him. Like every other time. Today I don't mind because I can hurry it along.

"What do you want to drink?"

"Water's fine."

He doesn't make a move to get anything for himself.

"Seriously, what's up?" I ask. I'm scooping noodles onto his plate. "You want it warmed up?"

"Cold's fine," he says.

"So? What's going on?"

"I had to get out of the office," he says. "They're driving me crazy. I'm supposed to have specs of the shoe we're doing with Cole Haan and I'm not finished yet."

"So you're…here?"

"Why do I get the feeling you don't want me here." It's more of an accusation than a question.

"No no no," I say. I try not to look suspicious or guilty or like I'm in a hurry, which I am. In a hurry, that is. "I'm surprised, that's all."

"I'm glad you're here," he says. He smiles at me. "I wasn't sure you'd be home or running errands or something. This is good."

"It is?"

"Yeah, it is," he says. "Is everything so bad that you can't believe I'm glad to see you? Wait. Don't answer that."

"Funny," I say. "Very funny."

The oven clock says 12:40. Ten more minutes.

"Why is spaghetti better the next day?" he asks. "Have you noticed that? It's always better the next day."

Hurry up. Hurry up. Shovel it in, I've got to get going, for God's sake. Of all days for you to come home, I think.

"Yes, I know," I say.

"I guess I just wanted to sneak out for a few minutes," he says. "I'm not even that hungry. It's getting to be like a pressure cooker there. You wouldn't believe all the shit."

Now? You're talking to me about all this *now?* It's 12:45. Can't you see *I've got to get going!*

"I bet," I say instead. I clear my throat, "Um, I've actually got to get going."

"That's fine. I'll walk out with you."

"But you just got here," I say.

I should feel bad that I'm rushing him. I should be happy he's finally making an effort to talk, even if it's about mundane stuff. I should pull up a chair and listen. This is the kind of conversation that could open up to more. This is the kind of talk I've been begging him for. I should embrace it. I should, at the very least, feel guilty. But I feel none of the above. I want him gone.

I can't risk him following me even by accident. The Starbucks is on the route back to his office so there's a real possibility he'd see me parking there. "Why don't you stay and eat some more."

"Nah, that's okay," he says. "I kind of just wanted an excuse to duck out. What're you up to this afternoon?" he calls from the bathroom off the kitchen. It's 12:48.

Come on, come ON. How long can it take you to go to the bathroom, for God's sake. Hurry up. Hurry *up*.

"Not much," I say back to him. "This and that. Bunch of errands."

He zips up his pants on his way back into the kitchen. It feels like he's moving in slow motion. Instead, I focus on looking laid-back, like *oh I guess I'll get going too*. My heart's beating a drum into my rib cage. I'm never late to meet Craig.

Our jackets are on. Bob pulls the front door closed behind us. We've both parked in front of the house. As we walk down the front steps, Ginny passes with her dog, Harry.

"You guys are such a gorgeous couple," she calls. "Look at you. It's like you've stepped out of a magazine ad."

For a split second I see us as she does. We do look like the perfect couple. To someone else.

"Aren't you sweet," I manage to say.

"I got your e-mail, Sam. So far we've got six coming next week."

It's got to be one by now, from the way my palms are sweating.

"Great," I say. "Let me know if I can bring anything." I whoosh past her while I hit the unlock button on my remote.

"Swear to God, you *are* the perfect couple," she says. "If I didn't love you I'd hate you."

My hand stops at the door handle. I look over at Bob getting into his car, starting it up. *You are the perfect couple* is exactly what I'd planned to say to Craig.

I drive slowly to put distance between Bob and me. Somewhere ahead of me I hear a honk and I'm sure Bob's the target. I cut over to Ashland because I know he doesn't take it, so I can step on the gas. By some miracle I'm only five minutes late.

I park and rush down the sidewalk. At the front door I shade my eyes to look at him through the plate-glass window. I love doing this. Even in a hurry I love to take him in when he doesn't know it. He's at our table. Warming his hands on his cup of coffee. He must feel a stare because he looks out at me and smiles, motions me inside.

I wish I could breeze in and kiss him. Of all the normal things I'd like to do with him—go to the movies, walk in the park in broad daylight, curl up in bed—most of all I want to be able to kiss him hello.

He stands until I slip into my chair.

"Is everything okay?" he asks. "Your e-mail sounded weird. It's never good to hear *we have to talk*. What do you want? Same as usual? Sit sit sit, I'll get it."

I have a few seconds to get nervous all over again. I reapply my lipstick by heart without a mirror. I don't know why but this feels like a pivotal moment. They're playing the new John Mayer CD and I remind myself I want to download it onto my iPod. I listen to it in the car now that Bob installed an iTrip remote. I watch the barista scribble code on the side of the cup even though no one's in line and mine will be made instantly. There's nothing to remember.

"There you go," Craig says. He slides back into his chair. "So? What's up?"

Here goes. I'm aware that I'm thinking that: here goes. I figure it's better to just dive in. Let the chips fall.

"I met Evie."

I'm burning holes into his head, watching for the slightest flinch or twinge. But there's nothing. It's not registering.

"Did you hear me? I met Evie. And Lexi."

It's his daughter's name that shakes him into understanding.

"How? What do you mean you met them?"

"It was at soccer last weekend. She didn't know who I was of course."

"How did you? I mean…" I can see he's trying to find the right questions. He's trying to act normal.

"How did I know it was her? Lexi's ball rolled over to me. I was at the boys' game and I guess her field was the next one over."

He looks down at his cup like he hasn't realized it was there. His wheels are turning. He's trying to decide what to make of this. What to make of me. Oh, God, he's feeling possessive of her. Maybe he's overstated their lack of intimacy. Maybe he does this all the time and he's busted again and he'll get up and say, "It was nice but it's got to end. No hard feelings."

I keep going. "She introduced herself and Lexi. They're beautiful. They're gorgeous actually. They took my breath away."

He looks up at me when I say this.

"I mean, wow. I don't know what I was expecting, but Jesus, Evie's a knockout. It was so weird knowing all about her. For a split second I wanted to ask her if her migraines were getting any better."

Weeks ago he'd told me she'd had blinding ones.

"Remember? You told me she had bad migraines. You're looking at me strangely. I didn't say that to her, by the way. Of course I didn't say that to her!"

I laugh a nervous self-conscious laugh. I try to cover it up by clearing my throat. "Funny, when I saw her I wondered what you were doing kissing me when you have her to go home to. Isn't that funny? That was my first thought."

Goddamnit, say something. How can you leave me twisting in the wind like this. Be a man and say what you're thinking! I don't say this out loud.

"You know what's weird? Meeting Evie, meeting your daughter, I didn't feel the slightest hint of guilt. You're probably feeling it now but I'm not. I know that makes me unattractive, but it's the truth. I should have felt guilt, putting a face to the name and all, but I didn't. I still don't. We're just friends, you and me. All we did was kiss. I mean, that part's not good but it's not like it'll happen again, right? We talked about that. So we're friends. It just felt weird meeting her. Knowing so much about her. And you. You know."

Nothing.

"Here's the part where you jump in and say something," I say.

Maybe this will be the part where he ends it. We'll stop talking. E-mailing. Too risky the way our lives can overlap at the most unexpected times, he's thinking. And he'll end it. This is when I realize that if he's not my friend I'll be heart-broken. I need him in my life. I need him, period. But maybe it'd be for the best. I need to focus on my family…on Cammy. That's right, it'll be for the best. I'll pour all the energy I have for him back into the family. He'll set me free. And it'll be for the best. I'll look back on this and be grateful to him for being the strong one. Then again: Oh, God, he'll set me free and I'll have to go back to my family. Please don't do it, Craig. Please don't send me back. He'll return me for his money back. Thirty-day refund policy. He won't be setting me free, he'll be throwing me away.

"Weird," he says.

"Weird, what? In what way? What do you mean *weird?*" I ask. I'm sounding desperate.

"Just…you know…weird," he says. In a shrug sort of way. In a tone that could go either way.

"Can you say anything more? Like what you're thinking right now? Weird as in weird but whatever, or weird like this is a wake-up call?"

"I don't know," he says. I'm leaning forward like I'm waiting for the jury to read the verdict. I correct my posture—I'd been hunching over the table like Cammy does when she's eating cereal.

"I better go," I say. I say this knowing it will force him to say something of substance. I say this hoping he'll stop me long enough to explain his silence. "I'm gonna get going."

I stand up slowly, to give him time to construct a sentence that will sit me back down.

"Wait," he says.

I lower to the chair quickly. Relieved.

I fight the feeling that I did something wrong in meeting her. Like it was my fault the soccer ball rolled to my feet. I should've kicked it a short way back to her. Smiled and waved. The way you do on sidelines at kids' games. But she walked up to me. It wasn't my fault. I didn't know who she was. How could I have? I never in a million years pictured her like that. Besides: *we're just friends.*

"I don't know what to think," he says. "I don't mean to torture you. I don't. I just don't know. In some ways I think it's amazing this hasn't happened before. We don't live that far away from each other. If we scratched hard enough we'd probably find we know people in common. But it's close to home. Don't take this the wrong way but I guess I feel protective of them."

"Of Evie and Lexi."

"Yeah," he says. Suddenly he doesn't like saying their names in front of me.

"That's cool," I say. I try to stay casual, as if it's not killing me that he's making me feel like the other woman or something. He's feeling guilty. He's feeling guilty and he chose them.

"Listen, I've really got to get going," I lie. "It felt strange keeping this from you. I knew I had to tell you. But..."

I trail off because I don't know what else to say. I'm hoping he'll jump in and tell me I did the right thing in telling him. I want him to ask me to stay a little longer. I want him to work out his feelings and thoughts aloud with me.

"Okay," he says. "I'll talk to you later."

He's lost in his head. He barely notices me sliding into my jacket and walking away.

I walk down the sidewalk to my car. The only space I could get was in the Sportmart parking lot almost three blocks away.

Why do I keep going back and forth? Every time I leave him I resolve to not see him again. This time I think I'll do it. This time I'll break free and I'll throw myself back into my family. Of Bob shuffling through his gloomy days. Of Cammy's troubles that aren't going to solve themselves. I've known that, of course, but I've been powerless. I have bursts of energy to deal with her. Just as quickly, I'm spent. For the love of God, someone please help me.

And then Craig e-mails. Come meet me. And I go back for more.

Here I am, in the smelly staircase up to the third level of the lot. Cigarette butts in every corner. What looks like spilled Coke on the first landing. Urine, too. I'm in a holding pattern. I don't belong in either world. Not in Bob's. Not in Craig's. I'm in limbo, like those dead souls who hover in despair until they go to heaven or hell.

I want to break free and make a decision for myself. I have to. Maybe now's the time.

Cammy

Jamie calls shotgun on his way to Mrs. O'Donnell's minivan. Yeah right. Like I'm really going to let that kid sit up front. It'll be the same as it always is: he races to the door handle and tries to climb in. I pull him out. He's so small it's a joke. I can pick him up with one arm.

Anyway, it's like I can say anything to Mrs. O'Donnell. Well, almost anything. I mean, if she knew what was *really* going on she'd totally tell Samantha so I don't go into *too* much detail but still. Today out of the blue she goes, "Do a lot of kids in your class do drugs?"

At first I was paranoid like does she know about me and is she trying to trap me? She could be a plant for all I know. But then she says, "I didn't mean to make you uncomfortable. I was just wondering."

"No, no, it's totally fine. I mean, you can ask. Um, I guess some kids do. I don't know. I mean, I'm not like *close* to everyone in my grade. Yeah, there's drugs."

"Huh," she says. It's like she's just interested in the information. She's curious. "What kinds of drugs?"

"I don't know. Pot, I guess. Some kids do coke or ex."

"Ex? Is that ecstasy?"

"Yeah," I say. "And mushrooms too." That's when my heart started beating fast. I snuck a look at her to see what she thought of that but she didn't seem shocked. I least I don't think she did.

"Wow," she says. "We're always hearing about it so I guess I'm not surprised. I'm just an old lady now. I had no idea. I mean, I figured pot but not the other stuff. Have you tried anything?"

I felt bad about lying to her but I had to. I told her I hadn't done anything. She seemed to buy it. Then again she switched topics pretty quickly so maybe she didn't want me to have to dig myself deeper into the lie. She probably figures someone who looks like me definitely does something. Everyone looks at me that way.

"Does it take a long time to do your makeup like that?" she asks.

First of all, Samantha would never ask me something like that. She hates my makeup and my clothes. She can't do anything about it but she acts like she can. What's she going to do, hold me down and strip my clothes off? Wash the makeup off my face? Even the school can't force me to wear something else since it's a *suggested* dress code.

Second of all, Mrs. O'Donnell isn't judgmental.

"Yeah, kind of," I tell her. "My skin totally broke out when I first started with the white foundation but now it's gotten used to it, I guess. The eyes take the longest."

"I bet," she says. "How'd you learn to do it that way? Are those black teardrops you drew on?"

"Yeah."

"Why teardrops?" she asks. She doesn't really look over at me. It makes it easier to talk to her.

"I guess I don't want to be fake, you know. I hate fake people."

"So the real Cammy is crying?" she asks. Damn, she's good. Samantha and Bob never ask me this stuff. They're all about *stopping* it not *understanding* it.

I look out the window and watch this woman walking a really fat dog. I mean that dog was obese. She stops every time the dog sniffs something on the sidewalk. She must feel me staring at her from the stoplight because she looks over at me. She looks sad but then—and this was totally weird—when the light turned green, she held up her hand. It wasn't a wave really. Just a hand. What's even weirder is I held mine up to her, too. I'd never seen that woman or her dog before. Just some stranger noticing me.

Mrs. O'Donnell didn't see that. She's sipping her Caribou Coffee.

"So the makeup," she says. Getting me back to what we were talking about.

"Oh, yeah," I say. "I don't know, I mean some of the music I listen to are groups who do makeup like this. It's kind of more than makeup though. People think we're freaks but it's more like a mask you put on. Everyone else puts on a show and acts all fake but you can't tell who's like that and who's not. At least we're honest."

"I never thought of it that way," she says. "Hold that thought. Boys, do you guys want Dunkin' Donuts? We have enough time for drive-through if you want."

"Yeah!" they all say from the back. Mrs. O'Donnell drives a Suburban so there're like fifty people stuffed back there and the noise is insane. That's how we can talk though. No one listens in on us.

"Can I have a chocolate frosting one?" "I want the sprinkles!" "Plain!" "It's honey dipped!" "No it's not." "Yeah it is, my mom says."

"I'm getting plain ones for everybody," she shouts over them.

"Oh, man" "Why can't we get like half chocolate, half plain?" "Yeah, half and half and some with sprinkles!" "Yeah, and a honey-dipped one" "You're such a retard, it's not honey dipped."

"It's plain or nothing," she says. "Tell me now or we'll keep going."

"Plain!"

At the window she orders a baker's dozen so everyone can have two. She knows I won't eat them. I'm trying to eat healthy. She passes the box back and they're like wolves they grab so quickly.

"Two each, that's it!" she says. "If you can't share I'll never stop for doughnuts again."

"So. Where were we?" She turns back to me before pulling out of Dunkin' Donuts. "Hey, I've been meaning to ask you, did it hurt to get your nose pierced?"

"Yeah. But it got better after a couple of days and now it totally feels normal."

"Did your mom and dad get mad at you?" she asks. "No offense but I'd kill my kids."

I looked out the window and for some weird reason I felt like telling her my shit. I was watching some woman with her baby carriage. She was folding the awning of it back so she could check on the baby and then there was this smiley coochy-coo thing and it pissed me off for some reason. She had rattles and plastic toys hanging from above the baby and they both looked so happy and shiny. I bet they look alike. So I told Mrs. O'Donnell.

"They're not my real parents."

We're driving past a dog day-care place called Citizen Canine when she reaches across the center cup holders and pats my hand. I look down and watch it. She keeps it there till we get to the next light. She doesn't say anything and that's good. What would she say anyway? I look out the window so she won't see the teardrop, the real teardrop.

My real mother would do something like that. She'd know that her touch was all I needed right then. She wouldn't get hurt or mad. She wouldn't force me to talk about it, like Samantha would. My real mother would know that this was exactly what I wanted from her.

I sort of wish Mrs. O'Donnell was my real mother.

Samantha

I'm glad Sally Flanders is out of the car-pool business. One day Lynn mentioned she smelled alcohol on Sally's breath when they bumped into each other in the produce section of Whole Foods and that was it. Today it's Lynn, and I wave thanks to her from the window, a signal that I don't have time for her to come in for coffee. Usually I'd go out and wave her inside. That's why my kids are the last she drops off. Her kids have half grown up here. They go right to the snack cabinet with mine. Today I watch the kids come bounding in, Cammy straggling in back. I can see her dreading every footstep that brings her closer to the house.

"Hey, guys, how was school?" I ask the boys.

"Fine. Mom, can I…" The questions bombard me and I say yes to all of them, not really hearing, waiting to have this talk with my daughter.

"Cammy, come sit down," I say.

Listless, she drops her backpack and drags herself over to the kitchen table.

"Oh, God," she says, sighing fatigue and disgust and not a little fear.

"I want to understand all this. I've waited to have this talk because I know you've been sick and I want you to be clear-headed."

She crosses her arms over her already concave chest and slides down the chair. Her jaw is set and her hair forms a wall around her face.

"I'm not fighting with you right now," I say. "I just want you to tell me what the hell's going on."

"Nothing's *going on*," she says. "I screwed up. Big deal. I'm, like, the last one of my friends to even try drugs."

"Well, it was just last week you were skipping down the sidewalk with Lauren when you guys thought no one was looking. You want to know where I've been? I've been in a dreamworld where I thought my kids were out of trouble and healthy and happy. That's where I've been."

"Whatever," she says.

"When's *that* phase going to be over? The *whatever* phase. I can't help you if you won't talk to me. You want out of soccer, talk to me."

Nothing. Just that Goth stare. With the lone teardrop drawn on.

"Fine. Have fun at practice."

"I don't know what you want me to say. What do you want me to say?"

"Anything. Say anything," I tell her.

For a second she looks like a little girl again. Her eyes open wide and there's no trace of sarcasm in them. The little girl who'd run over to me after doing a jackknife from the high board at the pool—*Mom, did you see me? Did you watch?* The girl who loved it when I braided her hair. I hold my breath wanting her to step out of this costume of hers back into the girl who sang along to the Beatles with me in the car.

I still can't take a sip of my coffee, it's too hot. I've got to remember to adjust the temperature of the hot-water dispenser at the sink.

"Am I still under house arrest?"

"You're kidding, right? You'll be under house arrest forever. Consider yourself permanently grounded until you can earn back our trust and until you get rid of this attitude and until you start turning things around. No computer. No cell phone. You'll go to school and come home and that's all you will do until we say different."

"Fine," she mumbles on her way out of the kitchen.

"So that's it? That's all you've got to say?"

"Yep," she calls over her back. "See ya, wouldn't wanna be ya."

"What*ever*," I say.

Geraldine Wilkes. The words, the name, scorches the dry ground between us, though, and besides, I'm not sure yet what to do about that part of the story.

"By the way—" she's back in the kitchen doorway "—I know you talked to my friends last night. You've ruined my life, you know that, right?"

"First of all, *you* have ruined your life, not me," I say. "Second of all, I thought the library-parking-lot kids weren't your friends. You called them *people you know.* You were very specific about that. Yet another lie. Are they Monica's friends, too?"

"I don't know," she says. "I'm not friends with her anymore."

"You're not friends with Monica? Since when? I thought you were like little peas in a pod."

Oops. I stumbled into a hornet's nest and I brace myself for what I know is coming.

Cammy shows restraint at first. An eyebrow shoots up, hair is shaken out of her face, her posture straightens in triumph.

"Peas in a pod. Cute. Typical."

I wait for part two.

"You think you know everything about my life but you don't know *shit*." She volleys this like someone who's not keeping a secret.

Do I tell her I know? Do I shout, I found the letter! I looked her up, too! I know your biological mother is five minutes away! Better not. Not just yet.

"Why the library parking lot, by the way?" I ask her, a forced look of innocence on my face.

"What difference does that make?"

"Just curious," I say. "Why, of all the places in the area to hang out, why would you pick the library?"

"It's empty at night," she says.

"So are about a million other places. The post office…"

"Federal property."

"The hospital," I say.

"The emergency room's open all night, remember?" She might as well be saying "ha!" after each comeback.

"The high school."

"Are you kidding? School property?"

"Okay, smartie," I say. "Why don't you cut to the chase and tell me why the library—just answer the question."

"Because," she says.

"Because why?"

"Just because," Cammy says.

At nine o'clock on the dot I log onto the computer and there is Craig's name.

Sorry about before. Just needed to think. I don't know why but it felt weird. It doesn't anymore. Hope you're having a good evening. And hey…I miss you. Tremendously.

TOY (thinking of you).

Now I can exhale. I e-mail back:

TOY.

Cammy.

Things aren't going well. I think I'm sick. Like mentally sick. I hate my family. Except the boys. I hate school. I hate my friends, if you could even call them friends. Ricky's dumped me. He's been acting like my goddamn parent for so long I think he got sick of it. Anyway, he's changed so much I don't even know who he is anymore. He's even talking about getting his tattoo lasered off. That's what this kid I don't even really know Johnnie said the other night at the parking lot. He told me he saw Ricky coming out of a dermatologist's office and he knows that doctor specializes in tattoo removals because his mom got hers taken off two years ago when she married her fourth husband who's a minister. Johnnie called Ricky my boyfriend and Will did some snorty thing and high-fived Paul. That was weird. I told him Ricky wasn't my boyfriend and I don't give a shit where he was. Johnnie goes *whatever* and flicked his lighter to the apple he made into a bong.

I hate Will and Paul and Johnnie and Monica and this weird-ass chick named Jess who's white but has dreadlocks that reach her butt. She doesn't shave her legs and one night she was so wasted she was dancing around the parking lot barefoot with her arms in the air and even in the near dark I could see a forest of underarm hair. So gross. I think I've said maybe three words to her ever.

I can't sleep and then at about five in the morning I do but it's only for two hours. I'm not hungry anymore. My heart feels like it's skipping beats every five minutes. It makes me short of breath. Last night Will came to the window and I pretended I didn't hear him knocking. I kept my eyes closed and after about five minutes I could hear him say "fucking cunt"—he didn't even try to whisper it—before he climbed back down.

Paul says *motherfucker* all the time. He never laughs. Johnnie says Paul never sleeps. *No one's ever seen him with his eyes closed, man,* Johnnie says. *He's like Yoda.* Will says, *How do you know Yoda didn't sleep?* Johnnie goes, *He's this little gnome dude and little gnome dudes don't sleep.*

I see Paul watching me when the library closes and the workers go to their cars. His head moves wherever mine does. He looks at whatever I'm looking at. He's never asked about it but I know he knows I'm looking for someone. I don't care, really.

I'm quiet but I feel like I'm about to explode and start screaming. When Samantha asks me what I'm thinking I feel like yelling:

It's written all over my face, how can you not see me?

I'm swirling into a vortex of hell!

I hate and I hate and I hate!

I didn't ask to be born!

I wish I'd never been born!

Some crackhead got knocked up and I'm forced into this fucked-up world!

Instead I say, *I'm not thinking anything.* And when she says, *it looks like something's on your mind,* I shrug and she's off my case. Thank God.

Everyone's shiny and sparkly and I'm a black cloud. Heavy

with rain that'll never release. The drops of water clinging to monster clouds woven from tufts of cotton candy bumping into one another. That was a line in a poem I was going to write. Kafka wrote poetry but he burned practically all of it. I want someone to burn this when I'm gone.

I wish I could just disappear. I wish I were dead.

Samantha

"You better hurry up or you'll be late," I say to Bob.

"Why are you so eager to get rid of me?" he asks. "Jamie, chew with your mouth closed, that's gross."

"I'm not eager to get rid of you," I say. "I just don't want anybody to be late, that's all."

"What, do you have a boyfriend or something?" he says. He blows on his coffee while he watches me and I wonder if guilty people have X-ray glasses that allow them to see other guilty people.

"You have a boyfriend, Mom?" "Isn't Dad your boyfriend?" "Mom has a boyfriend!"

"Very funny, very funny," I say. My heart's jackhammering, as Craig would say. I'm aware of trying to act like the idea's preposterous. "A boyfriend's coming over and I'm here in my sweats."

Bob looks up from his cereal bowl and it occurs to me I shouldn't have added that last part. If I weren't guilty I'd have sloughed the whole thing off with a laugh.

"Cam! Mom has a boyfriend!" Andrew announces when Cammy shuffles in, still in her pajama bottoms and ripped-up T-shirt.

"Yeah, right," she says. The only people she's not a bitch to are the boys. At least there's that. She's always been good with them. It's probably the age difference. There's never been competition between the three of them. She's never really complained about babysitting.

"Guys? Get your stuff and get ready, will you?" I say. I've finished packing their crustless sandwiches and Ziplocked baby carrots. I'm out of juice boxes so I throw in the small bottled waters I know will return unopened in their backpacks.

"Cammy? Why aren't you dressed?" Bob asks. He looks at me and raises his eyebrows in a question mark to see if I'm going to weigh in. I return the look with one that says "it's all yours" and I go back to pushing crumbs off the counter into my hand. I try to fold the tops of the cereal boxes, but the kids have ripped into the cardboard, so latching them shut is impossible. I scrunch the plastic bag inside and hope nothing goes stale.

"I'm not going to school," Cammy says. Like it's something we all talked about and agreed on and how could we have forgotten this development in the life and times of Cameron Friedman.

Bob shrugs his jacket on, pulling the cuffs out from under the sleeve of the suit. "And why is that, may I ask? Sam? Did you know Cammy's not going to school?"

"Nope."

I'm pouring milk from cereal bowls down the sink and loading them into the dishwasher.

"I'm just not going," Cammy says, pouring Cheerios into her bowl. She takes out the baking box of Domino sugar and scoops three heaping tablespoons over her cereal. Over at the fridge she shakes the carton of milk.

"Great. The boys used up all the milk," she whines. "There's, like, nothing left for me."

"You can't just decide you aren't going to school," Bob's saying. He's got what a writer would call a *beseeching* look on his face when he looks at me. "You aren't sick so you've got to go. Sam."

"I don't care what Samantha says, I'm not going."

When Jamie hears his sister call me by my first name he takes Andrew's arm and pulls him out of the kitchen into the living room. I don't know if I've noticed this before. Andrew hisses at him to stop pulling him away. He wants to stay and watch. Jamie finally tug-of-wars his brother through the doorway.

I'm aware Cammy and Bob are looking at me like I'm the tiebreaker.

"If Cammy doesn't want to go to school she doesn't have to," I say, shoulders up and down. Cammy tries to mask her surprise with indifference but Bob is flat-out astonished.

"Can I talk to you outside?"

He closes the door behind us. It's chilly out so I probably will have to wear a sweater on top of my blouse. No clouds in the sky, so hopefully it'll be a good hair day.

"What's up?" I look at Bob and he's got his hands on his hips with his legs in a V, Batman style.

"What do you think's up?" Bob asks. "What's going on, Sam? Seriously."

"I honestly don't give a shit if Cammy goes to school today or not."

"Why? What the hell is going on with you?"

"I'm tired of being the only one fighting the fight. I'm tired of trying to figure out why our daughter is unraveling. She's bottoming out and you're missing in action, Bob. You know what? If you want to try to get her to go to school today, be my guest. But I'm out of it."

"I've got to go to work, Sam. Remember? I work?"

"Oh, and I don't is what you're saying."

"I'm not saying that," he says.

"Yeah, you are. You always pull that one out of the hat when you don't want to deal with something."

"I'm dealing with it, Sam!" he says. "I'm *trying* here. I got her onto the soccer team. That wasn't easy, you know. I had to practically bribe the coach with new cleats for the team to get him to take her. I knock on her door and she won't open it. I don't know what else to do. Tell me what to do and I'll do it."

"I could be asking you the same question. Why don't *you* tell *me* what to do? How about that instead of me having to take the bull by the horns every time."

"Mom, Mrs. Lang's here." Jamie pokes his head out the sliding glass door that opens onto the deck. Carol Lang is driving car pool this week.

"Oh, honey, sorry," I say. "Daddy and I just needed to—"

"It's okay, Mom," he says. "Bye."

"Have a good day at school, buddy," Bob says. He waves through the glass at Andrew.

"Okay, so you get the gold medal for being the one to take care of everything. You win." Bob's smile faded in the turn from the boys back to me. "Happy?"

"It's not a competition, for God's sake," I say.

"So why do I feel like I'm being judged?"

"I thought you had to rush to work," I say.

"You got somewhere to be? What, the market has a run on kiwis?"

"Nice. Really nice. Perfect example of how you think I sit around doing nothing all day," I say.

"I'm just saying, you have more time to deal with Cammy than I do right now. I'm so overwhelmed at work it's not funny. This is about the worst time for Cammy to implode."

"I'll tell her she should plan her breakdown at a more convenient time for you," I say.

"You know what I mean," he says. "Stop twisting my words. What I mean is I'm behind on four projects."

"Oh, sorry," I say. "I didn't realize napping was considered a project."

Low blow. I know. I semi-wish I hadn't said it.

He looks down and pushes a clump of dead leaves through a slat in the deck with the toe of his shoe.

"I know about all the naps, Bob."

"I don't have to listen to this," he says.

"You're *depressed* but you won't do anything about it and you know what, I'm at the point where I don't give a shit anymore. Get help, don't get help. Whatever."

"So that's where we are," he says.

"That's where we are."

"I've got to go."

"What about Cammy?"

"If you don't care I don't care," he says.

"We can't take our shit out on Cammy," I say. I don't know why I haven't said this out loud to him before. Maybe I've only just now realized that's what we're doing.

"Yeah, well, you don't seem to give a shit so why should I?" he says.

"I care, Bob. I honestly do. But I'm out here doing this on my own. You're totally depressed. You hate work. You're sleeping all the time. We haven't had sex in almost a year."

"It was ten months a few days ago now it's a year," he says. He throws his hands up.

"So you *were* listening after all," I say. "Funny, I thought you were riveted by the Silvermans' house."

"Will you just get to the point?"

"If you'd just think about seeing someone with me. A counselor. I've got names…"

"*What?* You've got names? You've got names. How did we go from managing the Cammy crisis to seeing a fucking *marriage counselor?*"

"Shh, keep your voice down. It all fits together." This is not exactly how I'd imagined the therapy conversation would go. "If we could band together again. If we could communicate…"

"Here we go." He reaches for the door handle.

"Wait! Wait. Okay, okay, we don't have to get into it now. I know you have to go. Just wait. Let's figure this out."

"I'm done. You want to go to therapy, go to therapy. I'm not going. I happen to think we're fine. You've got a problem with your life, go talk your head off with someone. I'm sick of hearing about how I'm coming up short."

I haven't actually thought about marriage counseling in a while. I threw it out there to get credit. Like later on down the road I can say I tried everything. This is the dance we do now. Back and forth. Me trying and giving up, Bob trying and giving up. This is me now. Back and forth. Forgetting my family, remembering my family. The one thing I'm not back and forth about is Craig.

Cammy.

I found out who she is. There's a wall for peeple who have medils…wait, what the hell am I writng? I'm so fcked up rite now I can't type. Theres bird nests out front and little babies birds peeping and I want carmals to chew on. Oh man I am so wastd.

I found out which 1 she is. Aktually Paul did. Fcking Paul. He's a scumbag. I had no idea he knew about her but then last nite he comes up + sez he knows. I should aske him how he found about about the serch. I'll rewrite this latr. I've gotta crash. The wind is taking the subway in a city I dont know. Note to self…don't erase this tomorrw. Fuckng hilarius. Six seven eight nine ten one two…

OMG I just read what I wrote last night and I almost erased it but what the hell. So hilarious. Paul's deal was worth it but I think it screwed me up. It hurts to go to the bathroom. Plus I have a bruise where my butt hit the seat belt in the backseat. And my pants weren't all the way off so there's a rash on my ankles. I don't see why anyone ever wants sex. Especially in the places he did it to me. It was like a porno or something. Monica never told me how much it hurts back there. This morning I found blood on my pajama bottoms. I'll throw them out in the Dumpster behind school. It's too risky to throw them out here. The normal sex didn't hurt half as much.

At least now I know which one she is. I told him I knew already and he busted me when he goes, "Yeah? So which one is she? Here they come. Point to her." I pointed to this old lady who was the stupidest choice since she's like old enough to be my grandmother. I asked him how he knew I was looking for my real mother and he just blew me off like *everyone knows,* but I know for a fact no one but Ricky knows. Then again I tried talking to Will about it but he said he doesn't talk parent-shit. I feel bad I even brought it up with him since his parents were so fucked up. Now that I think about it I may have told Will her name. I'm always kind of out of it when I'm around Will, so there's a chance I got that much out.

Anyway, Paul asked me why I didn't just go in and ask who Gerry Wilkes is and I told him the truth: that I'm scared shitless. Whenever I've walked up to the front door my mouth goes dry and my heart skips even more beats, so I have to hold my left side because it's shooting pains now all the time. The only time I feel weak from hunger is when I walk up those steps to that glass door with the metal bars pushing into the main reading room. Plus I don't want her to see the bald spots where my hair's fallen out. Not that she'd care but still. I don't tell Paul any of that part but he was looking so nice, like a shrink would. He's asking me what I'm so scared of and I'm trying to come up with an answer when he goes, "I know which one she is."

"Bullshit you do," I say back. I have this habit of biting my fingers. Not my fingernails but the skin around them. Sometimes they get bloody. When he said that, I was holding my second finger to stop the bleeding. I guess I didn't wash my hands when I got home because I have brown cracked blood on my thumb. I don't even know how I got home after. I might have walked. I only have one of the shoes I wore. And my zipper on my pants is ripped. And the back of my hair is matted into rat's nests.

So he goes, "Let's get out of here and I'll tell you which one she is."

"How? You'll describe her?"

"Yeah. I'll describe her."

"Why can't you just tell me here?" I ask him.

"I do something for you, you do something for me."

"No way," I say.

"You're so pretty. I've been watching you forever. I think I'm falling for you."

"You don't even know me."

Sure enough he was totally lying about falling for me because he stood up from the ledge that looks out at the guys who were skateboarding at the time. He stood up and said, "Let's just get outta here."

"How about you tell me who she is and I promise I'll go with you after."

He laughed and I remember he said "pinkie swear" and I started to hold out my little finger and he goes, "oh my God you're so retarded." The only times I'm happy I have olive skin is when my cheeks burn. It's hard for anyone to tell that I'm blushing.

"What the fuck," he says. "Okay, we'll do it your way. She's the one who always wears short skirts. She's got fucking killer legs. Not much of a rack. But motherfucker she's hot."

"Does she have long hair or is she the one with curly hair?"

"Her hair's straight. Down to here." He holds his hand to my shoulder and it was sweet the way he did that. I thought he might have been using it as an excuse to kiss me since he could've held his hand up to his own shoulder but since the Ricky thing I didn't make any kind of move in to him.

Then he goes, "She's the one who looks like she's black but she isn't. She's like half and half."

For some reason when he told me who she was I felt nothing. I mean, this huge mystery's solved finally! After so long. The minute he said it I wanted to go home to my room and think about it. That's the only thing I was thinking: how good it would feel to be in my bed staring up at the ceiling listening to music. So I got up to go. I forgot my deal with Paul.

I remember weird things about last night. And the sound of him running up behind me. Weird. I remember how he called me a bitch when he reached me before I got to the main street at the end of the library but I don't remember whose car he shoved me into. I don't remember him dragging me back up to the lot but in my head all I can picture is my shoes rattling along the pavement and I think that's probably how I lost one of them. There are a lot of pebbles on the cement so my foot got cut up. I can see that now, I mean. I think my brain shut down during it. I remember the sound of my voice going *you're hurting me* but I don't remember what he did about it. I can't remember unlocking the front door when I got home but I can remember saying my address out loud a couple of times.

I hate my life. RAGE COMPANY. R.C. I fucking hate my life.

I just want to tune it out. It's all noise. I wish my head could be still and I could be blank inside for more than a minute at a time. The sounds are killing me. I seriously think I'm more fucked up than I first thought. Is there anybody out there?

Samantha

I've checked and I get a full signal so Craig hasn't tried to call my cell phone. Besides, I've been holding it so there's no chance I missed a call. He's never late. And he made a point of telling me not to be late. Fifteen minutes is a chunk of time I wish we hadn't lost because we only have an hour and a half together. I've got to get to the cafeteria by six-thirty to sign up Andrew and Jamie for Boy Scouts. Fifteen minutes feels like an eternity. I'm trying not to think the worst but I have these flashes of her stumbling upon his e-mail asking why he has so many from me.

"Who's Samantha Friedman?" Evie'd ask, not remembering we met at the park.

"Her? Oh, just a random friend," he'd tell her.

"She e-mails you a lot for just being a friend," she'd say. She'd try to click on one of my e-mails but he'd stop her, which would make her suspicious so he'd say:

"Oh, please. If you could see her you'd know."

"I know all your friends," she'd say. "How come I've never heard you mention her?"

By now I know we're not *just friends*. I replay our kiss so many times it's frayed in my mind. We moved in toward each other slowly. The air was charged like back in high school and I could barely breathe. Then, after our lips met and slightly parted, with his hand cupping my face he pulled back and said, *You're the best thing that's ever happened to me, Samantha Friedman.*

It was like a movie. Just like a movie.

I said, "That's not true. Lexi…"

My hand was on his thigh like it was something I always did. He kissed me again and said, "After Lexi. After her you're the best thing."

We felt each other's faces. We breathed into each other's mouths so we didn't have to break from kissing. Maybe it was ten minutes.

We shifted back into our seats and I turned to him and said, "We can never do this again."

He stared ahead at the lake. I got out of his car and back into mine. Five minutes later, at a red light, I fixed my hair in the mirror on the back of the visor. I put lipstick back on. I touched my cheek. I wondered if he thought my skin was soft. I wondered what he was doing. He hadn't started his car when I pulled away. He'd just sat there.

"Hey, sorry I'm late." He is breathless. The outside air clings to him.

"I was starting to worry," I say. "Everything okay?"

He's looking cagey and nervous. I feel my muscles start tensing up. He looks over his shoulder before he pulls the chair out and sits down. He doesn't take off his coat. I grip the edge of the table. She found out. He probably told her he had to run an errand.

When Craig leans across the table toward me all I can hear is a faraway ringtone version of "Staying Alive" and I turn in my seat to see whose cell phone is ringing. The song's getting to the falsetto chorus and it *still* hasn't been answered. I turn back to him and realize I want to be the one to break our hearts.

"Oh, God, wait," I say. A sourness in my stomach combined with lack of oxygen makes me feel like I am about to faint. "Wait a second."

"Sam…"

I am sucking in air like a goldfish out of the bowl. It crosses my mind this is not an attractive thing to do but I can't seem to help it.

"Are you okay? You want some water? I'll be right back…"

Wait! I want to call out to him. *Don't go! Every second counts! I don't care about water or your coat still being on! Come back! Tell me what's happening! Tell me why I can't seem to get enough air into my lungs!*

"Here," he says, holding a cup the Starbucks guy filled from the tap they use to rinse out the blenders.

I sip but I'm not sure I swallow the water or if it trickles out of the corners of my mouth.

"Just take a deep breath," he says.

"Tell me what's going on. What's happening?" I ask.

"She knows."

"I knew it," I say. "I *knew* it—I was thinking it before you came in. She found out about the kiss. Did someone see us or something?"

"I told her," he says. "Last night."

He's looking at me, wanting a reaction, but it doesn't compute. I nearly have to shake my head clear of it like a cartoon character.

"Oh, my God," I manage to say.

He is nodding his head.

"You *told* her?"

He looks down at his hands in his lap.

"Did you tell her we're just friends? I mean, we're just friends. You told her that, right? Did you tell her that?"

"No."

"What then?"

"I just told her. I couldn't take it anymore. It came out."

"Oh, my God, Craig. *Oh my God.* What the hell? You couldn't take it anymore? What does that even mean?"

I can see he's drawing a deep breath, about to launch into a play-by-play. He's come clean about the kiss and getting close to me and they're going to counseling and they'll reconcile and be even stronger because of it and la-di-da-di-da the sky will be bluer and the grass will be greener. I should want this for him. I should release him to his wife. Release him to his wife. Let him put his life back together. I'm unhealthy for him and even though it doesn't feel that way, I suppose he is unhealthy for me. I want him to be happy. I have friends already, I don't need him. I have Lynn. I can see more of her and that'll be great. I'm glad for him. Really. Glad. Happy happy happy.

"Wait, where're you going?" he asks. I am standing. I'm trying to put on my coat but one sleeve is inside out so it's more complicated than it needs to be.

"I've got to go" is all I muster. My hand gropes through my purse for the car keys. Where are my fucking keys?

Thirty seconds later the entire contents of my purse pour out onto the hood of my car. A lipstick rolls off onto the pavement, a tampon shines brightly in the middle of the mess and there, tangled up in a fistful of receipts and the white cord to one of the kids' iPods, there are my keys. I scoop everything back into my bag and as I walk around to the driver's side I feel his hand on my arm.

"You forgot this," he says, holding out my lipstick. "Sam, I told her I was leaving her. I can't live like this anymore. I'm in love with you and I can't not have you in my life. Sam? Do you hear me?"

I've never littered before but the travel pack of Kleenex is on the ground in a half puddle and I've decided I'll leave it there. Then his words make sense in my head. Like I'd needed to look at the Kleenex to figure them out.

"Wait, what? What did you just say?" I ask this because I want to be sure I'm not imagining things.

"I'm in love with you," he says. "And I can't stay in a marriage that's killing me."

Oh, Jesus. Oh, God. What the hell happens now?

I'm back to confusion and pressure to come up with something to say. The more I try to wrap my brain around this the less I can. "I don't know I don't know I don't know..." I say over and over again.

"Look, I should've said something but I honestly didn't think I was going to do this right now specifically because I hadn't talked about it with you. But Evie and I got in a massive fight and I started and once the words were out I felt this tremendous relief. She said she'd been suspecting something for a while. It's messy, I know. And it'll get worse before it gets better. But all I know is this one thing—I want to be with you."

"I'm going to go now," I say. "I've got to think about this. It's too much to take in. I've got to...I've got to think."

"Okay," he says. "Okay."

When I open my car door he stops me. "Just tell me, do you want to be with me? Even if you don't know what to do right now, do you at least want to be with me? Look at me."

"Don't. Don't do this," I say. I start up the car and drive away with my purse still on my shoulder.

Cammy

I got hammered last night at Dave's party. I don't even know how I got back into my room without anyone finding out I left. Will came by and I finally stuck up for myself. I was already kind of wasted on some yellow pill I got from Paul and when Will tapped on the window I could barely lift it open. It's one of those old windows with peeling paint and I think someone painted it shut a long time ago because it sticks and it's hard to open even if I'm not stoned off my ass.

Anyway, Will climbed in and I was like, "Let's get the fuck out of here."

And he was all: "Some guy Dave's having a party. His parents are away and everyone's there. Your girlfriend's there."

"What girlfriend?"

"That freak Monica something. She's hooking up with like everyone."

Every time we hook up Will's nice until we get high and he gets a BJ so I knew he'd take me to the party.

The branches scratched my legs on the way down. I almost lost it and started cracking up but I pulled it together and we took off in his car. He got his license six weeks ago. I told him that was cool and congrats and then, stupidly, I went and put

my arms around him and he was like *what the fuck're you doing?*
Whatever. I saw him with Stinky Ross the other day. Ricky
and I call her Stinky because she wears so much of this shitty
perfume that smells like roses mixed with mothballs. She smells
like the inside of a grandmother's closet. You can smell her
coming from a mile away. Anyway, Will and Stinky were
walking and he had his arm around her with his hand in her
back pocket. They walked by me in the hall and I thought he
saw me but it was between classes so it was crowded and he
didn't say anything when he walked by so maybe he didn't
notice me standing there by my locker.

So it's been six weeks since Will got his license and this was
the first time I drove with him. Turns out he's worse than Bob.
He doesn't stop for stop signs. I said, "You know that was a stop
sign back there, right?" and he goes, "What're you my
mother?"

We had all the windows down on our way to Dave's and it
felt like a wind tunnel but in a good way.

We walked up to Dave's house and someone was puking into
the front bushes but otherwise you couldn't really tell people
were over. Inside they were playing old Doors music. There
was Monica, sucking back her green Gatorade she spikes with
vodka or whatever she can get. Monica's always got Gatorade
with her. The first thing I saw at the party was her Gatorade.
She came over a few days ago. I called her when Samantha was
out somewhere. I did *67 so my caller ID didn't show up.
Maybe that's why she picked up. I'm so freaking bored under
house arrest. She came over to the house and the first thing
she says is:

"Where's the liquor cabinet?"

I showed her and she didn't even ask, she just took the
whole bottle of vodka.

"Nothing's been opened," she says. "Are your parents Amish or something?"

"Wait," I said, "*I'm* gonna get nailed for this, not you."

"It's a new bottle," she says. She barely makes a face when she swigs the vodka. She used to but now you'd think it was water the way she's drinking it. "They'll forget they even got it. They won't suspect you by the time they go for it."

"They don't forget things like that," I tell her.

"Are they having a party?"

"No."

"Do they have cocktails at night after work?"

"No. Well, my dad has scotch but that's in the kitchen. He'd totally know if the scotch was missing."

"So you won't get caught. They won't open the liquor cabinet for like months and they'll forget they restocked in the first place."

"How do you know they won't open it?"

"Every bottle in here is dusty. It's like where bottles go to die in here. When did you get so *fucking* paranoid?"

"I'm fucked up. Paul's weed is so strong and I get all freaked out if I smoke too much."

"Cool," she says. She pours some of the bottle into her Gatorade and puts the lid back on to shake it up. "I'm outta here."

"You just got here," I say.

"It's soul-crushing in here. There's nothing to do."

"We could get fucked up and we could watch a DVD."

"What about your mom?"

"I've got a lock on my door and plus she never comes in," I tell her. "I got some good shit from Paul."

"You've gone all Cobain," she says. "They said you were a pill freak but I didn't believe them. Good little Cameron Friedman."

"Shut up. Besides, my last name's Wilkes now."

"Friedman, Wilkes, what's the difference?" she said. She went up the stairs before me and since she didn't ask me I didn't tell her I'd just decided to take my real mom's name that morning. I haven't told Samantha and Bob yet.

I think we watched a Will Ferrell movie but I'm not sure. I don't even remember her leaving. I woke up when Jamie came in to get me for dinner and there was a string of drool to my sheets. I blew off dinner and no one seemed to notice. Sweet.

Anyway, this party at Dave's. Most people were passed out already and Paul was there asleep with the needle still in his arm. I said Will should loosen the rubber band but he was like *it's his fucking problem* so I went and did it. Then I went back to find Will but he'd disappeared. I looked around for him for a couple of minutes. Or maybe it was an hour. I don't know. I crashed on the couch Jess was curled up on. After zoning out for a while I got up to go find him because I was tired and kinda wanted to go home but not like in a baby way, more just that I wanted to sleep in my own bed and not next to Jess who kept kicking her legs in her sleep. I went upstairs and there's Monica giving Will a blow job. There's the Gatorade on the floor next to her. Her hair was all messed up in the back. She was on her knees and the soles of her bare feet were facing up and they were like caked with black. Like she walked on coal.

I went back down and Paul was awake. Even though the last time I saw him he like pretty much raped me, I went over. He scooted over to make room for me and it felt good to curl up next to him. I was cold by then, I remember shivering and he put his arm around me and I didn't want to move because I wanted us to stay that way all night. He was all dreamy, his eyes were glossy and he leaned forward to cut white powder.

"It's a new needle, I'm the only one who's used it and I'm

clean so it's basically new," he said. "Don't worry. You'll love it."

He didn't pull the rubber band too tight but it stuck to my skin and pinched anyway. I watched him like it was a science experiment. The lighter under the spoon. The boiling liquid. The syringe pulling it in. The tapping with his thumb and first finger. Him touching the inside of my arm, rolling a vein, patting it. Right as he leaned in I thought of Dr. Dann, the kids' doctor I used to go to. The bowl of lollipops at the counter was always full but they weren't the good ones with Tootsie Roll inside. Still. Blocks, toy fire trucks and *Highlights* magazines all around the waiting room. The last time someone patted a vein on my arm was when Samantha took the three of us to get tested for lead poisoning. The boys had their fingers pricked but I had to have a regular shot because I was old enough. Now it's Paul the burn boy sticking the needle into me. Maybe it's the same vein Dr. Dann used. Wouldn't that be weird, I thought. When I woke up he was on top of me. Right there on the couch. In front of everyone. His sweat dripped onto my face and he was grunting. I think I passed out again because I totally don't remember anything else.

Samantha

I have Damien Rice's "Cold Water" playing over and over in my ears. I'm shaking uncontrollably even though it's warm in the bedroom. It's a fluish shivering, where your bones throb and ache and your skin gets clammy. Your teeth chatter under the thickest comforter. I'm lying on my side on the bed, hugging my knees, and I still can't warm up.

I must've dozed off—suddenly Bob's towering over me. I take out one ear:

"What's wrong?" he's asking. He says it like he's impatient to get to the point of why he came in.

"I don't feel well."

"What's the matter?" He looks genuinely concerned.

"Nothing. I just want some alone time."

"Oh. Okay. Well, when you're done, can you come sign the taxes? I want to get them in the mail tomorrow so we don't have to wait until April or May for a refund."

He pads off in his Birkenstocks that have perfectly formed to his feet.

"Cold Water" has started over again.

This is what it's come to. A decision I think I always knew I'd have to make. Craig did it. He took the leap. He got himself out and he loves Lexi as much as I love my children. It's no different. If he can do it, I can, too. And maybe it'd be better for the kids. I've seen the way Jamie shrinks when Bob and I talk to each other. Andrew would adapt to just about anything. Cammy will be Cammy and frankly I wonder if she wouldn't do better without Bob. At least temporarily. I could concentrate on her. I could work on her instead of trying to breathe life into a dying marriage.

I could be alone for a while. I could be a better mother. Craig and I could date. Like real dates. We could do normal things like go to the movies. Restaurants. Out with friends. Lynn would like him. So would Mike, even though he'd pretend not to out of allegiance to Bob.

Otherwise I'll have to give up Craig. He's forced a choice I'd wanted him to make. I guess I never thought it'd come down to me. How can I live without Craig? How can I go back to the way things were before we met? But sharing the kids with Bob? Handing them over every other weekend. I see those couples in the McDonald's on Foster with the indoor playground. Overnight bags and backpacks dumped into the backs of other cars. The couples try to hide the tension when the kids run over to ask if they can do the highest slide. Or the twisty one. The parents force smiles and say *sure* because neither one wants to be unpopular. I can't be one of them.

But life without Craig? Unimaginable. Waiting until this marriage disintegrates like a piece of paper floating on the lake? Unthinkable. But that's what we're doing. We're sinking.

Cammy.

It's that almost-dark before the streetlights flicker on, the twilight where you can see figures moving but if you were throwing a pitch in the street you wouldn't be able to see the ball. Kick the can dark.

Stop pulling me. Get your hands off of me. Am I saying this out loud? I can't hear my voice. I can't recognize whose talking. Where am I? Can anyone hear me?

Behind my head it's warm and wet. I can feel it. Stop lifting me up. Why can't I say that out loud? Someone's pulling at my shoulders but my head flops back. Stop or it'll snap off like an old-fashioned doll's popping out of its torso.

I can't open my eyes but I can hear blurred words floating somewhere near me.

"Talk to me," it's saying. *The shadow over me. It's not a shadow it's the sound a blob would make. Charlie Brown's teacher waughwaugh-waugh.*

"The ambulance is on its way. Stay awake. Stay with me."

If I could just be left alone I could sleep. God, I'm so tired. Soooo tired. Let me be. Just back off, whoever you are. Can't you see I'm floating? Can't you see I'm dying? Finally…

"I'm lifting you into my car," it's saying. "We're not going to wait for the ambulance. It's taking too long. My car's right here. The door's open so all we have to do…"

Just leave me here. I'm in my bed, right? Why are you taking me out of my bed? It's cold. I'm so cold. I can't stop shivering. Where's my blanket? Why is my bed so hard? Wait, I'm in my bed, right? Or am I?

"I'm going to lift you," it's saying. "I'm going to get you in the car. The front of you first. On three. One–two–three…"

Ahhhhhh! Stop! Don't move me. Get your hands off of me. Can't you see I'm dying?

"That's good, that's good," it's saying. *Waugh-waugh-waugh.* "Now I'm going to pull you in from the other side. We'll get you in, I promise. Almost there."

I hear your footsteps. I can hear you. Why can't you hear me? Why aren't you listening to me? Can't you hear me? I'm talking to you!

Now we're moving. Or I'm floating. Bumpy-floating. I can see myself from above. I'm crinkled into the backseat of a car. My legs, even though I can't feel them, my legs are folded into a V against a door.

And the voice won't stop. It's a play-by-play.

"We're only a block away. Almost there. Now we're turning at the Exxon station. Here we go. Nice and gentle. I'm going through the light at the orthodontist office at the end here. If they stop me I'll finally have an excuse."

There's a laugh. A blob laugh. Shrek. Or a freak from Lord of the Rings. Mad Max. Matrix. *Blob. Blob blob blob. What's so funny, blob?*

Here's me saying Rage Company with Ricky chiming in.

SNAP: Andrew's and Jamie's faces when I tried on my soccer clothes: they're pumping their fists in the air like they'd been waiting all their lives for me to play soccer with them.

I'm dying. I'm not scared. I thought I'd be scared but I'm happy. It's a relief. I'm trying to tell you this. Can't you hear me? I'm happy now.

SNAP: It's the weight of Ricky's head on my lap under a gnarled Alice in Wonderland weeping willow.

Oh, my God, it's really happening. I'm dying.

SNAP: It's Dad letting me sleep in my new sneakers, tucking me in after stories and lullabies and good-night kisses. The look on his face when I told him I loved my new shoes and thank you so much Dad they'll make me run faster you know.

This is how it happens. This is how you die.

SNAP: It's Mom. Sitting on the couch watching the *The Wizard of Oz* with me on her lap, like it was the first time and not the fiftieth time she'd seen it. Her hand smelling like lilac, holding me into her chest when the Flying Monkeys flapped down and grabbed Toto. Talk to me, Cammy. That's all she wanted to do is talk to me. I couldn't do that for her.

Learning to ride a two-wheeler. Our old beagle, Felix, licking my face with his sandpaper tongue. Mom's pancakes. Playing Barbies with Hannah, my best friend in lower school.

Wait. There's more. Wait, just let me think of it. So much more to say. To remember. Wait, let me…

Let me think of some more.

Do they know I love them? Please let them know I love them.

This is how it happens. This is an overdose. I thought it would be fast if it happened. I thought people just passed out and didn't feel anything.

I'm dying. This is how you die.

Samantha

The phone rang a little after eleven at night. Shocking me bolt upright. I answered it quickly like it was the middle of the day and I'd been waiting for a call. This is how it happens, I remember thinking. This is how you get terrible news.

"This is Swedish Covenant," the voice said. I struggled to understand the words. *Swedish Covenant?* I don't think I said anything out loud.

"The emergency room," the voice said.

I knew it but I had left my body by then. I was watching myself from the ceiling.

"Who is it?" he asked from his side of the bed. The man I am married to. My husband, I thought. That is my husband's voice. He is about to be split in half, too, I thought. He'll leave his old self behind and we'll both be half of who we used to be. That's what I was thinking.

"Your daughter was brought in a few minutes ago," the voice said.

"Cammy?" I heard my question. *Cammy?* I asked. As if I had another daughter.

"What's wrong?" Bob pulled at my sleeve. I looked over at him.

I was holding the phone to my ear. Somehow I'd sat up. Against the headboard. I was sitting up as if we were watching TV.

"Sam, what is it?" I know he was saying the words out loud but all I saw was his mouth moving.

The phone dropped out of my hand. Bob fumbled to hang it up, reaching across me to put it back in its cradle. I looked at his arm stretched across my breasts. Foreign. Someone else's arm across someone else's breasts. Then, suddenly, we were fluid. Moving. Like this was a drill we'd been doing for years. Somehow I had sweatpants on. A sweater on top of my sleep T-shirt. Boots from the front hall closet. Somehow I was ready to go. Bob was moving around, scrambling too. I had entered a dream state. A waking nightmare.

Then Lynn was standing in the front hall in her coat over her pajamas saying *go, go, I've got it from here. Call when you know anything.* Then Bob and I were in the car. Then we were driving through all the red lights. At that hour some were blinking.

By the time the car screeched into the hospital parking lot the transformation was complete. The other me stepped out into the night. The new me ran across the lot in through the sliding glass doors of the E.R.

Then we were standing in the fluorescent light at a nurses' station. Listening to the doctor. The hollow me looking over his shoulder at an intern heating up leftovers.

This is what it will feel like from now on, I stood there thinking. I looked at a hand on my shoulder and wondered whose it was. I traced it up the arm then shoulder then the head of my husband. My husband's hand on my shoulder. This is what it will feel like forever.

When he said, "We're so sorry…" I finally focused on his face. I looked at this doctor who was so sorry. Sorry for what? I wanted to ask. Sorry that it happened? Sorry we weren't good enough parents to keep it from happening? Sorry sorry sorry. The word bounced in my head like a pinball.

"What happened?" I heard myself asking. "What are you saying?"

I felt Bob trying to lead me to a chair. I felt all their eyes on me, like *my* reaction would determine how this would go.

"But I don't want to sit down." I looked at Bob, bewildered that he'd suggest it, though everyone wants to sit down for bad news. I can't blame him for that.

"She had most likely slipped into a coma before she even got here," the doctor was explaining it further. Was that supposed to ease the pain for us? "We administered CPR and attempted to pump her stomach, but…"

He purposely trailed off. He avoided having to say the sentence again.

"But *what?*" I heard my words echoing down the white hallway. "But what? *What the hell are you saying?*"

Bob stepped into my field of vision. "Sam…" He spoke softly.

So I asked him: "What are they talking about? *I don't understand these words.*"

I hear a siren in the distance and I wonder if she heard them from the emergency room while they did CPR on her. Did she feel the pain of strong hands trying to beat air back into her lungs? Did they try everything?

She had enough Vicodin in her system to kill a horse, the toxicologist said. He hadn't put it that way at first. We'd asked him to translate the numbers he referred to on his clipboard. Her alcohol level was within normal limits. There was Oxy-Contin in her system but it appeared not to have been ingested at the same time. It'd been consumed earlier, maybe only by a few hours. The vomit was difficult to ignore when they lifted the sheet back. It had dried in her hair. I wondered what she'd eaten even though I knew food wasn't what made her sick. But what was the last thing she ate? Did she enjoy the taste of it? They had wiped her skin up but there was a little blood still caked toward the back of her right shoulder. They said she'd fallen, that she'd suffered abrasions at the base of her skull, that she'd hit the corner of the metal Dumpster on her way to the pavement. Some pebbles remained near embedded on the palms of her hands. Her lips were blue like someone had smeared frosted lipstick on them.

Drained of blood and soul, her skin had a pallor. It was gray. Pasty. Far from the Mediterranean olive she hated so much. She was pale.

She finally matched us.

I heard a moan. A howl. Like a werewolf. I covered my ears to drown it out but somehow that made it louder. I felt myself shaking. I felt my teeth chattering. The moaning ricocheted off the hospital walls. It wouldn't end. Nurses were rushing forward. That's when I realized I was the one howling. The moans were coming from my mouth. I felt hands in my armpits lifting me off the floor I wasn't aware I'd sunk to. Tissues were wiping my face and I realized my cheeks were wet from tears.

One Week Later

I found her journal a few hours after the sedative wore off. I tore through her room looking for whatever we'd missed. I reached in the pockets of the army pants she wore and pulled out a frayed book of matches. Only two left. A receipt for Snapple from the 7-Eleven. A crumpled dollar bill.

Her black skirt balled up and tossed to the corner of the room like it's in a time-out. The top corner of the Marilyn Manson poster curling in.

The journal. At first I thought it was a textbook. It was covered in a brown grocery-bag cover. She'd called the sparkly ones at office stores *retarded*. She'd drawn all over it like she had every other schoolbook. She'd traced her hand. I held mine patty-cake against it. Hers was smaller. Thinner. Delicate. I started crying thinking about those parking-lot pebbles and how it must have hurt to hit the ground full on. Once again I found myself on the floor. On the shag carpet she wanted replaced. I couldn't even do that for her. It wouldn't have cost that much…her room is the smallest. I wouldn't replace the *stained shag carpet she begged me to change.*

It took me an hour to read her journal. She didn't put the date on a lot of entries. Arrows pointed everywhere. So some early ones were in the back, some in front. It was impossible to find a rhythm. Some pages I had to read two or three times before I made sense of them. Some I could date from content alone.

I'm pretty wasted right now. But not too bad. Last night was an okay night. How bad could a night be when you get to pet a kitten? Seriously. It's hard to feel like shit when you're holding a tiny furry thing that's motoring just because you're petting it. And when you think about it, shouldn't we be the ones purring? And this is a total stoner thing to say but if you think even harder, isn't purring a fucking miracle? It's like your insides are smiling.

Wow. That's some deep shit. I sound like such a retard.

Paul found this tiny orange kitten at the far edge of the lot. It was wandering around a beaten-down bed of weeds next to a rotting Dunkin' Donuts cup.

"It was like he was in a pinball machine," he said.

"What're you, the frigging humane society?" Banana Smith said. I have no idea why he's called that but his last name isn't Smith, I know that much.

Paul's the kind of guy who doesn't have to tell people to shut up. They just do. He's that kind of cool. He was holding the kitten in the crook of his arm. Like a natural. Like he did it every day.

"Can I hold it?" I walked up to him holding my hands together like back when I went with my friend Olivia to her church and we went up to get wafers.

"Yeah, for a minute," he said.

Banana Smith came over to me and petted it too roughly.

"Dude," he said over his shoulder to Paul. "Let's get it high."

I twisted my shoulder around so he'd stop touching it.

"No, better one," another kid said. "Give her this. Let's blow her mind, man."

And that was it. I tucked the kitten in close and ran back home. I was wearing a hoodie with a hand warmer built in and she fit perfectly in there. I held her gently so she wouldn't bounce while I ran. I slowed down when I was sure no one was following me.

It was hard keeping her from waking everyone up but I kept stroking her until she fell asleep right next to my head on my pillow. I slept with my clothes on. If she mewed I'd start petting her again and she'd fall back asleep. I couldn't believe my luck. To have this tiny little creature right here, nestled up to me. I didn't want to fall asleep.

It was a different story keeping the boys from finding out in the morning.

"Mom! Mom! Cammy's got a kitten!"

"Can we keep it?"

"Mom!"

"Dad, did you see Cammy's kitten?"

"Cammy, let me hold it, Andrew, I called it!"

"Mom, why does Cammy get a kitten and I don't get a dog?"

"Can we keep it?"

"It's totally not fair. I want a dog."

That's the kind of thing I deal with every day. They're total tattletales. Samantha said Bob has allergies and we can't keep it. Even when

I said I'd keep her in my room so he wouldn't even know she was there, Samantha didn't let me. The boys named her Mia after the only girl they could think of who was half-decent. Mia Hamm. Soccer player. I fed Mia with an eyedropper for a few days. Then Samantha came home and said she found a home for her. Some family with a kid named Lexi. They renamed her Fluffy, which is more retarded than Mia. She says they love her.

I'll never forget that night when her little head was right up against mine on my pillow and we slept together on and off through the night. It's like we were in it together, Mia and me. So gay to write but it's true.

She may be with another family or whatever but at least she's not getting high with Banana Smith in the library parking lot. Thank God for that.

Then there was this:

DEAR GERRY WILKES:
HOW COULD YOU DO THIS TO ME?

My wailing was so loud Bob came running. All week long I'd cried, but he'd kept a distance. His pain was his pain. Mine was mine. On the floor in Cammy's room, holding her journal, the wailing broke through to him. I felt him reaching for me to pull me up but I wouldn't let him.

"You *bastard!*" I screamed. "*You goddamn son of a bitch!* How could you do this to her?"

"Sam," he said. He stood there, looking down at me. He saw the book open in my lap. Her handwriting. He leaned down for it.

"Get out." I clutched the journal to my chest. Mine. Mine, I wanted to say.

He left me rocking there on the floor of our dead daughter's room. His pain. My pain.

I crawl across the hall from Cammy's to our bedroom. I curl up on the floor by the old easy chair in the corner by the window. No one's sat in it for years. It's piled with stacks of catalogs I keep meaning to sort through. Clothes that need ironing. A pile of stuff for the dry cleaners. It's all meaningless now. It'll not be touched for years more.

The wool Berber carpet is pushing a pattern into my cheek. Craig. Craig Craig Craig. Just thinking his name stops my tears. Like meditation. Somewhere he is moving around in the world. He is worrying about me. Frantic probably. He might even be sleepwalking again. Sleepwalking through his days like he did before we were us. He is waiting for some word from me.

One of the last lucid moments I had was pushing past Bob out through the hospital doors into the night air. They'd pulled the sheet back over Cammy's face and Bob tried to put his arm around me. I felt him pulling me in close. My elbow lifted against him. My shoulder too. I didn't slough him off. It was more aggressive than that.

I was clear-minded. It was me before I shattered. Like a car window spiderweb-cracked but still in one piece, but if you poked the middle it would crumble into tiny pieces.

I spit words at him there in that sterile room.

"You didn't love her enough," I hissed. "You never even wanted her in the first place."

I remember him ashen. I saw the impact of my words. They punched him. He said *Sam, oh, Sam* before he started sobbing. His shoulders pumped along with the tears. His arms down at his sides.

"You're wrong," he choked.

"I can't look at you," I spat. "I can't breathe the same air as you."

I remember the sound of the hospital door sealing shut

behind me. I remember gasping. Like I'd held my breath until the outside so I really didn't have to share Bob's oxygen. I remember feeling for my cell phone.

I dialed the number. Craig answered right away.

"What's going on?" he whispered.

That's how I knew he had lied to me. The whispering. He hadn't left Evie and gone to a hotel like he'd e-mailed me the day before yesterday. Or maybe he *was* at a hotel and he was sleeping with another woman. Maybe the whole thing with me was just that. A thing. Either way he wasn't alone.

"Where are you?" I asked him. I'd called to tell him about Cammy. I'd called to beg him for help. And there I was in a cold foggy hospital parking lot trying to define us. Craig and me. As if there had ever really been a Craig and me.

"Where are *you?*" he asked. "What's wrong? Why are you calling me in the middle of the night?"

Was his tone defensive? I knew he was trying to shift the focus off himself back onto me. He'd wanted me to be sorry for waking him. He was feeling guilty.

"Are you at home?" I asked. "With Evie?"

I could tell he was moving to a place where he could talk and wouldn't be heard.

"Sam…"

I had my answer. It was the way he said my name. In a "let me explain" tone. He was at home. He was in bed with his wife. He was never going to leave her. He'd told me he'd moved out. He'd told me he'd gone to a hotel and had even started looking at condos and I'd thought it was quick but he's very decisive so it made sense. I hadn't questioned it. It had been a lie.

"So you lied," I said.

I stared at the glow of the blue neon Emergency sign.

"Sam, listen…"

I closed my eyes because I knew the rest. I didn't need to hear it.

"Cammy's dead," I said. Then I folded the phone shut and opened my hand and let it drop. It was ringing as it hit the pavement. Maybe he lied. Maybe he didn't. There was a story he had to tell me. Or, more likely, there were questions he wanted to ask. *Cammy's dead? What? Oh, Jesus, Sam…* He would feel bad about the start of the call, realizing the only reason I'd tried him in the first place was for comfort. He could justify that to whomever he was sleeping with.

Wait, Cammy's dead? *My Cammy? My Cammy's DEAD?*

Oh, Jesus. Oh, God. Oh, God.

"Ma'am? Do you need help? Ma'am? Help! We need some help over here!"

A paramedic on break helped me walk back in to the E.R. He asked if I had anyone they could call for me. I said no. He held my hand until the sedative kicked in.

Three Days Later

I sit on the couch like I'm an elderly person in a rest home. The house orbits around me. The sun beams through the front window in the morning. At some point I realize it's moved to the side of the house. I can see dust floating in the shaft of the afternoon light. Then a glow of light comes from all sides and I know it's nighttime.

I know I have to retrace our mistakes. I know I have to plunge into all the signs we missed. We'll yell and scream and cry and blame each other, Bob and I. These scenes wait for us. That's what we have in store. But right now? Right now I can't shake the stupor.

There's a relief in not caring. Halfway through brushing my

hair I realize I'm brushing my hair. I leave off and go to the medicine cabinet for my toothbrush and toothpaste but once I get there I forget what I was going to do there. I choke food down because my body is required to keep going. It's nothing but fuel, a plain white T-shirt kind of taste. Midway through the day I look down and see that I am dressed and I have shoes on but I have no memory of how I got that way. Did someone else dress me? How did I get out of bed?

Sunny days are dark to me now as if I've walked out of a matinee to the jarring brightness of a bustling workday. It startles me to see people moving around in the world. Driving, playing Frisbee, carrying briefcases, talking on cell phones. How can it be a normal day for them?

The locks confuse me. I stand at our front door with my key chain, fumbling for the right key. Do I turn it clockwise or counterclockwise? Did I lock the one on the doorknob or the bolted one on top? So much thought put into entering a shell of a home. The boys move around and whisper and sometimes I hear them laugh, but if I walk in they become quiet like they're in church.

Most things bewilder me. Food appears in the fridge but I have no idea where it came from. The laundry is clean and folded and I haven't a clue who's responsible for it. I find shirts in different stacks and I'm not sure if I've done this or if a stranger has. I'm aware of Lynn letting herself in and out every day. And Mike's voice mixes with Bob's off in the distance. Maybe another man is with them, I can't be sure. Somewhere in the house a TV is on and bursts of applause and laugh tracks make it feel like a creepy carnival.

Somehow the boys are taken to school and picked up. Somehow their lunches get made. Somehow mail is collected and neatly stacked.

Bob takes up smoking. Out of nowhere. I watch him pace

on the back deck. He taps ash into an empty Coke can that sits on top of the barbecue that hasn't been covered yet for winter. He's on the phone all the time this week. Making *arrangements.* I hear the lowered voices. A memorial service is being planned. Mr. Black says it will give students closure. The school was thrown into a tailspin with the news. Counselors were brought in to talk with shocked kids who never gave her the time of day. Bob walks back and forth with his cigarettes, talking into the phone about the music she would've liked played. About getting pictures blown up. Easels to set them on. The church next to school will host even though we aren't members. Even though we're lapsed Jews. Lynn brings Bob more Coke. She sets ice water in front of me but I don't drink it. It sweats and leaves rings on the wood coffee table.

I hear all this. I watch Lynn and Mike and other friends I no longer recognize move around in my house. I see them tiptoeing in and out past me like I'm taking a nap. All these *people.* In the middle of it, sitting in the vortex of the house of pain, I figure out the one thing Cammy would have wanted for the memorial service was her birth mother. She'd want Gerry Wilkes there. That I can do for her. I can give her that much. *That,* Mr. Black, would be closure. I will find her and ask her Cammy's question. *How could you do this to me?* I know the answer of course but I want her to suffer. I want her to feel what I'm feeling. I will leave that burden on her shoulders. I'll let her carry it around for a while. I'll let her see what it feels like to fail your child.

I can't keep the speech from replaying in my head. *She wanted to know you. She wanted to belong. She wanted you to show her how to be. And then you did and it was too late and she knew it. She died mad at you, Gerry Wilkes. She died furious.* I will say this to her, I think. But behind the wheel, turning in to the library, I know I won't.

The search was over in a two-second finger point across a quiet room. I watch her walk toward me, cocking her head, a friendly question mark on her face.

"I'm Gerry Wilkes," she says, holding out her hand for a proper handshake. I look at it in wonder. Those niceties are curiosities to me now. What a waste of time. She withdraws her hand as her smile flickers away to match my seeming unfriendliness. But it's not that, I want to tell her. I'm not unfriendly. I just don't care. I thought I was mad at her but seeing her in front of me I'm suddenly not.

"What can I do for you?" Gerry Wilkes asks me.

I knew she was a librarian but I'd expected someone else. A drug addict. Someone greasy, dirty, unkempt with slurred speech, shaking for anything to keep her head in the clouds. I thought she'd look like a runaway with Magic Marker words on a scrap of cardboard: *Help. I'm homeless. Anything you can spare. God bless you.* But no. She was probably never homeless. Somehow she'd raised a child for two years. Somehow she'd had the good sense to give her daughter away before she circled the drain. She'd loved her baby enough to want something better for her. The cliché of young mothers who spend all their money buying drugs and when there's no money they spread their legs to buy more. This was Gerry Wilkes seventeen years ago.

Here she is in front of me. Pretty with her brown hair brushed and pushed primly back behind her ears. I squint to try to picture her with Cammy's rage-black dyed hair. She's short—five foot three maybe. Petite. Clear skin and large eyes Cammy inherited. Shocking to see them on someone else.

"Can I help you with something?" she asks me.

"I'm Sam Friedman." I wait for the name to register. If she'd looked for her daughter she'd know the name. Otherwise it would hold no significance. Her face is expressionless. Not even a lifted eyebrow. She is searching her mind for a connection. High-school friend? she's asking herself. Old neighbor? She might even be worried I am someone from her not-so-distant past, someone she stole from? Someone she offended? All this might be playing out in her brain, but her face is frozen in blankness. She is standing on the other side of the front desk, so I can't tell if her hands are twitching with nervousness. Or maybe it comes out with foot tapping, which I can't see either.

"I thought you might want this," I say.

I put the newspaper clipping down and slide it toward her like a bartender. At the bottom I'd highlighted the date and time of the memorial service at the school. The one I had no part in planning. Cammy hated school. School hated Cammy.

Gerry Wilkes stares at the headline and the face in the picture. The freshman-class picture. When Cammy's hair was still naturally brown, her skin makeup free, a pink shirt underneath her favorite fuzzy cream-colored sweater she'd spent her allowance on. Because I'd told her I wouldn't pay for anything else since we'd finished all the back-to-school shopping. I'd wanted her to learn money management. I was pleased with myself that day. *I didn't buy her that goddamn fuzzy cream-colored sweater she wanted more than anything else in the world because I wanted to teach her a lesson.* I found the sweater in the back of her closet. She'd never let me have it dry-cleaned because she'd been afraid it would lose its softness. I held it up to my face and inhaled the smell of my dead daughter.

"I'm…" I can't speak. If I speak I will choke on tears I thought I'd tapped dry. I don't put on mascara anymore. Of course I don't wear mascara. I don't brush my teeth. I don't wash my face. I can't remember the last time I took a shower.

But here, in front of Gerry Wilkes, I fear I might have hit a vein of emotion. She looks up from the picture into my eyes and I know what she will say next.

"I know who she is," is exactly word for word what I sensed when she looked at me.

Just in case I say, "I'm not sure you do."

"I do," she says.

She hesitates and when she continues I can tell she's practiced what to say. Maybe she stood in the shower and had this very conversation. She's wearing a simple thin gold wedding band. Maybe she tried out different versions of the speech for her husband. Maybe he helped hone it. Then again, when she starts I see the edge melt and I realize she hasn't rehearsed it at all. She's trying to pick her words carefully. She's trying hard not to cry.

"You did a beautiful job raising her," she says.

She looks away and I can tell that number one, she regrets saying this, and number two, we're both thinking the same thing:

If I'd done—if *we'd* done—a beautiful job raising her she'd be alive right now.

Her eyes are filling. I'm heaving the weight of a dead child onto her just like I'd planned. *She* should know this pain, too, I thought on my way to the library. She should carry it for a while to see how it bends time and space. How hours can feel like minutes and days can feel overcast even in blinding daylight. She should suffer. She should cry. She should forget to eat and bathe and sleep. Facing her now…seeing my daughter's eyes staring back at me…I regret rubbing her face in it. I don't feel better. I have no idea what to say and while I'm aware of the silence begging for something from me I don't fill it. Those words, Cammy's words, are distant. *How could you have done this to me?*

Finally I say, "So you knew."

"I knew," she says.

"She died here," I tell her. "In the parking lot."

Then Gerry Wilkes says, "Who do you think took her to the hospital?"

One Month Later

I have to be careful. I try to watch every step because I have to. I've been pulled back to the curb by strangers pointing to traffic that hasn't stopped yet because I forget to look both ways before crossing streets. The boys, when I'm with them, take either hand and I'm aware they are reminding me to stop for traffic, not the other way around. They're the ones walking me across streets. When they're with me they're solemn. I feel sorry for this but I can't find the energy to do anything about it. I leave it to others. Lynn takes them to school. She still makes their lunches. She takes them to practices and games. She makes sure they laugh at least every once in a while. If I'm passing a window when she pulls up to let them off, I see them bounding out of her minivan. I see them calibrate their steps when they reach the front walk. They do this automatically now. Our house echoes with hushed voices and muted TVs.

Lynn asks me what I need and I want to tell her I need a do-over. I need to go back to the beginning. Before children, before marriage, before the inertia, the infidelity, the drugs, the missed signals. Back to my mother who would have been the only person to know how to stop my ache. A dead mother who did everything right. A dead daughter with a mother who did everything wrong. I need my daughter back, I have told Lynn. I need my Cammy back. The doctor has prescribed an Ativan a day. I take three, sometimes four.

Lynn asks me what I need and I say I need someone to make lists for me so I don't forget what I'm supposed to do to keep on moving through the day. On a pad that has "Memo from Lynn" in a cheerful circus font, she's written me daily instructions:

* Give the boys their multivitamins at breakfast.
* If you run out of something at night, write it down on the sticky pad by the phone in the kitchen and I'll pick it up for you at the market the next day.
* Andrew's dentist appointment is on Friday at noon.
* Remember the boys' birthday is on Tuesday next week. I will order the cupcakes from the Swedish Bakery and give you the ticket so you can pick them up on your way to school that day.

What I really need though is someone to tell me how I can pull myself out of bed in the morning. Someone to tell me how to close my eyes and not see her.

I no longer drive car pool, but on the boys' birthday I have to pull it together to bring in the cupcakes Lynn ordered to their class like the other parents do. I'm supposed to bring them at lunchtime because the teacher says the smell would be too distracting for the class if I dropped them off in the morning. *This way they have something to look forward to,* she said. She is chipper like all elementary teachers. The first time the boys went back to school after Cammy died, Bob and I walked them to class before the bell and she patted my arm and said, *I'm sorry for your troubles.* Troubles? I wanted to ask. My *troubles?*

Bakery. I'm going to the bakery. I'm pretty sure I have the claim ticket Lynn gave me but I'll check my purse again. There it is. Side pocket. Bakery. Side pocket. I watch every step. Step on a crack break your mother's back. Bakery. Side pocket.

The Swedish Bakery is a block and a half from Starbucks. Block and a half. I say this to myself so I don't pass it. Block and a half. I reach the corner and make a point to pause and look up. A guy in a U-Haul waves me to cross. On the other side I find myself in front of Starbucks. The green awnings, the circle logo, the huge pictures of frothy drinks on the plate-glass windows. I am moving slowly, mechanically. I don't know why I turn my head to look in. Force of habit from a life lived in a selfish fog.

I don't recognize him at first. From the side he looks different. His shoulders are slumped. He is staring straight ahead at the purple wall across the room. His elbows are on the table. His hands in a V fold over his coffee cup like he's praying.

I realize I've stopped moving. I am facing him and for the first time since the hospital called something in my brain snaps. It's as though I've come out of my coma. I've shaken off the trance. It's *him*.

Craig Riggs. Sitting at *our* table. Craig Riggs. I look at him and something in his hunched back makes me wonder if he lied after all. There he is, the same-size coffee in front of him. He hasn't moved since I stopped but then again I have no idea how long I've been standing here. Maybe it's been five minutes. Maybe it's only been a second or two. I wonder what he's thinking. I wonder if he's mourning me. The loss of me. I think he is. The way he's sitting. And it's *our* table. Oh, God, it wasn't a lie. He's alone like he's waiting for me. It wasn't a lie but he couldn't explain because I'd cut him off. I'd cut him out of me like a cancer. I hadn't replaced my cell phone that broke in the hospital parking lot. I hadn't checked my e-mail. I'd made him dead to me. The pills I'd been taking were numbing me against him as much as they were keeping me from feeling the ache of Cammy. Looking in at him, seeing him alone…he wasn't lying, was he? So I make a deal with myself: If he looks over at me, if he sees me, I will go to him. I will walk away from this life.

elizabeth flock

It's not too late, I'm thinking to myself. It's not too late for us. If he looks at me I will know we were meant to be together. If he looks over. Even a glance.

I think I see his eyes close a beat or two longer than a blink. I do the same thing and when I open them I think maybe that will be the moment he looks over.

Someone is tapping on their horn. A friendly kind of honk for a driver who doesn't realize the light's turned green. It continues, so I turn my head to it. Reluctantly I tear my eyes from Craig.

"Sam? You want me to run in?"

Like a tennis match my head turns from Craig to Bob, who is leaning across the empty passenger seat, reaching for the bakery ticket, then back to Craig.

"I can pick up the cupcakes," he says. "Here, pass me the claim thing and I'll meet you at the bakery. Will you grab me a tall cappuccino when you go in?"

Craig's shifted in his seat. He's sitting up straighter. He's looking toward the counter. I move my head along with his to see what he's looking at.

"Honey? Sam? Are you going in?"

Her hair is down this time. She's smiling, holding out his coffee, he's standing, pulling out the chair for her. Craig and Evie Riggs. Perfect.

A distant siren makes everything feel urgent. The wind's blowing my hair into my face but I don't push it back behind my ears. A bus is pulling up coughing exhaust. A homeless man calls out, *"Streetwise!"* and opens the Starbucks door for a tired mother pushing a double stroller.

"Sam, are you going into Starbucks or not?" Bob calls.

I need to wake up. Wake up, Sam. *Wake up.*

I look down at my shoes. I hate these shoes. Clogs. Ugly brown crunchy-granola clogs. I've always hated these shoes.

Then it hits me. I hate all my shoes. Every single pair. Even the black *Sex and the City*–ish pumps. They're no more me than these clogs are. I hate my clothes, too. And our couch. And the fake-distressed kitchen table that seemed like a good idea in the store where they called it a refectory table. I look up at the gray sky and yes, I think, *yes, exactly. My life is gray. I thought it would be Technicolor but it's gray.*

"I've got to circle the block," Bob yells. A MUNI bus is trying to squeeze by our car and gives up. I see the bus driver throw his hands up in frustration and deflate back into his seat because this is something he deals with a million times a day. Bob pulls forward and the bus driver takes hold of his huge steering wheel and the whole mess is straightened up just like that.

It's not too late. Maybe it's not too late to turn my life around. I could be the woman my mother was hoping I'd turn out to be. I could be the person I thought I'd be when I was a kid. *Yes, exactly.* That's it. I mean, when I was a kid did I long to wear sensible shoes? Did I wish I would one day be standing on a dirty sidewalk under a heavy sky while a husband I don't love calls out to me? Did I ever dream I would turn out to be a bad mother with a dead daughter?

This is how it happens. This is how lives change. Sometimes all it takes is a moment. A *defining* moment. Oprah would call it a *lightbulb* moment, an *aha* moment. This is that split second of clarity. This is me saying…enough. No more sleepwalking. Enough.

"Sam?" Bob's back. "Where're you going? Honey? The bakery's that way, remember?"

He's talking to me like I'm a child who's lost her way.

Someone honks at him and I've walked too far down the sidewalk to see his face but I'm sure he's saying "goddammit" and steering his way back around the block and I realize I will not get into a car with him again. Enough. I will not go back. I will take the boys and we will share them on weekends and they'll forget cleats and at the last minute Bob will swing by my house to grab them before the game. I will tell their teachers we will need two copies of announcements and school calendars and class phone lists. One for Bob. One for me. Not Bob and me. Not Craig and me. Me. I will not lose my way with the boys like I did with Cammy. I will not. I will be the mother to them I should have been to Cammy. And they'll be just fine. People get divorced every day. They'll be fine.

At the corner ten blocks away, in front of the fish store with aquariums in the windows and signs that meal worms are on sale, I realize I've stopped at the curb automatically. I may not have broken the spell altogether but I know now that I will. The light changes and I cross with the other pedestrians and I think to myself: this is how it happens. This is how you leave your life to start another.

I look down at these sensible shoes moving my feet forward and I'm actually glad I'm wearing them. I have a long walk ahead of me.

Acknowledgments

The writing of this novel took place during perhaps the most wrenching two years of my life and would not have been possible without the loving support of friends and family. To say they held me up and put me back together during a nearly unbearable time would be an understatement—they did so much more. For a multitude of reasons, both personal and professional, I will be forever grateful to Mary Jane Clark, Joan Drummond Olson, Bruce Fine, Mary Chase-Ziolek, Jodie Chase, Dotty Sonnemaker, Catherine DiBenedetto, Kat Mosteller and Kim Merenkov.

My heartfelt thanks to my editor, Susan Swinwood, and to my agent, Larry Kirshbaum, both of whom patiently and brilliantly guided and shaped this novel through its many incarnations. I am deeply grateful, too, to Margaret Marbury, to Kathleen Carter at Goldberg McDuffie, to John and Fauzia Burke and the team at FSB Associates.

There is nothing like the bond between siblings, who know you best and keep you anyway. I hope Peter, Katherine, Regi and Jill know how much I love them and appreciate them daily. My girls, Emily and Lizzie, fill me with pride and happiness. I love and adore them beyond measure. As I do their father, Jeffrey. That will never change. Ever.

My parents are without question the strongest, most generous and loving human beings I have ever encountered. Their arms and hearts are open to all their children and grandchildren, but I fear I may have tested this more than the rest. My one hope is that they know how deep and profound my love is for both of them. Their marriage has lasted more than four decades and is the gold standard for how to do it right. Because of them, I believe in love.

And in the end that is what this book is about: love. Plain and simple.

Questions for Discussion

1. *Sleepwalking in Daylight* opens with a very provocative look at sex and the modern marriage. Where do you think sex ranks in terms of importance in a relationship?

2. Do you believe there is a greater amount of dissatisfaction in today's marriages than there was in the past? What role do you think people's expectations play in the success or failure of their relationships?

3. Statistics show that more and more women are marrying later in life. Do you think couples who marry after age thirty have a better chance of having a successful marriage than those who marry young, as Samantha and Bob did?

4. When do you think Samantha started to lose her connection with Cammy? If her relationship with Bob had been on better footing, do you think Samantha would have let her daughter withdraw as much?

5. Do parents ever really know their kids? We like to think so, but when it comes to independent teenagers, can we be sure? How confident are you that you would know whether or not your child has tried alcohol and/or drugs, and what would you do if they had?

6. It can be very easy for us to blame the parents for a child's mistakes. At what point does a teenager "own" her actions and decisions? Discuss how much of the responsibility you feel falls on Cammy's shoulders, not her parents', for her choices and behavior.

7. Discuss the novel's structure. In what ways do the alternating narratives between mother and daughter enhance the story? How do the scenes in a teenager's voice give you further insight into the characters and their actions?

8. When it comes to adultery, some people claim their partner's lack of attention for "forcing" them into the arms of another. Was this the case for Samantha? Do you buy that argument? Given the circumstances, do you blame her for getting close to Craig?

9. How do you feel about Bob's actions (or inaction) throughout the story? Did you find him to be a sympathetic character? What role, if any, do you feel his supposed depression played in the novel?

10. How do you think the story might have changed if Sam had talked candidly with Craig's wife at the soccer game? If you were in Sam's shoes, would meeting his wife and child have been enough to prompt you to end the relationship?

11. Was the ending a surprise to you? How would you have changed it? Do you feel there was a way that things could have turned out differently for Cammy? How so?

12. How do you feel about Samantha's decision at the end of the story? Did she ultimately do the right thing, in your opinion? What other options did she have?